FROM CAPE TOWN
WITH LOVE

BLAIR UNDERWOOD PRESENTS

FROM CAPE TOWN WITH LOVE

A Tennyson Hardwick Novel

TANANARIVE DUE AND STEVEN BARNES

ATRIA BOOKS
New York London Toronto Sydney

ATRIA BOOKS

A Division of Simon & Schuster, Inc.
1230 Avenue of the Americas
New York, NY 10020

First Atria Books hardcover edition May 2010

ATRIA BOOKS and colophon are trademarks of Simon & Schuster, Inc.

For information about special discounts for bulk purchases,
please contact Simon & Schuster Special Sales at 1-866-506-1949
or business@simonandschuster.com.

The Simon & Schuster Speakers Bureau can bring authors to your
live event. For more information or to book an event contact the
Simon & Schuster Speakers Bureau at 1-866-248-3049
or visit our website at www.simonspeakers.com.

Manufactured in the United States of America

10   9   8   7   6   5   4   3   2   1

Library of Congress Cataloging-in-Publication Data

Underwood, Blair.
   From Cape Town with love : a Tennyson Hardwick novel / [Blair Underwood with] Tananarive
Due and Steven Barnes.—1st Atria Books hardcover ed.
     p. cm.
   At head of title: Blair Underwood presents
   1. African American actors—Fiction. 2. Private investigators—Fiction. 3. African American men—
South Africa—Fiction. 4. Cape Town (South Africa)—Fiction. 5. Intercountry adoption—Fiction.
I. Due, Tananarive, 1966–   II. Barnes, Steven, 1952–   III. Title. IV. Title: Blair Underwood presents.
   PS3621.N383F76 2010
   813'.6—dc22

                                                                    2010007764

ISBN 978-1-4391-5912-5
ISBN 978-1-4391-6494-5 (ebook)

To

John Due and Patricia Stephens Due
Eva R. Barnes and Emory F. Barnes

and

Col. (Ret.) Frank and Marilyn Underwood,
with gratitude and love

I like big families myself. In fact, my whole life
has been a crusade for larger families.

—Ali Karim Bey, *From Russia with Love*

You may know the right wines, but you're the one
on your knees. How does it feel, old man?

—Donovan "Red" Grant, *From Russia with Love*

Suggested MP3 Soundtrack

"Too Hot to Stop" (The Bar-Kays)
"Sihambile" (Mahlathini)
"Give It to Me Baby" (Rick James)
"Pretty Wings" (Maxwell)
"Unhome" (Miriam Makeba)
"Hate On Me" (Jill Scott)
"For the Love of Money" (The O'Jays)
"Good and Strong" (Sy Smith)
"Sexual Healing" (Marvin Gaye)
"Thula Mtwana" (Ladysmith Black Mambazo)
"Zingu 7" (Zola)
"Party Up (Up in Here)" (DMX)
"War Drums (Original Mix)" (EMC)
"African Woman" (Baaba Maal)
"Oya (Aw-Yuh)" (Babatunde Olatunji)
"Natural Born Killaz" (Dr. Dre, featuring Ice Cube)
"Another Way to Die" (Jack White and Alicia Keys)
"Demon Seed" (Nine Inch Nails)
"Welcome to the Terrordome" (Public Enemy)
"Sympathy for the Devil" (Rolling Stones)
"Red House" (Jimi Hendrix)
"Alive" (Pearl Jam)
"Chileshe" (Hugh Masekela)
"I Just Want to Celebrate" (Rare Earth)
"There's Hope" (India.Arie)
"Lean on Me" (Bill Withers)
"Africa" (Soweto Gospel Choir)
"Agent Double-O-Soul" (Edwin Starr)

FROM CAPE TOWN
WITH LOVE

PROLOGUE

THEY CALLED THEMSELVES the Three R's: R.J., Ramirez, and Reiter. Reiter was female, but not exactly the nurturing kind. I was sitting at a table in a cold, windowless room, in the worst pain in my life. I'd been in the same chair for hours.

Sitting upright wasn't easy because of the pain.

R.J. stood over me with a folder. He did most of the talking.

"The FBI is writing a book on you as we speak," R.J. said. "Usually that's the bad news. But in your case, that's the good news."

I couldn't resist. "Then what's the bad news?"

"You seen that TV show . . . ? What's the name?" R.J. asked Ramirez and Reiter.

"What show?" Reiter said.

At first, I thought he was talking about my old series, *Homeland*. I'd played an FBI agent working with the Department of Homeland Security. But I was as wrong as I could be.

R.J. snapped his fingers. "*Without a Trace*," he said. "It's about people who've disappeared, right? One day they're here, then *bam*, they're gone. That's a fascinating show."

There was wildness in his eyes.

"You ever heard of the Patriot Act?" R.J. asked me.

I suddenly realized how hungry I was. I wondered again if it was day or night.

"That's got nothing to do with me," I said. I wanted to force him to say what he was hinting at. "I'm not a terrorist."

"But you're an *interesting* guy," R.J. said.

"Fascinating guy," Ramirez agreed in a singsong voice.

R.J. went on. "And if we decide we want to talk to you for a while, get to know you better, we can keep you around as long as we need to."

"But nobody wants that," R.J. said.

"Pain in the ass," Reiter said.

Cold-steel reality unfolded in my head: I was in an interrogation room in an unknown location. My body felt butchered. I had been promised a long stretch in prison. I had just lost my oldest friend. I had barely survived the night, and a man had died at my hands.

No. Why mince words? I had *killed* a man. For the first time in my life.

I wondered how many people R.J., Ramirez, and Reiter had killed among them, or what measures they were willing to take when they wanted information. I didn't get along with most cops already—but they weren't cops, or anything like it.

I wished they were. I understood the rules with cops. There were no rules at all now.

ONE

SEVEN MONTHS EARLIER
NOVEMBER 5, 2008
SOUTH AFRICA

April Forrest's eyes widened. "Ten . . . what happened to your face?"

In the bosom of beauty, ugly comes as a shock. The swelling and bruises across my face made me look like I'd just been attacked by a prison gang. Might as well have been—although it was just one man. In the swamp.

When April left Los Angeles to teach in South Africa for six months, she'd left me, too. We had passed the one-year milestone right before she changed her mind about us, and an ocean and ten thousand miles had suddenly seemed like a small toll to see her again. I wanted to know what had scared her off—but maybe it was written all over my face.

"Long story," I said. "I tried, but I couldn't find flowers this late. May I come in?"

Apparently, *long story* wasn't enough to get the door open any wider. April was lithe and fine, with skin the color of ginger.

She was living in a tiny cinder-block house on a street of modest but well-kept homes in a middle-class section of Soweto, outside Johannesburg. In the bright light from the porch, I saw her jaw shift with uncertainty. Her delicate chin and gently swaying braids, adorned with regal white beads at the ends, reminded me of why some men could be driven to beg.

Two or three loose dogs I'd seen outside the gate were barking at me from the unlighted street. Two yipped harmlessly, but one sounded like thunder. A week before, I'd killed a German shepherd in the Florida swamp. The memory of the dog's last yelp, and his master's last labored breath, still iced my blood.

"You look like you almost got murdered, Ten. What happened?"

"The T. D. Jackson case." My investigation into the death of football star T. D. Jackson had taken me places that were hard to put into words. Dad had told me that an LAPD officer who had been through my ordeal might have been considered like an OIS, Officer Involved Shooting, and sent to counseling. "Like I said, April . . . long story."

April's look told me that I was failing my first test since our breakup. In her place, I might close the door on me. Dying hope flashed hot in my chest. I knew it then: I shouldn't have come to see April without calling her first, like my father and Chela told me before I left.

"Ten, I can't . . . I'm not alone."

She's already with somebody else? A foreign rage tightened the back of my neck. I didn't know if I was more pissed at her for moving on, or at myself for flying across the world to witness her new life up close.

When an older woman appeared behind April in the doorway, I wanted to hug her. April was boarding, so she was living with her hostess! The woman looked about fifty-five, but her skin was so smooth that she might have been ten or fifteen years older. Bright silver hair framed her forehead beneath her colorful head scarf. The slope of her nose and sharp cheekbones reminded me of Alice. Beauty, timeless. Another woman. A different time. Despite the severity of her frown, the stranger's face forced me to stare.

"I'm sorry it's so late, Mrs. Kunene," April apologized. A faint living-room light was on, but the woman might have been asleep. It was ten P.M. in Johannesburg, late for an unannounced visitor. I hadn't thought about the hour when I jumped into the taxi at the airport and told the driver to go to the address April had given me. A lot had changed since the last time I was in South Africa.

The streets were so dark, I had no idea how the driver found his way.

"This is my friend Tennyson. From the U.S."

April said *friend* as if it was the whole story. I could barely smile for her hostess—not that a smile would have helped my face. Mrs. Kunene looked like she was trying to decide if she should call the police right then, or wait for me to look at her the wrong way.

After a twenty-two-hour flight via Amsterdam, I couldn't fake pleasantries with a hostile stranger. "Come away with me for a long weekend," I said into April's ear, not quite a whisper. I'd planned a more elegant approach, but the sight of April's face had drained my memory. My palms were damp, like my virgin friends used to say in high school.

April touched her ear, coaxing away a strand of hair. "Ten . . . slow down . . ."

A broad-shouldered man with snowy white hair appeared next, wearing only his slacks, roused from bed. Mr. Kunene might be my father's age, but his motion was agile and his face was as smooth as his wife's.

"April, this man is your friend?" he said. "He looks like a *tsotsi!*"

I admired his lyrical accent despite the insult: He'd just said I looked like a gangster.

April planted her foot in the doorway to keep the door from slamming in my face. Her foot was as firm as her voice was gentle: "Yes, yes, he's a good friend. It's all right."

"Is he drunk?" Mrs. Kunene called, stepping back. The rolled *r*'s in the woman's accent were music. She made *drunk* sound like a state to aspire to.

"Sir and madam, I am not drunk," I said. "Please accept my apologies for stopping by so late. I have to talk to April right away." When they heard my reasonableness, and my American accent, some of the alarm left their eyes.

I pointed out the gate, where the tattered taxi that had brought me waited, a dingy gray VW Citi Golf that had once been white. One of the back taillights was missing, and the other glowed dimly. The driver sat inside, awaiting my verdict. The yipping dogs still barked, but the larger one had moved on. April saw the taxi and realized delays were costing me.

"I'll be right here on the porch," April said to her hosts, and slipped outside before they could object. The white curtains fluttered at the window as they watched us.

On the porch, I had an impulse to pull April close—but I followed her lead and kept a two-foot distance. If I tried to touch her and she flinched away, no words would rescue us.

"Sorry, but she's a minister," April explained, hushed. "They're strict with boarders."

Good. I hoped they ran the house like a damn nunnery. "I need a face-to-face conversation with you," I said.

April's eyes fell away, and my throat burned. A month ago, April would have fussed over my bruises, planting her soft lips on mine.

"Let me take you somewhere beautiful," I said. "Don't we deserve time, April?"

"Yes, but . . . I'm working until Saturday."

"Make up an excuse."

"Lying comes easier to some people, Ten." No irony or malice, just a fact. And she was right. If I'm not careful, lying is my nature.

"Then meet me for coffee tomorrow." The exhaustion shredding my voice must have sounded like desperation, but I hadn't had a good night's sleep in a week. "Tell me when you have a break, and I'll come pick you up."

Silence again. I'd envisioned myself staying with April—*yeah, right*—so I didn't have a reservation at a hotel. Another hassle waited, and the day was already ending on a sour note.

My driver, Sipho, was watching me through his open driver's-side window, eager to see me give him our signal: a thumbs-up if he could drive away, a thumbs-down if he should wait.

When I gave Sipho the thumbs-down, I heard him click his teeth with disgust. "Eish! No woman wants the nice guy!" he called from his window, repeating his mantra from our ride.

When I'd told Sipho the story of how April left the States to teach and then broke up with me by telephone, he'd let out a shout, as if she'd shot me. *A rich man like you, treated this way by a woman!* Maybe he was merely angling for a tip, but he was my only friend that night.

I was getting mad, and so far anger had nothing to do with April and me. I hoped I wouldn't have to scorch April in those flames. Neither of us would salvage anything from that.

"April, if you're through with me, help me wrap my head around it."

April touched my forehead, just above a bruise, and her touch extinguished my anger. "Where would we go?" she said. "If I get the days off."

I stepped toward April and cradled her cheeks with my palms. Her chin sank against the heels of my hands. For a precious few seconds, she trusted me to hold her up.

I did not try to kiss her. Holding her face was enough.

"I know the perfect place," I said.

Cape Town might be our last chance.

APRIL WAS ABLE to go with me Friday morning, and I didn't mind a day's wait. April was in her late twenties, but she was built like a nineteen-year-old, willowy and deceptively resilient. Most people she met underestimated her, including me.

We caught a flight at nine A.M., spent most of the trip talking about my most recent brush with death, and landed right after eleven with plenty of day left. It felt good to be a *we* again, even if only for a while. We were extra polite, careful with each other, not wanting to trip over any land mines too soon.

I was glad that November is summer in South Africa, because there was no fog to obscure the grand vision of Table Mountain's flat summit. The coastal town is designed to worship the mountain. I'd booked us two cottages at a quaint Cape-Dutch bed-and-breakfast near Stellenbosch, but I wanted April to see the view from Table Mountain right away.

The summit of Table Mountain might be my favorite place in the world. In sufficient quantity or quality, beauty is an intoxicant. When I close my eyes and visualize a safe, meditative space, Table Mountain is where I go.

As our crowded cable car climbed alongside the majestic, craggy mountain that rose to the sky, life's concerns shrank beneath us. The rock was riven with the lines showing how long the mountain predated us, and how long it would be standing after all of us were gone. Cape Town spilled across the green basin and coastline.

South Africa is beautiful.

The multilingual babble around us rose to an excited pitch as the Atlantic Ocean unfurled below us like a vivid dream through the cable car's glass floor, the edge of the world. If beauty were evidence, the ocean in Cape Town could convince you that Heaven is a shade of blue.

April squeezed my hand, hard. It was the first time she had touched me on her own since I'd arrived at her doorstep. So far, so good.

"Thank you for this, Ten," April said. "It's like looking straight at God."

I didn't always speak April's language where God was concerned, but I knew what she meant. "See the sand on those beaches?" I said, pointing out where the ocean licked the white sands of the shoreline below. "It's soft as sugar. Barefoot never felt so good."

My late lady friend Alice had given me South Africa like a box of chocolates, piece by piece—from jazz clubs to discos to wineries to she-beens in the poorest townships—flying me out to meet her without notice. Alice had been dead for years, which seemed impossible on the Table Mountain cable car. She had been a part of another man's life.

April looked at me as if I were a charming stranger she wanted to get to know better. "We'll have to go to the beach," she said.

Good. She was making plans for us. "Definitely."

April's smile made me light-headed. When her face came close to mine, I savored the smell of her. I had only two days with her, and I wanted them to count. Most tourists headed straight for the view of the water. Outcroppings of rocks surrounded us, and a colorful souvenir shop waited to help us buy back our memories when it was time to go.

A blinding glint of sunlight deified April. Her thin braids were dozens of gentle fingers fanning across her chin and jaw, framing the dimples that had called to my eyes when I first saw her in front of the Hollywood division police station with her reporter's notebook. She was a princess.

"Wait," I said, and I took her picture. I'm not a big photo collector, but I already knew I would want to keep that picture of April, even if it might be hard to look at one day soon.

April squealed, gone from the camera's frame. "Ten, what's that?"

She pointed. Brown fur blurred between two boulders. An animal about the size and shape of a mole skittered away on short legs, hiding.

"They're rock dassies," I said. "They rule the kingdom up here. Don't get too close. They can bite, and they might be rabid."

I remember asking Alice about the rock dassies, and she had looked as bored, too. "They're closely related to elephants, believe it or not," I said, just like Alice had told me.

"They're so adorable! Like gophers . . . or giant squirrels!" She laughed.

"They're not so adorable when you see their teeth. Wait—don't feed them." But April had already fished a snack bag out of her purse. She sprinkled Goldfish on the ground, making clicking noises. The rock dassie's head popped out from behind the rock.

"Take a step away, April. He'll come to the food. Don't get too close."

Five rock dassies from five directions were making their way toward April. To me they looked like an attack party, but April was holding her breath, watching their approach with wide, childlike eyes. The animals didn't walk in a straight line—they took a few cautious steps toward her, then zigzagged in another direction before walking toward April again. Like me, maybe.

"Hey, precious baby . . . ," April said, and I wished she were talking to me. "You're a sweet little boo, aren't you, huh?" I wondered if anyone else, in the history of the world, had ever been jealous of a rock dassie.

I instantly thought of him as Goofy. Goofy inched within a foot of her. Grinning wide, April froze like a statue as she waited. I made a mental scan of the area around us, just in case I would need something to beat Goofy away with. A rock would do the job.

Goofy realized that April wasn't a threat, so he raised the cracker with practiced paws and started munching—*Thanks, doll, you got any peanut butter to top this off?*

"Ten, look!" April said. "He's so cute! Can you take a picture of us?"

Goofy did not push my Cute button. Every instinct told me to shoo him away.

"That's great!" I said anyway, and snapped the photo.

The other furballs in Goofy's crew renewed their advance, their tiny legs scuttling toward April and her bright orange crackers. A lot of people would have jumped up to run for cover, but April didn't move from where she knelt in their path. I opened my mouth to warn April to back away, but I was stopped by her grin.

I snapped another photo to try to capture April's face—a barely harnessed joy that you rarely see in adults. A quiet thought surfaced: *April would make a great mother.*

Until that day on the mountain, I'd never had that thought about anyone.

When you go to South Africa, don't expect to find Africa right away.

The first time I landed in Johannesburg, the rows of glass-paneled skyscrapers made me think I was back in L.A. Johannesburg is hamburger stands, malls, and movie theaters—more bland than L.A., actually, but you get the idea. Considering my exotic visions of Zulu warriors wrapped in zebra pelts, and lions roaming the savannahs, Jo'burg was a letdown. Cape Town feels eerily like San Francisco at first glance, down to the wineries and nightclubs, but its character feels less American than Jo'burg, more English influenced with colonial B and Bs.

April and I hung out on Long Street, where the Cape-Dutch Victorian buildings and wrought-iron balconies made me feel like I was in Europe, especially the south of France. South Africa offers wealth and poverty with equal zeal, and much of Cape Town is a playground for the rich. Even on Long Street, it's strange how few black faces you see—usually it's white and Indian South Africans, or tourists from the world over. Apartheid might have ended in 1994, but the average black South African remains a long way from the mountaintop.

The past is hard to overcome.

But South Africa was celebrating while April and I were there; in 2010, it would be hosting the first World Cup ever held in Africa. In Soweto, especially, soccer madness had been everywhere, a rainbow of colors for teams like the Swallows and the Pirates. Stadiums were being built in ten South African cities, including Cape Town. The brand-new Green Point Stadium had views of Table Mountain and the ocean, majesty to suit the coming battles among nations.

When Alice took me to Cape Town the first time, it was two years after Nelson Mandela had been elected president after twenty-seven years at nearby Robben Island prison—and the energy felt similar when I returned with April thirteen years later. But there was one major difference: Now, instead of just the colorful South African liberation flag, street vendors sold American flags, too.

"Hey—Obama!" a man called from a passing bicycle that afternoon as April and I walked down Long Street, where black Africans, backpackers, and bohemians congregated. Even in the midst of soccer euphoria, I was a star in my black Barack Obama T-shirt.

Grins flashed at me. Laughing children ran up to me. Women young and old gave me hugs. Strangers honked their horns as they drove past. A vacationing couple from Germany begged me to pose for a picture with them while April and I shared bemused smiles.

It was 2008, only three days after the November election that changed American history. Our American accents triggered excited conversations about American politics. The phrase "president-elect Barack Obama" sounded odd, dreamlike. There was a world party going on, and I felt lucky to witness how important the election was outside America's borders.

Cape Town made us smile a lot, just as I had hoped. My swagger was back.

I was such a good catch, it boggled my mind.

Who else would fly from another *country* to try to win back his girlfriend after the way she'd cut things off? Shit, that girl would be crazy to walk away from me! Bruised or not, my face made most women lose their concentration.

On top of that, I might have at least a quarter-million-dollar settlement waiting for me at home—since an amoral studio exec named Lynda Jewell wanted my sexual harassment suit against her to go away. *And* I could put a few sentences together, too? April had better claim me back while she could, before I was out running wild.

To seal the deal, I chose the Nyoni's Kraal on Long Street.

Kraal means a small rural village in southern Africa, but in Afrikaans, a kraal is a pen for livestock. That may be all we need to know to understand the history of race relations in the region. The South African brother who owns Nyoni's grew up poor and built his business from nothing. Now it's one of Cape Town's most popular eateries, with room for hundreds.

Nyoni's Kraal had a faux thatched ceiling, African-inspired brass lamps shaped like masks, and mock crocodiles hanging on warmly colored stone walls. A prominent South African flag bore the black-and-gold triangle and stripes of green, white, red, and blue. The employees wore traditional dashikis. Our round-faced waitress, Nobanzi, wore a thin beaded headband and a wide beaded bracelet with colors that entranced my eyes. Xhosa, I guessed.

I ordered a 1999 Klein Constantia sauvignon blanc, and April couldn't hide how impressed she was by my knowledge of wine. I had my mojo back!

We joked about ordering mopane worms and chicken feet as appetizers, but we ended up with marinated snoek, a long, bony, saltwater fish I thought she would like. For my entrée, I ordered the kingklip, an eel-like local fish with firm white meat. April ordered African roast chicken. Heaven. For the first five minutes after our food arrived, we forgot about talking and enjoyed the taste of Africa.

"Mrs. Kunene might have a job for you," April said.

"A job?" I said, sampling my bread. "She doesn't know me."

April shrugged. "She asked about you last night, so I told her you're an actor and bodyguard in Hollywood. When I said we were going to Cape Town, she told me her sister-in-law runs an orphanage near here, in a township called . . . Lango?"

"Langa," I corrected her.

"Langa. An American actress is visiting, but they're worried they might not have reliable security. Mrs. Kunene thought I should ask you, since we would be here."

I'd been to Cape Town's townships before, including Langa and an even poorer township called Crossroads. Alice took me to see an amazing children's orchestra playing in a shebeen built of drab brick and entombed in razor wire. The area looked like Fallujah. But a music teacher invited neighborhood children to play instruments, and they took up scales instead of trouble. I heard those kids play a blast of Duke Ellington bright enough to light up the block. Anyone who heard it had no choice but to smile. Jazz is everywhere in Cape Town, even in the 'hood. I wondered if the bar was still there, if the band still played its sweet, silky songs.

"We only have a couple days here," I said. "When's she going?"

"Tomorrow."

"Who's the actress?"

"Sofia . . . Maitlin?" April said casually, as if she'd never heard of last year's Oscar-winning best supporting actress. "Mrs. Kunene gave me a number for her assistant, or whatever."

April was downplaying it. For some reason she didn't want me to take the job. When I held out my hand, April reluctantly pulled a slip of paper out of her purse. The name *Rachel Wentz* was written on the scrap she gave me, with the number for the Twelve Apostles Hotel.

Definitely legit. Rachel Wentz was Maitlin's *manager,* not her assistant. A manager is a professional who hobnobs with the upper echelons of Hollywood to manage your career—an assistant gets your coffee. Big difference. Having a license to call Sofia Maitlin's manager was reason enough to take the job. I'm an actor first, and access is everything. After being fired from my series, I was out of circulation.

But I'm no fool. "I came to Cape Town to spend time with you," I said, slipping the paper in my back pocket. "I didn't come to work."

"I told her you probably couldn't do it," April said, relieved. But her face brooded, suddenly dangerous. "You get hurt so much, Ten. Like you're . . . punishing yourself."

Here it comes, I thought. April didn't mention Serena's name, but her ghost was suddenly at our table. I first met April after a friend of mine was murdered, and we had recently passed the one-year anniversary of Serena's death. I clamped back the rage and sadness always simmering near the surface; I wanted my thoughts clear for the new tragedy unfolding.

Slowly, April continued, "The lengths you go to when you're on these cases feels . . . self-destructive—like you *want* to hurt yourself. That scares me, Ten. When you took the T. D. Jackson case, I started to think you're chasing something else. That maybe you're looking for something you can't fix by finding the bad guys. Forgiveness, maybe."

The suspicion that April might be right only made me angrier. "Or, maybe I'm just good at solving fucking cases."

"I know you're good at it—you're *great* at it—but I think it's about more than that for you. You put yourself in reckless situations, and then you have trouble moving past them. I see these patterns in your history, Ten."

April sounded like she had just finished a course on me, with charts and graphs. The phrase *your history* hurt. "Haven't I shown you that I'm not that man anymore?" I said softly.

April was my first monogamous relationship, my first true girlfriend. I literally don't know how many women I've had sex with—I stopped counting long ago, when I passed three hundred. In my twenties and early thirties, when acting work was dry, I spent years as a professional "escort," servicing wealthy women in Hollywood and overseas. I racked up a big body count.

Not long before I took April to Cape Town, my past mistakes caught up with me. A powerful female studio executive tricked me into a meeting and started taking off her clothes, offering me money for sex. Lynda Jewell knew about my history, and found me through my agent when my face started showing up on TV. She'd offered me a lot of zeroes to forget, but like they say, money can't buy love. The damage between me and April had been done.

April still couldn't look me in the eye. "This isn't about your past."

"What, then?" I said, my voice rising, as close to shouting as I came. "You've never had your ribs cracked, so you don't know how patronizing it is to say I *like* getting hurt. Did you pull that out of a college psych book? Or is it some *Dr. Phil* bullshit?"

A black African couple at the table beside us glanced over to see what the ruckus was. The moon-faced young woman in sunflower yellow was holding her date's hand, but he looked bored. The woman's forlorn eyes begged us to show a better example of courtship.

"Do we really want to make this harder, Ten?" April's voice flowed like a yoga relaxation tape. She had already started moving on.

I thought of the old Richard Pryor routine where the calmer his woman got, the more he had a fit. I closed my eyes, forcing a deep breath. "I need to understand," I said, opening my eyes. The lights stabbed my sudden headache. "We were fine before, and now we're not? What changed?"

April stared at her plate of half-eaten food. Our talk should have waited until dessert.

"I've really been praying about this, because I started writing you letters and couldn't find the words. There's a quality you have—riding the chaos wave, seeing where it takes you. It's so beautiful and free and brave, just like you. It's the first thing that attracted me to your spirit. But now . . ." She didn't finish. When April first met me, I was a suspect in Serena's death; I'd been a vote against her better judgment from day one.

April went on. "Some people can handle it—I *know* you'll find someone who can—but I can't anymore. I can't sit around worrying about whether you're going to get killed, or if you'll have to kill somebody. I can't live that way—or raise our kids that way."

I was about to promise April that I would never take another case, but the phrase *our kids* nearly made me choke on my bread. I tried to recover before she noticed, but I was too late. April gave me a resigned, heartbroken glance she tried to hide by drinking the last of her wine.

"We have kids?" I said. I felt like Rip Van Hardwick. Had I missed something?

"In two years I'll be thirty, Ten. I want to be headed somewhere."

I don't know how guys feel when they're ready to discuss marriage and kids, but I wasn't there yet. I was too tired to keep talking, so I should have kept my mouth shut—but I thought I knew exactly what to say. What every woman wants to hear.

"All I know is . . . ," I said, pausing for effect. "I love you, Alice."

For the first few seconds, I was confused by the horror on April's face. *You called her ALICE,* my memory whispered, and my insides shriveled.

"Shit," I said, honestly shocked. "Jesus."

Blasphemy was just for good measure, since April was a church girl. My words were gibberish to me, as if someone had hijacked my mouth. I couldn't think of an apology worthy of the transgression. I suppose my faux pas could have been worse. We could have been in bed.

There's no good way to call your girlfriend by the wrong name—but Alice was a former client from my working days. She was one of my steadiest clients for years, despite an age difference that made her old enough to be my mother—older, really. When she died, she left me her house, and I'd been living there ever since. I'd insisted to April that I'd kept the house only out of convenience; it was worth $2 million even in a recession.

The past was the past, I had promised April. But it wasn't. It never was.

"I can't do this anymore," April said again, near tears. "I'm sorry, Ten."

Now I was the one who couldn't meet April's eyes. The bright colors all around stung me, their celebration quietly mocking. I reached across the table and took April's hand, grateful when she held on. Her palm melted into mine. I stared as our sad fingers danced.

I was wrong about the ghost at our table: It had been Alice all along.

Since I had booked us two cottages at the B and B, taking nothing for granted, I was surprised when April gently held my hand after I walked her to her cottage's doorstep. She squeezed, a silent invitation to the Garden of Eden. Just before I got cast out.

My hand burned inside April's. My stomach had sloshed acid since we left the restaurant, but not from the food. April's hips swayed toward the pink-crimson bougainvillea blossoms guarding her door, and my eyes followed. *Forget all that bullshit I just said about you,* April's hips said, soothing me. *This is how I really feel.*

"Do you want to spend the night?" April said, taking my other hand.

A mercy fuck. I understood the concept, had even administered a few, but had never been offered one. Night skies hid most of the beauty around us, and in the dark I was just very far from home. I could hear Sipho's voice in my head, insisting that I walk away with my pride. If she was horny, she could buy a damn dildo.

"Why would I come this far to be anywhere but with you?" I said instead. She smiled, ignoring the pained rumble I had never heard in my own voice.

April dug through her too-big woven purse, looking for her room key.

My agent, Len, once told me that he'd ended up drunk on champagne, puking in the men's room when he went to his ex-girlfriend's wedding right after college. Walking into April's cottage, I was sure I should know better, just like I'd told Len.

The rooms were small, hardly big enough for the high queen beds that were their centerpiece. April's buttocks flared out when she leaned over to turn on the gourd-shaped light on her nightstand. I would miss April's ass; it was a minor miracle. She rarely wore a bra, since her breasts were small and perfect. Through the thin white cotton of her tank top, her nipples' black pearls stared back at me in the thirty-watt light.

April sat beside me, her hand on my knee. "It's hard for me, too, Tennyson."

"You seem to be doing all right."

"I'm not," she said. "I smell you on my pillow—even here. I see people everywhere who look just like you. The way you flew to South Africa will probably always be the most romantic thing anyone ever does for me. Thank you for trying so hard. I'll never forget it." I shrugged, tired of the postmortem. "I miss you, Ten."

I didn't say *I miss you, too.* Talk of missing me pissed me off. I played with the strap of her tank top, sliding it from her bare shoulder.

"What else do you miss?" I said, on cue. She could have been a client.

April slid her hand to my thigh, kneading hard. She knew exactly how to get my attention. Suddenly, April's cruelty was sexy. I felt taut arousal below my navel. Most of the heat baking my skin was pain, but I wanted her.

April pulled my T-shirt up, and I ducked to help her glide it over my head. The fabric stung when it snagged my bruised chin, but I hid my wince.

My chest offered a new array of bruises. On one side, my ribs were battered purple.

"God, Ten . . . ," April said. Her eyes flooded with tears.

"*Shhhhhh,*" I comforted her. "Don't do that. I'm all right."

"You just went through hell, baby . . ."

I just got to Hell, baby.

April lightly traced the trail of welts and marks on my chest with her fingertip. Pain sizzled, mingled with longing. People who like to be whipped are looking for the feeling April's finger gave me as she prodded my injuries. That night, I understood anew.

"Does this help make it better?" April said. Gently, she kissed my raw ribs. My skin fluttered against her lips, a wave of soft pain. "Yes." I clutched her shoulder. *Harder.*

She kissed my ribs again, less gently. Real pain that time. I gritted my teeth, remembering the tree trunk that had smashed my ribs in the swamp. "Like that," I said.

After she'd kissed my bruises, April unbuckled my belt. My jeans collapsed to my ankles. My knees and legs were scabbed from the swamp, but the erections have always been easy for me.

"*Sssssss*," April hissed, admiring my trophy the way I'd admired her ass, like a beautiful tragedy—my nickname isn't "Ten" just for brevity's sake. April stared and mourned. Her hands stroked me into her memory. Next, her mouth buried me in warm, earnest wetness.

April's lips were sweet agony. Her tongue had learned its way along my hidden ridges. She knew how I loved her fingers to roam across my testicles and deep between my thighs. We had trained each other's bodies well. Every hot swirl of April's tongue stole my breath. My legs buckled back against the bed.

I groaned, only partially from pleasure. A deep stab of grief made my seed surge and burn, until my groans had nothing to do with pain. My sore knees shook.

I kissed April so hard that my mouth ached from the pressure. I stole her lips and tongue, sucking so fervently that I expected her to push me away—but she never did. "You're gonna remember me, girl," I said, nuzzling her earlobe before I bit it.

April whimpered, surrendering to punishment. She pressed herself against me as if she wanted to climb inside my skin. Our fingers tangled as we fumbled at her clothes. Then she was naked brown skin, smooth as a college sophomore. Her nakedness lashed me. *One last time.* A guttural sound rose in my throat, and I collapsed against April to bend her over the bed, propping her ass high. Hot skin trapped hers as I pinned her beneath my weight. We'd tried anal sex once before, and my size made it too painful. I'd always wanted to try again, no matter how tight the fit, but instead I inched past the Forbidden Zone to slip through her moist, swollen folds.

"Oh, Lord," April said, trembling beneath me. "Oh damn, Ten. You're . . ."

April felt a little dry, but her insides welcomed me, grasping as I thrust. *So* tight. She pulsed against me with every breath. I bucked, and April's hands clutched at the bed as she cried out. I braced myself with my arms locked, rolled my hips deeper. Stirring her up inside. April's back squirmed against me, and my rib cage screamed.

I pounded back at her, ignoring the pain from my cracked ribs. The air was thick, hot soup. I thrust blindly, chasing the ring of pleasure that could make me forget about breathing. I thrust so hard that my hips snapped loudly against April's ass, whipping her. *SLAP-SLAP-SLAP.*

"God . . . God . . . God . . . ," April said.

I felt the tremors across April's shoulders, up and down her legs. Her insides snatched me, greedy and strong. I cried out when April's body bumped my ribs, losing track of which cries were hers and which were mine; which were pleasure, which were pain.

April howled and screamed. Her body danced and then went rigid, her first deep orgasm shuddering through her. I wondered how I didn't break us both in half.

We cursed each other, called to each other. We wanted to leave something behind, take something back. Our cries sounded so violent that I was sure the owners would call the police. But we couldn't be quiet. We couldn't go slow. When I climaxed, I yelled until my throat hurt. My legs gave way, and I sank to the floor.

Then, it was over. Quiet.

We lay nude the rest of the night, and I fought the feeling that I was in bed beside a cooling corpse. Both of us dozed, but neither of us slept for long. I could feel April's microscopic hairs brushing against my skin. Since I couldn't have April, her nearness chafed me. I wanted to leave so badly that I could barely lie still. *I love you, Alice.* Ugh. I was afraid I would vomit.

When the first pale sunlight peeked beneath the door, I checked April's face and found her eyes closed. She was asleep, or pretending to be; either one was fine. I kissed her forehead and climbed out of bed. Silent as a cat burglar, I found my clothes and dressed.

I left a note of apology on her table, explaining that I would slip her plane ticket to Johannesburg under the door. *Thank you for helping me understand,* I wrote.

The room reeked of us. April's sweet, sharp scent, like no one else's.

I couldn't glance at April's nakedness one last time before I walked away.

THREE

SOON AFTER DAWN, I was driving toward the airport to look for a standby flight when I remembered the scrap of paper in my back pocket, a glimmer of good karma. I had planned to spend the day touring wineries with April, but instead I was leaving her stranded at our B and B. I'd left money for cab fare along with her plane ticket, but I didn't expect her to be happy when she got up and realized I had cut our trip short.

Rachel Wentz's telephone number was a promise of diversion—and insurance against running into April at the airport. April and I might be friends again one day, but I needed to shake *I love you, Alice* out of my head. *You twisted, stupid-ass motherfucker.* If I flew straight home, I knew I would beat myself up all along the way. No thanks.

I pulled to the side of the road near the entrance to a winery on Route 44 and dialed my iPhone. I don't always pull over when I make a call, but I had nowhere else to go. The near-empty roadway was flanked by towering oaks, and the mountains and valleys around me burst with green life in the golden tendrils of the morning light. I could almost smell wine in the air.

"Who the hell is this?" said the woman who answered in Rachel Wentz's room, her voice angry and wide awake. "It's six o'clock in the morning."

I almost hung up. Since I'd called a hotel switchboard, she would never know it was me.

"This is Tennyson Hardwick. I—"

"We were looking for your call yesterday."

"I'm calling now." My interest in the job was circling the drain. After the night I'd just had, I would have a low tolerance for Rachel Wentz.

"Why should I let you within ten feet of one of the biggest movie stars in the world?"

Go fuck yourself. It was right at the tip of my tongue. Instead, I looked at my watch, still set to Los Angeles time. "It's nine o'clock last night in L.A., but you might be able to catch my agent, Len Shemin, on his cell—"

"Bodyguards have agents?" Her New York accent suddenly became pronounced. She liked being a character, and abrasiveness was her routine.

"I prefer Close Protection Services," I said. "But I'm an actor, too."

"Right, you live in L.A., so of course you are." The woman laughed, overly amused. I don't like being laughed at, but it changed her tone. "Okay, so I'll give Len a call. I've already got his cell and home numbers. How do I reach you?"

I told her, and she hung up without saying good-bye.

Ten minutes later, she called back. My phone rang before I could finish a cup of Caturra coffee I'd picked up from a roadside café. I've been Len's client for more than a decade, and I've never reached him that fast. But I'm not Rachel Wentz.

"You may be a godsend, Mr. Hardwick," she said when she called back; whatever Len had said had sealed the deal, given me instant respect. My caller ID beeped to announce that Len was trying to reach me, too; I wished I could see the look on his face. "We'd given up on you! Come to our hotel. We're leaving for an orphanage in the township in two hours. Sofia will be glad. You'll see our white van outside the lobby."

She never asked my rate, not that it probably mattered to her.

An orphanage would be the perfect reality check, I realized. Instant perspective.

I couldn't wait to get back to work in Cape Town.

✦   ✦   ✦

"What is it with adopting these African babies?" Len said when I clicked to his call. "Do they poop Botox, or what?" Rachel Wentz must have mentioned the orphanage to Len, because I wouldn't have. Any time I spend with a client is their own business.

"What is it with folks who don't want *any* kids, but feel free to judge people who do?" I said, a bit sharply. "Orphans need homes."

"Ten, you're so damn naive. Sofia Maitlin doesn't do anything unless it's been plotted by three publicists, two managers, an agent, and a partridge in a pear tree. Expect a red carpet at the orphanage door—this is probably her new Oscar campaign. And gee, what a coincidence, Rachel Wentz is there. This is disgusting. That kid will need therapy."

Len's cynicism was hard to stomach first thing in the morning.

"At least he'll be rich enough to pay for it," I said. "I say live and let live."

"Yeah, we'll see. Hey, I almost forgot: What about April? How'd it go?"

I love you, Alice.

"Didn't."

There was a long silence on the other end. Len had had a minor nervous breakdown during his divorce, although I was one of only two people who knew. I'd found him sobbing under his desk one day, but we never talked about that. Only two months before, I'd taken April by his office to meet him—the first time I'd brought a date out into the light. Len had beamed at me like a proud father, gushing about how good April was for me.

"Shit. I'm really sorry," Len said. "You know I mean that."

"Thanks. Next subject."

"Ten, I've been there. Your guts just got stomped to dogshit, and you need a boost. Boy, do I get that head space."

"You stink at pep talks. Move on."

Len pressed on with his true agenda: ". . . but no matter what, do *not* bump uglies with the boss—Sofia Maitlin is very engaged. To be honest, too many people know about the Lynda Jewell thing. You get tied to Maitlin, you're the *Enquirer*'s poster boy for a year."

"Fuck you very much, Len."

"Tennyson, promise me you will not screw Sofia Maitlin."

Len only called me Tennyson as my friend, not my agent. He'd watched me flush my career away once. He knew I had sex with every woman who came near me, mostly because I could. The grieving woman I'd coaxed into bed in L.A. soon after April cut me loose was engaged, too. I was still a whore, whether or not I charged money. April had just helped me forget for a while.

And Sofia Maitlin was one of the most beautiful women in the world.

"I promise you," I told Len, "nobody will know if I fuck Sofia Maitlin. Especially you."

"Ten, this isn't a joke—"

I hung up, realizing the harsh truth: I could easily start working day and night again, like the Michael Jackson song. It wasn't so far behind me. *So what?* my mind challenged. *At least you'd get paid. You should send a damn bill to April. She was joyriding you, man, and in this world, joy comes with a price tag.*

Anger was my medicine, softening the bite. I drove faster on the nearly deserted road, creeping far beyond the 120-kilometer-per-hour speed limit. My iPhone was on shuffle, and Lynyrd Skynyrd's "Freebird" played on the car's speakers next. The Southern-fried beat of liberation suited me fine. I jammed on the accelerator while the electric guitar whined and raged.

Free! I sang along at the top of my lungs, vowing never to change.

The Twelve Apostles Hotel was sandwiched between the mountains and the endless rocky shoreline, almost an island unto itself. The only vehicle parked outside was the well-shined white van Rachel Wentz had mentioned. I expected to find paparazzi, but I didn't see anyone lurking. *Good for her.* There are worse problems in life, but I feel bad for actors with swarms of paparazzi. Why would Sofia Maitlin want a circus in the middle of an adoption?

I hate tabloid culture. I haven't bought a tabloid since the nineties, and here's why: I once had a costar who was one of my mentors, an older man I'll call Raul Garcia. He played the assistant principal on my old series, *Malibu High*—a stern Edward James Olmos type. He was far from a household name, just a working character actor who'd been in the business for years, delivered his lines, showed up on time, and loved his work. He often brought his nephews to the set, and I used to shoot hoops with them. (I played a basketball coach.)

Our series came and went, so we didn't see each other for about a year. I called to have lunch with Raul and found out he was dying. Too far gone for visitors, his family said, but we spoke for ten minutes on the phone. His voice sounded awful, but he cracked me up with jokes, and the single most blasphemously filthy limerick I've ever heard. Buy me a drink sometime and ask me. I refuse to write it down.

Raul was an immigrant, and his family was proud and protective. In his home country, his success in American television gave him a stature beyond the size of his roles. His family might have suspected he was gay, but he never told them—only a few select friends. It was nobody's business. At his funeral, where his parents wept over his casket, no one acknowledged the lonely white-haired man I guessed to be his lover, and no one said the word *AIDS* aloud.

A week after the funeral, I was walking down Wilshire when a tabloid on display at the newsstand stopped me: RAUL GARCIA AIDS SECRET, a giant headline read. The photo was worse: an emaciated Raul celebrating his sixty-third birthday only two weeks before he died. A private photo someone had stolen or sold. Apparently, grave robbing is alive and well.

I refused to read the story inside, but a grainy image of the sad, white-haired man I'd seen at the funeral bore the caption RAUL'S SECRET GAY LOVER. And a large, boxed quote from an anonymous morgue employee confirmed that Raul died of AIDS from his *toe tag*. The toe tag was pictured beneath the quote—exhibit A.

It was an assault, as if someone had dug Raul up out of the ground and violated him. Maybe his family shouldn't have cared—and it's too bad Raul felt he had to hide—but grief is hard enough. If that tabloid story had been about my father, I would have wanted to skin the reporter and roll him in salt.

Thank God no reporters will be calling to ask me about April, I thought, the bright side of anonymity. *Yeah, Ten—lucky you! You're not an Oscar winner worth fifty million dollars.*

The parked white van was empty except for the wiry driver, who looked about fifty. He was so preoccupied with his cell phone, speaking Xhosa with clicks and dizzying speed, that he didn't notice me standing by the passenger-side door. I scanned the license pinned to the visor—his face matched the photo. The van was owned by an agency called Children First Mission. The insignia, children's hands clasped around a traditional shield, was on the door.

Rachel Wentz had asked me to wait by the van, but I wanted to meet my client before we faced the public. I used to know the hotel security managers in Cape Town, but I had to wait at the desk while the skeptical concierge called up to the room. She was a matronly woman with blond hair in a severe bun. When she got the okay, her eyebrows shot up high with surprise.

Not surprisingly, Sofia Maitlin was in the Presidential Suite—14,000 rand a night, or about $1,800. Loose change for members of the one-name club.

The three staff people who met me in the hotel room looked like they were dressed for a safari, not a visit to a township. All three wore oversize beige camera vests and hiking boots. Someone had read way too much Hemingway.

Rachel Wentz was about fifty and short, five feet tall, with a wide, jolly face that belied her phone manner. The other woman was Pilar, a tall Latina with merry hips who welcomed me with a bright smile. Pilar's skin was two shades lighter than April's, but she was about the same age, with a similar shape. My restless eyes lingered on Pilar's mouth.

The sole man was wiry, about thirty, and glued to his Bluetooth. He interrupted his conversation long enough to shake my hand and mumble his name—Tim—before his back was turned. He wouldn't be any help in an emergency.

The room was huge, about eighteen hundred square feet, with a décor in vibrant white and gold. The white dining-room table was a centerpiece, with six tall matching chairs. The glass sliding door in the rear was open, so the room was a bit muggy, but the ocean lay right beyond the balcony, and the water was the room's best feature. The rooftop suite floated on the world.

I liked the vibe already. No drama. Except for Tim's constant chatter, they felt like a group of friends on vacation. South African pop music played from the bedroom.

"Sophie's on the deck," Rachel said, beckoning me.

It had been a long time since I'd been in the presence of a star as big as Sofia Maitlin. Trust me, we don't get invited to the same parties—at least not anymore. If you don't believe there's any such thing as magic, you haven't floated near the inner sanctum of the Hollywood A list. These actors are no longer individuals, they're corporations with poreless skin. Movies fail or succeed on the basis of their allure, and their misadventures can kill box office or even a career. Ask Meg Ryan if Russell Crowe was worth it.

According to those ugly tabloids, Sofia Maitlin had been enough of a party girl to frighten producers who kissed Lindsay Lohan's butt. That was, until she had some kind of a spiritual breakthrough and found meditation or yoga or something. At that point, they only had to worry about her trips to Bali and Tibet, and not her screwing the offensive line of the New York Jets on YouTube. God is good.

"Where's her regular bodyguard?" I asked as we walked the length of the room.

"Food poisoning," Rachel said quietly. "Solid two hundred and ten pounds, Force Recon Marine, and a bad bowl of stew put him on his back. She's saying, 'We don't need a bodyguard.' Most times, I wouldn't be too concerned, but today's a special occasion, so we're worried about a leak bringing out the weirdos. Maybe you can talk some sense into her."

"Hello . . . ? I can *hear* you," a woman's voice said ahead of us. She sounded playful.

When I stood in the balcony doorway, I saw olive brown legs twined down the length of a rattan lounging chair. The calves were slender, sturdy, and athletic.

And bare feet. Sofia Maitlin's toenails were painted only with a light gloss, but she had magnificent feet. Long, lovely toes. Smooth, shiny heels. I'm a foot man, so she might as well have been lying on that lounger naked.

"Tennyson Hardwick, this is Sofia Maitlin," Rachel said.

The wide brim of a white straw hat peeked from behind the lounger as Maitlin leaned around to look at me. Two pairs of gold-brown eyes found mine. When she smiled, I felt a primal part of my brain slowing down, refracting to one word: *woman*.

Sofia Maitlin was a petite ball of pheromones, glowing at the center of her own force field. Raven hair coiled down her neck and shoulders in a loose ponytail. If her face had an imperfection, or if she was wearing makeup, I couldn't see it. I saw very faint freckles across her cheeks that the camera missed, a humanizing detail that only made her more appealing.

She had an ethnicity that was hard to place; skin dark enough, and light enough, to be from almost anywhere. She was wearing casual khaki shorts and a button-down frilly white blouse that hugged her bosom, open low enough to show subtle cleavage. Her all-natural chest is her hallmark; it was hard to forget the steamy waterfall scene in *The Vintner* that some critics believed was the sole reason Sofia Maitlin had won last year's Oscar.

Reason enough, from what I could see.

I was surprised when she stood up to greet me. She was only about five-two, shorter than April—typically, much smaller than I would have imagined. Her dancer's body moved with fluidity as she gave me a firm, businesslike handshake.

"May I assume the other man is in worse shape, Mr. Hardwick?"

Damned bruises. I felt as self-conscious as a schoolboy, wishing I could hide my face.

"Much," I said, remembering the cloudy eyes in the swamp. "It all worked out fine."

"Yes it did." Her eyes pulsed at me. Subtle, but I saw it.

"I really enjoyed you in *The Vintner*," I said, picturing the waterfall scene.

Her eyes glimmered, knowing. "Did you? How sweet of you to say so. Have a seat."

When I glanced around, I realized that Rachel Wentz was gone— or suddenly invisible to me. Not sure which, but I never saw her leave. Below us, the mightily blue ocean massaged the shoreline with a gentle, private song. It felt like the deck of a private cruise ship. I sat on the dark gray rattan lounger beside Maitlin's while she picked at the breakfast plate on her glass-top lounge table. She popped the last strawberry into her mouth and seemed to swallow it whole.

"Are you familiar with Langa?" she said.

"Yeah, and it can be a tough place," I said. "It's like any other poor section of town. There are houses, schools, stores. Some sections are better off than others. You definitely want to be aware, but you should be fine. There are regular tours through Langa. People invite you right into their homes."

"Then why do I need you?" she said, smiling.

"Because you know life is full of surprises, Ms. Maitlin. Someone in your position, with your fame, must be prepared for any scenario."

I saw a veil lift from her eyes, deeper penetration. For an instant, she was Sophie Echevarria—half Greek, half Cuban, the girl who'd set out from meager roots in Miami to try to conquer Hollywood. Her father had come to the States on a raft, nearly drowning at sea. Both of her parents died in a car accident soon after her first major film role. During last year's Oscar frenzy, her biography had been everywhere. She was Hollywood's favorite Cinderella story.

Even without reading the tabloids, I knew more about her than I was supposed to. Sofia Maitlin was a gossip magnet, the perfect combination of beauty, eccentricity, and vulnerability. Shooting *The Vintner* had been draining enough to send her on a six-month retreat in Mysore, India, to meditate and practice yoga with her master. Her off-again-off-again relationship with a Greek shipping billionaire only fanned the tabloid flames. She had famously dumped him when the *Enquirer* ran photos of him and a blonde playing naked Twister on the deck of his yacht.

That might have been some of the most expensive tail in Hollywood history. The billionaire missed Maitlin so much after she dumped him and went to India that he offered to marry her with a quarter-billion-dollar prenup. And if she caught him with his pants down again, she'd make another $20 million just on the side action.

That was either true love—or nice work if you could get it.

Up close, I realized Sofia Maitlin *might* have pixie dust between her legs. It was possible. Her smooth skin crackled, even from a distance.

And now, here we were.

She stood up abruptly. "Come with me, Mr. Hardwick," she said.

She walked toward a different glass door—leading to her master bedroom. I fell behind her, stopping just inside the doorway to leave plenty of space between us. Lynda Jewell had told lies about me that cost me my job on my television series, so I was still in High Caution mode with women I didn't know. For all I knew, Sofia Maitlin might still be looking for revenge sex after her billionaire humiliated her on *TMZ*.

In Maitlin's bedroom, there were framed photographs on the bureau, alongside stacks of books and magazines. Her iPod dock was playing Afro pop by Brenda Fassie, a late legend Alice and I once saw in concert.

"You know South African music?" I said.

She nodded. "We shot *Vintner* here a couple of years back, and I was out dancing every night. The Cubana in me, I guess. I breathe music, and the music here is exquisite."

"Maybe the best in the world," I said. Alice and I had once agreed on that. The harmonies of Ladysmith Black Mambazo and the Soweto Gospel Choir are awe-inspiring.

"Come in," Sofia Maitlin said. "I want to show you something."

I hesitated, but I walked beside her since she was near a small table and chairs instead of the bed. I smelled lavender, maybe from her hair. Maitlin pulled up a bottle of wine chilling in mostly melted ice cubes in a silver bucket on the table. The bottle was from Stellenbosch, vintage 2006. She pulled out the well-used cork.

"What do you think of Viognier-Roussanne blends?" Maitlin said.

I looked at my watch: seven thirty in the morning. "I think it's best to wait for breakfast to break out the wine."

She gave me a sarcastic smile. "Touché. Rachel and I didn't quite finish this one off last night, and if you love Cape Town, then I assume you must love wine."

"Let's say I do." I still had Alice's impressive wine collection at home.

"It was great to win the Oscar, but the biggest perk for six weeks at a vineyard? A lifetime supply of the most delectable wine," she said. "You'll have to try this."

"I'd love a taste," I said. But my eyes were on her, not the wine.

Mailin smiled when she poured me half a glass. It was way too early for wine, even good wine, but I sampled the blend to be gracious. The white wine was so golden, it might have been glowing. The pear scent hit my nose as soon as I raised the glass. With a sip, I tasted apple, apricot, a touch of citrus. Floral notes. It had a strong, sweet flavor, with a hint of minerality. Memorable. I made a mental note to buy a bottle.

"Very nice. Perfect for a spicy curry. The mineral taste . . . ?" I couldn't help trying to impress her.

Maitlin's smile widened. "Cement barrels. It's special, isn't it?"

I set my glass back down after a lone sip. "But I don't drink on the job."

Maitlin nodded, pleased. I'd figured she was testing more than my knowledge of wine. Any bodyguard who would get buzzed at the interview wasn't a good hire.

"My guru has been saying for years that it's time for me to be a mother," Maitlin said, her voice quiet. "She says a strong family is the only way to safeguard against the negative vibrations in Hollywood, and I agree. That's why I'm going to Langa."

Maitlin wasn't the first person to expect a child to cure her life's ills. But hell, maybe Maitlin's guru was right. I wanted to tell Maitlin how I'd met a teenage prostitute while I was investigating a case, how I'd taken her into my house to keep her away from the streets. And how Chela was almost eighteen, and I was going to pay to send her to college. I wanted to tell her all about me.

"Sounds like a good reason," I said.

Maitlin picked up a photo frame from her bureau, which she stared at for nearly thirty seconds before she gave it to me. The frame held a stylish black-and-white photo of a white-haired man and a woman with Maitlin's nose, both in their sixties. I saw the pieces of them in Sofia Maitlin, jumbled and rearranged. The photograph had caught them laughing at something off to the side.

"Mom and Papi," she said. "They weren't perfect—an artist and an activist trying to raise a kid?—but they gave me everything they had. Mom was always bugging me about having kids. I saw so many beautiful children the last time I was here, and I haven't been able to get them out of my head. But the time wasn't right. I'm ready now. Today, I want to see those children again. I want to bring a child home and give her everything I was blessed to have. More."

It was only my imagination, but in the photo I thought her mother's eyes laughed.

"Children First?" I said, remembering. "Are they reputable?"

"They've only done two transnational adoptions, but my lawyers said they check out. It's a very small agency run by a private mission."

"Will you take the baby home today?" It didn't seem likely; there were no toys or baby gear in sight. But the baby would change our scenario, so I had to ask.

Maitlin sighed, gently removing the photo from my hands to return it to its place. "I wish! But it's not possible. There are piles of bureaucracy ahead. It can take five years to get approved here, they told me. But a journey of a thousand miles begins with a single step."

I hoped it would work out for her. I didn't want Sofia Maitlin to leave South Africa with my kind of disappointment.

Maitlin looked up at my face, studying me.

"Want to see the real reason I always book this room in Cape Town?" she said, and moved away, expecting me to follow. I did. She took me to the spacious bathroom's doorway.

There, in a corner by a large white soaking tub, were two huge picture windows that made the room feel like it was built entirely of glass. I could imagine her bathing with nothing but the sky above her and the ocean below. The view was breathtaking from the living room and balcony, too, but the bathtub made it a private peek show. Spectacular.

There were no words for it. We stood in silence a moment, humbled by the vision of morning in Cape Town.

"This doesn't happen often, does it?" she said thoughtfully.

"What doesn't happen?"

"An instant spark."

She was standing two feet from me, but suddenly the distance seemed much smaller.

"Excuse me?" I said.

"The spark between two strangers. It's a rare, delightful thing." Her voice was soft.

I had two warring instincts: The first, and strongest, was to lock the door and pull her into that tub with me. My next instinct was to take two steps back, toward the doorway. Training overcame them both: I did neither. I didn't move. This was a game, and I wanted it to play out.

"And because it's so rare," she went on, "we're supposed to think it means something. We're two attractive people, two polite people, and we want to think that's a license to act out the dirty pictures in our heads. I'm sure you could make a woman lose her mind for a while."

Since I hadn't lost my mind, I had heard enough to understand where this was going. I became ice, and ice could not smell the lavender in her hair. Or wonder how her skin tasted.

"Ms. Maitlin, I don't know what you think you've heard about me . . ."

"I didn't have to hear anything." She laughed. "Sex drips off you, Mr. Hardwick. And if I can see it, the others can, too. Rachel will see it, and you don't want that. She'll bounce you off the job before you get started. My manager is Moses to me."

My face wanted to go hot. I lowered and slowed my breathing, putting an end to that.

"You're a beautiful man," she went on. "I hear you're an actor."

"*Malibu High,* some commercials," I said. "Nothing like you." To amuse her, I adjusted my facial muscles into "actor" mode. " 'The future looks bright!' " I said; the catchphrase had paid my bills for months.

"I remember," she said in a voice that made me doubt it. Her lips drew into a thin line. "You'll want to listen to me very carefully, Mr. Hardwick."

"I'm listening."

"The spark between us is there. I know and you know. But I'm engaged to a wonderful person. Greek, very proud. He gives me freedom, but he's old-fashioned. He's very patient with me. And he is in love with me."

She didn't mention that she was in love with him, too. Her fiancé, Alec Dimitrakos, could be excused for an old-fashioned streak—he was twenty years older than Sofia Maitlin. But his two billion dollars went a long way toward erasing wrinkles.

"So I've heard," I said. "Congratulations."

"I would never do anything that could hurt or shame him," she said. "And I couldn't work with someone who might give that appearance. I'm in the process of building a family, which I intend to carry out with the same tenacity that built my film career. *Punto.*" Period.

"I understand." I had entered my professional space. Maitlin was testing me again. She wanted to make sure I was thinking about her safety, not her ass. Actually, I approved.

"So you'll call me Ms. Maitlin, never Sophia. You are not to be photographed walking beside me. I don't need you to open doors for me or carry my umbrella in the heat. And if you can stop oozing sex, we might work together again."

I smiled. "I'm not concerned about working with you again."

She raised an eyebrow, surprised. "No?"

I had a test of my own. "All I care about is you coming back from Langa safe and whole," I said. "That means I'll judge my distance from you depending upon the situation. You'll agree to follow my directions, and trust that I won't ask for anything I don't need for your protection. You have your professional and personal standards, and I have mine. I can't take responsibility for your safety unless you let me do my job."

Either I had just lost the job, or I had just sealed it. I didn't know which until Sofia Maitlin smiled. "Agreed," she said.

I wasn't finished with her.

"And I can't take the job if you go to Langa this morning as scheduled, Ms. Maitlin," I went on. "The driver in the van? I can't allow an unknown second party to drive us. And I've never laid eyes on this orphanage, so I can't—"

"Roman, my head of security, has left a folder for you," Maitlin said, ready for my objections. "All that paranoid stuff is on the dining-room table. Information on the driver. Photos. Maps. Schematics. I'll give you time to digest it."

"I may need more time than you want to give me," I said.

"How will we know unless you get started?" she said, winking. "I'd like to get dressed."

We made our deal without a handshake. Touching her would have been a bad idea.

"*Sí, como no,*" I said as I turned to go, an homage to her Cuban roots. *Yes, right.*

"In the next life, *guapo,*" she said, almost to herself.

With that, my head slightly spinning, I left Maitlin alone with her ocean and the morning sky. We were both actors, but unless she had figured out how hard I was from the moment I set foot in her bedroom, I deserved the Oscar more than Sofia Maitlin ever had.

FOUR

ROMAN'S RESEARCH WAS meticulous. He had collected the names and photos of every orphanage worker who would be present, attaching their clean police records. He had photos of the two-story Children First facility from several angles, including the front and rear doors, with a detailed risk analysis. The facility reminded me of a well-kept inner-city school, and it had an impressive playground. Brand new. Crime was fairly low in that section of Langa, and local police had promised an escort. I called Langa police to verify that six officers would be waiting.

By ten A.M., I was ready to go.

When I climbed into the front seat with the black African driver and shook his hand, I leaned close enough to try to smell his breath. His driving and criminal records were clean, according to Roman's file, but everyone has secrets. No alcohol, from what I could tell. Good start. Princess Diana might be alive today if her driver hadn't been drunk.

"My name is Toto, like the little dog," he said when he introduced himself. Two missing teeth transformed his smile into a leer. There was an old doll on the passenger-side floor, a nude white Barbie with blond hair cascading down her back. The doll's grubby face told me that she had brought nameless little girls more joy than her current condition could convey.

"Is Langa home to you?" I asked the driver as he pulled away from the hotel, although I already knew from Roman's file.

"From birth." He glanced in the rearview mirror at his passengers with curiosity.

"Do you work for Children First?" Again, I already knew.

"When Mama Bessie calls, we all work for her," he said. "She knows I don't lose my head over silly things." Another glance in his rearview mirror. I couldn't blame him; I wanted to stare at Sofia Maitlin, too. But I also wanted him to keep his eyes on the road.

"How are things in Langa?" I said.

"You can see for yourself," he said, shrugging. "It's Saturday. Burial day."

While Maitlin and the others chattered excitedly behind us, Toto explained to me that Langa had one of the highest HIV rates in South Africa. On any given week, he said, there are forty burials in a township of two hundred and fifty thousand.

There are contrasts of wealth and poverty in the States, especially in L.A., but somehow it never feels as stark to me as it does in South Africa. When we reached Langa, a hush fell over the van. I almost felt sorry for the passengers trying to process the visual whiplash of African poverty. They sat close to the windows, gaping.

Like I said, in the bosom of beauty, it's hard to fathom ugly.

A brown dog lay bloated and forgotten at the road's dusty edge, forage for flies. A skinny boy, too young to roam alone, strolled in scuffed and laceless shoes past the corpse without turning his head or holding his nose. A clutch of teenage boys who looked fourteen and fifteen drank beer in a circle, pouring out the first drops as a libation to ancestors or absent friends. At a makeshift barbecue grill—a barrel sliced in half, propped on its side—a skinned, spotted lamb carcass lay in the sun. When we passed more closely, I saw that the spots on the lamb were a mantle of blue flies seeking shelter and nutrition for children yet unborn.

The man in Maitlin's entourage made an *ewww* sound. "Garçon, may I see the vegetarian menu?"

"Like I could eat for the rest of the day now," Rachel Wentz said.

"Hey, hey, are we at the zoo?" Toto muttered, just loudly enough to be heard. He definitely wasn't used to driving tourists. I almost smiled.

The van went quiet again.

There are sections of Langa with paved streets, brick homes, and street signs—locals, ironically, call it "Beverly Hills." Other sections, with blandly painted apartment buildings, look just like American projects. And there were signs of recent improvement; I noticed more colorful murals and newer construction than I'd seen during my last visit. But even in the so-called New South Africa, too many of the township's residents live in overcrowded hostels, or ramshackle lean-tos built of strips of plywood and corrugated tin. On some streets, Langa looks like the new South Africa; on others, the poverty seems as ancient as the rocks in Tanzania's Olduvai Gorge.

At the corner, the two-story white brick orphanage stood out on its drab street—a professionally painted sign hanging on a well-kept fence, and walls hosting a parade of convincing Disney characters, although Snow White and her seven dwarves had deep suntans. *April would get a kick out of that,* I thought, and then I banished her from my mind.

No children were in sight in the large yard behind the fence, but there was plenty of playground equipment. The orphanage looked better off than any of the shabbier buildings in sight, with at least a quarter of an acre on its grounds. It could have been a school in Compton, except for the razor wire.

But when we rounded the corner, with a better view of the orphanage entrance, Children First didn't look the way it had in the photos.

"Shit, shit, shit," Rachel Wentz said behind me. My thoughts exactly.

Word had gotten out. A crowd of more than fifty people had gathered, and there was only one white-and-powder-blue police car parked on the street near the gate. As soon as the onlookers spotted the van, the crowd congealed and surged toward us.

Two police officers in dark blue uniforms and caps—one male, one female, both black—were trying to keep the crowd contained. A quick scan didn't turn up anyone who looked dangerous, but I didn't like the growing numbers. Doors were opening at homes and businesses up and down the street as more people came running. Soon, our crowd could number in the hundreds.

Toto honked angrily. "Move!" he yelled from his open window, precariously close to clipping two teenage girls as they ran up to the van.

Maitlin didn't look happy as she craned to peer through her window, where eager palms slapped the glass with cries of "It's her! It's her!" It sounded like a hailstorm.

Locals, not media. The only video camera was a small Sony in the hands of a grinning teenage boy who probably had *The Vintner* etched on his eyeballs. I searched the crowd for more cops, but there were only two.

"Ms. Maitlin, we don't have the police we were promised," I said. "If we come tomorrow, I can coordinate—"

"No," Maitlin snapped, sounding angry. "Today. I'm not turning back."

"The bodyguard's talking sense, Sophie," Rachel Wentz said, playing mother.

But Maitlin had made up her mind. "Pull up," she told the driver. "We're going in."

I didn't have a choice, at that point. She would have gone in without me.

The female police officer waded through the crowd to the driver's window, so I leaned over to talk to her. She was probably a rookie; she looked about twenty-three. "I was promised more manpower!" I said, raising my voice over the thumping hands. Would six be enough?

"There is a funeral today, much bigger than expected," she said, apologetic. "We're sorry, but there have been some problems. The others are delayed."

"How long?" I said. I'd just confirmed an hour before.

"Indefinitely, I would say," she reported matter-of-factly.

"Officer, do you see this crowd?"

Her apology veered quickly to irritation. "What do you want me to do—shoot them with rubber bullets? It isn't every day a movie star comes to Langa."

Yeah, no kidding.

"Can you and your partner help us make a ring around Ms. Maitlin?" I said.

She nodded, satisfied with my plan. She motioned for her partner, who was husky but looked even younger than she did. Slim backup, but better than none.

I climbed into the backseat so that I could be the first one out of the van's sliding door. Four pairs of attentive eyes stared at me as if their lives were in my hands. Tim, in particular, looked terrified.

I didn't want anyone to get hurt, of course, but I was only one man with one client—Sofia Maitlin. I hate to put it this way, but her entourage, to me, was just cushioning between Maitlin and the bad guys. Strategic cover. I couldn't protect Maitlin from front and rear simultaneously, so I chose to take the lead, stick close, and wrap her up snugly in her entourage.

"Those are fans, so don't panic," I told Maitlin and her entourage. "The police are here to help with crowd control. Here's the plan: We'll put Ms. Maitlin in the center. I walk first, Ms. Maitlin behind me—Tim, you're behind Ms. Maitlin. Until we get in, you're her shadow. Rachel and Pilar, stay at her side. Walk close together, and don't stop moving until we're inside. Any questions?"

Nervous silence. Tim had paled two shades; maybe he'd figured out I wasn't *his* bodyguard. He obviously wanted to ask Maitlin to call it off, but he didn't have the nerve.

I gave Maitlin a reassuring bodyguard's smile. "I got you," I said. "Let's do this."

I slid the door open and climbed out. Autograph seekers waved paper scraps in my face as I helped Maitlin climb out, holding her hand. The police officers held the crowd back, and the rest of us formed a tight circle as we made our way toward the open gate. It was only a ten-yard walk, but the growing throng made it seem a football field away.

"Clear the way! Make room!" the male police officer shouted. His voice was almost lost in the excited shrieks as Maitlin smiled and waved to the crowd with her pro's public face.

Someone bumped against me, hard. I spun a portly, wild-eyed man around and pushed him back.

"Sofia! I love you!" he called, ignoring me. On closer glance, he looked sixteen, his scalp covered with tight, tiny ringlets that glistened in the sun. The female police officer gave me a disapproving scowl, so I let the boy go. He panted with elation that he had been within a few feet of Sofia Maitlin. I knew exactly what he would think about when he went to sleep that night.

"Open the gate!" I called out. I couldn't be a doorman and a bodyguard; my eyes had other work to do. Milliseconds count. The female police officer ran to the gate, keeping it open for us while she barred anyone else from going in.

A glint of light and quick motion in the corner of my eye made me look to the right as a boy lunged at Maitlin. He was screaming something, and I saw nothing but blurred limbs. I moved into the space between his limbs, my palm tapping the point of his chin. His teeth clicked together, and he stumbled back. In that instant my eyesight resolved, and I was able to actually see who I faced: perhaps fifteen, thin as a rail, bright eyed, and with teeth like Chiclets.

And the dark shape he held in his right hand was a black, wallet-size autograph book. *Damn.* Just a fan trying to get a souvenir. I didn't have the chance to apologize, because his right hand flashed to his belt to grip the hilt of a seven-inch black blade.

He glared and crouched, holding the knife with an ice-pick grip.

I remembered my Filipino Kali knife training, and the number of times master instructor Cliff Sanders had warned me about proper hand positioning. The reverse grip was for suckers and Michael Myers wannabes. I seriously hoped I wouldn't have to dance on this boy.

"*Go,*" I said, giving Tim's back a shove toward the open gate. I wanted Maitlin clear as long as that knife was nearby. We were closer to the gate than we were to the van. No one else in our group had seen the knife, including the cops. The boy's crouch nearly hid him in the pushing and shoving gawkers in Maitlin's wake.

My eyes tricked me as I watched the kid: The slender blade dissolved into a blur as he wove a web in the air, hypnotic and disorienting. Quite a display. He sliced the air two dozen times in three seconds, from every angle imaginable.

But he never lunged at me, and he wasn't tracking Maitlin. Even when he rose to his feet, his demeanor seemed more playful than threatening. He was politely warning me off, that was all. And I was receptive to his courtesy. That was us, just two gentlemen passing the time.

I slid back a step as the nearest witnesses in the crowd cheered. He danced, enchanting them with the fastest knife techniques I'd ever seen, his arms weaving like snakes. The boy must have been a local celebrity, because they called his name: "Ganya! Ganya! *Ummese Izulu!*"

"Boy!" the driver shouted, annoyed. "Stop showing off!"

Ganya, if that was his name, ceased his dazzling display, panting. His smile was thin, tight, proud. Ganya made a little bow to me, then slipped into the crowd.

As I had stood with my back to our party, the others had slipped through the gate. I could only stare where the boy had disappeared. I'm fast, especially when I need to be, but the way he moved was a primer on how to bleed.

Toto, the driver, grinned at my unease, patting my back. "Kids, eh?" Toto said.

Like hell. I would be watching for that "kid" on the way out.

As soon as we crossed the threshold of Children First, the noise was gone.

The orphanage smelled like a school *and* a home, piles of fresh laundry and well-seasoned, roasting chicken and mystery meat. I would have known it was clean with my eyes closed. The building was brand new, probably less than a year old. Everything gleamed.

"Welcome, welcome," said the black South African woman who met us inside the small foyer, clasping Sofia Maitlin's hands warmly. "We have looked forward to this *soooo* much!"

The woman had full, round cheeks and a whisper of gray hair in her cornrows. Her records said she was fifty-five, but she looked like she could be in her thirties. She was heavy for her height, but she commanded her weight with youthful energy.

Maitlin hugged her as if she were an elder relative. "I'm so glad to be back, Mrs. Kunene."

Bessie Kunene was the sister-in-law of April's hostess, I remembered. Since April's hostess was a pastor who helped run a school for girls in a desperately poor area of Soweto, service apparently ran in the family.

"You know you must call me Mama Bessie! I'm sorry for that craziness outside. One of the girls who cooks for us, Buhle, told some friends at the high school. You see the result."

"I just feel terrible for disrupting the children," Maitlin said.

Mama Bessie clicked her teeth. "We're paying no attention."

The building seemed secure. I glanced left at an empty classroom well equipped with wooden tables and chairs for children of all ages. Bookshelves were lined with toys, books, and crafts. The walls exploded with colorful artwork, maps of Africa, and posters picturing Nelson Mandela and Barack Obama alongside Elmo and Barney.

But the room was deserted, eerily quiet. Where were the children?

There were rapid introductions to Maitlin's entourage. Tim was an assistant to Maitlin's agent, but they also seemed to be friends.

Mama Bessie gestured for us to follow her, grinning. "They've been waiting," she said. "We're so proud of how patient they've been. They want to show off for you."

Mama Bessie led us down a long hallway with two more activity rooms—one supplied with drums and other traditional musical instruments—and a staircase that led upstairs to what I guessed was the sleeping quarters. Toward the end of the hall, the smell of food got stronger; baked chicken, bread, vegetables. My stomach growled. Lunchtime. I had forgotten to eat.

The dining room was brightly lighted, with three tables of twelve children each, all seated before plates of food with their hands in the prayer position, most of them smiling wide except some of the youngest, fussier children. At the table closest to us, the children were as young as three, and the rest were seated by age. The table on the far side of the room had mostly eight- and nine-year-olds, but two girls at one end looked as old as twelve. They were all dressed in bright white T-shirts and dark blue shorts, like school uniforms. Two female servers in the back were filling the elder children's plates. Clanking spoons were the only sound.

After an invisible cue, the students suddenly spoke in unison: "*Molo, Miss Maitlin!*" they said. A three-year-old trailed the rest, and everyone laughed. Then the children sang in three-part harmony: "*Jesus loves me, this I know . . . because the Bi-ble tells me so . . .*'"

The room was washed in a pure brightness that had nothing to do with the sunlight.

The two older girls at the end of the table tittered to each other instead of singing, glancing my way. One of them was biracial, like a younger version of Chela, even in her rebel's attitude. Her hair was Chela's loosely kinked spirals. The similarities gave me goose bumps.

I glanced at Maitlin, and tears were running down her face. Same for Rachel Wentz and Pilar; Tim kept his tears in his eyes. I've never cried over something beautiful, but I came close. Suddenly, the answer to the question *Why do celebrities adopt these children?* was obvious.

Because the children need them.

Because they can.

FIVE

AFTER THE CHILDREN'S song, we applauded and cheered. Somewhere close, a baby was crying. "Thank you, Ms. Maitlin!" the children said, in near-perfect unison. "*Enkosi!*"

"We are so glad you could come visit with us!" Mama Bessie said.

Maitlin moved through the room, lingering at each end of each table, stroking the children's heads, feeding them spoonfuls of vegetables and collecting colorful crafts they had made for her. *Thank you for giving us a place to live!* one card read, with smiling stick figures.

I guessed that Maitlin had the new facility built, and my respect for her jumped a notch. For twenty minutes, she gave them all reason to smile as they ate.

Then we went to the baby room. In the next room, there were eight babies in plastic high chairs. Two women took turns feeding the babies mashed food. The youngest baby looked only a few months old; the oldest, nearly two. A small, snowy TV played *Sesame Street* to catch their eyes.

The baby room was different. The sheer helplessness of children who couldn't feed themselves was mind-boggling. One baby's limbs were so spindly that I wondered how he didn't break. He looked at least nine months old, but he could barely sit upright in his high chair; his bird's neck fought to support his head. His nostrils were clotted with mucus. One of the women saw me staring, and quickly wiped it clean.

Mama Bessie named the children chair by chair, stopping at the end.

"And this," Mama Bessie said, "is Nandi. Isn't she a beauty?"

The girl, who looked more than a year old, was also Chela's *café con leche* complexion, with intricately braided hair that showed time and care. She had full cheeks, big pink lips, and round eyes, nothing short of angelic. She was an orphan, but she'd had a much gentler passage than the boy who sat nearby.

I wasn't surprised by the way Maitlin's face brightened when she saw Nandi. Beauty can take you a long way in the world.

"Look at how fat she is!" Maitlin said, delighted.

"The parents are unknown, presumed dead," Mama Bessie said. "She was abandoned."

The child gurgled happy words in Xhosa or Zulu, holding her chubby arms out to Maitlin. Her grin outshined Table Mountain as her stubby fingers twined with the star's.

Maitlin's eyes misted over. It looked like love at first sight.

"Beautiful," Maitlin whispered, lost in the baby's eyes. "You're *mine*, sweetheart."

"God showers us with blessings." Mama Bessie rubbed Maitlin's shoulder.

One of the caretakers helped Maitlin unlatch the high chair, then Maitlin lifted the child into her arms, cradling her as if she were spun glass. Maitlin's face was afire with devotion, a natural mother. She would be devastated if she couldn't take that child home.

"Everyone . . . ," Maitlin began, ". . . this is Nandi."

Rachel Wentz, Pilar, and Tim crowded around Maitlin to admire little Nandi.

"Oh God, Sophie, she's an angel!" Pilar said.

"This is definitely the little girl for you—I can feel it," Rachel Wentz said. "I swear, she almost has your eyes!"

I was intruding on a private moment, so I excused myself back to the main dining room. It was also a good time to think about a plan of egress, given the complications. One glance outside the nearest window confirmed that the crowd was still growing.

Some of the children shrieked with delight when they saw me. I had forgotten how little it takes to make a kid happy. One of the boys there—I swear, his name was Oliver—looked like a happier version of me at his age, nine or ten. I had met Chela when she was fourteen, but she hadn't been a kid anymore, with good reason to be sullen and cynical. I wondered why some kids forgot how to smile and others didn't, even in an orphanage in one of the world's poorest neighborhoods.

I checked out rear and side exits, in case of emergency. One of the kitchen doors led to an alleyway on the far side of the building, and an adjoining vacant lot. If necessary, if things got unpleasant, I could send our driver away as a decoy, and call for a taxi.

I used the telephone in the orphanage's tiny, cramped office to call the local police station and ask for additional crowd control. The three people I talked to were all surprised to hear that Sofia Maitlin was in Langa. The man I'd spoken to earlier wasn't available. We struggled mightily with each other's accents, and they all lost interest when I said there was no riot.

"It's not a crime to stare," the highest-ranking man I reached told me before he hung up.

So much for police assistance.

We stayed at Children First most of the day. Maitlin sat in on classes, read storybooks to the younger children, told Hollywood stories to the older children, and toured the neatly kept living facilities. The rooms were large, four beds and two pine desks in each. The children's belongings were meager, but photographs and artwork were taped to the walls.

During our tour, Mama Bessie told us the story of her orphanage.

"So many children, so much need, so many orphans from this horrible disease," she began, not mentioning HIV or AIDS within the children's earshot. "Ninety percent of our children are here because the disease killed everyone who loved them, and whom they loved. Two of our little ones are afflicted, but we are able to afford medicine for them, praise be to God. We are well endowed because of Miss Maitlin. But it wasn't always so! It started as a small dream—a phone call here, an inquiry there—and I completed the licensing procedure. Before I knew it, I had twenty-five children and a staff of mostly volunteers. Then Miss Maitlin came . . ."

"I'm not the hero of this story," Maitlin said. "It was your vision, Mama Bessie."

". . . and now, thanks to her, the children have new clothes. And this new facility. And now I can pay my staff—which makes them much happier with me!" She laughed.

Under Mama Bessie's watchful eye, Maitlin carried Nandi on her arm during most of her stay. Even when Maitlin put Nandi down, she never toddled far from Maitlin. I'll swear it to this day: It was as if the child had divined exactly where she belonged.

Oliver trotted behind me, imitating my walk and mannerisms, desperate for a man to model himself after. It was far too easy to imagine Oliver sleeping in Chela's room after she went away to college.

"Do you know Wesley Snipes?" he asked me.

"I've met him."

"Can he really fight like Blade?" I almost told him he was too young to have seen Blade—but unsupervised TV was the least of his problems.

"Close enough. Wes and I know the same karate instructor," I said, and the boy's eyes grew as big as dinner plates. "The one time I met him was on the mat." Fast, strong, with outrageous improvisational skills and an artist's flair. Trading lumps with Wes was the very best kind of evil fun. "I feel sorry for anybody who thinks Wes is playing. But a real warrior knows his art isn't about the fighting—it's about being strong enough *not* to fight." An oversimplification, but a damned good lesson for a ten-year-old boy.

"What if I'm afraid?" His eyes hung on mine. To him, fear was an up-close concept.

"Here's a secret," I said, crouching next to him. "Fear is fine. Fear is great. The best fighters in the world feel fear—they just *also* believe they can kick your butt."

The boy's eyes shined at me like I was Disney World cubed. For the first time since our private talk in her hotel bathroom, Maitlin gave me a small smile.

Visiting hours were over at five.

"We don't want anyone to think we're giving you preferential treatment," Mama Bessie told Maitlin, eyes on the clock. "It wouldn't look good for the commissioner of child welfare."

"Yes, you're right!" Maitlin said, nearly panicked. She raised the child's hand up to her cheek, her eyes closed.

"She's fine, she's fine," Mama Bessie clucked, reaching for Nandi.

When Maitlin gave the baby back to Mama Bessie, she let out a small sob she tried to disguise as a cough. Rachel Wentz put her arm around her, consoling.

"We'll take good care of her," Mama Bessie told her. "All of the babies get held every day. You see how happy they are."

Her words were supposed to be a comfort, but I could guess the questions in Maitlin's mind: The babies were held for how long? And were they held just once? She hid her eyes behind pricey Dolce & Gabbanas, but tears dripped from her chin. She had enough love to commit to a long adoption process, but enough distance to leave the baby in the hands of others. If I had been in her place, I'm not sure I could have walked out through those orphanage doors.

Out in front, the waiting crowd had grown to two hundred, maybe more. The late-afternoon sun was bright. An official news crew had shown up with video equipment, and all it took was a cell phone camera to post it on YouTube. By morning, the internet gossip sites would buzz with Sofia Maitlin's visit to Children First.

"Miss Maitlin?" I said, stopping her just inside the doorway. "I can take you out from the alley in back. A taxi can be waiting in five minutes."

"No, thank you," she whispered. "This is easier than giving Nandi back."

She had faced crowds all over the world. In a real sense, this was her job. I felt no threat from the worshipping crowd, and if she didn't either . . . maybe we could do this. "Do you want us to try to shield your face from the cameras?"

"No," she said. "I want the name of this orphanage in every paper in the world. Privacy is overrated." Her voice was full of resolve, but her chin quivered. Her slumped shoulders told me how weary she was. I was glad to see there were two police cars instead of one, at least. We had been promised an escort through Langa from a police car this time.

"You're doing great," I told her. "From the gate, only eight steps to the van."

"Seems like fifty," Tim said.

"These are children from the high school," Toto said from where he was waiting in the foyer. "They only want to see a movie star with their own eyes. Don't believe everything you read, how everyone is a car-jacker."

"That's not what we're worried about," Rachel Wentz said, defensive.

"Ready for your close-up, Miss Desmond?" Tim said.

He opened the door. When Sofia Maitlin stepped outside, the crowd cheered. She waved once, shyly, and stared straight ahead. Her subdued, hopeful smile was Oscar worthy.

No sign of Ganya and his knife. Good.

The cameras were mostly cheap, or cell phones, but two bright flashes bespoke professional photographers. Paparazzi. There were two video crews, not just one. As I surveyed the scene, I realized what the cameras would capture: Sofia Maitlin's pale skin afloat in a sea of grinning, dark-skinned Africans, many of them reaching to try to touch her. Maitlin's designer sunglasses contrasted with the bland Western hand-me-down clothing of world poverty. And Maitlin's wave—a polite reflex that would be captured on film to look like a politician's pitch.

"Stupid, stupid, stupid," she said as the van drove off. "I *had* to wear these glasses today." Maitlin looked sick.

"That little girl is so amazing," Tim said. "How did she end up there?"

"It's terrible," Maitlin said. She stared out toward the orphanage as it grew more distant, unwilling to let it out of her sight.

"Mother dead, father unknown," Rachel Wentz said. "When you see this little girl, it boggles your mind. She's a beautiful, healthy, little human being. And that's why the adoption will go through like a breeze, Sophie—everyone's gonna be rooting for this kid. I'll post the pictures I took of the two of you, get them out. We'll let everyone fall in love with her."

"Her name is Nandi—not 'this kid,'" Maitlin said sharply.

"Hon, I'm sorry this is so hard," Rachel Wentz said. "But we *will* get Nandi."

"Sophie, your hands are shaking," Pilar said, offering Maitlin a bottle of water.

Maitlin drained her bottle in one pull, pausing only to catch her breath. "I don't feel well right now," Maitlin said. "I need to close my eyes."

No one said a word the rest of the drive back to the hotel.

+ + +

Sofia Maitlin's wave to the crowd outside Children First had made international news by the time I got to Johannesburg the next day. On CNN, the viewer question popped up on the screen: *Should celebrities receive special treatment in overseas adoptions?* Ninety percent of viewers voted no. The war for public opinion was under way.

No clear shot of my face showed up in the video footage. I hadn't really tried to avoid the cameras, but people like Maitlin seem to get what they want, whether the rest of us like it or not.

I boarded my plane back home to Los Angeles with a check for five thousand dollars in my pocket. Not bad for a day's work; it was more than I would have asked for. I decided I would send half the money to Children First, where a couple thousand dollars would go a long way. Remembering Oliver made me smile.

I couldn't wait to tell April about my day.

Liar, my memory whispered. April had called me twice the day before, after I left her stranded, and I hadn't called back. I wasn't interested in either the pity or the anger in her messages. If she was pissed at me, maybe it was better that way. Give it all a clean break.

We were gone.

Grief came, so crisp that it shocked me, maybe the worst of my life. If I hadn't been surrounded by strangers, I might have screamed.

At long last, I was in love.

Fuck.

Two months after our visit to Langa, Maitlin messengered me a wedding invitation and a phone number to make travel arrangements for two to São Paolo in March. In a handwritten note, she thanked me for donating money to Children First. I'd asked for anonymity, but Mrs. Kunene must have told her. I didn't mind.

My father didn't feel up to a trip overseas, so I took Chela with me instead. I could write a book about my adventure with Chela at the wedding of the year in São Paolo. Let's just say that Chela gained a newfound respect for me and my growing clout; and I wouldn't go back there without a bodyguard of my own.

But that's another story.

Maitlin's wedding and its guest list whipped the tabloids into such an orgasm that they forgot her pending adoption. But two days after the wedding, when the news was reporting that Sofia Maitlin and her new husband were honeymooning in Cape Town, I got a text from an unidentified number, a one-line message:

WE GOT HER!—S.M.

The next day, the television screens were full of visions of Nandi on Sofia Maitlin's arm. It was the most satisfaction I'd ever felt after a job.

If only real life had fairy-tale endings.

SIX

JUNE 2009

DON'T WORRY—CHELA HAS BEEN GOOD. YOU SHOULD BE PROUD!
CAN "DADDY" COME OUT AND PLAY?—A FRIEND INDEED

The text message blipped across my phone on a Friday night, on a rare evening when I was thinking about going out. Dad had company, so I didn't feel any pressure to stay and keep him company while his lady friend, Marcela, was at her book club meeting.

I had a spy in my life, and now she knew my cell number *and* my email address. It was the third message in seven months, arriving as unexpectedly as the first—I'd gotten the first one right after I solved the T. D. Jackson case, while I was sitting on the plane bound for South Africa. My "old friend" knew things about my life he, or she, shouldn't.

And two of the messages mentioned Chela, which made me nervous. Outside of a very small circle of people who had a stake in keeping their mouths shut, no one knew how and why Chela lived with me. But my spy knew.

I cursed myself again for not working harder to make Chela's adoption legal. I'd traded calls with a lawyer as soon as I got back from South Africa, inspired by my visit to Children First, but I'd let it slide. My case had complications: Chela was a runaway and a fugitive, and I had been harboring her illegally. I was also a single man trying to adopt a teenage girl with a history in the sex game. Trying to adopt her might cause more problems than it would fix, especially with her eighteenth birthday only a year away. I had kept her out of trouble, for the most part, and I hoped that was enough.

But someone out there wasn't willing to forget about us.

I walked across the hall to Chela's room and knocked. Through the door, techno music played with the wildly earnest drone of hormone-drenched dance clubs. Chela cycled between techno and Metallica; I longed for the days when it was nonstop rap. When she didn't answer, I knocked louder and tried the knob. The door was locked. Strictly verboten.

"Hey," I said.

The door flew open. Chela had her phone to her ear and her Gucci bag on her shoulder, ready to go out. At seventeen, Chela looked years older behind her dark eye makeup, her only girly concession. Her style was baggy jeans, sweatshirts, and Dodgers caps, but her height made her look like a runway model undercover. She was five-ten—a five-inch growth spurt in two years.

Chela tried to close the door before I could get a good look at her room, but I saw the mountain of clothes. I wished I'd kept my own room, but I probably handed over my prized space because Chela had so little, and had lost so much. Yeah, I spoiled her. Guilty as charged.

"I just got a weird email," I said. "You gotten any messages from someone you don't know? Won't say who they are?"

I hadn't mentioned my previous message. With a few choice key strokes, my unknown ally had disentangled Chela from an internet chicken hawk.

"Weird messages?" Chela shook her head blankly, listening to her phone.

"Where you going?" I said.

"Check the board."

After our spring adventure in São Paulo, Chela had to write her whereabouts on a schedule posted outside her door—the green marker scrawl said she was going to a M (movie) with B (her egghead/wrestler sometime boyfriend Bernard). In São Paulo one night, she'd ended up in a room party with a herd of Texas millionaires. I found her drinking shots and regaling cowboys with dirty songs, a life-of-the-party version of Chela I had never seen up close.

And yes, that's tangentially related to why I can't go back. And no, I won't say more. But it did involve a variant of Texas hold 'em that gives new meaning to the term "No Limit."

"What movie you going to?" I said.

"Wow. This is really a whole new level of pain in my ass."

"I'm just curious."

"Curious like a prison guard."

Every shard of information was a battle with Chela, so protecting her was hard work. Soon after I rescued her from a madam I once worked for myself, two dirty-as-they-come LAPD officers abducted Chela in Palm Springs. To them, Chela was nothing more than a rich man's property and plaything. Both of us nearly died that day. I still had bad dreams about it.

"Let me holla at Bernard," I said, trying to sound casual. When I held out my hand for the phone, Chela's eyes said, *Negro, please.*

"B., Ten says hey," she said to her phone. I heard an insectlike voice that might belong to the long-suffering kid who was struggling manfully to be Chela's boyfriend. "Great—B. says hey, too, so we're all happy. Okay, Officer?" Chela's voice was smiling, but her glare told me to fuck off.

I hated my father when I was Chela's age, so I understood that glare. But Chela was too good a liar for me to trust her, and I couldn't pretend I didn't know better.

"Just think . . . ," I said. "When you go to college, I'll be off your back."

Chela gave me an exasperated shrug. "Yeah, right. See you at midnight," she said, and breezed past me to the stairs. Midnight was her curfew, though neither of us used that word. A promise to adhere to one of my rules was as good as Chela saying, *Good night, Ten, I love you.*

I'd been so pleased with my plan to put Chela through college that I'd forgotten to bring her on board. Chela had ignored her chance to take the SATs as a junior, and I hadn't noticed in time.

"We need to talk about college!" I called after her.

"Says the guy who dropped out."

Then she was gone. The front door opened and closed nearly silently while Chela made her hasty escape. There was a cop in our house, after all.

Loud men's laughter floated from the living room, a reminder of why I'd avoided going downstairs. Dad was free to entertain anyone he chose, but LAPD Lieutenant Rodrick Nelson was no friend of mine. I couldn't remember the last time I'd heard such a braying, carefree laugh from my father's throat. Hell, maybe never.

I walked downstairs, noticing Alice's collection of movie posters and memorabilia hanging on the stairwell walls. Josephine Baker in a banana skirt. Signed photos from Count Basie and Sidney Poitier. Every item was fascinating, but nothing was intimate—just like April had once told me.

". . . and then the nigger said, 'I thought it was *you*,'" Nelson finished in his wall-shaking basso. Another gale of laughter from my father, and Nelson wiped tears from his eyes while my father slapped his knee.

"Stop, man," Dad said. "You oughta be 'shamed."

Dad and Nelson were on their second round of Coronas, as cozy on the living-room sofa as two homeboys on the stoop of a corner liquor store. Or like a father and son, except for the laughing. The sight of them together pissed me off.

Nelson was my age, a dark-skinned brother who could double for a *Shaft*-era Richard Roundtree. He was my father's protégé, had served with Dad for fifteen years in the Hollywood division before Nelson got promoted to Robbery-Homicide and my father's heart attack forced him to retire. This was Nelson's first visit to my father in five years—except for one time in a Ventura County hospital that had been an interrogation, not a visit.

Turns out Dad was keeping the wrong company. Long story.

Grins and teeth faded fast when I appeared. Were I the paranoid type, I might have thought they were talking about me.

Nelson glanced at me as if I'd brought an odor. "Okay, I gotta run, Preach."

I'd solved two cases for him, so Nelson should have hugged me; instead, he was too tight to speak my name. Nelson thought he knew the *real* Tennyson Hardwick: booked for prostitution at Hollywood division, my father's old command. Maybe Nelson was the reason that arrest had been wiped from my record—that *and* the trumped-up attempted murder charge during a bodyguard gig.

But if Nelson was my blue-winged guardian angel, it was only to spare Dad the scandal. If not for Dad, Nelson would have sent me to prison without a thought. He itched to tell Dad who I really was, or maybe he already had. It hardly mattered anymore. After I lost April, I vowed not to let anyone else hold my past over me.

"Come by anytime, Nelson," I said with a too-friendly grin. "We missed you." *What took you so long, asshole? Easy to laugh when the mess is cleaned up.*

Nelson saw my thoughts, and shame made him blink away. He knew all about dispensing shame: After Serena died, he orchestrated an army of cops to swarm my house, a spectacle my neighbors were still talking about. That shit had been plain unnecessary.

Nelson rose to his feet and my father followed, pushing himself up with help from the sofa's armrest. Dad walked across the living room, toward the door. *Walked.* The man had been bedridden when I moved him into my house.

Dad was showing off for Nelson, so he levered himself off the dining-room table, the back of the recliner, and the corner wall, making it to the foyer. Nelson matched my father's pace, pretending not to notice Dad's struggle to stay upright. Dad needed his wheelchair or walker in public, but at home he was a man on his feet again.

Dad's health struggles had allowed me to witness his mesmerizing calm in the moments before his heart surgery—and then his quiet, tenacious battle to rise from the dead. Nelson had missed the most important lessons. *Asshole.*

"I'll get back to you on that dinner, Preach," Nelson said from the open doorway.

"Naw," Dad said, resting his back against the wall. "I don't get out much these days."

"C'mon," Nelson said. "You can't miss this! Dolinski's finally retiring."

"Damn, Dad, get out of the house," I said, grudgingly agreeing with Nelson. Hal Dolinski was one of the few cops who'd kept in touch with my father, and he'd come through for us when I was a suspect in Serena's death. I owed him big time. "I'll go with you."

Nelson gave me a Look: *The hell you will.*

My Look: *Try to stop me.*

"Sure, come fellowship with us, Tennyson," Nelson said. "But be warned: We'll be real cops using big words that might go over your head."

"Like 'I indisputably fucked up my cases'? Or 'I conclusively have my head up the boss's ass'?"

The cords in Nelson's neck tightened. Nelson would never have solved the deaths of Serena and T. D. Jackson without me. He didn't know everything I knew about either case, but I'd given him enough to clear the files and look good to the police chief. And he hated that.

"Like a couple damn kids . . . ," Dad said, pleased that we were fighting over him.

When Nelson finally left, I told Dad about the mysterious email I'd received—so I had to tell him about the first one, which I'd kept quiet for Chela's sake. I told Dad that a stranger had flushed out an internet predator seven months before—I just didn't mention how pissed off Chela was when I made her stop flirting with the forty-six-year-old married prick.

I showed Dad the email I'd received the previous fall:

Hey, Ten—

Long time no see.

I'm sorry to pop into your mailbox unannounced, but I seem to have done a bad thing. You should know about it. You may recognize the man in the attached photos. I know it was naughty, but I intercepted them on the way to Chela's secret account, one you don't know about. Don't worry; she hasn't used it in quite a while, he's somewhat frantic about that.

Was it naughty of me to send the pictures to his wife, with an exhaustive history of their "relationship"? I told her to ask about Bomb346@Quickmail.com. You might ask Chela about that account, too, but don't worry, she hasn't used it in quite a while. On the other hand, the musician is getting desperate. I suspect Mr. and Mrs. Cradlerobber will be having a heart-to-heart right about now. Your problem is probably over, but let me know.

What do I want in return, you may ask? Only a smile.

Who am I? Wouldn't you like to know . . . ?

—A friend indeed

Sure enough, Chela never heard from internet guy anymore, but mysteries make me nervous. I told Dad how I'd tried writing my "friend" three
times, trying to get more information, especially a name, but received only
an oddly cryptic response two weeks after my last note:

> *Nope. Can't tell you my name, Tennyson. It's a shame, because I
> think we could have been friends. Maybe people like us don't get
> friends, and those dreams remain deferred. In the old days, I thought
> I could have it all, but we learn as we go. Sometimes you just got
> to know when to give up some things . . . and hold on to what you
> got . . .*
>
> > *Why? I could tell you, but I'm afraid you wouldn't understand.
> Like Mama said once, there ain't nothing left for me to say.*

"What the hell's *that* mean?" Dad said.

The words in the second note rang eerily familiar.

The messenger probably was connected to one of my clients from
my prostitution days, women with power and influence. The reference to
"Mama" made me suspect a woman I called Mother, the madam Chela
and I had both worked for. Email and internet companies weren't her
style, but Mother could afford to diversify. I just couldn't figure out her
angle.

But that was more information than my father needed.

"Whoever she is, I think she knew me," I said. "Maybe a long time
ago."

Since my spy knew Chela's computer password, my only lead was
SecureGuard, the computer security company I'd engaged when I first
suspected that Chela had a secret cyberlife. The customer service number
on the SecureGuard website, *if* you could find the number, always led to
voice mail. I had a buddy in Chicago check out the company's listed street
address, but he found only a tiny storefront full of twentysomething temps
with no idea how to answer our questions. I cut off my SecureGuard sub-
scription, but by then, as Dad would say, the horse was out of the barn.

"Why you think it's a 'she'?" Dad said.

"See how she talks about being 'naughty'?" I said. "Only wants 'a
smile'? Dudes don't talk to other dudes like that."

"They do in West Hollywood."

"This is a woman. And she's keeping an eye on Chela. I just don't know why."

"So . . . when are you gonna tell me?" Dad said. "How you got mixed up with Chela." Dad spoke in clipped sentences. His speech was much better now that some time had passed since his stroke, but long sentences tired him. Until now, Chela's missing pieces hadn't seemed a problem.

"She doesn't want you to hear, Dad. She's afraid you'll think less of her."

"Think I haven't guessed?"

"The woman Chela worked for . . . ," I paused, and Dad nodded, ". . . was worried when she didn't come back from her client. I was hired to find Chela, and I crossed a few lines to get her. I had the choice of taking Chela back to the devil's doorstep or bringing her home with me."

"Third choice, too."

"Who? The police? Hell, I was a murder suspect. Nelson wouldn't have let that go. And Chela wasn't going back into the system, Dad. You know that."

Dad nodded; there were plenty of nights we wondered if Chela was going to run away from us, too. But Dad saw the gaping holes in my story. "And the people who had Chela?" His eyes were clear, ready for anything. "What happened to them?"

Probably best not to mention the man I'd tied naked to a chair.

"I didn't kill anybody," I said. "But believe me, I wanted to."

"No police? No justice, then." *Justice* was Dad's favorite word.

I shrugged. Despite everything I'd taught Dad since he moved in with me, he still believed police intervention was always the answer. Did Mother deserve to be in prison? Hell, yes, unless you think pimping fourteen-year-olds should be filed between jaywalking and prank calls. But she'd given me shelter the only way she knew how when I was low, and I couldn't be the one to turn her in. Not that Chela would have co-operated anyway. To Chela, Mother was a savior who had yanked her from the streets. We didn't talk about Mother, if we could help it.

"You're not telling it all," Dad said, so I would know *he* knew.

I changed the subject. "I want to adopt Chela." I'd never said the words plainly.

"In for a battle, I expect."

"Got a helmet."

"Guess you do." I had earned the admiration in my father's voice. He recognized how good I was at getting a job done—and unlike Nelson, he didn't resent me for not having a badge. On the T. D. Jackson case, Dad and I had become something like partners. The memories weren't the sort you sit and laugh over, but that case had put our bad days to rest.

Dad's mouth gave a tic from discomfort. "Don't know what's at the end of that road, though," he went on. "What'll come out."

"Good thing I can afford a lawyer, then. First thing Monday. Chela deserves that."

Satisfied that he'd warned me, Dad nodded and grinned. "'Bout damn time." He took a deep breath, gazing toward the ceiling rafters. "Like the book of James says: 'Look after orphans and widows in their distress and keep oneself from being polluted by the world.'"

Too late on that last part, I thought. Dad had no problem speaking when he was quoting scripture. "You got that book memorized now?"

"Just about," Dad said.

I won't claim that I felt God's approval, but having Dad in my corner was enough for me. I longed to tell Chela my plan, but not before I talked to a lawyer. Chela had suffered enough disappointment in her seventeen short years, losing everyone she loved way ahead of schedule—even Mother, in the end.

I hoped our budding family would get a second chance.

Mystery Lady's latest puzzle kept me up late Friday night. What did she want from me?

Her latest text message was from a private number, so that didn't help me. I was staring at her first two emails on my computer, looking for clues, when I realized I'd overlooked a huge one: I had her email address! Even if she had a half dozen more, she might have used FIDO26 before. And if she had . . .

I Googled the email address and held my breath.

Ten listings popped up. The first two were obvious scams: *"Looking for sale prices on FIDO26?,"* the name obviously dropped in at random. I hate that.

Three looked really good. Two were on a guns-and-ammo–type site. She was making comments about reloading shells as opposed to purchasing factory loads. I didn't understand the jargon, but it seemed to be something about an exotic propellant that provided more foot-pounds of energy with less noise. *Whoa.* The other was a cooking site, a recipe for fudge cookies she said she had learned in home ec at Hollywood High.

Hollywood High? On Sunset and Highland? My Mystery Lady and I had gone to the same high school? *Whoa.* Could we have been there at the same time? Was that where we'd met? Had we had a class together?

I don't want to brag, but even in high school, I had the kind of face girls remember long after they've become women. I'd gotten fan mail and notes from at least a hundred women who claimed to have gone to school with me, and almost all of them mentioned incidents we'd shared—most of which I'd forgotten. Mystery Lady might have had that compulsion.

I examined all three notes again, especially the second one. It was the only one that didn't feel breezy, spontaneous, and a little superior. The note was labored, trying hard to say something without quite saying it.

> *It's a shame, because I think we could have been friends. Maybe people like us don't get friends, and those dreams remain deferred. We start out thinking we can have it all, but we learn as we go. Sometimes you just got to know when to give up some things . . . and hold on to what you got . . . Like Mama said once, there ain't nothing left for me to say.*

Dreams deferred. A Langston Hughes reference, of course. We could have been in poetry class, or black lit. Or participated in an assembly during Black History Month.

But if Mama wasn't my former madam, who was she? My Mystery Lady's mother? Then I realized why the phrases sounded so familiar: Although the wording had been slightly changed, she was quoting the immortal Lorraine Hansberry's *A Raisin in the Sun.*

I've appeared in three different stage productions of *Raisin,* and the first was back in high school. In high school, I'd played Walter Younger,

Sidney Poitier's part in the 1961 film. Maybe my Mystery Lady had been in that production with me.

I leaned back and closed my eyes. Had anyone from *Raisin* or my high school drama class stood out? Someone I'd slept with or flirted with? Someone who might have been Brainiac enough to either run or work for a high-tech security firm?

Most of the dialogue she'd quoted was Mama's, I realized.

Who had played Mama in the show? June Middleton, and a girl named Marsha . . . something. I remembered her getting teased for having a name straight out of *The Brady Bunch*. Bit of a geek.

Marsha had been the understudy, since she had bad acne and a stilted delivery. But she'd had a steel-trap memory. She'd nailed her lines for three roles in three weeks, and she finally got her chance to take the stage after June got stomach flu on closing night. Marsha didn't bring the house down, but she saved the day. And I remember really clicking with her during one scene, in the zone, so deep in those characters that the footlights disappeared.

We'd made a connection. I hadn't thought about it in more than twenty years, but it was true. I hadn't collected yearbooks, so I couldn't flip one open to find a last name, but I was willing to bet that my Mystery Lady's name was Marsha.

I sent her an email:

You're either June or Marsha from Hollywood High. I say Marsha. You're just playing a new role. I already know your secret.

See how *she* liked being unmasked, I thought.

Mystery Lady didn't answer right away, but I went to sleep with an evil smile.

SEVEN

SATURDAY, I WOKE up to find that I'd missed an email late Friday night. I thought it was from my Mystery Lady, but it was from Rachel Wentz, Sofia Maitlin's manager. *Finally!*

It had been three months since the wedding, and in case no one's told you, every social event in Hollywood is about networking. Period. I've seen people work the room at Forest Lawn Cemetery. If you think I'm lying, ask somebody who knows.

I'd introduced myself to every producer I recognized in that banquet hall in São Paolo—with tact and grace, of course. By the time I left, half of Maitlin's wedding guests knew that I had just been cast in *Lenox Avenue*, the highly awaited prestige film penned by an Oscar-winning screenwriter. I didn't tell them I'd won the part only under the threat of a lawsuit against studio exec Lynda Jewell, but that's my business.

Every two weeks, *Lenox Avenue* was in the news because of the dream cast. Denzel, Halle, Leonardo, *and* Christian Bale were on board, not to mention enough black actors for a remake of *Roots*. (Yeah, John Amos had a part, too!) And the script—which I'd finally gotten my hands on after months of delays—was so fine it should have come wrapped around an Oscar. It wasn't only the best script I'd ever been attached to, it was one of the best I'd ever read.

My set call was in little more than a week, and I couldn't wait even though my part was minuscule; *Lenox Avenue* is set in Harlem, where most of the movie was being shot on location, but my scenes were being shot on a Hollywood sound stage. Remember that scene in *GoodFellas* when Joe Pesci gets pissed off at the poor kid serving him and his buddies drinks and then shoots him, saying, "Dance, you cocksucker! Dance!" That was basically my part: I'm the guy in the bar who rubs someone the wrong way, and I end up with a bullet between the eyes. I had three lines, literally, and one of them was, "Oh, shit!" Hell, I'm the king of the three-liners. But when I was working Sofia Maitlin's wedding, anyone would have thought I was Denzel.

I hoped the email from Rachel Wentz meant my schmoozing had won me some acting work, a fantasy that lasted the two seconds it took to read it: *Call me Mon. S. wants you on security at Nandi's birthday party next Sunday.* Not exactly what I had in mind. Was Maitlin only being a protective mother, or did she have reason to expect a problem at a kiddie party?

When I think back on it now, it's as if I knew what was coming.

Since I was lining up a bodyguard gig, I had an excuse to call my martial arts instructor, Cliff Sanders, and try to squeeze in a private class. He hadn't heard from me in months, and this after I'd committed to a lesson every week—my strategy for finally getting my black belt after ten years of intermittent agony, humiliation, and glory. So far, it hadn't happened. I'm not good at finishing what I start.

Cliff laughed when I called. "Come on and bring your sorry ass up here, boy."

Cliff lives north of L.A., in Canyon Country, out near Magic Mountain, and it might as well be on the moon. It's only a half-hour drive north of my house "without traffic," as if there's any such thing, but it's in the wrong direction—away from the Los Angeles heartbeat, on the way to Palmdale. Thirty years ago there was hardly anything out there except parched rocks and sun-faded grass. Brush fires came and went, taking only weeds. Now it's all strip malls and housing developments, growing as fast as the weeds used to.

Cliff was waiting in his driveway. The garage yawned open.

"Whassup, Hollywood? Ready to get that pretty face messed up?" Cliff called out. You never want to hear those words from Cliff unless he's smiling.

Cliff is in his midfifties, but you'd have to carbon-date him to know it. He's built like a double-wide refrigerator, and his wrists are as thick as my forearms. He has a gut, but it's as solid as a sack of rocks. Unbelievably strong: Once upon a time he benched five hundred. As flexible as Gumby, he's just one of those prodigies who started with an infinite pain threshold and the body control of a reincarnated yogi, then added an ocean of sweat and a bucket of blood. Not all of it his own. One of those sleepy, bemused guys who always seems to know a secret worth dying to learn. He's one of the deadliest men in the world.

Cliff has worked as a bodyguard for everyone from Muhammad Ali to Hugh Hefner, and is one of only two men in the world to complete Master Instructor Masaad Ayoob's Lethal Force Institute pistol-shooting classes back-to-back.

I was with Cliff in Vegas eight years ago for a mixed martial arts event the night three ultimate fighting behemoths tried to intimidate everyone off the hotel elevator. I got off. Cliff stayed on. He got off three floors later, the only one still moving under his own power. He had a bloody lip, a torn shirt, and a Buddha's contented smile.

As soon as I was within Cliff's reach, his palm shot out, snake quick. A playful sting vibrated against my cheek before my hand was up to block. In terms of pure speed I'm faster than Cliff, by maybe a tenth of a second. It doesn't matter. He doesn't telegraph at all. There's just no body language, nothing to react to. No aggressive tension to trigger the hindbrain. Your conscious mind is on its own, and, brother, that's just not fast enough. By the time it occurs to you to move, you're napping.

"Hey, man, save it for the garage." I laughed. "Been awhile."

"Whose fault is that? Get your lazy ass in here."

"Well, move your big ass out of the way."

Cliff laughed. "You're a sad SOB, Hollywood."

Cliff had converted his garage to a dream martial arts studio—mirrored wall, heavy bags, and a twelve-by-twelve red-and-blue jigsaw mat.

We caught up on what had been happening in our lives in the past few months. Cliff told me about his new fiancée, and I told him about some of my adventures on the T. D. Jackson case, keeping it vague. I don't like to talk specifics about my cases, even with the man who taught me how to be a bodyguard.

"Heard you worked a gig for Sofia Maitlin." His eyes twinkled.

"Not from me you didn't."

"I've known her regular guy Roman awhile—former Marine, good man. Ask him about Larry Flynt's wife sometime. He told me he ate something that messed up his stomach in Cape Town, so they called you. You must be moving up in the world. She as fine as she looks in the movies?"

"Seen worse," I said. Cliff laughed.

When Cliff turned on his massive iPod dock, it was time for class. That day, Cliff was all about the motion and music of percussion, so West African drumming filled his garage. With Cliff, once the music starts, the chitchat is over. The buddy thing went bye-bye, and we became teacher and student. I bowed, he nodded.

He ran me through some of the moves he'd last worked me on. Cliff has more black belts than a clothing store, and like many genuine masters, from Ueshiba to Bruce Lee, he had created his own art, a stripped-down synthesis called WAR, an acronym standing for Within Arm's Reach. It was designed for bodyguards, and its specialty is efficient dismemberment without exposing a cowering client to harm. Not a lot of spinning and circling in WAR: You fought as if you had been backed into a corner or pressed against a wall.

It reminds me of Javanese Pentjak Silat Serak, one of Cliff's areas of expertise, a beautiful movement system based on pure mathematics. And as in Silat, WAR's blows are designed to disrupt balance rather than merely damage the body. When Cliff moves on you, it's as if you had an invisible third leg you'd never known was there, and he knows how to kick it out. When you watch him do it to someone else, it looks like they're just falling down for him. It looks fake. Until your butt bounces off the floor. The man is a genius, and swears that if I'd just be a little more serious, I'd have a major breakthrough in six months.

Maybe I *would* keep coming to class this time. Maybe.

I worked hard, breaking the forms into self-defense applications, improvising, moving to and against the music. But no matter how hard I tried, Cliff knew I wasn't totally there.

"What's going on with you today, Hollywood?"

I mopped sweat from my face. "Guru," I told him, using his formal Indonesian title as a Silat instructor. He liked that more than *Sensei* (Japanese) or *Sifu* (Chinese), although he'd earned the right to both. "I feel pretty strong overall—but I saw some knife action a little while ago that kinda freaked me. I'm not sure I could have coped with it, and I hate feeling like that."

Cliff nodded, face as smooth and impassive as an Easter Island statue. He went to his shelf and brought back two black composition-plastic practice knives. He handed one to me and kept the other, twirling it around his fingers like an evil parlor trick.

"What'd you see?" he said. "Show me."

I did my best to imitate the rapid-fire jabbing motion I'd witnessed in Langa. Watching, Cliff nodded slowly, his eyes sparking. "Where'd you see that?" he said.

"South Africa."

"Guess so. Not Japanese, Chinese, or Filipino." And he'd know. It isn't just that Cliff has trained with the best, all over the world. It's that he's become the one the best come to, when they really want to train. "It sure the hell don't look like anything I've seen. Show me more."

As I imitated the knife's dance, Cliff improvised within my jabs, gently pushing my wrist right or left, up or down, as he deflected me. Cliff moves so well he sometimes seems to be in slow motion. I couldn't get my knife near him, especially with an unfamiliar movement pattern.

"Fast as you?" he asked.

"Faster."

His smile flattened a little. Playtime was over. "How much faster?"

"Ten percent, maybe."

"Rhythm?"

"Broken. Staccato. Maybe based on Jo'burg jazz. Reminded me of Max Roach on the drums, man."

"This, my brother, is some deadly shit."

"Tell me about it." My breathing was already accelerated.

"If I were you, you see this thing again, I'd use furniture-fu."

"What?"

"Tossing lamps and chairs. You ever see this stuff again, don't even think about fighting fair. You don't wake up, you're in for a dirt nap. You're a primate: Use a tool."

"And what if I were you?"

He smiled. "Silly question."

For the next ninety minutes, Cliff woke me up. The drummer's frantic *djembe* flowed through both of us as we lunged and darted. Knives scare the hell out of me. Anyone who tells you they're easy to deal with has never met anyone who could use one. An hour of decent blade instruction transforms a cheerleader into Black Belt Barbie.

So Cliff worked with me on attacking the legs, improvising weapons out of lamps and newspapers, putting power into my fastest low kicks and more accuracy into my eye jabs. Cliff always works out with a Cheshire cat grin, but I was too busy sweating to smile.

"Okay, young man," Cliff said. "We're about to go live."

He returned to his shelf and returned with two real knives.

The edges were wrapped with black tape, leaving just a half inch of point. Give you enough of a scratch to keep you mindful. I wouldn't trust just anyone to spar with me using a real knife, but I trusted Cliff—and he trusted me. There's a bond between martial arts teachers and students that reminds me of men who have experienced combat together, something hard to communicate to someone who hasn't been there.

Without warning, Cliff began the dance. We started slow, finding a smooth flow together, with Cliff constantly reminding me to concentrate on my exhalations, to let the inhalations take care of themselves. Controls fear, and engages the core muscles to increase power.

My mind floated away into flow, and I lost myself in the glittering *pas de deux*. We worked forty-five- and ninety-degree angles, the geometry of destruction. Concentrating on imaginary triangles and squares beneath our feet kept my mind off being punctured. The Moors knew this, and their insights birthed the great Spanish circle Antonio Banderas mastered in *The Mask of Zorro*. The calculating mind shuts down emotion, increases your chances of survival.

I was allowing myself cautious pride in a particularly canny riposte when Cliff tapped the back of my right hand with his knuckle, like a live electric wire. My knife fell to the mat at the same instant his blade touched my throat.

"Shit," I said under my breath.

Cliff's grin waited. "It's not all flow either. Don't get hypnotized."

I was lucky to walk away with only a nick.

I didn't know it then, but Cliff Sanders had just saved my life.

EIGHT

MONDAY AFTERNOON, THE towering royal palms against the bright blue sky made me wonder how Oliver was doing in Langa. I was on my way to an appointment at Sofia Maitlin's house in Beverly Hills to go over the plans for the birthday party when my cell phone rang: WILDE LAW CENTER, the ID said. My lawyer had called back right away.

I'd left a detailed message with Melanie Wilde's secretary to avoid confusion about why I was contacting her. Melanie Wilde and I had fallen into bed after she hired me to find out how her cousin T. D. Jackson died, so I didn't want her to think I was trying to mess with her new marriage. She'd betrayed her man for me once.

"Hope you didn't mind hearing from me," I said.

Melanie sighed on the phone. Her memories of me weren't happy ones either. "No, it's okay," she said. Silence filled the space when we might have recapped old times. "So you're looking for a referral to adopt a teenage girl, huh?" Skepticism drenched her voice.

Red light. I braked my Prius. "You think it's a problem?"

"Young, single guy—might raise more than eyebrows. How long has she lived with you again?"

"Two years."

"And she's seventeen? What's the rush, Ten? Here's the best advice I can give you: Wait a year. Adult adoption is much easier. You have no idea what a hassle you're in for."

I felt disappointment so keen that it reminded me of losing April in Cape Town—final and irreparable. I hadn't told Melanie much about Chela's history, or mine, but it was as if she already knew. Never mind that Chela and I also both had arrests that might appear in the system if someone started digging. If I couldn't win Melanie over, I'd have no chance with any adoption lawyer she referred me to.

"She's a handful, Mel, and she needs a father." The word *father* felt odd to my tongue. "I think adopting her would help me be a better guardian. Build her trust. I want her to have a solid place to call home before she turns eighteen. Maybe it's just symbolic, but . . ."

"You are full of surprises, Tennyson Hardwick," Melanie said. The tightness and distance evaporated from her tone. "You really want this kid."

"Yeah. I really do. We've been through a lot together. I'm all she has."

"Well, good for you. Our adoption just went through, by the way." After T. D. Jackson died, Melanie inherited his two young children. I wondered how the grandparents who'd squabbled over the children felt about it, but I didn't dare ask. A war zone, no doubt.

"How are Maya and Tommy doing?" I said, glad I was so good at remembering names.

"One day at a time. But much better, thanks. We're definitely a family."

"So are we, Mel. Me, Dad, and Chela. We just want to make it official."

I could feel her smiling at me through the phone. "I love it, and I'll do what I can to help. I know a great adoption lawyer, and I'll tell her it's not what it looks like. You know . . ."

"Understood. I don't sound like a good bet." And she didn't know the half of it.

"It'll be rough, Ten. And a long process. You'll be lucky if you wrap it up before her birthday. Where are her birth parents?"

"Father's dead. Mother's a meth addict who vanished almost ten years ago. *Poof.* Thin air."

The sigh came again. "That's a problem, then," she said.

"Why?"

"You can't get past square one before the mother signs off. She has to relinquish her parental rights."

"You're kidding me! She's completely AWOL. I thought after all these years . . ."

"Doesn't matter. The state will need to exercise due diligence, advertise, the whole nine. You'd save yourself time and money if you could find her first. Go in armed and ready."

Shit. Lawyers never have good news. Chela had been trying to find her mother, on and off, since she was eleven, and I would need Chela's help to learn where the trail had gone cold. Even bringing up the idea of looking for her mother might stir up more hurt than it healed.

"Life's never easy, is it?" Melanie said.

"You know better than most, hon." With the violence that had ripped her family apart, I wouldn't want Melanie Wilde's life for a day. The tendrils of her cousin's case hanging between us made me queasy. "I'm glad you have those kids. I know you're a great mom."

"And I'm sure you're a great dad, Ten," she said. "The rest is just a piece of paper."

If only paper didn't matter.

I shook off my disappointment about Chela when I pulled up past the guard gate along the aged cobblestone driveway to Maitlin's mansion on ten secluded acres near Mulholland Drive. My grass was turning brown from the intense late-spring sun, but Maitlin's immaculately maintained yard looked as green as artificial turf. A swarm of gardeners in bright orange shirts were giving the bright bougainvillea and hibiscus bushes a trim. In the circular driveway, two frozen cherubs in the three-tiered marble fountain played water-spewing flutes.

The ten-car carport was empty except for three cars at the far end, all of them draped in tarps, so I had my choice of parking. The sprawling Spanish villa was almost hidden behind huge royal palms and ficus trees, but from what I could see I assessed the value at about $30 mil, even in a recession. Much more, with all of the land. The house looked like about fifteen thousand square feet, give or take.

Maitlin's head of security met me outside. He looked like Hulk Hogan's svelte younger brother, about thirty-five, with bright blond hair he kept cut as if he were still in the Marines. His uniform was black slacks and a black T-shirt, and he had both a Secret Service–style earpiece and a handi-talkie strapped to his belt. He was also discreetly strapped; I saw the tiny bulk from the gun strapped to his ankle, probably a .38.

His handshake was a crocodile's jaws. "Hardwick? I'm Roman. Sophie says you did a hell of a job out in Cape Town. Thanks for stepping up. I was shitting pea soup for a week."

Too Much Information. I didn't ask if Roman was his first or last name, but his buried accent might be Swedish or Norwegian. Despite a friendly grin and easy praise, his poorly hidden scowl told me that it wasn't his idea to call me. Maybe he wasn't the type to share.

"Just trying to live up to expectations," I said. "Cliff Sanders says you're the man. Honor to meet you."

"You know Cliff?" A genuine smile this time. A little less bass in his voice. Knowing the right badass is instant cred in these circles. Roman gave my shoulder a pat and led me toward a golf cart parked beyond the car shelter. "The party will be around back. Me and my team will pretty much have things handled, but I'll show you the lay of the land. Sophie mostly wants you to mingle and blend in. You won't be working unless there's trouble."

I almost smiled. Of course. She'd mostly invited me as a networking gift. But Maitlin didn't know me well. If I'm on a job, I'm on a job. I wouldn't be there to socialize.

The golf cart took us along an unpaved, shaded path along the side of the house, and it was like vanishing into a jungle. Then we rounded the corner and met open sky in the expanse of the backyard, which could have doubled as a golf course. Roman gave me the tour of the grounds: tennis court, atrium, pool house, guesthouse. Closer to the main house, the narrow swimming pool looked like it was the length of a football field, ringed by pure coral rock.

"How many guests?" I said.

"About two hundred. She's keeping it intimate." Not a drop of irony. "Swimming's out—she's paranoid after the Tommy Lee thing. Damn sad, a kid drowns like that. She's doing a carnival theme for the kids instead. Water slides, bouncy house, clowns."

It sounded extreme for a two-year-old, but what did I know? I didn't have Dad papers.

"You got kids?" Roman said.

I barely hesitated. "A teenage girl."

Roman laughed. "Yeah, good luck with that." Then he reached into his pocket and pulled out his iPhone. He showed me backlit images of two sandy-haired children, both under ten. Their cheeks were so rosy that I would have sworn they were wearing rouge. "Those are mine. Six and eight. They'll be here."

"Sounds like fun."

His smile withered, his eyes scanning the property. "We're gonna have a lot of contractors in and out—rental companies for the carnival stuff, caterers, a clown, a deejay. A logistical nightmare. Fun? Maybe for the kids. I'll be working." He put his phone away.

"How many other guys on security?"

"I have my own crew, guys I've trained. You'll make six."

The backyard suddenly seemed three times the size it had on first glance, full of shadows and nooks in the foliage, behind the outbuildings, between the trees. I was glad to see the fence ringing the backyard, nearly hidden in shade. At least that would keep sugar-intoxicated kids from wandering back into the driveway, which would be busy.

Even with six of us, it would be a task to watch the property—especially since some of the personnel would be needed inside the house, no doubt. Personal security, perimeter watch, property damage. We needed to watch for paparazzi, interlopers, drunks, and thieves. Six was barely enough.

As Roman steered the golf cart along the length of the pool, I saw the woman and child splashing in the water at the far end about thirty yards from us, in a section cordoned off for wading. They had been obscured by a huge potted sable palm. A child's laugh pealed, carried across the water's green-blue surface. Maitlin and Nandi were in the pool.

Roman followed my eyes. "There's the boss lady," he said.

In a splendid white bikini, no less, set off against bronze skin. Like most of the moviegoing world, I had already seen Sofia Maitlin naked—

but her bikini was sexier, leaving room for the imagination. The bikini top was overrun by her spilling breasts. *Damn, I love my life.* I put on my mirrored aviator sunglasses so my eyes could roam.

"It's a tough job—," Roman began.

"But somebody's gotta do it."

We pounded fists beneath the dashboard, out of sight, before we climbed out to walk to the pool's far end. Back to business. Maitlin waved, as if we could have missed her, climbing out of the pool with Nandi. The toddler shrieked a complaint, and Maitlin cooed to calm her. Once Nandi was safely on the tiles, Maitlin pulled on a white terry cloth robe.

Nandi's stubby legs pumped as she ran toward us.

"Ro-man!" she squealed. Her pattering feet were no more than six inches from the pool's rim as she ran with a toddler's unsteady gait. The girl could run fast.

Alarm shadowed Maitlin's face. "Nandi, *no!*" she cried, chasing her.

One swoop, and Nandi was in my arms. I lifted her from the armpits, raising her until she was at my eye level. Wet ringlets framed a tawny, fat-cheeked face that matched the fountain cherubs. Nandi's brown eyes were big and six feet deep, easy to fall into. Those eyes would be hard to say no to.

But I tried anyway. "Your mom said *no*. That means you stop—right?"

Nandi laughed as if I'd just told the world's funniest joke. *Mister, you've got a LOT to learn about me,* her laugh seemed to say. She leaned so close that her nose nearly touched my face. "Look, Mommy, I see *me!*" Nandi cried, captivated by my mirrored sunglasses.

"Very bad, Nandi!" Maitlin said, finally catching up. "What have I told you about *listening?*" Her cheeks were flushed from the scare. The wading pool was one thing, but the Mexican-tile marker at our end said that the pool was eight feet deep. I expected Maitlin to take Nandi right away, but she didn't.

"Good—you two get acquainted," Maitlin said. "Nandi, this is Mr. Tennyson."

Nandi's face scrunched into such a comical expression of confusion that Roman and I both laughed. I suddenly wished I'd had the chance to give Chela a fraction of the childhood Nandi apparently had. Could Chela have looked much different as a two-year-old?

"Mr. Ten," I said. "That's easier to say."

"Mis-ter Ten!" Nandi said. "I can count! One, two . . . ten!"

"Mr. Ten is coming to your party," Maitlin said.

"I'm having a birthday!" Nandi held up two fingers. "I'm two years old. One, two!"

"Two is the best birthday there is, Nandi," I said, and Nandi nodded as if this were common knowledge. "You've grown a lot since the last time I saw you. You were just a baby."

"I'm not a baby!" Nandi said.

"Not anymore, kiddo." I was a little stunned by how much a few months had matured her. In Langa, I hadn't heard her speak a word of English. She already sounded like a native speaker.

A black woman in her midtwenties, whose hair was in a tightly curled natural, appeared from the back of the house, dressed in jeans and a Jill Scott concert T-shirt. The nanny, I guessed. If Sofia Maitlin was like most celebrity moms, she had at least one nanny, likely two—and the nanny probably lived at the house.

"Should I take her, Ms. Maitlin?" the woman said. I recognized her accent right away: She was from southern Africa.

"Yes, Zukisa, please get her dry and fix her lunch."

Zukisa gave me a shy smile, barely meeting my eyes before she gathered Nandi into her arms. Zukisa's smile made her cheekbones leap to life. Pretty girl. Nandi chattered on as Zukisa walked with her toward the house, the rest of us already forgotten.

"Did she work at the orphanage?" I said.

"No—Mama Bessie couldn't spare anyone," Maitlin said. "We interviewed nannies during the adoption process. I wanted a Xhosa speaker, so Nandi will keep up with her first language. I'm working on mine, but the clicks are killing me. She's so good with Nandi! I hope she'll stay until Nandi graduates from high school." Maitlin suddenly clasped both of my hands. "Thanks for coming."

"Anything to help. I'm happy everything has gone so well for you and Nandi."

"Life is a blessing," Maitlin said. I was glad she'd covered her bikini, because her body would have been a distraction. I remembered our odd encounter in her bathroom, wondering if she was testing me again.

My iPhone vibrated in my front pocket. *Is that a phone in your pocket, or are you just happy to see me?* I had received a text or an email, but it would have to wait. Probably Len, wanting a recap on our meeting at Maitlin's house. Len couldn't let go of the notion that Maitlin was secretly orchestrating my next career bump. Stranger things had happened.

"I was bringing him up to speed, Sophie," Roman said, and Maitlin let my hands go.

"Good," Maitlin said. "Then you know the basics. We're not expecting a problem, but we're not accustomed to so many people at the house. How's *Lenox Avenue*, Mr. Hardwick?"

I was glad she remembered. "Have an early set call on Monday, as a matter of fact. The dailies look like money."

"Congratulations."

I shrugged. "Just a start."

"And not the end. You'll see." She winked at me. At least I would have a bone to give Len to gnaw over when I called him back. "Remind me to introduce you to someone Sunday." My heart did a minor flip until she went on, "Nandi's birth father will be here."

That was a surprise. "But I thought . . ."

"He showed up during the adoption process. Apparently, he'd fallen out of touch with the mother, and never knew he had a child."

"How . . ." My brain was stuttering. "How did he find out?" *Who sold you out, lady?*

"Her face was on every television station and magazine. Apparently, she looks just like his kid sister. After the DNA test, we needed his consent, so we worked it all out. Now he's living in San Diego. He has visitation for birthdays and holidays."

She said it cheerfully, but I could only imagine the stress that had added to her adoption process. I almost said *I'm sorry*, but maybe it was for the best. Hell, maybe it was a sign: If Maitlin could do it, so could I.

"I'm about to adopt my teenage ward," I said. The phrase *teenage ward* sounded as if it should be followed by *Quick, Robin! To the Batpole!* "I need consent, too."

Maitlin's face melted into approval, joy, admiration. Her eyes misted.

"That's so wonderful! Good luck, Ten," she said, squeezing both of my hands again.

It was the first time Maitlin had called me anything except Mr. Hardwick, exactly as if she thought we were becoming friends. I hoped so.

Sofia Maitlin would be an excellent friend to have.

Well, well, well—I'm impressed. I have to admit, I wasn't expecting you to catch on so fast. I'd planned for a series of maybe ten notes, and thought if you were really smart you'd catch on by number six. If you hadn't gotten it at ten, I would have been bored. Now I'm . . . intrigued.

By the way, you're keeping lofty company these days, aren't you? I'm jealous, but if Sofia Maitlin trusts you, then maybe I can trust you, too. I need help, and you might be the only one who can deliver. I don't have her $$$, but what I'm offering is worth more than cash. Meet me at Hugo's West Hollywood at noon on the dot Tuesday.—A friend in need

I was wrong about the message on my phone: The email was from my Mystery Lady. I was idling my car in Maitlin's carport when I checked my email, and the words on my phone's screen made me so paranoid that I looked over each shoulder to see if someone was watching me. Had Marsha followed me to Maitlin's house? I didn't think so. Only the gardeners were in sight, still fiercely trying to order nature's progress.

I read the note carefully and caught the subtle change in her signature: In her previous notes, she had been A friend *indeed*. She might be in trouble, or she wanted me to believe she was. She had done me a favor when I had a problem with Chela that might have gotten me locked up if I'd tried to fix it myself—and I don't expect favors to come for free.

If Marsha was playing me, she was definitely plucking all the right strings.

"You want to play?" I said under my breath. "Then let the games begin."

NINE

TUESDAY

I love Hugo's on Santa Monica Boulevard in West Hollywood—Chela and I ate there at least once a month for the terrific salads—which I assumed my Mystery Lady already knew. As I walked beneath the restaurant's green canopy, I was on familiar ground. And in new territory.

I was a minute early, but I didn't see anyone sitting alone at a table, or anyone who looked like she was waiting. The crowd huddled near the door included three young office girls on an adventure away from their cubicles, two agent types arguing over the Lakers, a family of Asian tourists, and a band of high school girls in a competition to look the most like Nicole Richie or Paris Hilton, waifish bodies beneath faces hidden by gigantic sunglasses.

The assistant manager, Ricardo, smiled and waved me through, and observers assumed I must be "someone." I heard one of the cubicle dwellers whisper about *Homeland*, the series I'd been fired from, so I cast her a grateful grin: *Thanks for remembering.*

Sigh.

My favorite table gave me a view of people approaching from outside and new arrivals at the door. Once my iced organic peppermint tea arrived, I decided I wasn't going to sit waiting like an anxious schoolboy. I was hungry. I ordered a grilled chicken sesame salad and looked forward to the orange slices, almonds, snow peas, and jicama.

By twelve fifteen, my food had arrived. But instead of my waitress—an efficient but unchatty woman who had her mind on her Hollywood dreams—the assistant manager came to my table with the plate. Ricardo had thinning, stringy hair that wouldn't stay in line; when he leaned over to speak to me privately, a swath fell across his eyes. He rested my salad in front of me and held up a sealed, unmarked, standard-size envelope.

"I'm a bad person, Ten," Ricardo said.

"What's this?" I was already taking my first bite.

"I wanted to tell you as soon as you walked in . . . A woman came in about a half hour before you and gave me this envelope. She said I should only give it to you if you took off before twelve thirty, but you look damn pathetic sitting here. It sounded like psycho bullshit to me, to be honest, but she said she was your girlfriend, and it was a joke."

"I don't have a girlfriend," I said, looking around. Cubicle Girl smiled at me as if she thought I was seeking her out. If my Mystery Lady was Marsha from high school, she was far older than twenty-two. "Is she still here?"

"Naw, she took off. Like I said, she got here way before you. I almost came over here ten times before now."

I slid my index finger across the sealed lip of the envelope. "What did she look like?"

"Five-six, maybe. Longish hair. Dark skin—black or Latina. Thirties? Super fine."

"Super fine?"

Ricardo winked. "Why else you think I went along, compadre? Hope she at least put her phone number in there!" And he left me with my puzzle.

Super fine, huh? A phone number would have been great, but I knew better than to expect anything that simple. Inside, the handwritten note was two lines of elegant penmanship: *Some encounters are best kept Secret. Meet me near Maxella and Del Rey in Marina del Rey. I'll make the drive worth your while.—A friend in need.*

I didn't recognize the intersection, but it sounded close to the harbor. Was she inviting me to her place?

I guessed she was about twelve or thirteen miles from Hugo's, which might mean forty minutes in traffic. Not a quick drive. Some guys would have torn up the note and walked away, and maybe those guys are smart. But I wasn't that type, and Mystery Lady knew me already.

I finished eating and drove south as swiftly as the traffic would allow.

I was within two blocks of our designated meeting place when a groan rose in my throat, and I pounded my steering wheel with frustration. "Shit!"

The corner of Maxella and Del Rey brought me to the bright tropical colors of the Villa Marina Marketplace, a shopping mall laid out in a giant, multilevel strip and swimming with humanity. I'd shopped there at least a dozen times with female companions, but Mystery Lady's joke hadn't dawned on me until I drove up. *Okay, you got me,* I thought. It was a mall.

I idled and kept watch for about five minutes before I parked. Scores of women passed me, but few were dark skinned. I gave every sister careful scrutiny, but no one registered recognition. They were either too young, too old, or definitely would not fit Ricardo's definition of *Super fine*—and I allowed for a broad definition. I could almost hear Mystery Lady laughing at me.

"Oh no, baby, we're not done," I muttered. I had been talking to her without realizing it, like she was my imaginary friend. I *hoped* she was a friend, anyway. I scanned the street and read the note again. I found another clue I'd overlooked: *Some encounters are best kept Secret,* she'd written, with a capital *S*. It wasn't a mistake, so it had to be a puzzle piece.

"Secret . . . ," I muttered, scanning the street again.

There, right near Starbucks and Rubio's Fresh Mexican Grill, I saw the sign for Victoria's Secret. Bingo! "You *are* a naughty girl . . ."

Not counting São Paulo, where the Brazilian women cast a spell on me, I'd hardly been laid since April and I had broken up. Opportunities abounded, but interest was lacking. On the days I felt restless and irritable, I called my fine selection of booty calls—a couple of actresses, a comedienne, a photographer—women I'd known for a long time and was attracted to, but who held no mysteries or expectations. After April, I wasn't in a hurry to start that dance with someone new. And it had been years since I'd found any joy fishing in the barrels of L.A.'s nightclubs. Too easy.

But my Mystery Lady had awakened the part of me that enjoyed the hunt. I felt the first stirrings of a hard-on as I walked into the lingerie store.

As soon as the bell tinkled, I knew I was in the right place. A thin, statuesque saleswoman with a slightly horsey face grinned widely at me as I walked past the rows of skeletal mannequins in sheer lingerie who could be her twins. The cheery blond woman beside her was shorter and cute, slightly older than Chela.

"Damn!" said the shorter girl. "I only had five minutes to go!"

"But he made it, so pay up," said the tall one.

A five-dollar bill exchanged hands as I stood before them. The tall girl giggled; her name tag read CHLOE, and the shorter one was KATE.

"I'm looking for someone . . . ," I began, and Tall Chloe giggled again. She reached behind the counter and pulled out a midsize store gift box.

"A face that could make you forget your own name?" Chloe said, and they both laughed.

"Definitely fits the description," said Kate. She had a fading English accent.

Chloe met my eyes. "And you made it before one thirty, so guess what . . . ? We have a package for you, Tennyson Hardwick."

She gave me the gift box, which had my name written in a corner with a bright red Sharpie, the same handwriting as the note. I shook the box, and something fluttered inside. It was light, but it wasn't empty. "And the woman who left this . . . ?"

"She's long gone, mate," Kate said. "More than an hour ago. She dropped in, did a little shopping, and left that for you. If you'd gotten here five minutes later, she said to put the box in the rubbish bin and forget we saw her."

Chloe grinned. "Very mysterious."

Mystery Lady liked deadlines. The physical description I gathered from the clerks was consistent with what Ricardo had told me at Hugo's.

Chloe touched my wrist when I began to open the box. "Oh no. Use a changing room. She said you should be alone."

"Go on, there's no one back there now," Kate said.

"Alone, huh?" I shook the box again—this time I listened, as if for a bomb. No ticking. "All right then, ladies. Lead the way."

While the saleswomen chortled, we walked past the lingerie promising sex. The changing rooms were spacious, with saloon-style doors, moody pink lighting, and a tiny doorbell for emergency consultations. I had visited a changing room at Victoria's Secret once before, but that particular time I wasn't alone. Twins, in fact. Another story. Ask me sometime: I don't kiss and tell, but I have been known to allude.

With my saloon doors closed behind me, I finally opened my Mystery Lady's gift.

A black teddy. Underneath the sheer black fabric, I saw the blurred outline of a white envelope. *Please let it be her hotel room number,* I thought.

Instead, I found a photograph: a brown-skinned model wearing the black teddy in the box, only strings except at the breasts and crotch, with a thin strip of satin to hold it together. Her body made the regular Victoria's Secret models look like amateurs. She had one hand on her hip, nails painted bright red, her hip slung to one side in a dare. Tantalizing shadows fell across the flat, slender sides of her abdomen. She had a triathlete's build, and natural breasts as nice as Sofia Maitlin's. My mouth watered, as if that photo was a hot lunch from Aunt Kizzy's Back Porch, the soul food restaurant just down the street. *Woof.*

I eagerly read the handwritten note underneath:

You'll be my #1 if you meet me where you first got high. Look north if you want a hummer. Let's see if you're Up to finding me—A friend in need

She wasn't finished with me yet. Shit!

It was almost three o'clock, and I had blown my day. I'd planned to throw the box away as soon as I got outside the door. But I didn't. Instead, I sat in my car staring at the last clue. And the photograph.

The first part was easy enough: I was just off the Pacific Coast Highway, which is also called CA-1. *You'll be my #1.* But follow it where? *Meet me where you first got high.*

Even as I merged into the early rush-hour traffic headed back home to paradise on the Pacific Coast Highway with its spectacular view of the ocean, I had no idea where I was supposed to be driving. Bright white foam cascaded against sandy shoreline and craggy rocks, and cars laden with coolers and surfboards were parked up and down both sides of the highway. The view from the PCH always brings to mind that great line from *Roots* as Kunta Kinte holds his firstborn child up to the night sky: *Behold—the only thing greater than yourself.* Beautiful.

Meet me where you first got high. I could barely remember the first time I got drunk, much less high. It would have been back in high school, but I was hanging out in South Central Los Angeles in those days, not the PCH. Had I driven out to meet Marsha and some other students for a party on the beach where someone passed a joint? *High school.* I racked my brain as I drove.

When the answer hit me, I laughed aloud. "Good one, girl," I said.

My first major break in television was a semiregular part as a basketball coach on a *Beverly Hills 90210* clone called *Malibu High,* so many years ago that the residuals checks were down to double digits. The highway would take me straight to Malibu. The last time I'd visited Malibu, I'd risked getting myself killed when I rescued Chela from a rapper's rented beach house.

I was hunting pleasure this time, not business. I'd almost been late once, and I didn't want to give my Mystery Lady the chance to throw me off her trail. I gunned the accelerator, passing majestic rows of royal palms. "Oh, I'm coming, baby," I said, posting her photo on my sun visor. I was eager to finally see her face.

"You find her?" Dad said when I called to tell him not to expect me home early. My life was his favorite new soap opera.

"About to."

In my father's silence, I guessed that he was disappointed I hadn't asked him to be my partner on this new case; he spent most of his time watching TV, so any drive was a diversion. But there are some women you just don't bring home to Daddy.

"Any problem, let me know," Dad said finally. "Keep your eyes open, Ten."

"Oh, I'll keep an eye on her, all right," I said, staring at the photo. Her curves blotted out the mighty Pacific. After I hung up, I posted her note beside the photo so I could study them side by side, a recipe for a car crash. But my clock was running.

Three twenty.

Look north if you want a hummer. I shifted in my seat to release the pressure of the erection fighting to break out of my jeans. I guessed I would find my treasure somewhere up Route 1, Pacific Coast Highway, which actually runs northwest. Close enough. Malibu feels more like a village than a city, with a population of only eighteen thousand, and the PCH carves straight through town. Malibu is best known for its celebrity residents and gorgeous houses near the beach. What did she have in mind? An adult bookstore?

I passed a rainbow assortment of six gleaming Hummers parked in a row. *Look north if you want a hummer!* I slammed on my brakes so hard that the car riding on my tail was forced to honk and swerve. My Little Head had taken over the steering wheel of my Prius long ago. I waved an apology, but I got the finger in return.

The Hummers and two or three Jaguar convertibles were parked in front of an office building built on a bluff to my right. A discreet sign in the window read: MALIBU LUXURY CAR RENTALS. I would have missed the sign, but I couldn't miss the Hummers. The owners had hauled in piles of sand to give the impression that the massive vehicles were racing across sand dunes. The two-story office building behind the cars was a converted beach house.

It felt like the right place, but where was she? I saw only a salesman sitting in a lawn chair behind the Hummers, as if he was at the beach. *Last chance,* I lectured my erection. *If all you find is another bread crumb, game's over. Don't let her drag you all over the map, man.*

The salesman looked about fifty, slightly overweight, hiding his paunch beneath a loose-fitting Hawaiian-style shirt with a sailboat pattern. He was so deeply tanned that he looked like he was on his way to skin cancer treatments, probably from spending too much time sitting on his phony beach. The back of his neck was broiled and spotted.

He pointed out the Hummer closest to me, an H3 with paint the color of a fiery sunset. "Chicks love these babies," he said. "Keep it all day for a hundred bucks."

"Sorry, man. I'm looking for someone . . ." I thought about showing him the photo in my pocket, but I described my Mystery Lady instead.

"Can't say I've seen her." He spoke slowly, a verbal wink.

If I'd been chasing anyone else, I would have ignored his cue. "You seen her or not?"

"Can't say I have."

Now I was sure of it: He was speaking in code. I tried to keep my patience. "This lady you can't say you've seen . . . where would I find her?"

"Can't say that either," he said with a convincing shrug. "Sorry I can't be of more help. But be sure to check out our selection in the rear."

He went back to his chair to soak up the UV.

I began to doubt that I'd read the car salesman's meaning right, but I followed a gravel footpath to the rear of the building. The path had a steep incline, since the office building was higher than the makeshift car lot below. Behind the building, a bike covered in sand dust leaned against the storm fence between the building and the rocky cliff pressed behind it. The strip was narrow, without a blade of grass—never mind a living and breathing female. The windows were shuttered from the inside, and the rear door was locked. End of the line.

Sighing, I glanced one more time at my treasure map. *Let's see if you're Up to finding me.* Why was the word *Up* capitalized? Way too deliberate to be a coincidence, so I looked up. Beneath the dizzying blue skies, I noticed fire-escape–style stairs from the rooftop on the opposite corner of the building. The stairs were painted white to blend in with the paint.

Was that a piece of paper up high, waving at me in the ocean breeze?

My heart gave a tentative leap. I climbed up the stairs, which rattled enough to make me glad the walk was only two stories. At the top of the stairs, I grabbed the paper, which was anchored by a rock. CAN YOU HELP ME? the same handwriting said.

The modestly sized, flat rooftop was a makeshift beach-watching and hangout spot, with faded deck-style wood flooring and observation benches and a large umbrella facing the sea. I was only a few feet behind two lounge chairs side by side, their backs raised high. A few discarded Coke Zero cans were strewn near the stairs. From the rooftop, the shoreline stretched as far as I could see in either direction. The view of the water across the highway would have been perfect except for the large beach house smack at the center of the vista, far below.

"Hello?" I called.

Silence. Or did I hear a faint whimper? And R & B music playing very low? It might be Marvin Gaye's "Sexual Healing," or my horny imagination. Two steps, and I heard Marvin's familiar whisper: *Wake up, wake up . . .*

"I'm glad you finally made it," a hidden woman's silken voice said. "It starts to cool off up here before long, and then I'd really be in trouble." Her voice came from one of the loungers.

I saw two bare brown legs first, one outstretched, one bent at a knee that glimmered with oil in the sun. The photo hadn't done my Mystery Lady justice: Her feet were small, with brightly painted red nails, but hard, not dainty. Exquisitely toned calves, and legs a mile long. She lived in the gym: Her body hadn't bloomed that way by accident.

When I stood over the lounger, I recognized her Victoria's Secret teddy—but she wore it in red to match her toenails. Her breasts were more impressive in the flesh, ripe and round, bare except for the nipples. It was hard to look away from her chest.

Her face was a disappointment only because it didn't unlock any memories. The new face was a hell of an improvement, but except for maybe the nose, it was hard to see high school Marsha in the lovely woman she had become. The acne was gone without a trace, and time had been generous to her smooth face, perhaps in compensation for her awkward high school years. Her hair was long and bone straight, almost the way Cher wore hers—a weave, obviously, albeit a good job. She wore reflective sunglasses that hid her eyes except for a glimmer of sea green that had to be contact lenses. She was strong jawed like Mike Tyson's ex, Robin Givens.

Her kind of beauty could be both a lure and a weapon. If she was my age, she didn't look it. She and Halle had the same timeless genes.

"What took you so long, Ten?" she said, smiling playfully.

My mind was slow to respond, deprived of blood flow after the sudden surge to my groin. As far as the Little Head was concerned, we'd already spent way too much time talking.

"Lousy directions," I said.

"And yet, here you are."

"Funny—you don't look like a car salesman."

Without unclasping her hands from behind her head, she nudged away her sunglasses with her elbow, displaying her full face. Her eyes were so large and striking, with or without contacts, and they seemed to swallow me. I longed to see their true color. The true window.

Her nose brought her surname back to me.

"Marsha Willis," I said. "You played Lena Younger in *A Raisin in the Sun*." Acne or not, I'd thought it was a shame to hide Marsha's face under so much stage makeup to make her look like Mama. Her face didn't stir memories, but her body, height, and voice seemed right. I hadn't known her well, but she'd been a sweet girl. And she'd been so determined to be an actress that she had routinely outshined more talented actors who were less motivated.

Her eyes sparkled. "Impressive. I knew you were the right man."

I showed her the HELP sign. "What's this about?"

With a mischievous grin, Marsha shifted position to bring her hands into view, her wrists bound in handcuffs with red, feathery padding. "I'm afraid I'm in a bind, Ten."

I expected to hear the denim in my jeans rip. I don't want to complain, but men who are well endowed have a tough time in close quarters. It's a curse, but I suffer in silence.

"First things first," I said, trying to keep my brain power switched on. "How do you know so much about my life? Are you with SecureGuard?"

"You have to *make* me talk, Ten."

"Too bad I left my waterboarding kit at home."

"You're wearing a belt, aren't you?"

Not for long, I hope. I lifted my T-shirt so she could see my leather belt and its copper belt buckle. From her appreciative smile, she was happier with what she saw beneath it.

I yanked off my belt with fluid speed, and it snapped against the chair, close to her shoulder. Clutching the heavy buckle safely in my palm, I twined the aged brown leather once around my hand for a firm grip, pulling it taut. *What's she up to . . . ?*

"So . . . ," I said. "Are you my guardian angel?"

"Guardian, maybe. Angel? Don't count on it. How's Chela?"

"She's great. Now tell me why you care."

Her eyes swallowed me again. "Make me."

My belt flew in a blur, snapping against Marsha's bare thigh. Marsha didn't flinch or blink; she had flawless control of her reflexes. Her smile was engraved on her face. "Is she still Chela to you? Or do you call her Lauren?" she said.

Even my father didn't know Chela's given name, which Chela had confided to me right before I went to Cape Town. Chela was only her street name.

The *SNAP* was louder, and Marsha recoiled from the belt's sting. Wouldn't leave a welt, but it had to burn. Marsha's fixed smile broke, giving way to a fresh one—surprise and delight. She thrust her chest out, as if in reward. "I like you more all the time," she said.

"How do you know so much about Chela?"

Marsha's eyes narrowed with defiance. She shifted her position on the lounger, one hip down, the other thrust high, offering me more skin. Her eyes watched me, anticipating. My fingers twitched on the belt. Hurting women isn't my thing, but nothing turns me on more than giving a woman exactly what she wants. *SNAP*. The belt bit into the meat of her back thigh. Lots of nerve endings. Marsha hissed, closing her eyes as she squirmed.

"How do you know Chela?" I said again, speaking slowly.

"I run a security company, Ten. Trust me, I know a lot of things." My biography shined from her eyes. "Where do you want me to start?"

"Start with Chela."

Marsha hesitated, not hiding her teasing smile. "My memory's a little foggy . . ."

SNAP. The belt found her right buttock, jiggling a strip of firm flesh. Her ass was slick from oil, which brightened the pain.

Marsha's face glowed, ecstatic. "I remember now . . . Lauren McLawhorn, from Minneapolis. Struck out on her own, getting into trouble. Until she met Tennyson Hardwick."

I was so startled, I lowered the belt. "Go on."

"You shared an . . . employer. And you were Chela's black knight. Although I'm surprised you left your mutual friend free to do business. You could have sent that old bitch to rot in jail."

My mouth went dry, and my erection was fading fast. I glanced around the rooftop, and for the first time I noticed a high-powered camera with a tripod at the far edge, pointed toward the beach. I almost hadn't seen the camera behind the beach chair and umbrella shading it. Marsha might be a photography buff, or she might be in law enforcement; I was beginning to fear the latter. And she'd brought me right to her. The day's colors were changing.

"What's this about?" I said.

"My chest this time," she said, puffing out again. Her breasts bobbed in the teddy.

"That's gonna hurt."

"It better."

LASH. I gave her what she wanted. The belt must have grazed her nipple, because she whimpered and sat ramrod straight. "*Shit, that's good,*" she gasped, wide eyed, as if she'd just snorted a line of fine Colombian.

"Keep talking."

"I saw your name when you registered with SecureGuard, I remembered it from high school, and I got curious. I know people, and I did some checking. There was some guesswork, but you'd be surprised by how much information is out there—even when it's supposedly expunged. About you. And Chela. And your mutual old lady friend. That's the part I still haven't figured out—did she give you a finder's fee to keep you quiet?"

"I know everyone makes mistakes. Even old ladies."

"Like sending fourteen-year-old girls to do things you wouldn't want to see?"

There was more than a ring of judgment in her voice, and I took a step back. Marsha's body suddenly looked like the dangerous weapon it was. "You want to arrest Mother, go ahead. I won't shed any tears. You don't need me for that."

Marsha laughed. "Oh, please. You think I'm a cop? That's cute."

"What, then?"

Marsha pointed to the belt. "Try my ass again. That was nice, too." She lay on her stomach to present her lovely brown buttocks, so shiny that they reflected the sunlight. Her ass was a ripe dark cherry, parted by the red teddy's thong. *Be careful what you wish for,* I thought.

LASH. I was a tad careless with my strength, so I knew that last blow would leave a welt. Something to remember me by.

"*Yes!*" Marsha cried. "Damn, you're good. Again?"

"Not until I hear more."

Marsha pretended to pout. "I'm in security, plain and simple. It's my job to know things, and you're my new hobby. It's nice to see an old friend doing good things."

"We were never friends."

She smiled. "We're friends now, aren't we?"

"Depends on what you want."

"It's not rocket science, Ten. I want to fuck."

She splayed herself in the lounger with her ass posed high in the air, her eyes calling to me. Since I was no longer worried about arrest, blood rushed back into my groin so fast I thought it would explode. Dangerous sex used to be my favorite pastime; consequences always seem meek from a distance.

I gave her a last lash across her ass, more softly this time. Then I tossed the belt away. "What about Joe-Bob the Car Salesman downstairs?" I said.

Marsha laughed. "Forget about him. But remember his advice."

"What advice?"

"Think about it," she said, flipping over to massage my crotch with the heel of her foot. Her practiced pressure alone was enough to lock my toes. "It'll come."

"Oh, I remember now," I said, unsnapping my jeans to be free of the binding. With my briefs and T-shirt off, if I walked a few yards closer to the edge of the roof, I would have been flashing the motorists.

I sat beside Marsha on the lounger and whispered into her tiny ear: "He told me to be sure to check out the selection . . . in the rear." I slid my hand across her ass, where hidden muscles flexed beneath my touch. She smelled like the coconut oil she had doused herself in to give her skin its irresistible shine. My finger toyed with the strip of satin nestling her crevice.

"Two can play that game," she said, plying her bound hands between my legs, slippery fingers sliding past my testicles. Feathers from her handcuffs tickled me. She found her spot, and suddenly a single sturdy index finger plunged past a ring of muscle. I gasped, my breath trapped in my lungs when my body tightened around her, so rigid I could imagine snapping her finger off.

Most guys would rather cut off their own finger than allow a sexual partner to explore with hers, but a woman's touch is a woman's touch. I had given up my squeamishness during my working days, when my lady clients taught me the secret of prostate stimulation. Marsha knew how to work her finger around. Her nail must have been cut short, because all I felt was pleasure.

Still sliding her finger inside me, Marsha cradled herself over me and slipped my shaft between her lips, welcoming me with an endless throat. I would choke most women who tried, but Marsha could have been a circus act. I closed my eyes, my mouth open wide. I thought the loud wail from a nearby seagull was mine.

The cascading sensations of pressure and moistness from front to back were devastating. Marsha worked her finger back and forth, up and down, side to side, and her tongue mimicked her finger's motion as she stroked me with her mouth. My hands were claws against the lounger's edge. I hadn't felt anything like it since . . . since . . .

A white hole gaped in my mind, my memory. Pleasure was all.

When Marsha's mouth and finger set me free, I tugged her teddy off so my skin could celebrate hers. She was hot from the sun, slipping beneath me like an eel. Coconut oil is one of the best sexual lubricants there is. I swam across Marsha's hot skin.

Marsha had a Brazilian wax, so her nakedness was striking and true. Her bare clitoris was large and dark, its base as bright as blood. Only a hint of coconut taste between her legs. While my tongue played, she swelled to greet me. Her clitoris felt like a separate creature, squirming with new life. While I bent over her to tease her with my tongue, her fingers tortured me with light strokes of replenished slick oil, coating me inch by inch. Lubricating me.

Marsha was a moaner, with no apparent concern about being overheard. When she had her first orgasm at the mercy of my tongue, she screamed. I knew what Marsha wanted—it's a human tendency to give others what we ourselves crave. Marsha wanted what April couldn't handle.

I rolled Marsha onto her stomach. Her hands were still bound, and she clung to the raised back of the lounger with her leather handcuffs. With a strong arm around her middle, I hoisted her beautiful ass high in the air.

Marsha hissed, squirming with anticipation. I pressed my rounded swelling against her tight, puckered skin, spreading the oil to smooth my passage. My fullness quivered against her, craving the tightest embrace her body had to offer.

I pushed and retreated, then pushed deeper, an inch at a time. My belt had been her first sweet torture; now, she had a new one. Marsha made a sound midway between animal and human as she sank down into the lounger from my weight. While I invaded her, prying her open, my fingertips rubbed and massaged her slick areolae and nipples. Marsha screamed again.

"My . . . neck . . . ," she whispered. Begging.

Say no more. I wrapped a tight hand around her throat, pressing in rhythmic, deep strokes above her. Breath control heightens sexual response, creating a kind of tunnel vision, a world of pure sensation. I concentrated my grip on the sides of her neck, pressing only slightly against her windpipe with my palm. With breath control, it's not about pain—it's about pressure. I would never choke out a woman, or completely stanch her breath. I gave her exactly what she wanted, no more, no less. Don't try this at home. Hey, I'm a trained professional.

Marsha whimpered and yelped, her voice thinned by my grip. The tighter my hand squeezed her neck, the more her body opened itself up to me. Finally, my pelvis reached the satin mounds of her buttocks, and I was as far inside her as our bodies would allow. My breath was shallow, too—Marsha's tightness pulled and snatched at me, a dizzying massage.

I thrust, and the lounger squeaked against the wooden deck. After each partial retreat, I pushed myself a little deeper. Marsha surrendered more with each squeak of the lounger, raising herself against me with whimpers and moans.

Only the rare woman can tolerate anal sex with me.

Years ago, a philatelist client had shown me her proudest possession, an 1856 "Black on Magenta" from British Guiana, one of the world's most valuable, and rarest, stamps.

At that moment Marsha was rarer, and more precious still.

TEN

SUNDAY

"New girlfriend?" Chela said, blocking me in the upstairs hallway.

She was just getting up at twelve thirty when she met me on my way to Nandi Maitlin-Dimitrakos's birthday party. The party didn't start until two, but I'd been asked to arrive an hour early. I would have preferred another hour's prep time at the house, but Roman had insisted that he didn't need me sooner. Maybe his hospitality was wearing thin.

The rest of that week, my major pastime had been sex with Marsha. We both had matching appetites and empty calendars. I'd been home for dinner with Dad and Chela every night, but Marsha usually paged me by ten. Since the Chateau Marmont was only a fifteen-minute drive, I didn't mind the late-night booty calls. She always got straight to the point, and each night was a new adventure. Visiting her made me as horny as a teenager.

"Uh . . . not a girlfriend," I said. "Just a friend. Why do you ask?"

Chela smirked. "Check your neck. Is your friend a vampire, or just a freak?"

Shit. I ducked to peek in the bathroom mirror, and found a huge purple hickey on the right side of my neck, too high for a summer shirt to hide. I remembered Marsha gnawing on my neck the night before, but I had no idea she'd left a mark. Now I *looked* like a teenager, too.

"Damn!" I said.

Chela laughed. "Real smooth, Ten."

"Thanks for the heads-up." I didn't have makeup on hand, so I was stuck with it.

"This is your last chance to invite me to your dumb kiddie party," Chela said, trying reverse psychology. Chela had been begging me to take her to Sofia Maitlin's party for days.

"Sorry, but this is work. No distractions, Chela. I'll try to take pictures."

"Right. It's *way* better if I'm not there when the helicopter commandos swoop down to kidnap her baby."

That's exactly what she said.

"Next time. I think we're becoming friends. I told her about what we talked about a few days ago." The same day I'd heard from Melanie Wilde, I told Chela about my adoption hopes. She seemed surprised and pleased, until I said we needed her mother's consent. *Well, screw that, then,* she'd said. She had been somber the rest of that night, and we hadn't mentioned it since.

"You told Sofia Maitlin you want to adopt me?"

"Hope that's okay. I just—"

I saw Chela's girlish smile in her reflection in the bathroom mirror. "No, that's cool," she said. "I just didn't know you . . ."

"What?"

She shrugged. "I didn't know you were that serious about it."

Maybe the plan wasn't dead! I turned to meet Chela's eyes, which were uncharacteristically soft and open. "Yeah, girl, I'm serious. You think I would play with something like that?"

Suddenly, Chela darted out of the bathroom doorway. Had I said the wrong thing?

"Chela?" I called after her as she disappeared into her bedroom. I found her squatting on the floor beside her bed, and she opened her bottom nightstand drawer. She pulled out a dirty white manila envelope, stained with everything except tire tracks, bound by a frayed string.

She handed me the envelope. "I promised myself a long time ago I wasn't gonna spend another second of my life looking for that lame bitch, but go for it. That's all I've got."

It was already ten minutes later than I'd planned to leave, but I peeked inside. The envelope was stuffed with loose scraps of paper—scribbled telephone numbers, a photocopy of a birth certificate for a woman named Patrice Sheryl McLawhorn, and a single four-by-six photograph. In the photo, a grinning blond-haired white woman with Chela's nose cradled a lovely brown-skinned toddler whose forehead was hidden by an unkempt mop of curly hair. As I'd suspected, the resemblance between Chela and Nandi at that age was uncanny.

Chela had never told me that she had a picture of her mother. The woman was acne scarred but pretty. The photo had been taken at a kitchen table in what I guessed was Chela's grandmother's house, a rare moment of joy in a home filled with chaos. The camera's flash made a starburst against the microwave, and I could see the reflection of a portly woman, Chela's grandmother. When Chela was ten or eleven, after her mother had been gone for more than two years, Chela's grandmother had died after a long illness.

Chela lived in the house with her corpse for days.

She'd had no one to call and nowhere to go.

"She never went by Patrice. She hated that name," Chela said. "I called her Sherry, from her middle name, like her friends. My grandma called her Bunny. Don't ask me why. Pretty dumb nickname for a grown woman, if you ask me. I kept every phone number I ever got for her in there. She was so heavy into the meth, I figure she's dead by now." No emotion in Chela's voice. "You wanna look? Fine, whatever. Just don't expect me to talk to her. We've got nothing to talk about."

Carefully, I closed the envelope, as if it might break in two. "Are you sure?" I said. "Like you said . . . she might be dead. Or . . . she may not want to cooperate with us. She hasn't been here for you, but she still may try to fight."

Chela's eyes sparked fire. "Then let's hope she's dead. And if she tries to cause a problem . . ." Chela shrugged. "Hey, you could always kill her."

"I don't kill people. And you wouldn't want me to."

"I wouldn't?"

"But if you're ready, I'll start looking for her," I said.

Chela nodded. "I'm ready . . . *Dad*." And she grinned.

No word had ever sounded better to my ears. I would have hugged

Chela, but hugs weren't a part of our repertoire. *Dad*. As mighty and mysterious as my father had been to me when I was a kid, the word *Dad* was profound to me. During the drive to Maitlin's house, I thought about nothing except finding Chela's mother, dead or alive.

I thought I was having a good day.

The only helicopter at Nandi's birthday party had been rented by paparazzi, a mutant mosquito buzzing overhead to try to get photos despite the cover of treetops, huge balloon bouquets, and large white tents. A long white canopy protected the identities of celebrity guests as their drivers deposited them on the same shaded path I'd walked on my first visit.

Think of a celebrity couple in L.A. with young children, and they were there: Tom Cruise and Katie Holmes. Will Smith and Jada Pinkett-Smith. Harrison Ford and Calista Flockhart. Angela Bassett and Courtney B. Vance. Ben Affleck and Jennifer Garner. Even celebrities *without* kids came to Nandi's birthday bash. The party was the summer's hottest ticket, the lead story on the entertainment tabloid shows and the celebrity coverage on CNN Headline News—but not for the reasons it should have been.

None of the guests learned the true story that day.

Red flags were waving in my mind as soon as I arrived. I was surprised by the army of support staff on the grounds: valets, caterers, animal handlers, jugglers, and clowns. I counted at least thirty; I hoped that Roman and his team had done their homework to give them security clearances. A lone nutball can ruin a party.

"Where do you want me?" I asked Roman when I found him at the check-in table beside a red-haired security staffer with freckled, thickly muscled forearms. Roman introduced the man as Carter. Roman's staff could be a wrestling team.

Roman patted my back. "Just work the room. Eyes wide open." Pretty vague, especially since "the room" was several acres large.

The sound of the helicopter propellers beating overhead made my teeth grind. "What about the chopper?" I said. "We can get the police to—"

"Already done," Roman said. "LAPD's bird will chase 'em off. Just make sure nobody bothers the guests. Absolutely *no* photos by staff."

There were twenty tables with ten seats apiece in the backyard, which had been transformed into an amusement park with carnival games, a mini merry-go-round, strolling clowns, pony rides, and two massive in-flated bouncy houses shaped like pirate ships, one mostly red, one mostly yellow, prows poised for battle. The gift table was a mountain, more toys than most children would see in a lifetime. Children swarmed every-where, laughing and shrieking at imaginary peril. I recognized Roman's children from the picture he'd shown me, romping alongside the princes and princesses of Hollywood.

For the first half hour, the birthday girl and her parents were nowhere in sight. Scanning the guest tables, I found a printed placard with my name—my neighbors were Halle Berry and Jennifer Garner (and yes, it's true: Halle has no pores)—but I stayed only long enough to smile politely and sip from my glass of lemonade with frozen mint-leaf ice cubes.

Murmurs, coos, and applause wove through the crowd.

The sky was finally quiet when Maitlin's family walked outside through the back-patio door, past the pool. Maitlin had waited for the helicopter to leave. She was carrying Nandi in her arms, and two men trailed behind them. Maitlin and Nandi were dressed in matching casual backless white summer dresses, their hair pinned up with crowns of white ribbons. Nandi's wrist sparkled with a diamond bracelet I guessed was one of her birthday gifts, easily worth ten grand.

Maitlin's husband was on her heels, a balding and frumpy dark-haired man in reading glasses who tried to smile but looked uncomfort-able under so many eyes. Maybe the inanity of a lavish party for a child who wouldn't remember it was sinking in, even to a billionaire.

I didn't recognize the second man, who was black and in his midthir-ties, so giddy that his grin was nearly bigger than his face. His off-the-rack suit didn't fit quite right, and his eyes seemed dazed. *The birth father*, I realized. He was tall, with a thick, cut frame like LL Cool J. Nandi hadn't gotten her looks only from her mother's side. If the birth father had been an actor, he could have found an agent that day.

I could only imagine the impact of the deal he'd made with Maitlin and her billionaire husband. Overnight, he'd been transformed from a

Cape Town local with a daughter in an orphanage to a man worthy of a seat at the table with Hollywood's upper echelon. His eyes were bright enough to burst.

Maitlin's husband, Alec, headed straight for the discreet bar near the pool, a clove cigarette dangling between his fingers, meeting a huddle of other men who also looked Mediterranean, probably relatives.

Maitlin walked from table to table with Nandi on her arm, flanked by the birth father and Zukisa, the nanny. Zukisa looked watchful and anxious, as if she expected Maitlin to drop the girl. As guests exclaimed and hugged Maitlin and Nandi, a hired photographer snapped photos of Maitlin's table-side visits.

I didn't expect Maitlin to notice me, but she grabbed my arm.

"Steve, this is Tennyson Hardwick!" she said, as if it were critical for Steven Spielberg to know my name. "He's costarring in *Lenox Avenue,* and he was an absolute lifesaver in South Africa. We never would have found Nandi without him."

An exaggeration, but it won me beaming smiles and hearty hand-shaking from people I don't usually get to shake hands with. I won't name them all, but you get the picture. *Yeah, Steve-O, so why don't you sign me to star in your next movie? Here's my card,* I told him in my imagination, which my agent would kill me for not saying aloud.

"Mis-ter Ten!" Nandi said, remembering me with shining eyes. It was oddly moving to hear Nandi say my name. "It's my birthday!"

"I know it is, kiddo. Happy birthday."

Maitlin's attention stayed on me. "Tennyson, say hello to Paki Zangwa. This is Nandi's birth father. We just helped him move to San Diego, and he's visiting for the party."

Up close, the man's genetic stamp on Nandi's long forehead and eyes was obvious. I assumed he'd had a DNA test months ago, but except for complexion, Nandi was his clone.

"*Molo,*" I said, the traditional Xhosa daytime greeting. "*Ndiyavuya ukuwazi.*" I'd only said I was pleased to meet him, but with pronunciation good enough to make him gasp.

"You speak Xhosa?" he said.

I laughed. "Hey, man, that's all I remember from my travel book. Welcome to the States."

Zukisa looked at me with fresh eyes, ready to take me home to her parents. Her gaze found my camouflaged hickey, and she tried to hide a small smile.

"A pleasure!" Paki Zangwa said, speaking to the entire table. "This is all so very special. From a nightmare, a dream has come true for Nandi. Thanks be to God. And to Sofia and her very good husband, for this home that is . . ." He blinked back tears. ". . . beyond words."

To my surprise, I liked Paki. Had he abandoned his daughter, then resurfaced when little Nandi started pooping in gold diapers? Maybe. But I found myself wanting to believe in him.

It was a beautiful day for a party, cloudless but not too hot, and children's laughter tickled my ears as they scurried between the carnival games and the massive bouncy houses, their faces smeared with clown paint, melted ice cream, and ketchup from their gourmet hot dogs. Clowns dispensing hot dogs and ice cream strolled the grounds with catering carts.

I monitored the support staff, and everyone seemed efficient and businesslike, without much open gawking. I caught a frozen-lemonade guy trying to snap cell phone photos of Halle, but he was embarrassed when I caught him, blushing and apologizing profusely. He looked like a college student, or maybe a young actor between gigs. The right photo would fetch thousands of dollars from the tabloids. Roman probably would have fired him, but I confiscated the phone and sent him back to work.

In the days afterward, I would mull over every decision I made at Nandi's party, with a firestorm of regrets.

What could I have done differently? What had I overlooked?

Maitlin stayed close to Nandi's side most of the afternoon, taking her own photos of Nandi with the clowns, on the ponies, or on the merry-go-round. Maitlin's husband made token appearances, but it was easy to guess that he'd been much less interested in adopting a child than his younger wife. One of the men he spent most of the time with at the poolside bar might have been his son, probably close to thirty himself.

But marriages are all about accommodating each other's needs, and celebrity marriages take that model to a science. Sometimes love even has something to do with it. Yeah, a quarter-billion dollars' worth of love. I invested in a brief, silent, cynical speculation that her half-year "spiritual retreat" had been suggested not by her guru, but her lawyers.

"I want to jump!" Nandi said, pointing to the brightly colored pirate ship. Its thirty feet must have looked like the *Titanic* to her. While a generator kept it inflated, I counted nearly two dozen children romping through its mazelike portals, throwing themselves against the rubbery walls and launching themselves down the huge inflatable slide modeled after a pirate's plank. Children could leave and enter from the aft, the stern, or the side, and they wriggled in and out at dizzying speed. It looked like a recipe for trampling, but so far, no ambulance. My attitude toward kids is simple: no transfusion, no foul.

Maitlin looked like she was having doubts about the ships. Nandi was small for her age.

"*Please*, Mommy?" Nandi said. "I want to go in!"

Maitlin motioned for Zukisa, who was a few paces closer than I was. "She wants to jump. Will you make sure she doesn't get hurt? I need to eat."

"Of course!" Zukisa said, taking Nandi's chubby hand. The diamond bracelet glistened in the sunlight, even from my ten-yard distance.

"Wait," I said, stepping closer. "Better take off her jewelry."

"Alec would kill me if she lost that!" Maitlin said. "Thank you, Tennyson. My brain must be fried from the sun."

I wanted to mention that Alec had been crazy to give Nandi the bracelet in the first place, but I left that unspoken. Zukisa and I shared a look: *These rich people!*

I didn't follow Zukisa and Nandi into the closest bouncy house, but I peeked inside, noticing how many places she could vanish and reappear in the ship's elaborate layout, like the rooms of a small house. Nandi was fearless, flinging herself down the slide while Zukisa tried to keep up with her. Zukisa was only in her twenties, but she was perspiring after ten minutes of chasing Nandi. Luckily, Nandi avoided collisions with other children, nimble as a running back.

"Ooh, that girl!" Zukisa finally said, sitting on the grass beside the slide. "She can go all day long like this. I can barely stand up in there!"

When Nandi was inside the bouncy house for the first time by herself,

Zukisa and I both waited twenty seconds for her to appear at the top of the bright yellow slide. This time, she rode down on the lap of a sturdy tomboy who looked about ten, both of them screaming with laughter. They landed in a tangle on the pad on the grass.

Zukisa leaped to her feet, alarmed. "Be careful with the young one!" she scolded.

Nandi sat up, red faced with laughter. "Again!"

And so it went on. I checked my watch: It was almost four o'clock. Only an hour to go. I couldn't wait to get home and start poring over the information about Chela's mother.

"Hardwick!" Roman jogged up behind me. "What are you, the au pair? I've got caterers who need watching. They want to heat some food in the kitchen, so make sure they only take what they brought in."

Call it instinct, or maybe premonition: I didn't want to leave the ship. I almost said so.

He pointed to a caterer's table, in the shade of the trees near the path back to the front yard. Theirs was the only table that offered anything except kiddie food, styled after a South African barbecue called a *braai*. Spicy sausage called *boerewors*, dried strips of meat called *biltong*, and Indian samosas. Their table smelled like Cape Town. I speared a piece of sausage with a toothpick and wolfed it down. Yum. I made a note of the restaurant's name on a small placard on their table: SOUTH AFRICAN SUN ON MELROSE.

"You need the kitchen?" I asked the man in the chef's hat.

"Yeah, yeah." The stout, ruddy white man had a slight Afrikaner accent. He was overseeing a staff of three black workers, two men and one woman, who might have been South African, too. "The stew's not heating fast enough on our burners, and the first batch is going fast."

He motioned authoritatively to two of his workers, and they lifted a huge iron cooking pot filled with stewed meat and potatoes. It looked like it weighed a ton. One of the black men was short but stocky, with broad shoulders. He seemed intimidated by me, casting his eyes down from mine. He was the only cook who looked over forty, and his grip on the stew pot nearly slipped more than once as they made the long journey across the yard. I wished Roman had offered them a golf cart.

I barely knew my way to the kitchen, but I dutifully led them. Their arms had to be aching by the time we crossed the property, but they never complained. As we walked, I cast another glance at the pirate ship in time to see Nandi dive headfirst down the slide. Watching her made me smile.

On the way to the kitchen, we passed Maitlin at a table with her husband, Rachel Wentz, and Nandi's birth father, all of them enjoying a toast of golden wine. The wine bottle caught my eye: a big yellow smiley face grinning at me from the label. Their table was a cozy portrait. Rachel Wentz grinned at me and waved, and I waved back.

In Maitlin's immense kitchen, tiles, marble, and stainless steel glistened like Nandi's diamonds. A housekeeper in a gray uniform and white apron was waiting inside to instruct the men on how to use the stove, a middle-aged Latina who was glad for the company. She gave us a crash course on the kitchen's endless features. The children outside were laughing so loudly that I could hear them despite the closed windows and the grounds that separated us.

"Who gives a baby *diamonds*?" one of the men said to me as he stirred the stew, his voice laced with a ring of contempt I didn't like. "Nice life, eh?"

"Nice lady," I said.

There was a sharp clap, and the shorter, broad-shouldered man gestured angrily at the first worker, who looked nervous about having angered him.

"It is not our concern," the angry man said to me, apologizing in his lyrical accent. His brow was knit with focused attention as he tended to the stew. He wore nondescript black slacks and a white shirt, but he carried himself like a chef, not just a cook. "We are not paid to gossip."

While the food heated up and filled the kitchen with exotic scents, I stood at the kitchen's picture window and watched the backyard's flurry of activity. The party looked more chaotic from a distance, and I yearned to be closer to the crowd. The cooks didn't need another babysitter. Why was I wasting my time?

I had been exiled in the kitchen for about fifteen minutes when sudden movement through the window caught my eye. Zukisa and Roman were running toward Maitlin's table, near the pool. Zukisa's erratic body language was loud and clear: Something was wrong.

Roman leaned over Maitlin to say something to her, and Maitlin leaped to her feet so quickly that her chair fell over behind her. In unison, everyone at the table turned toward the party crowd, as if they had heard someone call to them. The group left the table, heading toward the party. Did one of the child swarm fall down, go *Owie*?

I looked at my watch. It was 4:10.

"Excuse me," I interrupted the housekeeper, who was trying to educate me on the precise temperature range of the freezer. "I need to go back outside."

The housekeeper looked offended, but she shrugged and turned her back to me, continuing her recitation to the cooks. Both cooks gave me pleading looks.

In the time it took me to get back to the party, I lost sight of Maitlin, Roman, Maitlin's husband, and Zukisa. The gaiety was still in full swing outside, but I didn't see Nandi.

From a distance, I spotted Roman's children rolling down the pirate ship's slide, laughing. A clown was pulling an endless stream of scarves out of a (presumably) stuffed rabbit, so I had to wade through a crowd of twenty-five children in identical Bozo makeup while I searched their faces for Nandi's.

With the climbing rope hanging beside the pirate ship's side entrance, I climbed up into the giant red bouncy house where I had last seen Nandi playing. A half dozen screaming children ran past me. My heart raced, until I noticed their grins.

"Hey, mister—no shoes in here!" a boy scolded me as he pushed past. I ignored him, nearly losing my balance while the inflated floor gyrated wildly beneath my feet. I searched the colorful holes and passageways. "Zukisa?" I called. "Nandi?"

No answer.

"Who wants to see me make this little rabbit disappear?" the magician bellowed from outside, and an army of children shrieked, "*MEEEEEEE!*"

At the far rear of the ship, a child-size archway led to a cubbyhole large enough for three or four children to climb into, or a couple of adults. Something pale against the corner of the red floor caught my eye, so I picked it up. One of Nandi's white ribbons. Outside, nearly buried by the cheering children, Maitlin was calling Nandi's name.

Behind me, Roman stuck his head into the archway, anxious. Zukisa was panting beside him. I didn't have to ask if Nandi was missing.

I held up the ribbon. "She was here."

Zukisa clutched her cheeks with horror, as if the ribbon were a corpse.

Roman took the ribbon and pocketed it. "I was about to call for you."

"This was the last place I saw her," I said, wriggling out of the cubbyhole. "How long?"

Roman checked his watch, struggling to keep upright as the floor swayed wildly. "Almost fifteen minutes." He nodded toward Zukisa, disapproving. "She waited ten minutes to tell me."

She must have disappeared almost as soon as I left, I realized.

"She likes to hide!" Zukisa said, defending herself. "It's like a maze, looking for her in these things." But Roman's glare silenced her.

There was no reason to believe the worst—not yet—but I used my imagination.

"The pool?" I said. I'd once read about a family on vacation who searched for their child all morning, only to find him drowned in a shadowed corner of a motel pool.

"Checked there first," Roman said.

Someone could have snatched Nandi. *Is anyone watching the front gate?*

"We just shut the gate," Roman said, reading my mind. He clung to a balancing rail as he space-walked toward the closest exit. Outside, he gave me a handi-talkie that matched the one strapped to his belt. "I'm going around front. Start a full sweep out here."

A young security staffer who looked like a college football player ran up to us, slightly red faced. His name tag identified him as LEVITT. "Where do you want me, Roman?"

Roman studied me, a barely noticeable hesitation. "Hardwick's on point back here, so what he says goes. I'll be up front with Carter. Every nook and cranny. *Find her.*"

"Yessir," Levitt said as Roman hopped into his waiting golf cart and drove off. Levitt had seemed surprised when Roman put me in charge, but he obediently awaited his orders.

"Clear both bouncy houses," I told him. "Ask about Nandi, but don't start a panic."

Levitt nearly saluted before bounding into the ship. He was former military, too. *"Okay, kids, I need everybody out!"* Levitt boomed, loudly enough to be heard over the playing children.

I liked the efficiency displayed by Roman and his staff, but Zukisa looked ready to faint in the flurry. I put my hands on Zukisa's shoulders and tried to calm her wide, frightened eyes. She wouldn't be any help if she was panicking.

"I'm sure we'll find her," I said, so convincing that her face visibly softened. "Call to her. Tell her she's not in trouble. You know Nandi: Try to think of where she might go."

Zukisa nodded, inspired. *"Nandi!"* she called, wandering away, eyes low to the ground.

I glanced at my watch: 4:17.

My day had not yet begun.

ELEVEN

4:30 P.M.

The magic show was over. No one ever tasted Nandi's three-tiered birthday cake. The gifts on the table were never unwrapped. No one sang "Happy Birthday." Roman radioed me to say that Maitlin and the housekeepers were searching the house. Outside, I had every tablecloth lifted, every hot dog cart opened and examined, every bush and tree searched.

Levitt and I scoured the pirate ships for Nandi: inside, outside, underneath. I had the bearded vendor who'd brought them escorted from his truck, where he was waiting. He reminded me of a nineteenth-century carny, with thick eyebrows and a bulbous nose from too much alcohol—although I didn't smell any on his breath. He looked scared to death of a lawsuit when I told him to help us deflate his bouncy houses. "I've been doin' this twelve years," he said, shutting off his generators. "Kids don't get *lost* in here. She's gotta be somewhere else."

The bouncy houses were slow to deflate, the progress almost imperceptible.

By four thirty, my stomach felt as if someone had dropped it into a freezer. Time to call the police. If the party was a crime scene, it was being trampled beyond recognition. I cursed myself for touching Nandi's ribbon with my bare hands and giving it to Roman.

The ribbon was evidence.

I was about to tell Roman I was dialing 911 when the commotion came: Another one of Roman's men was driving Maitlin and her husband back past the pool, and Maitlin waved with a luminous smile. Relieved murmurs lightened the guests.

"Told you she just probably ate too much ice cream," I overheard someone say behind me, maybe Tom Cruise. I didn't look to see.

Maitlin and her husband climbed out of the cart hand in hand. Alec's dark sunglasses hid his eyes, but Maitlin's smile never faltered. Guests matched Maitlin's smile as they gathered near her, expecting good news. Maitlin made a glass sing with raps of a knife handle. Even the children were quiet.

"Please forgive us for the commotion, everyone!" Maitlin called. "We feel like such fools. Nandi felt sick, and one of my staff took her back into the house!"

There was a round of *Awwwwwwws*. Maitlin quickly went on, her smile wider. "But she's fine now! And she wanted me to come out and thank you for making her birthday so special—and especially for all of the *presents,* which she can't wait to open." Rounds of easy, relieved laughter, Maitlin loudest of all, almost manic. "Thanks so much for coming today, and we hope to see you all again soon!"

The block of ice in my chest was melting when my handi-talkie beeped.

"We need you up front—*now!*" Roman's voice crackled.

Roman wasn't laughing.

5:49 P.M.

It took more than an hour to clear the guests and service vehicles out of the driveway, until nearly six o'clock. Tom Hanks's limo was missing, and he ended up catching a ride with Angela and Courtney. Later, when it was much too late, we heard that his car was found a couple of miles down the road, the driver asleep behind the wheel.

I was sweating through my clothes, and not from the dying sun. Roman and I barely made eye contact as the line of service vehicles passed.

Smiling politely was a Herculean effort. I was a better actor than I thought.

But I had learned from Maitlin, who was one of the best.

A search of the grounds turned up a hole in the backyard fence concealed by a nest of sago palms, at ground level, just big enough for an adult to move through for clear access to the driveway. Wire cutters. Since it was an internal fence, it wasn't electrified or attached to the alarm system. That hole answered a lot of questions, but it wasn't the answer we wanted.

After we found the hole in the fence, Roman took me to see Maitlin.

The house looked too peaceful to be home to so much turmoil, all arched windows, aglow with late-dusk light. Roman took me past an endless array of rooms including a yoga room with a hardwood floor, strap attachments on the wall, and a shrine complete with a portrait of a saintly Indian woman whose eyes were rolled up to Heaven. Two blue yoga mats lay side by side, a false portrait of serenity.

Roman led me upstairs on the winding marble staircase. I heard a woman sobbing from a hidden corridor. Not Maitlin—maybe Zukisa? Her sobs were of miserable, hopeless grief.

The sitting area at the top of the stairs was cluttered with dolls and toys, the first sign that Nandi lived in the house. Roman led me to a closed door painted light pink. He knocked.

"Come in!" Maitlin said. Her voice was tear stripped.

It was Nandi's room. Maitlin sat on the edge of a four-poster toddler bed with a pink canopy to match the door and carpet, her lap buried in a pile of crumpled tissues. Her nose was beet red. She was nearly unrecognizable.

"Here," Maitlin said, and handed me her cell phone.

The display showed her text field. Roman had briefed me, but the words seared my eyes:

WE HAVE NANDI. SEND THE GUESTS HOME, BUT MAKE NO FUSS.
YOU WILL SPEAK TO HER SOON AT THIS NUMBER. IF YOU DO NOT
FOLLOW THESE INSTRUCTIONS—AND IF YOU CALL THE POLICE—
WE WILL CUT HER SWEET LITTLE THROAT.

There was a video attachment, and I clicked on it. A video, shot on a narrow road I didn't recognize until the camera tilted up to show a Mulholland Drive street sign. A bit of background, enough to ensure we'd know it was real. And a man whose face was turned away from the camera, wearing a dark windbreaker. Over his shoulder slumped a small child. A girl. Nandi. For a horrible instant I thought she was dead, then the cameraman's gloved hand moved in and tickled her nose. She leaned up and batted at his hand sleepily, then relaxed again, but not before I saw the little smile curling her lips.

Nandi was alive.

The message's time stamp was 4:20. The note made me dizzy from the mistakes already. I gave Roman a withering look; he'd known about the kidnap note since soon after he found me in the bouncy house.

"You've talked to her?" I asked Maitlin.

Maitlin forced back a sob. "Yes. They called, just like they promised. She sounded like . . . she was in a car. She was . . . crying." Her last word was an agonized sob.

Ice froze out my feelings. I didn't have time to feel. "What did she say?"

"She said . . ." Maitlin sobbed again, wiping her nose. "Oh, God!"

"Ms. Maitlin, what did she say?" I said, more gently.

"She said . . . 'Mommy, I want to come home!'" Maitlin wailed. Her fingers shook so badly that she had to clasp her hands together to still them.

"Did you hear any other voices?" I said.

"After Nandi, there was a man's voice. He said, 'Stay by the phone for ransom instructions. If you call the police, FBI, *anyone,* Nandi is dead.' His voice was . . . muffled. Distorted."

It might have been a handkerchief, or even a voice-changing device. Ninety minutes had passed since Maitlin received the note. A lifetime! They could be anywhere.

"Is there anything you can tell me about the voice?" I said. "Anything at all?"

"Maybe . . . an English accent," she said. "I'm not sure."

Roman spoke up. "She said the voice sounded robotic. Voice changer, I'd say."

Maitlin's knuckles were white from clutching her cell phone. The kidnappers had called her private number. Did they know her?

Maitlin had shut down, staring with dead eyes into the heart of her worst fears, so I turned to Roman. "When did they call?"

"About thirty minutes after she broke up the party," he said.

Thirty minutes! I was amazed by how Maitlin had laughed while she assured the guests that Nandi was fine, all the while knowing she had been kidnapped. The Academy had missed Maitlin's greatest performance.

"Who was the last person with Nandi?" I said.

Roman made a chuffing sound. "The nanny, and her story's full of holes. If she was watching her, how did Nandi vanish in thin air, in a yard full of people?"

I saw exactly how Zukisa might have lost sight of Nandi on the massive ship. And a yard full of excited children might be the perfect cover for a kidnapping.

"Where's Zukisa now?" I said.

"In her room," Roman said. "She's not going anywhere until Nandi gets home. That Paki guy either. It's not good enough she got him into the country? I always said—" But Maitlin's pained grimace cut him short.

I remembered the crying I'd heard. "Is she *locked* in a room?"

"No," Maitlin said. "I told you *no*, Roman."

"The door's not locked, but she's not going anywhere," Roman said. "Neither one."

"It's easy to paint suspects," I said. "I was watching Nandi play on the ship, too." *Until you sent me to the kitchen*, I thought, but I kept that to myself. "Let's focus on the facts."

Roman bristled, counting off a list on his fingers. "One, the nanny was the last person with Nandi. Two, she has Sophie's private number. Three, she knew the party was today."

"Phone numbers are easy to get," I said. "All of Hollywood knew about the party."

"And so did you," Roman said, standing closer, as if my scent would be telling.

"*Stop it*, Roman," a voice said behind me, surprising me. For the first time, I noticed that Rachel Wentz was in the room with us, sitting on the floor in a large nook by the window, beside a child-size tea table and two chairs.

"We're not going through this again," Wentz went on. "This man is a private detective. He solved the Afrodite and T. D. Jackson cases. A friend I trust implicitly assured me that Sophie's life was safe in his hands, or he never would have come to the orphanage with us."

"I'm not licensed," I said, for the sake of candor.

"Who the fuck cares?" Rachel Wentz said. "We want results, not your goddamn paperwork. It's better if you're not on anyone's radar. If they find out we've told you . . ."

She didn't finish, but she didn't have to. Maitlin buried a sob in Nandi's pillow.

A sudden, authoritative rap on the door made Maitlin gasp and jump. I took a step back, poised to face an intruder. The door opened, and Alec was there with the man I'd assumed was his son. The younger man looked skittish and heartsick, but I couldn't read Alec's expression, empty except for shellshock. He only glanced at me before addressing his wife. "Well?" he said.

Maitlin shook her head. "Not yet."

Alec muttered to himself in Greek, then to Maitlin, "You're being a fool, Sofia! If you care about that child, we're calling the police right now."

Rachel Wentz couldn't speak for Maitlin to her own husband, so Maitlin leaped to her feet, facing off against Alec with her chin thrust high. He was more than a foot taller. "We are *not* calling the police. They said they would kill her!"

"And when someone takes her again next week—then what?"

A rapid-fire exchange began between them in Greek. Until then, I'd had no idea that Maitlin spoke the language. Then I remembered that one of her parents had been Greek.

"He's right," I said, raising my voice to be heard.

Maitlin and her husband both looked at me. Tears shimmered in Maitlin's eyes.

"Yes, yes, tell her!" Alec said. "Tell her she's being a fool."

"Ms. Maitlin, I don't think you're being a fool—far from it. You want to protect your child. But all kidnappers say, 'Don't call the police.' They want to keep all of the power, because they know that the FBI will get in their way. *That's* how you protect your child. To be honest, we've already lost too much time."

"There's your detective," Roman said to Rachel Wentz, an I-told-you-so. "Didn't I say the exact same thing?"

All of you shut up!" Maitlin shrieked. "*I'm not calling the police!*"

The cell phone in her hand rang. I hoped the police were calling *us*.

Maitlin sank back down to the mattress and stared at her ringing phone. Roman and I both ran to try to see the caller ID: UNKNOWN CALLER, the lighted display said. Rachel Wentz joined us at the bed, leaning over, too.

"It's them!" Maitlin said, sounding helpless. "That's what it said before!"

"For Christ's sake, answer!" Alec said. "If you can't, let me."

"Ask Nandi where she is," I whispered as Maitlin opened her phone with trembling hands.

"Hel . . . Hello?" she said, her voice unsteady.

Loud static. Maitlin had pressed her speakerphone button. *Good girl!* I held my finger to my mouth: *Shhhhhh.* But I didn't have to. No one in the room drew a breath.

A raspy, metallic voice growled from the phone: "Take me off the goddamn speaker." An English accent? It was hard to tell with the distortion, but it was possible.

"I'm sorry!" Maitlin cried out, fumbling to find the right button to push. Instead, the phone flew out of her hands, to the foot of the bed. With another cry, Maitlin lunged to grab it.

"Hello? Hello? . . . Please answer!" She looked at her telephone display, and her eyes widened with terror. "Oh, God—*I hung up on him!*"

"Let me see," said Alec, and he took the phone. "Hello? Hello?"

The keening from Maitlin's throat belonged at a child's funeral.

"Don't worry," I said. "Everyone stay calm. He'll call back. They want your money."

"Oh God oh God oh God . . . ," Maitlin whispered, rocking like a lost child. Rachel Wentz sat beside her on the tiny bed with her arm around Maitlin's shoulder, her lips pursed as she fought tears. Alec looked at us helplessly, a powerful man reduced to waiting.

"Hardwick's right," Roman said. "Panic doesn't help us, sir. They'll call back."

We waited in a silence as thick as the walls. I readied the small notepad and pen on the bed beside Maitlin where she'd already scribbled her first conversation with Nandi's kidnappers, writing only NANDI and NO POLICE. She took the pad, but barely noticed.

"Listen for anything," Roman said. "Noises. Engines. Airplanes. Water."

"Try to recognize the voice," I said. "It may be someone who knows you."

Maitlin sobbed, nodding.

Alec stood over Maitlin and rubbed the back of her neck, whispering tenderly, "It's all right, love . . . It's all right. Just breathe. It was an accident. It's not your fault." *Good.* Maitlin would need all of the support she could get.

After two excruciating minutes, the phone rang again. Same caller ID.

This time, Maitlin seemed calmer as she answered. "Hello?" Quickly, she picked up her pen. "Yes, I'm sorry. I dropped the phone . . ." Her face clouded. "No, I swear—we haven't. It's just me and m-my staff. I d-did exactly what you said." While the caller spoke, she looked at us, shaken. "No . . . It's me and my husband, and my m-manager. They were with me when I got the message. And the nanny . . . and Nandi's birth father. And my private security men, but they're not police. That's all, I swear."

From the doorway, Alec's son raised his hand as if to remind her he was there, but Roman and I both waved to keep him quiet. Maitlin already had been way too specific.

Maitlin nodded wildly, writing on her pad. I couldn't make out everything upside down, but I saw the word MONDAY. Shit. They were planning to keep Nandi overnight!

"But can't we do it now? Tonight?" Maitlin whined. A pause, and I heard the vestige of a voice snapping at her. "No, whatever you say. Just please . . ." The caller cut her off, and she began writing furiously again. I saw the number 5. Gazing at the pad, Alec winced.

The kidnappers wanted five million dollars. I felt grudging admiration for their logic: By asking for so much less than Maitlin and her husband could afford, Maitlin was less likely to seek police help. The bastards were more likely to get their money.

"Can I just . . . c-can I just please talk to her again?" Maitlin said.

We all forgot to breathe. The caller said something that lifted

Maitlin's mouth into a sickly smile. "Sweetie? Are you there?" The barest whisper.

"*Mommy!*"

Nandi's voice on the mouthpiece was so clear that I wanted to look over my shoulder for her. Maitlin choked on a laugh. "Nandi—hello, my sweetheart! Are you okay?"

Nandi's chipper voice said something about *pizza*.

They weren't hurting her. She didn't sound frightened, so maybe she hadn't been traumatized yet. *Thank you, Jesus.* Prayers didn't come to me often, but I was learning fast.

I took Maitlin's pad and scribbled a note to feed her dialogue: *Where are you?*

A single word could help. Water. Boat. Truck. Anything.

Maitlin's anguished eyes came to mine, but she shook her head defiantly. "Have a great time, sweetheart," she said to the phone, as if Nandi were at her grandparents' house. "Just be good, all right? Do what they say—no talking back. Mommy and Daddy will see you soon."

"*Okay, Mommy!*" Nandi sounded like she was in the room with us again.

"Sweetheart, where are you?" Maitlin said quickly. She believed she had comforted Nandi and given her enough skills to survive the night, so she was ready to take a chance.

"It's *fun* here—" I heard Nandi say, and then silence.

Maitlin's skin suddenly looked like chalk. "Hello? Nandi?" she said. "*Hello?*"

She looked at her phone display, wide eyed. I peeked, too. CALL ENDED, it said.

As Maitlin wailed, the phone jittered in her unsteady fingers. "Oh G-God, they're going to hurt her! They're going to . . . to . . ." Her bones seemed to be dissolving. Alec and Rachel Wentz stroked her, trying to comfort her, but she was sinking out of the room.

I knelt down to meet Maitlin at eye level. I took her hand and squeezed it, almost hard enough to pinch. "No. They're *not* going to hurt her," I said. "All they want is their money. They don't get anything out of hurting her except feeling like monsters." I hoped I was right. I was rusty on my kidnapping statistics, but plenty of kids don't make it home.

I saw a film leave Maitlin's eyes, but the worry remained. "I told her to be good, but what if she doesn't listen? What if she makes them mad?"

"She's a baby, Sofia," Alec said. "They won't hurt a baby."

"Nandi is fine!" Wentz said. "She thinks she's on vacation. She's eating *pizza*."

Despite herself, Maitlin let out a strangled laugh.

"That's right, Sophie," said Roman. "It's all gonna be fine."

But if Maitlin had seen the look Roman gave me, she would have wailed again.

The household staff had been sent home except for the security team, so the house was eerily quiet. The only voices downstairs were ours.

"Moment of truth time," Roman said as we rushed down the staircase. "No bullshit."

"Works for me."

Roman glanced at me with red eyes, and his voice shook. "I didn't want to bring you in on this. When all hell breaks loose, you look at the new people first. Or, you could have been a dickhead who'd say, 'No police necessary, leave it all up to me,' charge a shitload of money, and shrug your shoulders when Nandi comes back in a body bag. I've put all that aside now."

I had done something to impress him, apparently. I hoped he would listen to my advice: "We need the cops, Roman," I said.

Roman nodded. "No fucking kidding. These pricks are pros. Snatched her in plain sight. But it's Sophie's call, just like it was her call to bring you in. She says no police."

"Sometimes you gotta make the *right* call, man. Not what the boss wants."

We stopped in a foyer so large that it felt like a Spanish courtyard. Ten-foot potted palm trees lined the walls, beneath a massive skylight glowing only faintly in the dark. Hidden crickets chirped from the trees' large ceramic planters.

"I think we got a fifty-fifty chance with this thing," Roman said, his glassy eyes on mine. "These motherfuckers might take the money and run. Nandi's old enough to say too much."

I wanted to argue with him, but I couldn't. Anything was possible.

"Another vote for the FBI," I said.

"Fuck it, you're probably right. But we're gonna agree on one thing right here, right now: We're doing it her way. Period. It's her kid, so she calls it. If Alec and Sophie can live with their decision, so can we."

I didn't know what we could live with, but I shook Roman's hand on it. His palm felt clammy, ice cold.

"The drop's tomorrow night at eleven, and that means me. You, too, if you want in," Roman went on. "No way Sophie's going out there, or Alec. If we don't walk away with Nandi, we go to the feds."

Let's hope any of us walks away, I thought. *Let's hope Nandi will get a second chance.*

"How'd they play us?" Roman said, pacing. When he looked at me, his eyes went straight through me, watching something distant and unspeakable unfold. "*Fuck, fuck, FUCK.* This shit . . . ," he said.

"What?"

"I thought I'd never have to deal with this again."

"Deal with what?"

"Not a what. A when." He wasn't making sense. "April 2004. Al Anbar Province, Iraq. A bad month for Marines. A *very bad* month. FUBAR. Fucked Up Beyond All Recognition. IEDs. All battle-dressed up and nobody to kill in retaliation." He slapped the banister hard enough to echo. "Not again. Not here. Not a child placed under *my* protection!"

Roman was losing it. I should have called the police right then.

I tried to bring Roman back into the room with me. "Someone could've been waiting for her in the bouncy house—maybe where I found the ribbon," I said, and Roman's eyes focused back on home soil. "Maybe they rendered her unconscious. Maybe nitrous oxide. Dental supply store . . . hell, even a catering supply: They use it for whipped cream. She's small, so she wouldn't be tough to conceal or carry. A man, woman, or older child could have made the initial grab. They got her to the broken fence—maybe a bag, maybe a cart. Handed her off. Then . . ."

The scenario was getting blurry, but I pressed on. "They loaded her up and drove off," I went on. "But not in a service truck. I'd say it was a private car, or a limo. Five minutes, they're out."

Pain seared Roman's face. "Shit." We had argued about searching the guests' cars, but in the end it hadn't mattered a damn.

"Nandi could have been out on Mulholland before Zukisa knew she was missing," I said.

"And I sent you to the fucking kitchen," Roman said, his eyes flinching.

"Hindsight's a bitch."

I wanted to know more about South African Sun on Melrose. Roman might have sent me on a fool's errand, but the restaurant could have orchestrated it. And I wanted to know more about Roman, too. He wasn't a full-blown suspect yet, but I hadn't crossed him off the list.

Roman studied me. "I'm head of security, I send you away from the scene right before the grab . . . ," he said. "That doesn't knot up your balls?"

We thought just alike. Roman was pulling himself together.

"Like I said before, it's easy to paint a suspect," I said.

"Like the guy I found with Nandi's ribbon in his hand?"

"Just like that."

Roman nodded, and we pounded fists. "Until Nandi's back home, you live here. If you don't have a piece, I'll lend you one of mine. We're gonna work the office phone and computer to stick a microscope up the ass of anybody who was here today—and that's a long fucking list. You're gonna come up with ideas I don't. If we're lucky, it works both ways."

"So far, so good. Partner." I didn't want him to think he was my boss.

Roman's eyes bored into mine. "Right, partner: And if evidence convinces you that I had something to do with this, fuck the FBI. Shoot me in the head."

I remembered Nandi's laughter as she rolled down the slide, a happy angel. "I could handle that."

"Same here, Hardwick," Roman said. His eyes reminded me of Hannibal Lecter's death stare from *Silence of the Lambs*, unblinking intensity. "Not a doubt in my fucking mind."

If we didn't kill each other first, I had a partner. It was a start.

Roman led me toward his security room, which was a small, virtually windowless room off the front foyer. Inside, he had two desks, a swivel chair in front of a bank of small video screens, a console, and a computer and monitor. One security man I'd met only since the kidnapping—a thin-faced man in his forties with active eyes—was scanning the footage, cycling between cameras. With at least ten cameras on the grounds, that was a lot of footage for one man. But we were spread thin. Too bad we weren't the FBI.

One camera had captured Zukisa frantically running out of the bouncy house, looking right and left. The man paused the tape, which was marked 3:55 P.M. "That's when she's thinking, 'Oh, shit,'" the video man mumbled.

I saw movement in the dark shrubbery from one of the upper video screens marked LIVE FEED. My heart did a war dance when a flashlight's beam flared like the sun. But it was only our security patrol. Levitt. Roman had spread the rest of the team throughout the grounds.

"Talk to me, Skeeter," Roman said to the video man.

"I don't have shit," Skeeter said. "Damn clowns."

"What about the clowns?" Roman said, anxious.

Skeeter shrugged. "I just fucking hate clowns."

My cell phone vibrated, and I checked the caller ID: SEXUAL HEALING, it read.

That could only be Marsha. I slid my phone back into my pocket, but Roman waved to say *Go on*. Still, I almost didn't pick up. I could barely remember what Marsha looked like.

"Mmmmm . . . ," Marsha purred when she heard my voice. "What are you doing tonight?"

"Tonight's no good." The ice in my throat made my voice curt. I glanced over at Roman, who was listening to his video man's soft-spoken update—but Roman was as interested in my conversation as I was in his. I would have been curious about his phone call, too.

"Everything okay?" Marsha said.

"Just busy," I said. "Call you in a couple days."

"Relax, Ten," Marsha said, her voice smiling. "Tomorrow, you'll die just fine."

An ice pick jabbed the base of my spine, and the floor dropped from beneath my feet. *First Marsha shows up, then Nandi's gone. Do the math!* my Evil Voice screamed.

Now my mouth felt frozen, too. "What?"

"Bang—you're dead?" Marsha said, laughing. "Your movie shoot's tomorrow, right?"

Lenox Avenue, I realized dimly. My set call was first thing Monday morning. I'd told Marsha all about it.

So much for my film debut.

TWELVE

SUNDAY NIGHT WAS interminable. The office was claustrophobic with so many men in and out, so I walked the grounds and visited the kitchen coffeemaker when I needed fresh air. We kept busy because we didn't want to admit the truth: Someone had stolen Nandi, and there was nothing we could do.

Every half hour, I almost called the police. Or my father. To this day, I wish I had.

I liked Roman, but he was a stranger. And there's no such thing as truly knowing someone; we're lucky if we know ourselves. If Roman was smart, he'd give his own men closer scrutiny, too. I had already collected their names, running cursory searches to see if anything caught my eye. I'd been searching the companies involved in Maitlin's party, too. Aside from a zoning problem with South African Sun on Melrose and a consumer complaint about high prices for the bouncy houses, I had zilch.

We didn't have much luck reaching any of the vendors on a Sunday night, so we left a lot of phone messages. Nothing specific, but we said it was an urgent matter regarding Sofia Maitlin. The limo company never called us back, but callbacks trickled in; first came South African Sun on Melrose. The owner's demeanor was cool after we told him we'd had a theft, but he answered our questions. *Are there any new employees at your company? Did you notice any unusual activity before or after the event? Do any of your employees have a criminal record?* The answer was always no.

The owner was annoyed when we asked him to fax us the names of every employee, whether or not they had attended the party.

"Call the blacks first, is that it?" the man said. He was the Afrikaner I'd met earlier, and he definitely wasn't black. He read my silence. "Oh go on, you know what I mean," he went on, annoyed. "My cooks are black. Wasn't it enough that you had to escort them? We're not thieves. We've cooked for the mayor." His indignation sounded real enough, but it's easy to fake.

Most of the people we reached weren't as testy, but no one was happy about being asked to name their employees. Especially since we couldn't tell them the real reasons. The sleepy vendor from Big Tent Carnival Services meekly asked about a warrant, but he backed down when I warned him that his next call would be from Sofia Maitlin's lawyers. Warrant enough.

Still, we were a long way from anywhere. From time to time, Alec and his son, or Rachel Wentz, came down to hover; but they stopped asking for news. Maitlin, we were told, had taken a Valium and fallen asleep. I bet she'd washed it down with wine.

On my two A.M. coffee run to the kitchen, I found Zukisa sitting alone at a table in the breakfast nook, staring out toward the pool. She was still dressed from the day. The skin beneath her eyes was puffy and dark from hours of crying, as if she'd just gone three rounds.

"Sofia's gonna need you alert tomorrow, darlin'," I said.

The flirtation in my voice was so mild that she might not hear it consciously. After Roman's grilling on her last minutes with Nandi, Zukisa was eager for a friendly voice. That's why good cop—bad cop works so well. People who feel trapped crave friends.

Zukisa had an impeccable background check: Before she worked for Maitlin, she'd spent nine months as a nanny for a high-ranking politico in Pretoria. Maitlin hired her away. She'd been thoroughly vetted in South Africa.

I didn't think Zukisa was a suspect, but I could understand why Roman did. Those crucial minutes Zukisa had waited helped the kidnappers succeed with their grab.

"He's never liked me, from the start," Zukisa said. "He is so overprotective of Sofia."

"Just doing his job. To prevent a situation just like this one."

"I must resign," she said.

"Not so fast. Unless you've been asked to resign, there's no need for that right now. You have no more reason to resign than Roman does. Don't try to make this about you."

"He will have me fired," she said, tight lipped. "He said I waited too long."

"About how long?"

I'd already heard her recounting of events, but I wanted to listen for inconsistencies.

"Maybe only five minutes, or six!" she said. "It seemed like only a moment to me. I went back and forth from those ships. There were so many children—so many places to look. And all the while . . . I wanted it so badly—to see her face. I wanted it so much that I believed she was there. I *believed* I would find her. I expected that any moment, she would be there."

Zukisa still sounded amazed that Nandi had never turned up. She'd been in denial. And she didn't have to say the rest: Going to Roman—who already disliked her, in her mind—would have been her last resort.

More tears filled her eyes. "I don't know how I will ever sleep again. I see Nandi every time I close my eyes. Roman treats me like I am nothing to Nandi, but that girl spends three times as much time with me." Her voice shook.

All the more reason you might want to snatch her to take her back home, I thought. But if Zukisa was faking the grief that wrenched her face, she was in the wrong business.

"Nandi will be fine," I said. "We'll bring her back."

"Yes," Zukisa said, nodding eagerly. "You *must* bring her back. God is with you."

"What do you think of Paki?"

Zukisa clicked her teeth, shaking her head, snapped from grief. "What do I think of a man who only steps forward when a wealthy woman chooses his child? What *should* I think of him? I think he is despicable. Half a thief! I can't stand the sight of him."

With a sigh, she went on. "But a kidnapper? I do not think so. He is a very simple man, still wide eyed and confused, like a child, about everything in America. Whoever did this . . ." Her eyes sharpened with icy rage at the thought of the kidnappers. "These are awful people, but they are not simple. They are sophisticated. They are not wide eyed. They know all about how things work. They know all about Sofia."

She had good instincts, or she was good at deflecting suspicion. That assessment could potentially eliminate her as a suspect, too, except for the inside knowledge of Maitlin's life.

I toured the sitting rooms until I found Paki watching soccer on TV, a six-pack of Newcastle Ales ready on the coffee table. I had sat in while Roman questioned him, too—*Do you know of anyone who would want to kidnap Nandi?*—and I still wasn't sure how to read him. His worry seemed genuine, but he also rubbed his armpit in uncomfortable moments, which made me wonder if he was hiding something.

Was it a cultural quirk, or what poker players call a "tell"?

"Mind if I join you?" I said.

Paki nodded and gestured at the empty half of the sofa, but he didn't look eager. He rubbed his armpit. It might be too late for the good cop–bad cop approach, but I tried.

"Real hard-ass, that Roman. Huh, brother?" I said, reaching for one of the bottles. "Bet you're used to that back home."

Paki glanced at me, as if to be sure of my meaning. I winked. Roman and his Nordic features probably reminded Paki of every bad experience he'd had before the end of apartheid—and every story his father and grandfather had told him about police interrogations.

"His job is to find Nandi," Paki said, shrugging. His speech seemed self-conscious as he enunciated carefully over his accent. "He should ask as many questions as he chooses, all night long, if he thinks that that will bring her back. I only hate to waste his time." Paki wasn't taking my race bait.

"Yeah, well, he was riding you and the sistah pretty hard," I said.

"Zukisa?" Paki said, surprised. "That lovely woman adores Nandi! How could anyone think she would do this terrible thing? Zukisa has nothing to do with this awful business."

I wasn't surprised by the way Paki flew to Zukisa's defense. He had seemed smitten with Zukisa from the first time I saw him looking at her, despite Zukisa's obvious disdain for him. He seemed *very* certain she couldn't be at fault, considering that she was the last person with Nandi. But he wasn't rubbing his armpit.

"So how'd it happen, Paki? You and Nandi?"

Paki sighed, flipping through the channels. The volume of the television was too low to hear, as if he didn't want to disturb the household. He flipped at random, never stopping long. "Ah . . . you want to know about the princess I did not deserve?"

I took a swig of beer, making a mental note not to drink more. I just wanted Paki to feel at ease. He followed my example, twisting off the cap from another bottle.

"The price of lust. What did I know? I met a girl at a nightclub." Paki flicked his hand at his face as if the memory were a bug biting at him. "She gave me a 'club name,' not her real name. We went to the back of her car, both of us drunk. That was the last I saw of her until I heard from some friends that she was pregnant. I could not find her, or even learn her real name. I went to the club every night. I found a girl who knew her, but she said she had moved away. What should I have done?"

"I don't know. Maybe you did everything you could. How did you hear about Children First? Why did you suspect Nandi was yours?"

Paki looked up at me with hangdog eyes. Unblinking. "Imagine you are me: You walk past a man reading a newspaper and you see a child who looks exactly like your sister, on the arm of an American movie star— exactly! *Haw!* And Children First is well known in the township. The age and coloration were right, and I stepped forward, demanded a blood test. Sofia's people paid for the DNA test, and for that I thank them. I could not stay quiet. I had to claim her. I wanted her to remember she had come from somewhere." His voice quivered with emotion. "Do you understand this . . . brother?"

I nodded. I also understood that anyone would be tempted to get a piece of Sofia Maitlin and the life she could offer Nandi.

"I get no stipend!" he said, objecting to my unspoken thoughts. "She pays me nothing. She only helped me get a work visa and find a place to live, and enough to move. That is all. Aside from these things, all I asked was to see my daughter from time to time. On her birthday. At Christmas! Does it make me a criminal to ask for these things?"

"No one said you're a criminal, man."

"No one has to say it," Paki said, and switched the channel again. *The Golden Girls* was on, its laughter frozen in time. Paki seemed to forget I was there, sinking into the soft pastels with glazed eyes. "So much to watch!" he said. "Hundreds of channels. Everything here is choice after choice. There is so much! How do you make the right choice?"

Paki had nothing left to teach me, and his choices were his own.

MONDAY
7:10 A.M.

I hadn't slept when my cell phone rang the next morning. Barely past dawn.

It was Len Shemin, my agent. I was walking the grounds outside, relieving the night shift's patrol. I was tired of my thoughts, so I picked up the call.

"Hey, man, I can't make the shoot today," I told Len.

"Really?" Len said. "Nice afterthought, Ten. Think you could have waited any later to let me know you're blowing off your career's biggest shoot? The one you hired a lawyer to fight for? It's still ninety minutes before your set call. Sure you're cutting it close enough?"

"Look, I can't go into it, but—"

"Never mind," Len said, chuckling. "I'm just giving you shit. I got an email from Rachel Wentz. I don't know what kind of voodoo you're practicing over there, but the whole shoot's been pushed back because Sofia Maitlin's production company wants to invest in the project—if he can spare you for a couple of days. Apparently, that's just fine with Spike. He emailed me, too. Sofia Maitlin. Whoa. I just called to say to remember us little guys, okay?"

"Ain't even like that." Len is a genuine friend, so I wished I could tell him more. I wished the real picture was half as rosy as the one Rachel Wentz had painted for him.

"You okay, Ten? You sound like shit."

"To quote Ving Rhames in *Pulp Fiction*, I'm pretty fucking far from okay. But I'll live."

Len laughed. "What's this I'm hearing about a kid going AWOL from the party? Someone must have been shitting bricks."

"And Angelina Jolie gave birth to a two-headed calf. Bullshit tabloid rumor," I said. "Gotta go, Len. Thanks."

I didn't give him the chance to ask any more questions. I can weave lies with the best of them, but I never enjoy lying to friends. I was deep in the bosom of celebrity life, but I wasn't in Hollywood by far. I didn't need an agent that day.

Sometimes, life becomes instantly clarified.

Mine was all about Nandi.

There was a call at noon. Four of us crowded Maitlin's phone, straining to hear Nandi's small voice. Nandi didn't sound happy, whining about how she didn't have any apple juice, so we were left with an image of deprivation before the kidnappers took the phone. When we heard Nandi's cries, Maitlin hugged her stomach, as if she had been speared. Maitlin's ghostly face reminded me of the painting *The Scream* by Edvard Munch.

"Don't hurt her!" Maitlin begged her telephone.

"We'll call with the drop-off location at ten," a man's mechanized voice said. "Bring five million dollars. No invisible ink. No booby traps. Unmarked bills. If you are late, if you fuck with us, if I see any police . . . I'll slit her throat myself." *Click.*

"Sons of *BITCHES*!" Alec roared, red faced, the most emotion he'd shown since Nandi's disappearance. I'd almost wondered if the man's stoicism was suspicious, but what was the point of kidnapping his own child? His son, Nikolos, convinced him in Greek to take a walk outside Nandi's room. Maitlin and her husband drifted to separate islands to suffer.

Maitlin never left her daughter's room. If she had slept, it was on Nandi's miniature bed. Maitlin's eyes were hollowed out, dark pockets. By Monday afternoon, she wasn't speaking to anyone, saving her energy for her phone calls.

The next call came at ten exactly, after an eternity. The room was crowded, all of us standing by for the endgame. News that would bring Nandi home to her bed.

The call lasted twenty seconds at most. Nandi was crying in the background.

I couldn't hear the caller that time, so I read Maitlin's scribbles: *11 P.M. Citrus College. Glendora. Football stadium. 50-yard line. Barranca entrance.* Maitlin was so nervous as she wrote, I could barely make out the last words. As I read, my heart knocked against my ribs.

"Yes," she kept saying, obedient. "Yes. Just don't hurt her. That's what you promised."

Beverly Hills is an hour from Glendora on a good day. Roman and I had mapped tentative routes to predictable sections of Los Angeles— the port, downtown, the beaches—but Glendora was a surprise. Forty miles east of us! And late was not an option. If the drop-off went badly, it couldn't be because we got stuck in traffic.

Maitlin's sob caught between my ears, a wounded, mournful surrender I would hear the whole drive to Glendora. I wanted to promise her that Roman and I would bring her daughter home, but there was no time for false assurances.

"Go, go, *GO!*" Rachel Wentz cheered behind us. We were racing down the stairs.

All we could do for Nandi was run.

THIRTEEN

10:15 P.M.

Five million dollars sat in the rear of Roman's black Mercedes SUV, in two large duffel bags stuffed with hundred-dollar bills. Each bag weighed at least fifty pounds. Roman and I had retrieved the pile of currency from Maitlin's bank that day amid curious gazes from bank employees but no embarrassing questions.

I hated what we were doing, but I liked my new partner. The disagreement about whether or not to call the police simmered between us, and sometimes he seemed too emotional, but Roman's mind stayed quick. *It's good when somebody's got your back,* I thought.

Then, he turned on DMX.

Don't get me wrong: I like rap fine. Sometimes it's just the right sound at the right time. But when I was driving with a carload of cash to retrieve a two-year-old child, the last thing I wanted to hear booming from the speakers was shit about losing our minds or acting a fool. Men have been psyching themselves up for battle with music since drums were invented. Roman cranked the angry bass, smacking his hands against the wheel in rhythm.

He reached under his seat and handed me a gun case. A SIG Sauer P226. A hyperfunctional weapon beloved of SEALs and Recon Marines. Never fired one, but it had killed more men than the flu.

"Ever zap anybody?" Roman said. The speedometer was creeping past ninety.

I remembered the life flickering out of a man's eyes in the Florida swamp—but I would have saved his life if I could have. His bad heart killed him, not me. "No," I said. "You?"

"Not sure of the exact count," Roman said. "Iraq. Some memories I don't want stuck in my head. Everybody thinks it's the men you kill who haunt you. That's not true."

"What is it, then?"

"It's the men you couldn't save," he said. "Boys and men who trusted me, and died."

I was glad I'd never been to war. Back when my father's doctors thought he was dying, one of Dad's oldest friends told me Dad was never the same after his tour in Vietnam in sixty-seven. I'd never met the playful, laid-back dude his friend remembered.

"Sounds rough."

Roman hunched over the wheel. "Shit was a long time ago."

I checked the magazine, counting the rounds I might need to save my life. Both magazines were full, but the black metal lip on the second looked a little off to me. I decided not to trust it. I fed the first back into the SIG Sauer. I held the gun in my lap, caressing it, my finger beside the trigger. Roman drove like a fiend, skating past changing yellow lights to get us to Interstate 10.

"In a perfect world?" Roman said. "Once Nandi's clear, we smoke 'em all."

This man is going to get us all killed. "Not what I signed up for."

"And this isn't a perfect world," Roman said. "So we eat it and bring Nandi home."

"We've got their five million," I said. "If they play fair, we'll get her."

"We'll get her no matter what," Roman said. He zagged across solid lines, trying to maneuver around the bank of brake lights that had suddenly appeared ahead. It was ten fifteen and we were nowhere close. We hadn't even hit the 60 yet, and Glendora was a long way northeast.

Roman nodded toward an index card on the dashboard. "Grab that. That's my number." The index card had a phone number with an 818 area code, and three names: *Wendy. Bryan. Caitlin.* He didn't have to tell me what the number was for. "Write yours down on the other side. Wife, girlfriend, your kid. It's better when they hear it from someone who was there."

Roman, obviously, had made this call before.

I wrote *Captain Hardwick*—it would annoy Dad if a stranger called him by his Christian name, no matter what the news. I was fine until I started writing Chela's name, when I realized what I was doing: I was volunteering to possibly walk away, just when I'd promised to take care of her. I didn't let myself think about April often, but her words from Cape Town came back to me: *I can't sit around worrying about whether you're going to get killed, or if you'll have to kill somebody. I can't live that way— or raise our kids that way.*

April had been telling the truth on me, and I hadn't wanted to hear. What was I doing speeding on the Santa Monica Freeway with five million dollars in cash and a gun in my lap? Riding the chaos, just like April had said. And I was taking my family along for the ride.

I wrote *Chela Hardwick* on the index card, hoping it would matter to her if the call came. I wanted to write more, but it felt like a jinx to plan on dying.

Roman's GPS showed traffic patterns; most of our route was clear, colored green, but we were close to a patch in yellow that meant a slow-down. No alternate route made sense. Our arrival estimate was 10:58, but we would add minutes in traffic. We might already be late.

The drumbeat in my chest wasn't from DMX. A wary voice whispered, *If you remember how to pray, this might be a good time to start.* Was the voice mine? My father's?

I watched the small wood-carved crucifix swing back and forth from Roman's rearview mirror. I wished it looked more like a comfort, less like an omen.

The campus of Citrus College was dark and deserted by the time we screeched to Barranca at exactly 10:59. The music was off.

We drove past the light on Route 66 heading north on Barranca, and the last lights were from a strip mall and a 7-Eleven. Ahead, there was a well-kept residential neighborhood and mountains shrouded in darkness. The navigator said we should have been sitting right on top of the football stadium, but I couldn't see it.

"Where the *fuck* . . . ?" Roman said, straining to see through his windshield.

When the clock showed 11:00, we were still on Barranca, lost. Maitlin's phone might already be ringing with bad news.

The colors black and white appeared in my side-view mirror, and I froze. A Glendora police cruiser approached from behind us, sirens off. The cruiser slowed and the driver glanced our way, trying to see through Roman's tinted windows. The massive luxury SUV looked out of place on an empty street so late.

"We better—," I began. *Get the hell out of here,* I was about to say. If we showed up with a police escort, Nandi might not survive the night.

Roman drove slowly, ten miles below the forty-mile-per-hour speed limit. Still, the police cruiser lingered. I braced for the flashing red light, scanning the dark streets for a cover story. There was a trailer park on my side of the street. Good.

"*Shit,*" Roman said. He was already wild eyed.

"Stay cool. We're looking for a friend's house on Barranca." I kept my body language neutral, looking toward Roman instead of the police. He was dripping in sweat, glistening in the glow from the navigator.

My heart flipped. Roman was freaking out. This could go all wrong, I realized. Maybe it already had.

The police cruiser drove ahead at last, turning east at the next light, on Foothill.

"That did not just fucking happen," Roman muttered.

The clock said 11:01.

"There's the parking lot," I said. On the driver's side, a huge parking lot sat empty. I still didn't see a football stadium, but the parking lot was big. An unlighted sign in white sat atop what looked like a grassy hill over the parking lot: CITRUS COLLEGE—THE FIGHTING OWLS. High above stood towering poles from dark stadium lights that were nearly invisible in the night. The stadium was behind the hill, camouflaged to blend into the neighborhood! A maze of gates penned it in. But the gate to the parking lot was wide open.

The empty parking lot stretched everywhere, a long drive snaking the length of the stadium before it turned the corner and led to a more traditional ticket booth and entrance. The parking lot abutted the strip mall we'd passed earlier, and college buildings were nearby, but the concrete was an ocean of isolation. Not a single other car.

We parked at the edge of the stadium's deserted ticket island and admission gates. The only lights were from Roman's headlights. The clock said 11:02.

Roman opened his car door, but left the car idling. Lights on.

"*Hello?*" he called out. "We're here for Nandi! We've got your money!"

No answer. They might be playing us, of course. A test. Maitlin might get a new location when we passed.

"They want us on the fifty-yard line," I said. "We better hustle."

We used the strategy from actors' base camp during a shoot, hiding the car keys on top of the tire on the driver's side—easy to find, but the last place anyone else would look. Roman opened the back of the SUV, and we heaved two and a half million dollars apiece across our shoulders in duffel bags, securing them with one arm. Those bags were *heavy*, like carrying fifty-five pounds of potatoes on your back. My P226 was in my jeans, hidden beneath my T-shirt. Roman tossed me a device that looked like miniature binoculars with an adjustable headband and chin strap, and I caught it with my free hand.

"Night vision," Roman said. "Better than a flashlight. Dark as shit out here."

"Thanks, man," I said. I fitted on the goggles, and hidden objects leaped into my green-tinged vision. Another maze of fences lay ahead. I scanned the parking lot again; I saw rows of painted lines, suddenly bright, but not a single car. Nothing moved. I took the goggles off and wore them around my neck. Too disorienting until I needed them. I would trust my own eyes.

We ran as fast as we could with the weight of the money, only at a jog. The gate to the stadium's main entrance was wide open, too.

We turned a corner past the gates, and the football stadium unfolded like a massive crater, ringed by a competition running track with marked lanes. Without my goggles on, all I could see were the shadowy rows of aluminum seats, rising like the Red Sea on either side of us, and the words

CITRUS COLLEGE spelled out with white flowers high above the goalpost.

Fingers toggling his goggles, Roman swept the field with his eyes. "Nobody," he muttered. "They better not think we're just gonna drop off the money and go. Kiss my ass."

"Hello!" I called out to the vast, dark space. "We're here for Nandi!"

Nothing. I checked my watch: 11:04.

"I don't like it," I said quietly. "We're wide open for a sniper. *Pow*, we're dead. Money disappears. No Nandi." I hoped they were professionals, and that this was just another day at the office. Amateurs might think it was worth it to shoot us. Just in case.

Roman hiked his bag up higher on his shoulder. "Let 'em try it."

We ran side by side, our shoes sinking into springy artificial turf as we made our way toward the fifty-yard line. Every yard was an effort; my thighs felt tight. The wads of bills shifted inside my duffel bag, making it squirm like something alive. *Please let Nandi be here,* I thought, even while the darkness and silence said otherwise.

Both of us were breathing hard when we flung our bags off on the fifty-yard line and tried to realign our joints. My left shoulder would be bitching at me for a long while.

Five minutes late, but we'd finally made it.

This time, both of us used our goggles to scan the stadium. I finally saw movement on the home side, near the announcer's booth. A flash of light, and then the world went dark. My goggles had shut off.

"*Fuck!*" I said. Or maybe Roman said it. Simultaneously, we took off our goggles.

Someone had turned on a spotlight, triggering the goggles' auto shut-off. The light was too weak to fully illuminate us, but it was more than bright enough to hide whoever was standing behind it. The light was on the home side, about ten rows high.

"*Empty your guns and throw them down,*" a man's voice said. He sounded like a megaphone, with a posh English accent, and he was nowhere near the light.

My heart tumbled.

"More than one," I whispered to Roman.

"He's at nine o'clock. Got my eye on the booth, too."

I pulled out my P226 slow as a snail, ejected the magazine, and raised it above my head. I tossed the magazine right, the gun about ten yards left. Roman threw down his nine, too, but he didn't reach down to give up the little .38 Special he kept strapped to his ankle. I envied him for his hidden weapon, but I hoped it wouldn't haunt us later.

"*Keep your hands raised high. Both of you.*"

We complied. Standing still with your arms raised when you just gave up your weapon isn't as easy as it looks, but we did it. My teeth were locked, expecting gunfire.

Footsteps. Three or four men were approaching us from different directions; they'd been hidden in the bleachers.

"*Now . . . open the bags, please,*" the voice said. The politeness was reassuring.

Roman unzipped his bag, and I unzipped mine. The sound of the zippers ricocheted through the empty stadium.

"*Show me the money,*" Megaphone said.

"Where's Nandi?" I called out.

CLICK. Our guns were gone, but three guns were on us.

My palms went cold, and wet. I heard whispered cursing, and realized it was mine. Roman and I both grabbed wrapped stacks from the bags and held them up high.

"There's the money!" Roman said. "No tricks. No bullshit. We just want the little girl."

In the endless beat of silence, I suddenly felt certain that Nandi was already dead. I mapped my flight in case any shooting started—I would run zigzag back to the gate. Stick to the shadows.

"*Put the money down and step away from the bags,*" Megaphone said. "*Go to the track on the opposite side of the field. The visitors' side.*" They wanted to send us away from the money so they could retrieve it. But then what?

"Sorry for being an asshole," Roman said, "but we need Nandi first."

My tone was gentle as I backed up Roman. "You asked for five mil, right? Well, here it is. Just bring us the little girl. She's a baby, man. Let's end this thing for everybody."

"*DO IT!*" Megaphone shouted.

I couldn't see Roman's eyes because he'd put his goggles back on, but I heard something that might have been a growl. I didn't like the sound of it, but I understood. The longer we were here with no sign of Nandi, the slimmer the chances that we would leave—with or without her. Why hadn't I called Chela and Dad from the car when I'd had the chance?

We were at the fifty-yard line, only a few feet from the sidelines, so we crossed to the other side of the field. After each step, I was amazed we were still both breathing and upright.

"This ain't gonna happen," Roman muttered.

It could have been a prediction, but it sounded more like a vow.

A child's cry from somewhere above made my neck snap up. Blackness. I fumbled to put my goggles back on, and I saw her: Nandi's tiny pale shape standing at the very top of the steps in the bleachers on the visitors' side, almost in the exact center. Alone and crying, afraid. Nandi was holding a child's cup in one hand, swaying back and forth as she cried. The stairs in front of her would break her neck with one slip.

I wanted to shout out to Nandi, but neither one of us did. She would try to come to us, and that would mean disaster. We forgot about the Englishman, or the men and their guns. We ran toward Nandi.

I ran up the endless stadium steps two at a time, Roman at my heels. When I dared to take my eyes off Nandi, I saw the four men swarming the field around our money bags, also dressed in dark clothes. *"Hurry!"* one of the men on the field hissed.

For one perfect moment, everything was going according to plan.

"Her ankle's tied to the bleacher," Roman said, the same time I realized it. I couldn't see what was binding her, but Nandi was struggling against it. I was glad they'd taken precautions so Nandi wouldn't fall. *We might survive this,* I thought. Jinx.

Twenty yards. Thirty more steps.

"Five million my ass," I heard Roman say.

"What?" With Nandi in sight, I had forgotten the money.

"You grab Nandi," Roman said. "Get her to the car."

Sudden motion as Roman tried to pivot away. Instinct made me shoot out my arm toward him, trying to grab his shirt to pull him back. My fingertips got his sleeve, but Roman yanked away, hard. Then he dove behind the bleachers, gone. Vanished in the dark.

"Man, come on!" I whispered sharply. "Don't get us killed over some damn paper."

I couldn't stop Roman. I'll have the rest of my life to wonder how the night would have gone differently if I had, but I had to keep my eyes on Nandi, who was stamping her feet with agitation. Even with the ankle restraint, she could fall and injure herself on the concrete. She saw me coming and seemed frightened, crying out.

What the FUCK is he doing?

"Nandi, *don't move!*" I shouted to her. "It's Mister Ten! Stay right there, honey!"

"Mister Ten?" Nandi called back, delighted. Her sobs stopped cold.

Then I was touching Nandi's hot face, wiping her tears and nose with my T-shirt. No one had combed her hair, which looked like a bird's nest of dark curls, but she was clean, and her matching plain red shorts and shirt were new. My heartbeat and adrenaline made my hands shake. I cradled Nandi's head against my shoulder, stroking her matted hair. Her tiny heart swatted at my chest, looking for safety.

As soon as Nandi was in my arms, I knew I couldn't live with myself if I let her go.

"*Shhhhh*, sweetheart . . . We're gonna take you home to Mommy. It's okay now."

Silence from the dark field far below, except for grunts as the men tried to lift their load.

"*Roman? I got her!*" I whispered, praying Roman had fought off the memories of missions gone bad.

I fumbled with Nandi's ankle restraint. Nandi had been tied only with a nylon stocking, but the knot was tight against her tiny ankle, with no wriggle room. The other end was knotted around a metal bar beneath the bleacher. I whipped out my miniature penknife. Not much of a weapon, but perfect for cutting nylon.

POW. A gunshot! And something that sounded like an Apache war cry. Roman's voice.

Frenzied shouting came from the field, and a howl of pain. Had that been Roman, too?

The world stood still for a moment, meaningless, before I remembered myself. My breath caught—*Oh jesus jesus jesus jesus NOT NOW*—and I sliced the stocking. Nandi's weight fell against me, a warm ball of cotton in my arms.

I whispered to her, crouching behind the bleachers. "Be real, real quiet, okay?"

While Nandi whimpered on my chest, I flipped on my goggles to look at the football field, where my future was being decided. A dark silhouette lay writhing on the field, two feet from one of the bags. Not Roman.

"Come on . . . where are you, man?" I whispered.

I found the huddle near the closest sideline, a group of four men in a circle. Roman was backing away from someone, disarmed. The man lunged at Roman with a knife that flared like a Fourth of July sparkler in my goggles. Roman stood in a nervous wrestling stance, rocking from side to side. The man with the knife squared off with him, his arms moving like an optical illusion.

Shit. Shit. Shit.

The knife was blurry, part ice pick, part pneumatic drill. The rapid fluidity of the motion was a bad dream unfolding. The man's body weaved as he chopped at the air with his knife, dicing it. I could run down to help Roman, or I could try to save Nandi.

Nandi's whimpers gave me only one choice.

"*Shhhhh . . . ,*" I said, desperate for her to stay quiet.

Sticking close to the far wall of the stadium behind the stands, I ran toward the stairs on the west end, closer to the main gate. *God, if you give me this . . . I'll finally believe you're real.*

Below us, Roman screamed. I pressed my palms against Nandi's ears. Her whimpers were getting louder, bordering on sobs.

"It's okay, Nandi . . . ," I whispered, and faked a laugh. "They're playing a game."

My laugh fooled her. "A game?" she said. Her smile startled me.

The scream stopped in midnote, but there was no time to mourn. Right away, powerful flashlight beams strobed up and down the stands, looking for us. I dove down to hide, banging my knee into the sharp corner of a bench. No sound. I swallowed my cry.

"Find them!" the Englishman said.

Heels thundered below us as the men ran up the bleacher steps, closing in. My heartbeat shook my body. Hiding wouldn't work. On to plan C.

I peeked around to get my bearings: We were only twenty yards from the gate, a straight run at a sharp descent. The gate was closed, but it might not be locked. From there, a winding sidewalk would take me back down to ground level.

A little luck might get us out of the stadium. Luck, and my new BFF, God.

"Are you playing a game?" Nandi whispered.

"Yeah, sweetie. We run really fast."

"*Really* fast?" Nandi whispered, grinning.

Hope to God, I thought.

"Stay quiet—or we lose," I whispered, and Nandi nodded like she understood.

I ran. My knee pulsed with fresh pain, but I ran. I landed cat quiet and ran as fast as I could without tumbling down. I crisscrossed my arms to hold Nandi firmly in place, supporting the back of her head with my palms so I wouldn't jounce her. I held her as if she were made of eggshells.

I dodged the flashlight beams, using my goggles to guide me to the gate I shouldn't have been able to see—but could, thanks to Roman. I smelled freedom wafting from the parking lot.

And then I stopped. Everything stopped. God went back to sleep.

Five yards ahead, a man was in my path.

The gunman was masked in black from head to toe. Even his eyes were hidden behind black nylon. He was an apparition.

But his gun was real. Through my goggles, his gun glittered so brightly in the moonlight that I thought it was a muzzle flash. I thought we were already dead.

I stopped running so abruptly that I almost pitched myself down headfirst. The soles of my shoes whined against the concrete.

He could have shot me already, so maybe he didn't want to.

"You really don't want to take another step," the Englishman said.

The one voice I hadn't wanted to hear. The devil was taking his turn with us.

"He's mean," Nandi whispered.

"Man, don't." He wasn't as tall as I was, with a thick neck and shoulders. I was well within his shooting range, but he was too far for me to disarm him. And how could I? Holding Nandi was as hobbling as missing limbs, or eyes. Any move I considered was too risky. She made me defenseless.

"Five million dollars—it's yours!" I told him. "Just walk away."

"Put the girl down," he said.

Nandi squirmed. She didn't like the way the game was going.

I stepped back. "I didn't see a thing. We're all done here, man."

Three other sets of footsteps were approaching from all sides. I sidled toward the gate, a six-foot fence penning me in. I hadn't seen the chain and padlock when I was running, but I would climb over if I had to. If he was going to shoot me, maybe he would have already. All the while I made plans, I never felt so much like I was in a cage. I flung my back against the gate, testing it. The chain clanked, but didn't yield.

Trapped. My heartbeat shook the stadium.

"No need to die like your friend," the Englishman said. "Put her down. Gently."

"Please let her go," I said. "Don't do this."

The gunman aimed lower, at my feet. Picking a spot clear of Nandi. My toes itched.

"When your boss asks you what went wrong . . . ," he began, ". . . and she *will* ask . . ."

"You got what you came for! Do you have kids? Do you have a mother? Take me, not this kid. Be the hero now—let her go."

The silence from the other waiting men made me wonder if they were on my side.

The Englishman went on calmly: ". . . report to her that now we will need another five million, just like the first five. That's my fee for my man getting shot in the leg, for breaking trust." His voice shook, betraying his outrage. It wasn't business anymore: It was personal. "We'll be back in touch."

I smelled stale cigarette smoke as the knife fighter slipped behind the Englishman, his blood-stained blade ready at his side, breath a little irregular, but no other evident reaction from killing Roman. He, too, was masked in what looked like a bodysuit. He was about five-seven and small boned, only slightly taller than the Englishman, but with an arrhythmic, angular quality that made my hindbrain scream *Danger!*

I tried to hide Nandi's eyes, but she pulled her face away from my palm.

I hoped she didn't see the blood. I hoped she wouldn't see mine.

"We can do this with crying and screaming," the Englishman said cheerfully, "or you can give Nandi a smile and tell her you'll see her soon."

A *CLICK* from the gun; his round was chambered, his mind made up. If I pissed him off like Roman, he would shoot me in the foot first, then probably shoot me in the head as soon as they had Nandi. Or leave me to his friend with the knife.

I lowered myself down to my throbbing knee so I could face Nandi at eye level when I set her down. I stroked her unkempt mop of hair. Nandi's wide eyes waited for me to explain.

"So . . . the game's over, and guess what?" I said, struggling to keep my voice light. "You won! Now we switch off, and you get to go have fun with your new friends."

"I don't wanna." She wasn't crying, but she was close. "He's mean!"

"No, no, it's okay. See?" I smiled for Nandi, just as I'd been instructed. My face hurt from the lie, but my smile didn't show a sign of trouble.

Still, Nandi gave a wail that crushed my chest. "I want my mom-meeee!"

The men were behind me, closing in, but I didn't break away from Nandi's eyes or abandon my smile. My smile was the only thing I could give her. "You'll see your mommy soon. Hear me? I'll come back and take you to your mommy. That's a promise."

I was close enough to see the quick spark in her eye: not a smile, but she believed me.

The sound of sirens rose in the night sky like an hallucination, too far to help.

While one man pulled me back, another swept Nandi up high. I yanked myself free, ready to fight, but somebody suckered me with the butt of a gun to the back of my head. I staggered, the world swimming.

I yelled out, my last resort for Nandi's sake: *"HELP! CALL 911—"* A flock of birds nesting in a nearby tree took flight. My anguish flew for miles.

I waited for the knife. The gunshot.

Instead, bright light flared all around. Dazzling white pain. I felt myself falling, pulled down into the depths of myself. I was drowning under the weight of Nandi's heavy absence. Crushed by the burden of her trust.

FOURTEEN

My head was a throbbing mess, but most of it wasn't from the pistol whipping that had left a walnut-size knot on the back of my head.

At the football stadium, I'd awakened in time to see Roman's body loaded into the coroner's ambulance. Nandi, gone. The money, gone. Vast, empty nothingness from end to end, except for the red lights of Hell flaring from the police cars and ambulances.

Two hours later, in an interview room in LAPD's Robbery-Homicide division, I remembered the index card in my back pocket. I still had my cell phone, so I dialed. I couldn't rehearse what to say. I wanted to tell her in person, but I wasn't free for a visit.

The phone picked up after one ring, anxious, silent waiting instead of a greeting.

"Is this Wendy?" I said, consulting the card. "Roman's wife?"

The woman's breaths fractured. "Tennyson Hardwick?"

He had told her I might call. What would I say if she asked me if he'd suffered?

Roman's wife coaxed me past my grim silence. "Please. Just tell me."

"I'm sorry to call with news like this . . ." I heard her suck in her breath, waiting for what she already knew. Each word was a labor greater than the last. "Roman was . . . killed tonight during our assignment for Sofia Maitlin. It happened fast, Wendy. He was trying to—"

Only a deep gasp told me she had heard. A pause, followed by a whispered question. "Did you get Nandi?"

My mind flashed on Nandi's anxious, wondering face. I closed my eyes.

"No, ma'am." My throat was seared raw. "They want more payment."

"God," she said. "Oh, *God*."

She repeated her prayer for the rest of our call, excusing herself when she lost her voice. I heard a child in the background, and remembered Roman's kids on the pirate ship. I was grateful when the line clicked dead.

Lieutenant Nelson was standing in the open doorway, at a polite distance. After I put away my telephone, he came in with a packet of extra-strength Tylenol and a cup of black coffee. I'd asked for the Tylenol, but I would have picked beer over caffeine. I was tired of being awake. Every time I blinked, I had to fight to open my eyes again.

Nelson's brow was severe, hiding his thoughts as he paced. He'd been roused from bed, and was dressed blandly in gray sweatpants and a USC sweatshirt. So far, he'd spared me the I-told-you-so tirade whirring behind his brow. Maybe he had a human streak.

"He asked me to call her," I said.

Nelson shrugged. "I've got nothing to add to that conversation, Hardwick."

"I'd like to go home."

Nelson sat at the edge of the table. "Forget it. You're in mighty deep waters—too far out for me to pull you in. I got you a few minutes to breathe, but that won't last long."

I nodded. I'd figured as much, on all counts.

"Can't get worse," I said, although we both knew that wasn't true.

"Oh, it can, and it will." Nelson chuckled sourly. "Now you're the FBI's problem. And the chief of police. And pretty much the whole damn world. You want to be famous? You just got your wish. Kiss your life good-bye."

Nelson walked away and closed the door. Human, after all.

+   +   +

5 A.M.

I thought I finally would be free to leave after my polygraph, but I was wrong.

"Explain to me again why you didn't call the police the day of the party?"

Special Agent Fanelli of the Federal Bureau of Investigation was whiny and incredulous, a posture that had worn thin hours ago. He was about fifty, small boned and craggy faced, with a shock of dark hair and an uneven hairline, wearing a stylish gray suit. His accent was straight out of Little Italy, like John Turturro. "To be honest, Ten, this is the part I still don't understand."

Five in the morning, and no end in sight. The agents were wide awake. At about three, Fanelli had started calling me Ten, as if we were buddies.

"If I'm being charged with something, I need to call my lawyer. If not, I'm ready to go."

"Are you serious?" The female agent, Garceaux, was a fair-skinned sister whose hair was lashed in a tight bun. Her blouse and skirt were so mismatched that I wondered if she'd gotten dressed in the dark. She was in her thirties, but her voice was kitten soft, like a child's, almost out of my hearing. "This little girl's life is at stake, and you're talking about a lawyer? You can't be bothered to help us conduct a thorough investigation? You and your buddy blew it, but you're just gonna kick back and see how it all plays out? Wow."

Her words were lashes, whipping me. I'd handed Nandi over to men I knew to be killers. Until that night, I hadn't known what guilt felt like, so thick in my lungs that it was hard to breathe the room's stale air. Maybe the polygraph had confused guilt with lies.

Now I understood exactly what Roman meant about those betrayed, those left behind.

"But sure, go on, put in a call to a lawyer," Garceaux said. "I'm sure Nandi's all comfy eating frosted flakes and watching Elmo while we wait for you to lawyer up." For the first time, she sounded angry. I noticed her wedding band, and I was sure she had kids. Maybe a daughter.

I stared at the table. I couldn't raise my eyes to stare a mother in the face.

"Everything else, we got it," Fanelli said, pressing on. "You take the money to the fifty. Your buddy goes Dirty Harry and starts shooting. He gets sliced and diced."

"His name was Roman," I said, my eyes snapping to his. Fanelli dehumanized Roman at every chance, trying to rattle me and force a discrepancy in my story.

Fanelli almost smiled, bemused that he'd gotten to me. "Pardon me— Roman. Then you try to grab Nandi, but they clock you and take her away. She's gone in a poof. I got all that. The part where I'm stuck, bear with me, is why you don't call the police. Like, *right away*. And your dad's an LAPD captain? It confuses me. As soon as the kid is missing, you say, 'Listen, I know you're a movie star, but there's common sense and there's stupidity.' Was it a mass outbreak of stupidity? Is that why a man is dead and this little girl is God-knows-where?"

"Sounds right—put it in writing," I said. *"WE FUCKED UP!"*

I don't know where I got the energy to shout.

Garceaux sighed. At last, maybe she felt sorry for me.

Fanelli finally had the confession he wanted. He gave me a contemptuous gaze over his shoulder before flipping through his notes. "Lucky for you, stupid's not a crime."

"Nothing else about the subjects?" Garceaux asked me, more gently. "Not even race?"

I went through my laundry list again: "Only one of them spoke. He had an upscale English accent, but it could have been phony. I can't tell you race, because they were covered from head to toe. The one who killed Roman used a knife, and his art looked like one I saw in Langa. That's where Maitlin found Nandi, in South Africa."

"His 'art'?" Fanelli said. "That's what you call it?"

I was tired, so maybe I shouldn't have said it—but the knife fighter was an artist. Once Roman was disarmed, he'd never had a chance. Almost no one would. "He's incredibly dangerous," I said. "About five-seven. He's not big, but his knife was like the needle of a sewing machine, jabbing from different angles. Fast as hell."

Garceaux was scribbling eager notes, but Fanelli wasn't impressed.

Anything I said was wasted on his ears. "You done with your briefing now . . . Detective?" he said.

Fuck you, I told him with my eyes, but ignorance can't be cured in a single conversation. I'd been underestimated my whole life—except by Sofia Maitlin, who'd expected far too much.

"Here's the new reality of your life . . . ," Fanelli went on. "My injunction says you can't go within five hundred feet of Sofia Maitlin. You are not to contact Sofia Maitlin. If you *dream* about Sofia Maitlin, you're going to jail. We'll tell your new roommates you aided and abetted in this kidnapping—so you'll get along great with the guys behind the wall."

I'd expected to be iced out, but it stung. My head felt too tired to hold upright. I had promised Nandi I would come for her. I closed my eyes, and her tear-damp face shined at me.

"Was anything I just said confusing to you?" Fanelli said.

"I need to tell Sofia what happened," I said.

"Trust me, she knows," Garceaux said. "Take that off your list of worries, sunshine."

"This is a federal investigation now," Fanelli said. "You're *off* this case. Until we contact you again, forget you heard Nandi's name. Do not discuss this case with anyone. Talk to the news about this case, or the tabloids, and you're going away. Have I been clear?"

He waited for an answer, so I nodded.

"Louder—for the tape, please," Garceaux said.

"Got it." A growl of surrender preserved for posterity.

They glanced at each other, deciding I'd had enough.

Garceaux slapped my shoulder. "Better hope we can clean it up. Get some sleep."

They left me alone in the interview room. Nandi's cries and Roman's screams rang in the small room's walls, inescapable.

Five minutes passed before I could rise to my feet.

Chela was the last person I expected to find waiting for me at Robbery-Homicide. She looked dressed up for Halloween, wearing oversize sunglasses, one of Dad's fedoras, and my trench coat.

"*Ten!*" she said, and wrapped her arms around my neck. I needed her hug, but I was so tired that she nearly pulled me off balance.

"What are you doing here?"

"What do you think? You scared the shit out of us!" Chela said, still hanging on. When Chela's hair brushed my cheek, I smelled Nandi in her curls. My stomach lurched. "Ten, why didn't you tell us Sofia Maitlin's baby was—" She stopped in midsentence, noticing the bandage on the back of my head. "Omigod! Did they take you to a hospital?"

A crowd was gathering as we attracted the attention of newly arrived detectives huddled near the coffee machine. Extra manpower. They weren't usually at work so early, and I didn't like their eyes on us. I wasn't in the mood to answer any more questions, spoken or unspoken.

"I'm fine," I told Chela, steering her toward the hall. "Who told you about—"

"Captain's cop friend called. We've been here three hours already."

I scanned the mostly empty office. "Where's Dad?"

"He's sleeping in the car. Ten, there's a buttload of news vans outside the police station, and the reporters are all asking questions about you and Sofia Maitlin's baby. It's surreal!"

I understood Chela's strange costume: It was a disguise. The story was out. The reporters might beat us to my house. A mounted television screen across the room with local news was showing a photo of Nandi. AMBER ALERT: MAITLIN KIDNAPPING!

What if we'd put out the word when the original trail was fresh?

My stomach rolled, twice. I was about to puke all over the floor of the RHD.

"Wait for me," I told Chela.

I'd given up on making it to the men's room when I almost ran by the sign on a door beside me. The bathroom was empty. I lurched to the first stall, and everything spilled out of my stomach: the coffee, the lone protein bar I'd had for dinner at Maitlin's, and a quart of pure acid. My stomach kept heaving long after the food was gone.

My phone vibrated in my pocket. I'd ignored my phone during the FBI interview, but I grabbed it. I was surprised by how much I hoped it was April.

PRIVATE CALLER, my screen said. Was it the kidnappers?

"Tennyson."

I recognized her sob before she spoke. "Are you all right?" Sofia Maitlin whispered.

"God, Sofia, I'm so, so sorry," I said. My legs folded beneath me. Suddenly, I was sitting against the wall, half a foot from the urinal. The smell was sharp, making me want to vomit again, but I couldn't move. The tiles were cold through the seat of my pants.

"Of course," she said. "I know you are."

"It was going fine, according to the agreement, and then Roman freaked out and went after them. He was gone before I could stop him. He shot one of their guys, and it went to hell."

I owed Maitlin the truth as I saw it.

Footsteps in the hallway brought me to my feet, and I leaned on the wall for support, the way my father did at home. The footsteps passed me, fast and sure down the hall.

"Nandi?" Maitlin said, whispering. I wondered if she was hiding, too.

"I *had* her. She wasn't hurt. I was carrying her in my arms before they took her back."

Maitlin sobbed quietly. "Everyone said to call the police. If I had, Roman wouldn't be . . ."

He wouldn't be dead if he hadn't lost his mind either, I thought.

"Roman made a choice," I said. "He knew the risks. So did I."

"But they said they would kill her if we told anyone! I thought it would be better to keep quiet. Can you understand?" Maitlin needed forgiveness, too. "Everyone knows now."

"The publicity's a *good* thing," I said. "She's everywhere because of who you are, and someone's seen her. It's the best weapon you have. It's exactly what they *didn't* want."

Unfortunately, the massive publicity would make Nandi's kidnappers desperate, and I knew they must be arguing about their next move. They might kill Nandi without ever wanting to. The next phone call, if another came, might be our last chance.

"Have you heard from them?" I said.

"Nothing." A tight squeak. "I borrowed this phone. I'm keeping mine clear."

"The FBI's shutting me out," I said. "There's a court order."

"That's Alec. My way didn't work, so now it's his way. How can I argue?"

"Don't argue. I'm glad the FBI is there, but I need somebody to keep me in the loop." I needed to fulfill my promise to Nandi's frightened eyes.

"Tennyson . . . ," Maitlin began. "Do you think . . . ?"

She'd be a fool not to wonder if Nandi was sleeping in a shallow grave.

"People who kill children don't let people like me live," I said, assuring myself as much as Maitlin. "They smell the money now. No matter what, make them believe you'll pay more. He talked like a businessman. He doesn't want to hurt Nandi. If Roman hadn't pissed them off, I believe it would have gone down just like we agreed. *We* broke the agreement first."

"I just talked to Wendy," Maitlin said. "Poor woman. With those kids!"

I didn't ask about her conversation with Roman's widow. Wendy would accept all the solace she could gather today; tomorrow, she'd probably file a lawsuit against Maitlin.

"Was Nandi wearing the same dress? From the party?" Maitlin said suddenly.

Red T-shirt, no logo. Red shorts. I told Maitlin what I'd told the FBI, and then I added details I'd saved for her. "Her hair wasn't combed, but she was clean," I said. "Fresh clothes. She looked fine. She was drinking juice. They're taking care of her." They were, anyway.

"Her hair!" Maitlin said, her tone lighter, far away. "Oh, I can just see it . . ."

"Nandi recognized me. 'Mister Ten!' she said. I told her we had to run, and she said, 'Really fast?'" When I mimicked Nandi's delight, Maitlin laughed, or sobbed, or both. My hushed lullaby went on: "She said she wanted her mommy . . ."

Sofia Maitlin finally had the chance to visit her daughter.

FIFTEEN

8:35 A.M.

Sleep was the last thing on my mind at home, but no one could have slept with so many helicopters beating overhead, an airborne assault. The FBI had sidelined me into a circus tent.

Inside, the house was silent. The television set in the living room was off. I'd tried watching TV for updates on Nandi, but it was too jarring. *Last person with Nandi. Held for questioning. Restraining order.* Fox News was already running clips of my old TV series, *Homeland*, and my image played above the bright red question: *Who Is Tennyson Hardwick?* In Hollywood, the caption should have said, *Who WAS Tennyson Hardwick?*

Nelson had put it best: Kiss your life good-bye.

Chela was upstairs monitoring her bedroom TV at a low volume; finally, she'd found the perfect job. I'd asked her to write down anything she thought I should know, but for the past two hours, all she'd reported was recap and supposition. No actual news. Chela was supposed to be in school, but we were having a family emergency.

Distraction can be deadly, so I put the noise out of my mind. When your day already feels like a bad dream, it's easy to pretend it isn't real.

The FBI had shut me out, but I'd been ready for them—just in case. I'd emailed myself the data Roman and I had compiled before the last call from the kidnappers. I'd stashed a flash drive in the glove compartment of my Prius, but my car was now a part of a crime scene, so I was glad I'd emailed the file as a backup. With FBI involvement, I'd probably lost my email and phone privacy, too, but I'd sent my data to an encrypted site they would have to hunt harder for.

I was never a Boy Scout, but I try to stay prepared.

My house was a command center. I'd built a makeshift office in the tiny panic room Alice had converted from a pantry before she died, one of our house's most practical features. Without the shelves, the panic room had space for a card table and two folding chairs. The room, hidden behind a massive wine shelf, had once sheltered Chela. Now the room sheltered me while I searched for Nandi.

I used Dad's laptop—a Christmas present that was still barely out of the box—just in case my desktop and laptop were confiscated later in the day. It had happened before, after my friend Serena was murdered. Dad's computer was a slim precaution, but at least I had an option.

Dad paced the small room with his cane, studying the pages I'd taped to the walls: lists of names and telephone numbers, and businesses hired for Nandi's birthday party. I was relieved to have my father standing over my shoulder. I'd made a horrible mistake in judgment with Roman, but I was in sure hands again.

"Tom Hanks's limo driver was found unconscious," I said. "Behind the wheel, apparently drunk, two miles down Mulholland. Swears he doesn't know how he got there."

"What do you think?"

"Someone at that party knocked him out, took his place, smuggled Nandi into that limo . . . and then just drove out the front gate."

"Description?"

"The driver never saw a thing. One minute he was smoking a cigarette, and the next . . . a cop was shaking him awake."

Dad nodded with a heavy, angry sigh. "Professionals."

"Wonder if they put her in the trunk. It's risky on a sunny day like Sunday. She could have died."

"Not if they weren't going far," Dad said.

Of course. A limo driver could have pulled into a gas station, or stopped at a corner, and transferred Nandi to another vehicle. Hanks would never have known anything was wrong until he had to hitch a ride with Angela Bassett and Courtney Vance. It was common for limo drivers to run errands during long waits.

"I need to look at the tape again," I said, firing up my computer screen. I'd made a digital copy of about forty minutes at the front gate, twenty minutes before Nandi's vanishing, and twenty minutes after. "We weren't looking for cars coming *in*, only going out."

"Leave that angle alone," Dad said. "I'll tell Nelson to follow up."

I looked up at him, but he kept his eyes away from me, reading the walls.

"Dad, Nelson's not gonna give a damn—"

"Whoever clocked this limo guy is long gone, Ten. You know why? 'Cuz ya'll made a damn phone call instead of sending a SWAT team. You did your best, but you needed more." Dad's voice was pained. My decision not to call the police baffled him.

"Nelson doesn't want to hear any leads from me," I said.

"Don't get caught messing with the FBI's case, Ten." Dad said it with hushed urgency, like the most important advice he had left. "You hear me?"

You hear? I had said that to Nandi, slipping into my father's language. Unexpected words and images took me back to the football stadium. To Nandi's tears.

"I'll take my chances," I said. "I don't know if Nelson is a real cop, or just a yes-man."

"How you gonna talk about *real cops*?" Dad said, so angry that he spat. "Nelson *is* a cop. Nelson and the FBI are three steps ahead." He swept his arm toward the wall as if my papers were preschool drawings. "This ain't shit! Snap their fingers, this is all done."

And all-night grilling by the FBI couldn't cut me like one sentence from my father. I'd suspected what he thought—now I knew. Richard Allen Hardwick spoke his mind.

"Go on and do this any way you want," Dad went on. "You're a grown-ass man, Ten. But if something happens to that little girl, you're gonna be in Hell, son. Hell is walking and breathing after you cost somebody's life."

"I'm already there," I said.

"Trust me, you ain't there. Not yet. You better weigh every choice you make today like gold. If the FBI locks you up, you don't *get* another chance."

No wonder my father's men used to call him Preach. My father had given me some powerful sermons in my life, but this was his first in a long while. My father knew about living in Hell. He'd always blamed himself for my mother's death, as if he should have seen the cancer inside her. Maybe he'd been in Hell since Vietnam, one way or another.

"I lost my chance," I said. My voice broke.

"Maybe so, son. But don't try to be the FBI. Stick to what *you* know. You were there. Get out of their way, look where they *won't* look. Or what good are you?"

Dad sharpened my focus. He was right: I had to concentrate on last night.

"The man with the knife," I said.

"What about him?"

I told Dad about the knife-fighting style, and how dismissive Fanelli had been when I described it. Dad nodded, and some of the grimness left his lips. "Might be something."

Dad's nod gave me hope. A growing hole in my gut was certain that Nandi was dead, or might as well be. But hope might keep me on my feet.

My morning got its first sunshine when Dad's lady friend, Marcela, stuck her head into the pantry. Marcela Ruiz was in her late forties, my father's former nurse, and she was hinting about marrying Dad. She had undergone a makeover since I'd first met her, with sassy haircuts and highlights to complement her shrinking waistline. Dad was twenty-six years older than Marcela, but she had seen something special in my father when the rest of the world saw only a dying man. For two years, Marcela had been like a stepmother.

That day, Marcela was answering my doorbell and telephone landline, shooing reporters away. I'd asked her not to interrupt me unless it was important.

"Ten, you have a visitor!" Marcela said. I couldn't understand her smile—until I saw who was standing behind Marcela's shoulder.

April Forrest was in my kitchen.

◆ ◆ ◆

April was wearing a dress, rare for her. Her dark office attire looked like grieving clothes.

When we hugged, I rested my chin on her shoulder and let my eyes fall shut. We hadn't kept in touch much at all since Cape Town, except when I answered her occasional polite emails—my choice, not hers. I knew people who stayed friends with their exes, like Jerry and Elaine on *Seinfeld*, but it hadn't worked for me.

That day, the past was a million miles behind us.

"You okay?" April said. I bit my lip, shaking my head, just enough for her to see. When she lightly touched my cheek, it helped as much as anything could. "What can I do?" she said.

"Are you here as a reporter, April?" Bluntness was all I had time for.

"*Ex*-reporter," April said, and I could give her only a confused look. "I got laid off two weeks ago. I'm a civilian now, just like you. I'm here for whatever you need."

We had catching up to do, but our reunion didn't last long. My phone rang, and my heart jumped. WILDE LAW CENTER, it said.

"Shit," I said. "My lawyer's a damn clock. She tries every thirty minutes."

"She knows you need to give a statement to the press. Someone should speak for you, Ten, even if it's just to say you can't discuss the case."

"I don't have time for that, April!" We were arguing already.

"Have you seen TV today?" April said.

"She's right, Ten!" Chela called from the stairs. "You worry about Nandi—we'll worry about you." That might have been the first time Chela and April agreed on anything.

"Your lawyer will know what to say," April said. "Silence doesn't look right."

My brain was so tired of the subject, I wanted to break something. But I surrendered my ringing phone to April. "I need it back if you get a call. It might be Sofia."

I hadn't heard from Maitlin since her call when I was in the men's room. She might have been indoctrinated by the FBI by now, but I hoped she would call again. April couldn't help the glow of wonder in the corner of her eye when I said Maitlin's name, but she took Melanie's call with snappy professionalism.

My house felt like a machine revving up. As soon as April handed me my phone back, it rang again in my hand. The room stopped breathing.

CLIFF SANDERS, it said. I would have smiled, if smiling had been possible.

"My martial arts instructor," I announced, and the others relaxed.

"Put Cliff on speaker," Dad said. He liked Cliff, who taught regularly at the police academy. He was on the short list of my friends who had Dad's approval.

I'd left a message for Cliff on the way home from the police station. My best hunch.

I had my own team, just in time.

Dad and I holed ourselves up in the panic room to talk to Cliff. I told him as much as he needed to know, a minute's worth of bad memories to last a lifetime.

"Greedy-ass motherfuckers," Cliff said, awed by the magnitude. Almost in reverence.

"The clock's running for Nandi, man. All I've got is the knife style."

"Shit, that might be enough," Cliff said, and Dad nodded. He thought so, too. "Like I told you, I don't know the African styles. But there's a South African brother you'll want to talk to. He *knows* his arts. I've got a name, but can't give it to you yet. These people are very private, and there is protocol to adhere to. But I should have permission to give it to you soon."

"I need him yesterday, Cliff."

"I'll hit you back when I can tell you something." Cliff knew the Los Angeles martial arts community better than anyone, so I trusted him to find what I needed faster than I could. We'd stumbled onto the battlefield I'd spent my life training for.

"Your ears only, Guru," I said.

"Goes without saying, Ten. I'm just doing recon. You'll make the contact."

After I hung up, I knew I had to get out of my house. I couldn't stay at home just waiting.

I went upstairs to glance down at the front yard from the protection of my curtains, the best view. There were two local news vans, a dozen video cameras, and thirty people trampling my pathetic strip of grass near the sidewalk. Up and down the street, my neighbors stared and shook their heads. Mrs. Katz, from across the street, was conducting a seminar on my vices, pointing out my house of the damned.

I couldn't look for Nandi with a circus on my tail. The paparazzi might follow me.

"It's crazy down there," Chela said behind me.

Thanks to my former profession, in part, I had experience dodging bottom-feeding photographers. But I would need at least two drivers to help me do it.

"You ready to help me wade out into the sharks?" I asked Chela.

I'd forgotten how beautifully feral her smile could be.

SIXTEEN

9:20 A.M.

The crowd stirred with excitement and closed in on us when I opened the door and appeared with Dad, Marcela, and Chela, all of us wearing sunglasses and dressed for an outing. Dad was in his gray church suit, using his walker instead of his cane, shuffling with painstaking movement to exaggerate his condition. I held his elbow to pretend to steady him as he walked down my stone porch steps, but it wasn't quite pretending.

At least the helicopters were gone. Mrs. Katz had probably called the police.

Men's and women's voices flew at us, shrill and desperate.

"Tennyson! What can you tell us about the kidnappers?"

"Why didn't you call the police after Nandi disappeared?"

"What's your relationship with Sofia Maitlin?"

"Tennyson—is it true you're a male prostitute?"

The last question, shouted by a man somewhere near Mrs. Katz's rosebushes, almost made me turn around. My face and ears burned hot. Since my name had made the news, someone was talking—for all I knew, it might be Nelson. Chela gave a start, glancing up at me, but she followed my example and kept her face stone. She squeezed my hand, feeling exposed. I was sorry I'd brought her outside.

We waded toward the driveway at awkward angles, penned in, to avoid my prickly cactus garden. Marcela's tiny white Rabbit waited alone. April was already gone.

"Start the car," I muttered to Marcela.

While Marcela walked around to the driver's seat, I opened the passenger-side door so Chela and Dad could climb in back. Chela hopped in, but it wasn't easy to maneuver Dad into the backseat of a two-door car. I needed to sit up front in case we got a tail.

I held the passenger seat forward for Dad as he tried to command his disobedient limbs. Someone bumped roughly against my half-open car door, and the impact jounced my father. He grabbed the headrest to keep from falling.

"*Hey!*" I said, and a pock-faced man behind me snapped a photo of my angry glare. I had an epiphany about why cameras get broken and photographers get punched in the face. My mind mapped the logistics of a swift attack on the six strangers closest to me, men and women alike.

A soft, compassionate smile beckoned me, snapping me out of my rage. A blond-haired newswoman, perfectly coiffed and powdered, thrust her microphone toward me, standing on her toes for height over the mob.

"Mr. Hardwick?" she said with gentle respect. "What can you tell us about Nandi?"

"I'm praying Nandi comes home soon," I said. I spoke to the newswoman and her microphone as if she were alone. "That's all I'm thinking about."

The mob exploded into sound, gathering behind our car in the driveway. I turned away, folded Dad's walker, and slid it into the backseat after him, across the floor. Then I climbed into the car, slamming my door. Chela sat in a childlike ball in a corner of the backseat. Marcela honked the horn at the mob, angry.

When Dad let his window down to lean out, the microphones and cameras closed in. "Please don't bring our families any more pain today!" Dad shouted.

The swarm shouted follow-up questions, but Dad put his window up again. Marcela floored the accelerator, and the car screeched backward. One photographer dove out of the way, cursing loudly. I hoped she clipped him.

"Well?" Marcela said, checking her mirror once we were at the corner.

Videographers were lowering their cameras, journalists and onlookers checking their watches or phoning in updates. The show was over.

"We'll see," I said.

As Marcela turned the corner, a black Kawasaki motorcycle and a small red car that looked like a rental weaved behind us, gaining speed. Paparazzi on the chase, probably guessing we were on our way to Maitlin's house. Their wet dream.

"I can't *believe* these people are such total, complete *ASSHOLES!*" Chela said, and Dad cleared his throat loudly. He hated profanity from Chela.

"This is what happened to Princess Diana," Marcela said. "It's . . . stalking!"

"I planned for company," I said. "Let's head to Sunset."

My cell phone rang. Len, my agent, was calling. I could have used a conversation with a friend, but I had to let him go to voice mail. There was nothing he could say or do. The only two people I wanted to hear from were Cliff and Maitlin.

I rifled through my leather bag, where I'd stashed my Glock, laptop, cell phone charger, and disguise: Chela's oversize Lakers jersey and baseball cap, and a stage mustache and sideburns. The phony facial hair wouldn't hold up under close scrutiny, but I could slap it on fast. I worked in my passenger visor mirror while Marcela careened around another corner.

"Slow down, sugar," Dad cautioned Marcela. "We're tryin' to get there in one piece." Chela gave me an amused look in my mirror, mouthing: *Sugar?*

Traffic on the Sunset Strip was predictably clogged during the Tuesday-morning rush hour. Bright sunlight sprayed across glass office buildings while power breakfasts geared up at Sunset's roadside restaurants. A young girl with an Afro, laughing while she rode her father's back, reminded me of Nandi.

Chela turned backward in her seat, staring out the rear window. "The car got stuck at the last light, but the motorcycle's right behind us!"

She was right; the motorcycle was only three car lengths behind us, and gaining between lanes. I couldn't ditch a tail if he was right on top of us.

"Change of plans," I said. "Don't stop at the House of Blues. Pull into the Mondrian."

"The . . . Mondrian? Where's that?" Marcela said.

"Next door," Chela and I said in unison.

I didn't ask how Chela knew where the luxury hotel was. I didn't have to.

The Mondrian is a stylish hotel with an exterior so understated that it's easy to drive past. I coached Marcela through the sharp left turn that took us to the narrow motor lobby and I pulled cash out of my wallet. "Give the car to the valet. You guys go in and have breakfast. Take your time."

"Ten, I wanna go with you!" Chela whined, a vision of Nandi.

I blinked. "Can't do that, honey." I glanced back at Dad. "I'll call when I've got something." He nodded. I'd nearly gotten Dad killed the last time I took him on a case.

"Keep your head, Ten," Dad said. "Don't get rattled."

Too late. "Yessir."

I jumped out of the car in time to see the Kawasaki stop abruptly in a lane across from the lobby entrance, waiting for an opening for a left turn. I hid my new mustache behind my palm. Motorcycle Prick saw me get out of the car, but he couldn't turn because of the heavy traffic flow. He revved his engine, impatient, as I vanished into the hotel.

I emerged from the hotel exit ten minutes later in my Lakers ensemble, blending into a group that looked like a young singer or rapper and his entourage. My mustache and sideburns were so convincing that I'd barely recognized myself in the bathroom mirror. I made it a point to walk right past Motorcycle Prick, who was hovering in the motor lobby, waiting for us to pick up the car from valet parking. I recognized his pocked face. *Adios, asshole.*

A quick hop took me to the House of Blues, and I spotted April's cream-colored PT Cruiser right away. It was early, so the parking lot was nearly empty. She'd parked close to the driveway, ready for a quick exit. April's windows were closed, but her radio was so loud that I could hear an irate female talk show host: "*. . . Yeah, but do you REALLY think Sofia Maitlin wouldn't have called the police PRONTO if that kid wasn't adopted—*"

I knocked on the passenger window, and April jumped, startled. She unlocked the door, switching off her radio. I climbed in, glad for the AC and the shelter of tinted windows. April's tropical air freshener, Wrigley's gum, and stale Burger King fries were the scent of my old life.

I couldn't stomach the pity, and questions, in April's eyes. I gazed out at Sunset. No sign of Motorcycle Prick.

"Thanks," I said.

"Where to?" she said.

"Anywhere but here."

April drove.

April kept glancing at the hickey on my neck. Marsha's mark had faded since Sunday, but it was a neon sign to April. April had joined the anonymous traffic flow, but she almost ran the light because she was staring. I didn't want to talk about Marsha or the football stadium, so we sat in a long silence.

"Sorry about your job," I said finally, remembering my manners.

"Thanks. Same story everywhere." April shrugged, controlling her emotions. I knew she must be reeling, but I was drowning in my own pain. Agony can be selfish.

"Let me know if you need to borrow money to tide you over," I said.

April looked embarrassed, as if I thought she'd come looking for a handout. "Thanks, but I got a job already—well, three months doing PR at a nonprofit. Who knows? Maybe I'll go back to South Africa. Mrs. Kunene would love that."

South Africa was a sore subject for us.

April sighed. "Ten, I hope it's okay, but I had to come when I saw the news this morning. I still can't believe it. I feel . . . responsible."

"Why?" I said, surprised. Then I remembered: She was the one who'd given me Rachel Wentz's business card, introducing me to Sofia Maitlin. And Nandi.

"None of this has anything to do with you." I sounded irritated without wanting to.

"O . . . kay . . . ," April said, choosing her words carefully. "I'm sorry, that's all."

"Yeah, me, too," I said. "I won't be good company today, April."

"I didn't expect you to be. I just want to help."

I made myself pause for a breath. No matter how horrible I felt about Nandi, I didn't want to miss a chance to clean things up with April. She'd claimed she wasn't mad about how I left her in South Africa, but I wanted to treat her with care. Maybe there was more to our story.

"Thank you, baby," I said. "If you weren't here . . ." *I wouldn't have anyone,* I finished silently. She smiled and patted my knee, a butterfly's wings.

"When's the last time you ate, Ten?" April said. "Or slept?"

The idea of food made me feel sick. I might have napped at Maitlin's house, but never for more than a half hour. "Been a while," I said.

"Where do you need to be now?" April said.

I blinked. I couldn't go to Maitlin's house. I couldn't go home. The futility of trying to find Nandi dimmed the morning sun.

"I don't know," I said, my voice hoarse. A confession to myself, at last.

April's hand touched my knee again. This time, it rested there. I hated how good it felt when she touched me. I didn't want anything to feel good until Nandi was home.

"Ten . . . ," she said. "My roommate's in Atlanta. There's no paparazzi at my place. Just a bite of food in your stomach and an hour to close your eyes."

April was offering me an oasis, and I was ready to say yes.

My cell phone rang. Cliff was calling, right on time.

"His name is Xolo Nyathi." He spelled it. I wrote the name down while Cliff spoke, every word a gemstone. "He isn't a friend, but we move in the same circles. South African. He knows African martial arts like nobody's business. *Saki* from northeast Africa, Senegalese wrestling, Zulu stick fighting of southern Africa, *Gidigbo* of Nigeria . . . he teaches them, and is respected by the entire community. Kalindi Iyi in Detroit is probably the best man in the whole country, and he sends West Coast students to Nyathi. That says a *lot*, trust me. My friends who've trained with him think he walks on water."

"Got it."

"You need backup?"

"Not yet."

"One word, and I'm there," Cliff said, to be sure.

"I know it, man," I said. "Thanks."

There was a pause, and Cliff and I probably were sharing an identical thought: *If I'd had Cliff with me instead of Roman, Nandi would be home now.*

"Okay, he's expecting you. Write down this address . . . ," Cliff said.

Finally, there was something I could do.

On weekday mornings, Xolo Nyathi worked at a boutique supermarket called World Feast in Little Ethiopia. I had the phone number, but wanted to go in person. Dad was right; we might have blown earlier leads by calling instead of showing up. Good cops don't just phone it in.

"Do you think this guy knows something about the kidnapping?" April said after I hung up and briefed her on Cliff's call. We were stopped at a red light.

"Probably not," I said. "But it's a start."

April's eyes flashed, intrigued; laid off or not, she was still a journalist at heart.

"I need to rent a car," I said.

"You just got your lead, and you want to rent a car? Use mine! I'll go with you."

"Bad idea," I said. We'd worked a case together in Palm Springs after Serena died, pretending we were a married couple—but only for a morning. That day, both April and Chela had brushed too close to the bad cops who nearly killed me. "I can't involve you in this."

But April had already turned south on La Cienega so she could make her way to World Feast. We were less than ten minutes away. "I know that place. It's on Fairfax. I eat at Nyala's, Merkato's, and Rosalind's all the time, Ten! There's nothing dangerous about Little Ethiopia. You're in a hurry, right? I'm just your chauffeur."

I sighed, leaning back against the headrest. *Fine, let April come. She's a big girl. Nandi's waiting.* "Okay. Let's go."

I must have dozed for a minute or two, because when I opened my eyes, a church loomed above me through my window, silhouetted by a bright sun. The foreign symbols on the wall confused me. Korean, I remembered dimly.

Bleary eyed, I saw April at the steering wheel, in her mourning dress, and Nandi's teary face came back afresh. Despair and weariness stirred in me so deeply that I moaned myself awake. April is the only woman who has heard such a wounded sound from me.

April rubbed my knee. "*Shhhhh,*" she said. "I know, baby. God will work it out."

I wasn't in the mood for God talk. I'd tried to bargain with God when Nandi was in my arms, and God had left me hanging. God could kiss my black ass.

Little Ethiopia in western Los Angeles is marked with official blue street signs, but it's a small block. The strip of Fairfax between Whitworth Drive and Olympic Boulevard is a self-contained village, a patchwork quilt of Ethiopian restaurants, thrift shops, and clothing stores, most of them alive with the green, yellow, and red Ethiopian flag.

"Park here," I told April as soon as we drove past Whitworth. "We'll walk the rest of the way, just in case no one should see your car."

April pulled into the nearest empty spot with a waiting meter. From habit, I reached for the stash of quarters she kept in her passenger-side drinks compartment. She gave me a small smile, and we both felt at home again.

Most of the restaurants weren't open so early, so the tourists, hipsters, and first dates weren't crowding the streets yet. Several stores were locked for the night. Still, the spicy scent of incense was strong as we walked in the shade of the storefronts on the street's west side. A sole man sat outside Rosalind's with his laptop, enjoying his morning coffee and a newspaper written in Amharic. Merkato's sat near the center of the block. I peeked inside the empty restaurant's picture window as we passed. The ceiling was a rainbow of colorful Ethiopian umbrellas hanging upside down. Baskets, artwork, and carvings bespoke another land.

World Feast was on the other side of Fairfax, closer to Olympic than Whitworth. We dodged cars instead of using the pedestrian crossing. GRAND OPENING, read a banner in the window. Other signs proclaimed bargains on mangoes, kosher meats, and fresh injera, the traditional spongy Ethiopian bread. The market was the length of three or four of the closest stores, a wall of large windows and bright fluorescent lighting.

"Whoa," April said. "This is definitely new."

I'd never seen the store before either. Little Ethiopia had grown.

Inside, the store reminded me of a Whole Foods market, designed for shoppers with very specific tastes. The store had three checkout lines, all empty.

Gentle Bob Marley played from the ceiling sound system. At the front of the store, fruits and vegetables were displayed in large, quaint replicas of traditional Ethiopian baskets. One basket held bound sage. The aisle closest to the entrance was lined with Ethiopian flags, hats, jewelry, CDs, DVDs, books, and T-shirts. In a concession to the marketplace, the large basket full of South African flags and beadwork jewelry was relegated to the far corner. At World Feast, Ethiopia reigned supreme.

At the end of the first aisle, ten yards from me, a full-size male lion made my heart drop.

The lion, on a platform, stuffed and preserved at its height of regality, guarded the wall. The eyes shimmered as if they were still living, staring me down. In the land of PETA, the lion surprised me. I gazed into the lion's dead, golden eyes and wondered who had killed him, and how. "This place will get picketed on a regular basis," April muttered, shaking her head.

A young brown-skinned woman wearing a bright scarf and a loose-fitting white dress emerged from one of the aisles, her face as lovely as morning. Her face was Ethiopian: smooth, rounded, and distinctive. "Hello, do you need something?" she said. She wondered why we were hovering near the lion, but her smile never failed.

I asked to see Xolo Nyathi.

Her smile twitched. "But he is the boss," she said. She eyed my rumpled Lakers jersey. "Do you have business with him?"

"Tell him Cliff Sanders sent me," I said.

She repeated the name to herself and went toward the back, where an iron-reinforced door led to the store's offices. She didn't invite us to follow her, so we waited.

"We should split up," I said. If we were together, we would need a mutual cover story, and we hadn't worked one out. Lies don't work well in bunches.

April nodded. "I'll get some Ethiopian coffee while I'm here."

April vanished into the aisles, where I was sure she would eavesdrop.

Xolo Nyathi came out right away, walking briskly. Unlike his employee, he wasn't smiling. He was wiry and tall, about six-four, with a long, thin face and nose. He had April's ginger complexion, was about my age, and wore scholarly round, gold wire-rimmed glasses with his beige linen suit and leather sandals. He walked with the slight stoop of tall men accustomed to being forced into small places.

He was too tall to have been on the football field. Most of the men I'd faced had been wiry, but none had been taller than me.

"Yes?" Nyathi said.

"Sorry to just barge in on you, Mr. Nyathi," I said. "My martial arts instructor, Cliff—"

"Ah, yes, Cliff Sanders," he said, recognition loosening his face. "I'm sorry, but my sister-in-law heard the name wrong. Warrior arts. Of course I know Cliff Sanders. An extraordinary man." He spoke rapidly, with a South African accent like Paki's. But Xolo Nyathi was an educated man; like Zukisa's, his speech was more casually elegant.

"Well, he was impressed with you, too," I said, relieved that Cliff had broken the ice. "I'm one of his students. My name is Tennyson Hardwick. I wanted to ask you about a knife-fighting style I ran across in South Africa."

"I know a bit about knives, yes," he said matter-of-factly. "Come."

He waved me to the rear of the store, past the lion.

"Did you take that lion down?" I said. I had to ask.

"Not me," he said. "My father. He grew up in a small village, and one day a lion came. You see the rest of the story. A taxidermy student did a good job, don't you think?"

I nodded, noticing how the lion's hungry eyes seemed to follow me. "Too good," I said.

He laughed. "That's what my sister-in-law says. But it has sentimental value! I flew it all the way here from Jo'burg. You have no idea of the cost, and all I hear is complaints."

The store was scented with incense, too. Some of the store aisles were labeled by region. Ethiopian. Korean. Mexican. Jewish. West African. The store carried matzoh, cornmeal, curries, and tortillas. World Feast, indeed.

"How's business?" I said.

He shrugged. "This economy! It's terrible. This is my second store— my first is in Pasadena—so between them, I don't embarrass myself too badly. We laugh about it, me and my neighbors. But all of us have lived through many storms, so we'll survive this one, too."

We stopped just shy of the office door, where there was a small area just big enough for sparring, out of sight of many customers or any passersby from the window. April's head peeked out from an aisle behind us. She was keeping an eye on me.

He took off his glasses and quickly wiped them with his shirt before replacing them. He searched for and found a plastic picnic knife on the rear deli counter.

"This knife style . . . show me," he said.

I didn't want to go back to the football stadium, but I had to.

I gripped the knife the way the stranger had, ice-pick style. Rather than trying to remember his movements, I closed my eyes and tried to *become* the masked knife fighter. I imagined Roman squaring off in front of him. I lunged, hacking at the air. My motion wasn't as fast, but I tried. I kept thinking of a sewing machine.

Xolo watched soberly.

"Wait, wait . . . go back," Nyathi said, mimicking my wrist's motion. His fluidity was unearthly, his timing chaotic. He was a casually deadly man. "Again?"

I re-created the move again. The knife man had used triangular footwork, what the Indonesians called Tiga. I borrowed Silat footwork, grafting it to the hand technique.

"Enough," Nyathi said. He took off his glasses again, but this time he slid them into his shirt pocket. His brown face might have paled.

"Do you recognize that style?" I said.

He hesitated before he nodded. "Where did you see that?" he said soberly.

"Like I said, I was working. I can't say more than that."

April made a quick dart to get closer to us by one aisle, still out of Nyathi's sight.

"There is no honor in that art," Nyathi said. "It's only for killing."

"Is it from South Africa?" I said, a guess. I had seen it in Langa, after all.

"Yes, it began there," Nyathi said. "I first heard of it a few years ago, from the prisons. In any nation, you see, there is the criminal element . . ." He stopped, uncomfortable.

My heart knocked against my chest. *I have something.*

"Go on, Mr. Nyathi," I said.

"It's from prison yards. They say it is related to Zulu spear work. Short spear, the *assagai*. The knife's motion is impossible to mistake. You say you encountered it? In a fight?"

I nodded.

"And you survived by . . . ?"

"The knife fighter went after the other guy," I said.

"Your friend Cliff?" Something sparkled in his eyes. He might never admit it, but he would love to see *that* confrontation.

"No. Someone I worked with." Past tense.

"I'm sorry to hear," Nyathi said.

We waited a moment, both of us feeling sorry. I pressed on, trying to keep my voice casual. "Do you know anyone who practices this style?"

"You would like to find the person who hurt your friend," Nyathi said, not fooled.

"Killed, Mr. Nyathi."

Nyathi took a step closer to me. Something rattled to the floor from April's aisle, and I heard her whisper curses. Her head peeked out, then pulled back again.

"These people are not the sort anyone with a sound mind seeks to find," Nyathi said.

"My mind is sound enough."

For the first time, I heard a muffled television on behind the office's closed door. A newscaster's voice was talking about Nandi.

"Mr. Hardwick, you seem a decent man . . . ," Nyathi began.

"I try to be."

"Then I feel obligated to warn you not to look for these people." His eyes, meeting mine, beseeched me. "This knife form is popular in the criminal class. It is a killing art called Ummese Izulu. The Knife of Heaven."

Nyathi reached into his pants pocket and brought out a handkerchief to wipe his brow, perspiring despite the cold air clutching us from the fresh meat and fish counter. Nyathi's sister-in-law was hovering in the aisle beside April's; he waved his handkerchief to her, impatient. "The register!" he said.

She scurried away to her post.

Satisfied that we were alone, Nyathi told me his story.

"The night in question was three years ago. Understand, the African immigrant community is small and scattered here, and our little family of African martial artists is smaller still. We all know each other. So we had a barbecue at a grandfather's house, a special night. All of us shared our favorite dishes from home, a couple of drummers brought their drums. We displayed our martial arts skills with sparring and demonstrations. No matter what you know, there is more to see, more to learn.

"Late in the evening, a drummer introduced himself as Spider. A young man, hair shaved off. No one knew him—everyone assumed he had come with someone else. But he had sought us out on his own. Spider begged our forgiveness for coming uninvited, but said he had brought food and wine for us, and he wanted permission to present himself to the elders in our community of warriors. Spider displayed skills in the shadow dance, the solitary play we use to demonstrate our skills.

"This is a major part of our gatherings: the introduction of young warriors to the spiritual elders. And we were very impressed!" He leaned forward, his eyes full of the memory. "*Very* impressed. The old men were reminded of themselves in their youth, and they shared stories of old matches, something that they rarely do before newcomers. He might have found harbor with us, if not for what happened next.

"He was drinking beer, and his personality changed as he grew puffed up from our praises. He became careless, rude. Several women were there, and he insulted a young woman in a very coarse way, the way someone might talk to a woman who was *isifebe* . . . a prostitute. Her young man challenged him, and they agreed to fight a practice match, using dulled knives. The young man was one of our best.

"And what did Spider do? He *destroyed* that young man, mentally—and almost physically. Even with a practice knife, Spider punctured him in the side"—Nyathi indicated a spot on his side dangerously close to the kidney—"and in the thigh, very close to his manhood. He did it laughing and taunting, so amused to give pain to another man. It was a sickening display.

"His venom repelled us. What this man knew, he knew from killing, not from practice. We are warriors, not killers. We tried to speak with him, would still have found a place for him had he humbled himself. Instead he cursed us, and fled."

Sounded like the right man to me.

"Do you know anyone he's affiliated with?" I said.

Nyathi looked at his hands, inspecting those impeccable fingernails. When Nyathi turned his attention back to me, he looked as weary as I felt. "From time to time, I hear talk," he said. His voice hushed. "Do you know of Umbuso Izulu? The Kingdom of Heaven?"

I cursed myself for not bringing a pad with me. I pulled my pen out of my pocket, ready to write on my open palm. "Who is that?" I said. "How do you spell it?"

"Not a who—it's a criminal enterprise here in L.A., but it originated in South Africa. Very organized, and growing." I remembered Zukisa's words when we discussed the kidnappers at Maitlin's house: *These are awful people, but they are not simple. They are sophisticated. They are not wide eyed. They know all about how things work.* I might have it. I might.

My heart was pounding. "What do you know about them?"

"I just told you," he said. "That's all I know, or want to know. I'm a businessman. No one worthy of respect would associate with Umbuso Izulu. I've only heard about the knives because they fight with this style you saw. Ummese Izulu—the Knife of Heaven. They say once you see the Zulu blade, you are a dead man. No one walks away."

Almost no one, I thought.

The television set's volume climbed, and the newscaster's words were suddenly audible through the door: "*. . . from FBI sources, Sofia Maitlin's longtime bodyguard, Roman Ferguson, died on the scene from multiple knife wounds. A second man, actor Tennyson Hardwick, was treated and released after being rendered unconscious by the kidnappers. While it is currently unknown what his role in these events might have been . . .*"

He gazed at me closely, studying my mustache. "Are you a bodyguard? Like Cliff?"

"Now and then."

Xolo Nyathi's jaw went to stone. Maybe he'd known from the start.

April and I had once talked about the magical moment when an interview subject decides to share, to say the thing that loyalty or fear made them hold on to. Nyathi had reached his moment. The look in his eyes made my heart thunder.

"This man," he said, speaking slowly. He rubbed the sole of his sandal across the floor, as if he were wiping clean an invisible mess. "Spider. He plays drums with a combo from time to time. I believe the art he showed us was Ummese Izulu."

God, please just do this for Nandi. Punish me instead.

"Where does he play?" I said.

"Shelter? Bamboo. Little clubs, parties. He's in demand. He plays salsa, ska, South African township, all the styles. I've seen him twice. I enjoy live music."

I was running out of room on my palm. I hoped April was taking notes, too. I had never heard of Shelter, but Bamboo was an African and Caribbean restaurant in Baldwin Hills.

"After the party, I saw Spider playing drums at a restaurant. His playing style on the *djembe* was fascinating to me because it reminded me of his motion with a knife. The quickness. Between beats, he seemed to pat at the air, as if he was doing drills even while he played. The same butterfly energy and speed. I fear no man, but if I had no weapon, I believe Spider would kill me in . . ." He closed his eyes. They vibrated behind his lids, as if he was choreographing conflict. "He would kill me in less than a minute."

"And if you had a weapon?"

Nyathi's lips curled into the slightest of smiles. "As I said, I fear no man."

Spider was the man I wanted. My bones felt it.

I asked Nyathi to list every venue he could think of where Spider might have played, or anyone who might have hired him. By the time he finished, my palm was full of scribbles. I would transfer the notes in April's car. Her backseat was littered with reporters' notebooks.

"It would not be good, Mr. . . . Hardwick . . . ," Nyathi said, ". . . if the wrong people were to hear that you got this information from me."

"I understand. Everything is in confidence."

"I have only given you suppositions. But if one businessman's thoughts might help you on your quest . . ." He gave me a sad, knowing smile. "Then God be with you."

By the time I finished interviewing Xolo Nyathi, April was standing nonchalantly at the checkout counter with an armful of purchases. I walked past her without acknowledging her, and back outside.

"Mr. Hardwick!" Nyathi called sharply from behind me as I began back toward the car.

He had run out behind me. He looked over his shoulder before he approached me, then he slipped something into my palm. "A souvenir from my shop," he said.

Silver gleamed in my hand: a small Ethiopian-style cross, with artistic flourishes around the traditional cross shape. I hadn't owned a cross since I was a kid. *Dad would love this guy.*

"Thanks," I said. "I'll take all the help I can get."

"I pray you find her," Nyathi whispered. And he went back into his store.

I beat April back to her car, so I hung out on the corner of Fairfax and Whitworth to wait, mulling over what Xolo Nyathi had told me. While I waited, I put in a quick call to Chela's cell.

"Hey, Ten—whassup?" Chela said cheerfully. She was enjoying her day's adventure.

"Where are you guys?"

"Waiting for the check. I love the food here! Did you ditch 'em?"

"So far, so good."

"We were just joking that if they keep trying to follow us, we'll drive to Palmdale."

On another day, I would have laughed. Palmdale was a long hike to nowhere.

April carried a loaded shopping bag and a large, thin object that looked unwieldy.

"Hey, could you put Dad on?" I said to Chela, keeping an eye on April.

"Thanks for the whole *Bourne Identity* escape thing," Chela said, trying to cheer me up.

I heard muttering, and Chela's voice was gone. I realized that if the day went wrong, I might never be able to speak to Chela again, but the cold knowledge was devoid of emotion. She would make it without me. She had a home.

"Whatcha got?" Dad's voice sounded far away, just shy of the microphone.

A passerby came too close to me on the street, a man with short dreads and an army jacket. I stepped away from him and kept my voice low. "Umbuso Izulu. Heard of it?"

"Mmmmm-hmmmm," Dad said. "Kingdom of Heaven. Gangs from South Africa, Zimbabwe. Moved over here in the nineties. Why?"

April's car *clicked* as she unlocked it with her remote key.

"Hold on," I told Dad, and walked to climb inside April's car. I didn't relax until my door was closed. "I think they're involved in this."

"Ambitious, ain't it?" Dad said, sounding skeptical. "A movie star's kid . . . ?"

April climbed into the car beside me, closing her door, too. She showed me a reporter's notebook, flipping to a page full of neat lines of notes. She'd written down everything she'd overheard from Xolo Nyathi, just as I'd hoped. I blew April a kiss.

"Yeah, but this movie star's kid is from South Africa," I said. "She put herself right on their radar. We need to pull Nelson into this. I'm calling him."

"Better coming from me," Dad said. "You two fuss and fight. Gets in the way."

"Fine. But he needs to jump on this even if the FBI won't. The guy on the football field knew the same knife art I saw in South Africa. I've found a lead, a guy named Spider, who knows the art. A drummer. I'm going to talk to him."

"All this from the knife?" Dad said.

"It's an uncommon fighting style," I said. "I got lucky."

"Tell you what I know: Kingdom of Heaven had a nightclub, mid-nineties. Hollywood. It's closed now, but those guys had a bad rep. Vicious, like the Colombian and Mexican gangs. From time to time we'd find a vic dumped in an alley, some poor African immigrant whose girlfriend or sister said he was at the club and never came home. Just kids, mostly. Twenty-one, twenty-five."

"How'd they die?"

I knew what my father was going to say before he did.

"Multiple . . . ," Dad began, and stopped. "Shit." *Multiple stab wounds.*

I stared down at the cross in my hand. I clasped it so hard that the ridges bit into my palm.

"Nelson was on at least one of those homicides," Dad said. "I sent him out so he could talk to witnesses. Black cop—you know, tryin' to blend. The investigation never took off, but Nelson will remember. I might've heard somethin' about abductions in South Africa, but I don't think they ever pulled that in the United States. They're smart. Like things quiet. Don't want headlines."

"They tried to keep the kidnapping quiet."

"Yeah, but they knew it might not stay that way." Dad sighed. He wasn't quite convinced. "I'll work on selling Nelson. What about you?"

I hesitated. Was I talking to Richard Hardwick the police captain, or to my father?

"I'm going after Spider," I said. "I got a couple of leads. Clubs where he plays."

April cast me a worried glance over her shoulder.

Up ahead, I saw a sign for a car rental company on the corner. When I gestured for her to stop, she looked disappointed, but signaled to change lanes.

"Don't go solo," Dad said. "Give me a minute with Nelson first."

"Nelson's gonna take more than a minute," I said. "Even if you sell him, he has hoops to jump through. I'll give you everything I have, but I won't wait for him. No time."

"Ten, if you move in too fast . . ."

I knew what he wanted to say. If I showed up asking questions about Spider, the kidnappers might get scared and any debates about Nandi's future would be over. But they also might kill Nandi in the next twenty minutes. In the next hour. Until I heard about another ransom demand, I would assume they weren't sending her home.

"Dad, moving too fast isn't the problem," I said. "We're not moving fast *enough*."

I read him the list of nightclubs Nyathi had mentioned, and Dad shared the names discreetly with Marcela or Chela, who wrote them down. Writing was still difficult for him.

"Remember what I said, Ten," Dad said. "Every decision matters."

"Yessir." A stone caught in my throat. "Thanks, Dad. Love you." It fell out of me.

"It's a solid lead, Tennyson. Be careful." Short silence. "I love you, too, son."

Some people grow up telling their fathers they love them, or hearing their fathers say it. Not me. Finally, after forty years, my father and I had run out of bullshit.

Better late than never.

SEVENTEEN

10:15 A.M.

April was still waiting in the parking lot of the car rental office when the salesman walked me outside to inspect my rented black Corvette 2LT convertible. The car gleamed like moonlight on wet asphalt, and I silently apologized for everything I might do to its perfect finish. The salesman was thrilled when I agreed to buy the insurance, but he wouldn't have liked the reason.

I'd asked April to go, but she was still leaning on a hand-carved Ethiopian walking stick she'd bought at the store. Once we were alone, she stood within six inches of me. She forced me to stand still and look at her. I hadn't realized how much my eyes were avoiding hers.

"I bought this cane for your father," April said. She knew how hard Dad had worked to walk again. When she first met him, he was confined to his bed. Our history was in that cane.

"Bring it by next week."

"I'll be there," she said, her eyes glistening. "Will you?"

"I'll try."

After hearing what Xolo Nyathi had to say about Spider, April hadn't broached the subject of teamwork on the case. She knew her limitations; she only wished I knew mine.

"I write for a living, Ten, and I can never think of the right words with you," she said. "But I'll try this one—*please*? I don't know what else to say. Because if you run out there and get killed, it will bust open a hole in me I'll never fill up again. And your father. And Chela."

"Now you're worried about filling a hole?" I said. I couldn't stop myself.

"Don't you get it, Ten? I was afraid of *this*."

"I'm adopting Chela," I said, out of the blue. I needed to change the subject. "I've talked to a lawyer. We're looking for her birth mother."

"That's great. Then you need to be here for her. Isn't that the point of adoption?"

That stung. I shouldn't have expected April to understand, but I wished she did.

"I promised Nandi, April," I said. "I held her in my arms, looked into her eyes and told her I was coming back for her." Saying it aloud sucked all the air out of my lungs.

April blinked fast, her mommy instincts afire, but she didn't miss a beat of tranquil reasoning. "And you can do that—with the help of the police and the FBI. The information you just brought Lieutenant Nelson can help bring Nandi home. *That's* what your promise meant. It doesn't have to be you. Don't keep repeating the same mistake, Ten."

I tried to look at her, but instead I stared at the sky.

April leaned against me. Her chest sank to mine, firm and familiar. I cradled my arm around her back, holding her in place. She inched closer to me, and our pelvises brushed. Warm arousal flared, a memory of touching. Her scent fogged my mind.

"You're barely on your feet," she said. "Come home with me. Climb into bed. Let me hold you, Ten. Please?" Her whisper was hot in my ear.

You fucked up, Ten, my Evil Voice agreed. *Leave it to the FBI. Go with April. LIVE.*

Had I been waiting seven months for April to give me a second chance? Had Marsha only helped me forget everything April made me remember?

Fresh misery clawed at my stomach as I leaned over to kiss April's forehead, like a brother. I took a step away from her, setting her free.

"Not today," I said.

There was much more to say, but no more time.

Somewhere, Nandi was waiting for me.

The day staggered on in dream time. I was so tired, I dozed at the lights. When my eyesight blurred, I reminded myself that I hadn't slept in two days, since Nandi vanished. The longer I was behind the wheel, the more sense April's offer made.

Then I could swear I heard Nandi crying, and I drove faster, blowing past speed limits with the car's gentle V8. Obstacles appeared out of nowhere, forcing me to jam on my brakes. I was half delirious, and April had known it.

I was also driving nowhere fast. What was my next move?

At the nearest 7-Eleven, I loaded up on Excedrin for migraine, craving both the caffeine lift and the pain relief. I ignored the throbbing most of the time, but it was hard to think. In the car, I kept the AC on full blast until my arms were covered with gooseflesh. I needed the cold air to keep my body and mind awake.

To keep alert, I lectured myself aloud: "Man, you can't just show up asking questions the way you did in Little Ethiopia. Your face is all over TV today. You need to vanish."

I hung on my every word. *That brother's talking sense.*

I stopped at a large thrift shop to find clothes for a character I could commit to all day.

Good thing I was in Hollywood.

By 11 A.M., Tennyson Hardwick was dead. I was a brand-new man.

To erase myself, I replaced every item of clothing except my briefs. I remembered I might need to run, and rejected a pair of sandals reminiscent of Xolo Nyathi's. I settled on plain brown loafers that looked brand new and fit fine. For clothes, I found a white guayabera and loose-fitting track pants. Business casual, and loose enough to give me freedom of movement. I topped off my ensemble with a fake Gucci bucket hat.

I drove to Ursula's Costumes in Santa Monica to complete my new identity. I've been to Ursula's a few times, so one of the salespeople, Heidi, recognized me right away. Her eyes widened in surprise when she saw my face, so she'd been watching the news. But Heidi only gave me a sympathetic smile and a half wave, and she left me alone to browse.

I'm gonna bring that girl flowers one day, if I survive the one I'm in.

Careful shopping and fifteen solid minutes in front of a mirror gave me a full beard and sideburns neatly trimmed down; enough facial hair to obscure my features, but not so much that I would stand out. Aviator sunglasses finished my new look.

It wouldn't fool the people closest to me, but I hoped it would be enough.

Next, I had to find my body language, and my voice.

I'm good with accents. I could pull off a decent southern African accent, but I didn't dare try it in the field. South Africans spoke English, but they also spoke Xhosa, Zulu, or Afrikaans, too, just for starters. As for the rest of the continent, I didn't know any Swahili, Wolof, or Amharic either. My cover story would have to steer clear of Africa.

"Hey, man," I said to the mirror. "What's your name?"

The man in the mirror mulled it over.

"I'm Clarence, mon," the man in the mirror said with a perfect Jamaican accent. His shoulders slouched down, his belly poked out, and he shoved his hands into his pockets. He was ten pounds overweight. He might have been athletic once, but had become bored with his body. He was no threat to anyone physically. He liked music, women, and smoking blunts.

"Clarence Love. I'm a singer, yeah? From Kingston. I'm new to L.A., just tryin' to find my way round. Looking for new places to spread the Love."

His voice was music. He extended his arms Christlike and grinned, inviting me to bask in his fabulousness. Clarence Love was born.

A text message vibrated in my pocket. I had to fumble for my phone; the pocket was deeper than I'd thought. My hand shook. *Please let it be Maitlin with good news.*

Instead, it was a text message from Marsha:

Stop hot-dogging B4 you get killed. I can help with the Kingdom. Come see me ASAP.

It didn't sound like good news, but it was the closest I'd had all day.

+ + +

The Chateau Marmont in Hollywood is notorious for bad behavior. The founder of Columbia Pictures, Harry Cohn, said in 1939, "If you must get in trouble, do it at the Chateau Marmont." The hotel was built on a hill above the Sunset Strip in the 1920s, an imitation of a French royal residence. With its private balconies and hasty escape routes, that place is screaming with gossip. I ought to know.

The hotel was living up to its reputation, yet again. How did Marsha know I was investigating the Kingdom of Heaven?

As my Corvette sped toward Marsha's suite at the Chateau Marmont, I made a mental list of everything I knew about the woman I'd been fucking for the past week. The list wasn't nearly long enough. The more I thought about her, the more nervous Marsha made me.

When I pieced together my history with Marsha, thoughts surfaced that crumbled my stomach to dust. *She's been spying on you and your family. She didn't find you by accident. Five days after you met her, Nandi disappeared.*

The first day we'd met had been a game, start to finish. She'd been conducting a sophisticated surveillance that probably was illegal, and her body did all of her talking. Luring a mark into bed is the oldest trick in a liar's book. Was Marsha using me? And if so, why?

One last, terrible thought persisted: *Does Marsha have something to do with Nandi?*

By the time I got to the hotel, I was pissed off six different ways. I unpacked my Glock, nestling it snugly down the back of my pants, hidden by my loose shirt. I wasn't going anywhere else without my weapon.

As Clarence Love, I asked the concierge to call Marsha's suite, testing my accent. He didn't recognize me from my earlier visits, so one thing went right.

When Marsha opened her door, she was wearing only a T-shirt above endless brown legs. "I like your new look, Clarence," Marsha said.

My Glock tugged on my waistband at the small of my back. "We need to talk," I said.

Marsha moved aside, untroubled by my empty eyes. "Yes," she said. "We do."

I never turned my back on Marsha as I walked into her foyer and she locked her door behind me. She was in a junior suite, about five hundred square feet, with a combined sitting room and bedroom, and a full dining area and kitchen. The furniture was 1940s style.

For the first time since I'd known Marsha, I ignored her prominent queen bed. I watched the corners for shadows, in case she wasn't alone. A fluttering curtain in the dining area made my fingers twitch to reach behind my back.

"You should sit down, Ten," Marsha said. "You're jumping at shadows."

Her sofa looked good, so I sat. From my vantage point, I could see the foyer, the balcony door, and the kitchen. No one would surprise me. Marsha bent over to pick up her jeans from the floor, flashing me her buttocks. For half a second, my eyes were caught.

"Start talking," I said.

She flung her hair out of her face, wrapping it into a ponytail. I'd never seen her with such a girlish hairstyle, softening her face. *She's changing her identity in front of your eyes.*

"I'm really sorry, Ten," she said, doe eyed. "I hated lying to you."

"Skip it, Marsha. How are you so deep in my business?"

"Guess—and I'll tell you when you're warm," she said, the barest twinkle in her eye.

"Lady, you need to be very careful right now . . ."

"All right." She sounded weary, suddenly. I hoped she was dropping her mask. "There's information I can't volunteer, Ten. Period. As long as you understand that, we can talk all you want. Ask me direct questions."

"Who are you?"

Marsha leaned closer to me, as if her scent would clarify it. "You know who I am. You've known me a long time."

"I knew you a long time *ago.*"

"You want to know what I do for a living? I do favors. I broker information. That's already saying too much, so don't ask for more."

"You broker information for who?" I said.

"You expect me to flash you my ID card, Ten? Come on. The little car rental place in Malibu is a front. Do a little research. And I'm crazy for telling you that."

She works for the government, I thought. Aloud, I said, "That's not good enough."

"It'll have to do."

"You've got nothing to do with Nandi?" I said.

Anger narrowed her eyes. "Of course not! I heard about it this morning, when I saw your beautiful face on TV. Now I know why you vanished this weekend."

I didn't believe her yet. Did she work for the CIA? The NSA?

"You're watching me." I was daring her to lie.

"To protect you. I sent somebody to keep an eye on you. You shook him. Not bad."

Motorcycle Prick hadn't been paparazzi; he'd camouflaged himself within the flock. Her story seemed more plausible.

"How did you know I was looking at Kingdom of Heaven?" I said.

Marsha blinked, her first hint of shame. "Your cell phone. You told your dad."

Rage made me shoot to my feet. "How . . . Why the hell are you spying on my private calls?"

I towered over her, but she only crossed her long brown legs, taking her time. "Because I could. I wanted to know more about the kidnapping." All pretense of shame was gone. "Look, Ten, you can be pissed off, or you can let me help you. You're in over your head. You're not gonna Rambo your way through the Kingdom of Heaven. Have no doubt of that."

"Did they kidnap Nandi?"

"I've heard chatter." Her quiet voice filled the room.

"Assuming I believe you, what can you offer me?"

"A little information. Off the record." When Marsha stood up, she casually slid her hand across my thigh and crotch. Although I took a step back, my body sang out for more. April was long ago and far away.

"Why?" I said. "What's that gonna cost me?"

Marsha went past me to her apartment's small kitchen, opening her refrigerator. She kept her back to me as she spoke, but her voice grew more intimate. "I'm not proud of everything I do, Ten," she said. "An unfortunate part of my job description. Now I get to do a good deed—and bring peace to an old schoolmate. Maybe save his life. You need something to eat."

"I couldn't eat if I wanted to."

Finally, Marsha looked at me. "If you want to chase down your friend Spider or Umbuso Izulu, you better eat, Tennyson." She pulled out a carton of eggs.

I sighed. If I wanted her to talk, I had to do it her way.

I moved closer, taking a seat at her dinette table. When she set down a glass of orange juice, I took a sip. It seemed to singe my stomach, so I pushed it away.

Marsha's motion in the kitchen was exquisitely precise, the same quality she brought into bed with her—every movement calculated, down to flicks of her wrist to crack the eggs. She had physical training I'd been too busy fucking her to notice.

"Okay," I said. "I'm listening."

"Your dad was right. The Kingdom isn't known for kidnapping in the States," Marsha said. "But in South Africa and Zimbabwe, kidnapping is one of their biggest businesses. They bully rich families into keeping quiet, so it stays out of the press. Nandi's kidnapping is straight out of their playbook."

"Do the victims go home?"

"Most of them," she said. "But not always. The way they convince families not to call the police is by making an example of the ones who do."

The smell of cooking eggs made my stomach cinch.

"Is Nandi dead?" I said.

"The family will know within twenty-four hours, Ten. That's their typical window after an abduction. So we need to know if Sofia Maitlin has a new ransom demand. And proof of life."

"Can't the FBI tell you that?"

"I'm not FBI," Marsha said. "There are serious limits to what I am allowed to do inside the United States. Despite what you see in movies, we don't get to do whatever we want."

"What about Malibu?" I said, remembering the cameras on the rooftop that had made me think she was a cop. "You're watching somebody."

"Touché," she said. "That's one of the things I can't talk about."

I ignored my flash of irritation. "If I can get the new ransom demands or proof of life . . . then what?"

"Then it's worth the risk. You try to find Umbuso Izulu. Learn what you can, fast. But not by yourself."

"Who's backing me up?"

Marsha brought me a steaming plate of scrambled eggs and set it on the table.

"You're in luck," she said. "I am."

Marsha sat astride me in the chair, hooking her legs across the armrests. Her crotch settled against mine like a missing puzzle piece.

I didn't touch her, pulling my face back. "You crossed the line, listening to my calls." I would have to be careful with every word on my phones, even if Marsha promised to stop listening.

"Let me make it up to you."

My palms took matters in their own hands, pressing to her buttocks, fingers clutching rounded flesh tight. She wasn't wearing underwear beneath her T-shirt. Marsha slid herself across my crotch, and my body wanted to let bygones be bygones.

Marsha nuzzled the spot on my neck where her mouth had left me raw. I flinched, but blood surged to my groin. My pants were so thin that her skin felt naked, and I had plenty of room to grow. Her body seemed to clasp at me through the fabric.

While she kissed me, Marsha's hand found its way inside my pants, and the magnitude of the pleasure from her warm fingers rocked me, a mighty current.

"We don't have time," I said.

"This won't take long."

Marsha slid to the floor and knelt between my legs. She took me into her mouth, and my legs stiffened into a V. I gazed up at her ceiling, my eyes fixed wide open. I felt liquified, overrun with sensation. I groaned, my battle against my body already lost.

Marsha's mouth was possessed.

I clutched at her table as my hot juices gathered, boiling. My plate of eggs fell to the floor.

I screamed when I came.

I'd been waiting to scream all day.

EIGHTEEN

11:30 A.M.

I had to reach Maitlin, or I would lose my mind. Was Nandi still alive?

I never had Maitlin's cell number, and the FBI was all over her phone anyway, so there was no way to call her directly. Maitlin told me she'd borrowed a phone to call me—and I knew there was no way in hell that her husband, Alec, would have helped her reach me. That left one obvious choice, and luckily, my agent, Len, had the number I needed on his speed dial.

It pays to have good representation.

No one answered, but I left a message. When my return call came, I mumbled thanks to whichever deities had lent a hand.

"I'm not comfortable with this," Rachel Wentz said when she called me back. Her voice had aged ten years. Like Maitlin, she sounded like she was hiding so she wouldn't be overheard. "I'm returning your call as a courtesy, but you can't talk to Sofia. I'm sorry."

"Rachel, I just need to know if she's talked to Nandi," I said. "Have they called?"

The line was silent so long, I wondered if she'd hung up on me.

"You can't picture what she's going through," Wentz said. "I've never seen her like this—even after her parents died. Sophie and I don't blame you, no matter what anybody says—you and Roman both said to call the police. But if the FBI knew I was talking to you like this, they'd put me *under* Guantanamo Bay. They could not have been clearer about the bad shit that will happen if we discuss this case—especially with you."

"They're trying to scare you," I said.

"It's working. Listen, I had all brothers, we grew up in Queens, I've flipped off cops all my life. These guys are making me piss myself." Pause. "I can't discuss the call with you."

I sat up ramrod straight. "They called?"

"And I can't discuss anything Sofia said to Nandi." Another pause. "An hour ago."

I sank against Marsha's sofa cushion, my strength sapped from a wave of relief. I wrote down TIME OF CALL: 10:30 A.M.

If Marsha's people were bugging my phone, she would hear it herself soon: *She's alive,* I mouthed to Marsha. I didn't trust her, but I didn't think I had a choice.

Marsha pumped her fist and started texting someone on her Black-Berry. I'd given up asking who she was communicating with. Whoever it was, I hoped it was the damn cavalry. I would help her shred the Constitution to pieces to bring Nandi home.

"I'm working a lead on the kidnappers," I told Rachel Wentz.

"I swear to God, I am not hearing this . . . ," she said.

"We may be looking for a gang called Umbuso Izulu, originally from South Africa. I need to find out if Sofia has had contact with this gang. If there's any chance they might have infiltrated her entourage."

"A South African gang? She would have mentioned something like that. And I told you, she can't talk to you—"

A rustling sound came, a tussle for the phone. *Please let Sofia be standing right there . . .* For the first time in memory, a prayer came true, like a genie's wish.

"Ten?" Sofia's voice said, hushed. "It's me. What are you asking about?"

"How did Nandi sound?" I diverted from my interview; I had to know.

Sofia sniffed. "Crying, mostly. She knows something is wrong. She wants to come home, like you said." Her voice was a shadow. "But she's alive."

"That's right. She's alive."

"Just a minute," Sofia said, an urgent whisper.

For thirty seconds, I was in a wireless, soundless stasis. As the seconds ticked by, I cursed myself for spending so much time on Nandi. I needed to ask her about Umbuso Izulu.

"What?" Marsha said, waiting.

"I'm on hold."

"Shit," Marsha muttered. "Like she's got more important things to do right now."

When Maitlin came back, I told her what I'd learned about Kingdom of Heaven and the knife-fighting technique. Her breathing quickened.

"Have you heard of them?" I said.

"I . . . no," she said. "Kingdom of Heaven?"

"They're also known as Umbuso Izulu. They specialize in kidnapping in South Africa, but they hadn't been doing it here. That's why nobody put it together."

"I've never . . . had any contact with anyone like that."

The way she paused between her words made my stomach knot. If Maitlin was hiding something, the case could fall apart.

"Sofia . . . ," I said, the way an older brother would. "What aren't you telling me?"

She exhaled loudly, and I could almost see her wriggling. "No, I . . . I'm just scared and tired and . . . Please, you can't jeopardize the exchange. They say they'll give her back tomorrow night. Don't do anything without letting me know."

"Where's the exchange? What time tomorrow night?"

"I can't talk about this, Tennyson! They're telling me you might have been involved."

"That's bullshit, and they know it," I said. "If I was a suspect, I wouldn't be walking around free. Sofia, you have to let me know if there are any major breaks."

She sighed. "It's ten o'clock tomorrow night, and that's all I can say. If there's an *emergency,* call me on Rachel's phone."

Another exchange in the dark. Déjà vu fluttered through my stomach.

"Sofia, if you remember anything about criminals in South Africa or African gangsters here—no matter how trivial it seems—tell the FBI. Tell them now, before it's too late."

"I just want my baby home," Maitlin said, sounding childlike suddenly. "He said if we bring his money, he'll give her back. He said everything will be fine. He promised."

I ground my teeth. "Sofia—"

That was all I had the chance to say before Rachel Wentz convinced Sofia Maitlin to hang up. Maybe Maitlin had sounded too upset. Neither of them wished me good-bye.

"Nicely done," Marsha said, impressed. She rubbed my shoulders.

"She's in denial," I said. "Or she's hiding something."

"Yeah, no kidding, lover," Marsha said. "Who isn't?"

Knowing that I had more than twenty-four hours before the scheduled exchange gave me breathing room I hadn't felt in days. Despite what I'd told Maitlin, I knew that Nandi's kidnappers were still holding out in the hope of getting paid, or Nandi wouldn't still be alive.

They don't want to kill her. It seemed more apparent all the time. Or, maybe Maitlin had passed her denial on to me. I didn't care which it was. I was glad to feel better.

"I hope that Glock in your pants isn't registered to you," Marsha said.

"Guilty," I said. "It's the first weapon I could grab."

Marsha shook her head, marveling at such an amateur mistake. "Leave it here."

When I laid my Glock on her table, Marsha stared down at it as if it were an old, smelly fish. "I don't like toy guns," she said. "But if nines float your boat, I can make you smile."

She led me to her bathroom. There, she pulled away the framed Renoir print of a woman sitting at a piano, revealing a wall safe. She spun the combination lock rapidly, with practiced fingers. The space in the safe was much bigger than it should have been; the safe wasn't wide, but it was deep. Marsha pulled out a long black tray and laid it across her closed toilet seat.

Six handguns lay side by side, nestled in custom-fitted foam. Other compartments were home to silencers and laser optic sights. I made a mental note never to piss Marsha off.

Marsha's buttocks peeked out again as she bent over her gun stash, her legs spread wide.

I would be carrying that screen saver in my head for a while. *Damn*, she was sexy.

The first gun I noticed was a Beretta, blue steel with a plastic grip. It was eight and a half inches long, with a five-inch barrel.

"It's loaded, sixteen rounds," Marsha said, following my eyes. "But let's not plan on making the news. Shooting is a last resort."

Marsha's philosophy was miles from Roman's, so I took the Beretta. It weighed about two and a half pounds. "I'll take good care of her," I said.

"You always do," Marsha said.

"Yeah, mon, you know it, baby," Clarence Love said.

I finally had the perfect partner. My new wife and I left for work.

1:30 P.M.

Three calls yielded a restaurant employee who knew Diaspora Beat was playing a lunch gig at Bamboo Restaurant, near Baldwin Hills. As my car raced on the 10 freeway toward Bamboo, we agreed on a simple cover story: I was a struggling singer, and she was my wife—accountant by day, manager by night. We had moved to L.A. two months before from Seattle, were living way out in the San Gabriel Valley, and I was still learning my way around the club circuit.

"Love?" she said. "Did you just make that name up?"

"Easy to remember," I said, shrugging. "I'm sure somebody in Jamaica has that name."

She shook her head. "Research is a good thing in covert operations, incidentally. But fine, I'll be Octavia Love."

"Octavia?"

"I knew someone from Jamaica named Octavia. Like you said, easy to remember. My favorite author is Octavia E. Butler. The science fiction writer."

That's ONE thing I know about you, I thought. Marsha's idea of sharing.

"Let's not engage Spider if he's here," I said. I had learned my lesson from Roman, and then some: Partners have to share a mind.

"Check. We'll keep a low profile and follow him." She paused. "In a . . . Corvette."

"Hey, in L.A., a Corvette is like a Toyota Corolla. Don't even trip."

Marsha smiled as I hit the gas to zip into a gap in the traffic flow to open road.

Bamboo was a nondescript restaurant on the southern side of the Baldwin Hills boundary. No one seemed to notice us when we walked in. Somewhere in the rear, the band was already playing. The thought of running into Spider gave me an adrenaline surge.

Inside, the black professional class was represented in full force, the tables crowded with men and women in suits, ties, and crisp dresses. Other patrons of all races had been drawn by the restaurant's ambience and varied menu of soul food, Caribbean, and African dishes. I still wasn't sure I could keep any food down, but my mouth watered in the doorway. I didn't have to look at the menu to know that jerk chicken and curries were cooking in back.

Clarence Love felt right at home.

"Now *that's* what I'm talkin' 'bout," Clarence muttered.

Marsha squeezed my hand. "Maybe we came to the right place," she said. Her Jamaican accent was prim and high bred, emphasis on her *t*'s. Marsha had costumed herself in professional attire; hair efficiently pinned except for strands across her ears, wearing a gray pants suit that reminded me of Hillary Clinton on the campaign trail. Unlike Hillary, her white blouse was low cut, nestling a gold heart-shaped necklace in her cleavage. She could flash her flesh at the right angles.

The hostess's long blond hair was braided into cornrows; I wondered if she wore these every day. She grabbed two menus and motioned for us to follow, with no wait. "Hope you don't mind sitting near the stage," she said apologetically. "It's a little loud for conversation."

"You can sit me *on* the stage," I said, winking.

Our table, as promised, was in a corner right beside a small raised stage with a four-man combo eking out an imitation of Baaba Maal's "African Woman." It's salsa with a Senegalese flair, although the lead singer couldn't touch the vocals of the original. *Hell, I can probably sing as well as he can.*

The drummer looked shorter than me, about five-nine, in his twenties. Thin. My heart sped. He *could* have been the man I saw on the football field! Keeping my sunglasses on, I watched the drummer out of the corner of my eye, pretending to study the menu. The drummer's hands were listless on the skins, keeping the rhythm without the dynamism or odd gestures Xolo Nyathi had described. *Shit.*

"What looks good here, C.?" Marsha said.

I leaned close to Marsha's ear. "I don't think it's him."

She laughed, throwing her head back as if I'd told a joke. "Fuck."

"We'll find out for sure at the break."

The band was on a budget, with only a keyboardist, drummer, guitarist, and singer. Instead of horns to fill out the sound, the song's brass was performed on the keyboard. Big difference. Their cover of Bob Marley's "No Woman, No Cry" was more convincing, but it didn't sound like a band Xolo Nyathi or anyone else would follow.

"What's the name of the band?" Marsha asked the waitress when she brought our jerk chicken wings, fried plantains, and black bean soup we'd ordered à la carte.

"Uhm . . . Diaspora Beat, I think . . . ?" she said. "Something like that."

I gently laid a hand on the waitress's shoulder as she leaned down to hear me. Marsha gave me a mock evil eye. "Who's the man to talk to if I want to sing for them?" I said.

"Oh, ask the guy on keyboard—it's his band. Simon." She leaned closer, intimacy inspired by my lingering touch. "Just between us? They could use the help. You should hear Simon's regular guys. Would I know your singing from anywhere?"

"No, not yet," I said. "I'm just learning my way round. I'm a little shy."

"Awwww," she said, as if I'd been transformed into a puppy.

Marsha made a *humph*ing sound. "Shy? Don't believe a word he says. You'll see how shy he is up on that stage. Remember his name: Clarence Love. His voice is triple platinum."

"Come on, Octavia . . . ," I said, as if I was embarrassed. "She doesn't have time to hear—"

"She asked, didn't she?"

Our mock argument continued after the waitress smiled and excused herself, and Marsha and I shared a satisfied gaze. Marsha wasn't an actress, but she was an easy liar who could read human psychology.

I had eaten half the food on the plate when the keyboardist announced a ten-minute break. Recorded calypso music filled the restaurant. I was ready to introduce myself to Simon as he climbed down from the stage, but our waitress took his hand and led him to our table. "It'll just take a minute . . . ," I heard her tell him.

Simon was tall, thin, and dark skinned. His hair, which he wore in long dreadlocks, was tinged red from either sun or dye. He stared at us warily.

Marsha and I both got to our feet, conferring respect. I hoped he wasn't Jamaican. The accent was one thing, but the Jamaican patois was another matter.

"Simon, this is Clarence Love," the waitress said.

"Yeah, mon, hey," I said, shaking his hand. When I introduced him to my "wife," his eyes studied her blouse with appreciation.

"We understand you could use a singer," Marsha said.

Simon looked puzzled. "I never put up any ads . . ."

Marsha went on. "Sorry to be blunt, but we heard it with our own ears."

I groaned inwardly, but Simon only laughed, covering his mouth as he checked over his shoulder to see if the singer had heard. The rest of the band had headed straight for the bar, following the age-old musicians' custom.

Simon gave me a look, almost pitying. "I see this one speaks her mind."

"Ev'ry damn day," I said, and he laughed again. Simon was African, I guessed. His accent sounded faintly English, with a dash of exoticism. But not South African. And he didn't sound like the Englishman I'd heard at the football stadium.

"Leave me a demo," Simon said. "I'll see what *my* ears say."

Shit. I'd forgotten to make a demo. Any singer looking for work would have one.

"No, mon, sorry," I said. "I give you a demo, it sits in your car. Let me sing for you. Give me an audition. Just five minutes."

Simon shrugged. "It's not exactly big time, you know? We play at parties and restaurants now and then. I've already got a lead singer for the night gigs. The full band."

"Yeah, yeah, I've heard good things about the band," I said. "Heard you had a wicked drummer . . . Is that Spider?" I indicated the drummer, already knowing the answer to my question. My heart's excited pumping made it hard to sound casual. Marsha's fingers tightened around my kneecap under the table; maybe she thought I was pushing too fast, or maybe she was just saying *Be careful*.

"No, not Spider. That kid's new."

"Where can Clarence do that audition?" Marsha said.

Simon glanced toward his bandmates again. Then he sighed and pulled out a business card. Before he gave it to me, he scribbled a word on the back. "Check us out at Skylight tonight. Spider'll be there. We start playing at nine, but catch me at about eight thirty. I'll let you sit in for a song during mic check."

Spider would be performing tonight!

"Great!" I said, grinning. "But I don't know the set list, yeah?"

"We'll keep it simple for you," he said. "Some Marley, some Tosh. You'll catch on."

Or YOU will, I thought, shaking his hand again. I would need to brush up on my Bob Marley and Peter Tosh lyrics. I hoped I hadn't pushed my cover too far.

"You just did a very smart thing," Marsha assured Simon. "Mr. . . . ?"

"Simon Odembo," he said. "I use Simon O. I like your name—Clarence Love. It's catchy. Easy to remember."

I gave Marsha a smug look. "See? And she's always hated my name."

"But I married him anyway," Marsha said with a demure smile.

Simon laughed again, amused by our private improv act.

My mouth opened before I could stop myself. "Hey, mon, d'you know if Spider's got—"

A loud *clink*, and Marsha's water glass tipped over, spilling ice water across our table. I scooted back to avoid cold water across my lap. "I'm so clumsy!" Marsha said. "Sorry, baby."

When I looked up again, Simon was joining his band at the bar. I grabbed paper napkins from the dispenser at our table to mop up the water. "I know," I said quietly. "Too much."

"I saw something on his face," Marsha said. "Too many questions. We don't want to get ambushed. Just show up tonight and sing your ass off." She paused. "You can sing, can't you?"

I read the business card he'd given me: his name, band logo, and an 818 number. On the back, he'd written *Club Skylight, Culver City.* That nightclub hadn't been on Xolo Nyathi's list. I just wished we didn't have to wait so long. *We'll follow him when he leaves,* I decided. *If he knows Spider, he might visit him.*

For show, I raised my water glass in a toast. "Here's to tonight," I said to Marsha.

"Let's hope it's worth celebrating."

The memory of Spider's knife and Roman's screams brought to mind a few moves banned in the dojo that ended with *crunch* sounds. I couldn't wait to try them on Spider.

"I'll drink to that," I said.

We clinked our glasses together, almost hard enough to crack them.

NINETEEN

2:35 P.M.

The band was scheduled to play until three thirty, which meant we spent an hour baking in the car. The crowds had thinned out, and we didn't want our stay inside the restaurant to be conspicuous. Parked at the end of a parking lot with mostly family friendly vehicles, I realized Marsha had a point about the Corvette. We were anything but covert. Admiring passersby grinned when they saw the gleaming car.

I checked in with my father, but he didn't have any better leads.

While we waited for Simon O., my phone rang every ten or fifteen minutes. Anyone who'd ever met me tried to talk to me that day. I would have turned my phone off, but I wanted Maitlin to be able to reach me.

PRIVATE CALLER, my phone read finally. That was the only ID I answered.

Rachel Wentz started talking before I could greet her, and she hung up before I could respond. "Meet us at the corner of Melrose and Westbourne in thirty minutes," she said.

Then there was dead air on my phone. When I tried calling back, I got no answer.

Dammit! Meeting Maitlin on that schedule would take me to West Hollywood before Simon O. was scheduled to stop playing! I would never make it back in time to follow him.

"That's it?" Marsha said when I briefed her on Rachel Wentz's call.

"Something's definitely up, or she wouldn't be leaving the house," I said. "She never left Nandi's room when I was there. She wants to say something she doesn't want the FBI to hear."

"Could be anything," Marsha said. "Maybe we should stay on Simon, Ten."

I suspected that Marsha might be right, but Maitlin's call intrigued me. I hoped that Maitlin was ready to tell me what she'd been hiding.

"I'll go catch up to Maitlin," I said. "You can stay on Simon."

"How? On foot? Don't count on renting a car in the time we have."

She was right. We didn't have time to split up.

"Look, we'll see Spider tonight," I said. "This was always a long shot."

"Tonight could be bullshit. It's a mistake to walk away from the bird in your hand."

I'd confirmed that Diaspora Beat was playing at Club Skylight that night, so it sounded like a solid lead. The employee on the phone had said Spider was expected to play, although he hadn't known how to reach him before the show.

"Maybe we'll get lucky and Simon will still be hanging out at the bar when we get back," I said. "Come with me and disappear into the store while I talk to Maitlin."

"What store?"

"The Bodhi Tree," I said. "It's right on that intersection."

The Bodhi Tree is Los Angeles's best-known New Age bookstore, a fixture in West Hollywood since 1970. I once saw Tupac browsing the shelves there years ago, but Sofia Maitlin wasn't going to the Bodhi Tree to buy incense or Eckhart Tolle books.

"Now it *really* sounds like horseshit," Marsha said. "She probably wants to chant with you and buy crystals, or some crap like that. Don't go for it, Ten."

Scanning the parking lot, I got an idea. "Simon's car is the Acura, right?"

Marsha nodded. We'd narrowed down the cars in the lot by location, and she'd run his plates through the contacts she refused to talk about. The car was registered in Simon Odembo's name. We'd found a listing for his home address by using directory assistance. Glendale.

"A flat tire might make him stick around," I said.

"I've got a better idea," Marsha said, opening her car door. "But I need to make a call."

While I watched the clock, Marsha strolled to the other end of the parking lot, chatting on her phone. She was ducking me the way I'd ducked April.

She was back in a couple of minutes, but it was hard to stomach more waiting. Marsha handed me a slip of paper with the numbers 674195. "You didn't get that from me," she said.

"Lotto numbers?" I said.

"Like any careful new car owner, Simon Odembo subscribes to CarAlert. One of the perks is that he can use a password if he gets locked out. *Voilà*."

Marsha was right. I called CarAlert, the new OnStar rival, and identified myself as Simon Odembo. I explained my dilemma and gave my password.

Ten seconds later, I was climbing into Simon Odembo's car. I popped the hood, fanning as if the engine had overheated. But my show was for nothing: I swear I don't think a single person glanced my way. I knocked a fuse loose from the terminal on the car's computer module. Hood back down. Done.

One minute after I called CarAlert, Marsha and I were on the road. Finally—no waiting.

The drive took thirty minutes, so we pulled up to the bookstore by three fifteen.

The black Mercedes SUV identical to Roman's was parked at a spot near the corner of the residential district that borders the Bodhi Tree. All of the SUV's windows were tinted black and sealed up tight, but I saw Rachel Wentz in the driver's seat. We drove past without slowing, and Rachel didn't seem to notice me.

"I see her," I told Marsha. "I'll jump out at the next corner. You can circle."

"Were those really her boobs in *The Vintner*, or did she use a body double?" Marsha said, and her joke irritated me. It was probably just her idea of graveyard humor, but it reminded me of the way the FBI agent had tried to minimize Roman's humanity. As soon as I found a spot to pull over, I left Marsha in the car to ponder Maitlin's breasts alone.

"This better be good!" Marsha called after me.

When I knocked on Rachel Wentz's window, she gasped loudly. She stared at me, wide eyed, as her hand reached for the gear shift.

"Hey, Rachel, it's me—Ten," I said, remembering my disguise.

Rachel Wentz was so relieved that she closed her eyes. The doors *clicked*. I opened one of the rear doors to climb in.

"You just scared the holy living shit out of me," Rachel Wentz said. "Nice getup."

"Close the door, Ten." A whisper from the rear passenger seat behind me.

After I closed the door, I leaned over to find Sofia Maitlin lying prone. She sat up slowly, checking the windows to make sure we weren't being watched. If I hadn't dodged helicopters and a motorcycle to escape my own house, her behavior might have seemed extreme.

The dark spots beneath her eyes were much worse, her skin impossibly paper thin. Her bright red nose looked chafed and raw. Sofia grabbed my hand and held on, hard. Her nails bit into my skin, but I squeezed back. Sometimes touch is the only mutual language.

"Drive," she told Rachel Wentz.

The SUV bucked into the traffic lane with a screech. I had lost sight of Marsha, but I hoped she would stay on our tail. Sofia Maitlin held my hand during the whole drive.

"What's going on?" I said. "Did they call again?"

She shook her head and held her cell phone up for me to see. "I'm always waiting," she said. "That's why I'm rushing right back. Nothing since we talked."

Then, nothing. Her long silence agitated me. "Sofia, whatever it is, just say it. Something about the gang from South Africa?" I rubbed the meat of her thumb with mine, gently. If we had been in bed, it might have been foreplay.

"Paki," she said. "The birth father. I didn't tell you everything about him."

My heart thundered. "What about him?" I said.

"There was more to the story in South Africa . . . Not just what was on the news . . ."

Rachel Wentz was noticeably silent. She obviously must know whatever Maitlin was about to say, but she didn't try to run interference for her client.

"What happened?" I said.

Sofia's face was wrenched with a bitter memory. "Everything was going fine with the adoption, the paperwork was almost finished . . . and then *he* came. I'll never forget that phone call. I thought it would be good news from my lawyer, and instead she said, 'Sofia, there's a problem . . .' Out of the blue, a man claiming to be the birth father showed up. Paki. He demanded that we help him come to America so he could be in his daughter's life."

"You know he's the father for sure?" he said. "You have proof?"

"Yes, we're positive, unfortunately," she said. "We helped him get a job, in San Diego. Close enough to visit his daughter . . . occasionally. But far enough not to be intrusive." Sofia brought her hands up to her mouth, as if she'd just made a horrible revelation. "Roman kept saying, 'What do you really know about that guy?' I couldn't bring myself to believe it."

"What makes you believe it now?"

Rachel Wentz spoke up. "He's been *real* jumpy since the FBI showed up. Pacing. Nervous. He couldn't wait to get home."

That didn't prove anything. He might be nervous around authority figures, and Nandi was his biological daughter. I would have been pacing, too.

"What else?" I said.

Maitlin sounded breathless. "He knew a lot about the party. He was very interested in the planning—making suggestions. Alec didn't like it, but I didn't see the harm. He recommended that restaurant, South African Sun."

"The FBI has this, then," I said. "They're looking at the employee lists. Anything yet?"

Maitlin shook her head. "They're talking to Paki, but nobody's said he's a big lead."

They wouldn't necessarily tell her if Paki had turned into a suspect.

But with Spider's trail to follow, I couldn't get mired in a diversion fueled by Maitlin's anger toward Paki. "What makes you think Paki might be tied to a criminal gang?"

"Something he said when we ran into each other in the hall before a hearing in South Africa: 'I'm a little guy, but I have big people behind me.'"

"Was he threatening you?"

"I thought he meant the South African *government*. Rule of law. I'm wealthy, Mr. Hardwick. I was a celebrity, but I couldn't trump the power of his nation. Now . . . I don't know. What if he meant he was connected to that gang? Right before he left with the FBI this morning, he looked me dead in the eye and said, 'I'm sorry.' The sound of his voice chilled me, Ten."

"It's an expression of condolence, not a confession," I said. "He's Nandi's birth father, but he knows you're the one who's raising her."

Sofia was shaking her head. "No. It *wasn't* that. My mind is clearing up, past all the crying—I don't have time to sit and cry. Nandi needs me, and I'm noticing things I didn't before. Things about Paki. I make my living from voices and emotion, and he meant it when he said 'I'm sorry.' He *knew* something."

The validity of the theory was too dependent on Sofia's state of mind, but I wrote Paki's name down and circled it.

"Where's Paki now?" I said.

"With the FBI. I think."

"You've told them everything you told me?"

Maitlin hesitated before she nodded, the way a bad actress might have played a lie. "Yes, but they're looking in so many directions, like you said. Half of the city was at our house Sunday. I'm afraid you're right: They might be getting lost."

"Are they searching Paki's house?"

"Yes, I think so. I don't know if they found anything."

"So you want me to give him a closer look," I said. "As if he's the main suspect."

Maitlin nodded fervently. "Yes—if you can! I'll give you his home and work addresses. You'll know if he's hiding something. Make him tell you the truth." A fire in Maitlin's eyes said *Even if you have to break his bones to get it.*

"If I ask Paki too many questions and he's involved, it might be bad for Nandi," I said.

"If I'm right, don't let him go," Maitlin said. "Not until she's home."

Maitlin had already decided Paki's guilt, and she wanted me to break him. I almost told her my name was Tennyson Hardwick, not Jack Bauer. If Sofia Maitlin was circling the crazy drain, I couldn't let her drag me down with her.

I looked at Rachel Wentz, waiting for her assessment.

"I've known Sofia a long time, before we were working together," Wentz said. "I know this woman like I know myself, and she's not crazy. If she says Paki's not acting right, you can bet your ass he's hiding something."

An inside job could explain everything. Paki had helped plan the party, and he could have funneled information to the kidnappers to help them execute such a flawless abduction. His *Aw-shucks* act might have fooled Zukisa, the nanny, or she might have purposely deflected suspicion from him for her own reasons. Maybe Zukisa was in on it, too.

"What about the nanny?" I said.

They both shook their heads.

"No way," Maitlin said. "That poor woman was the one who first came to me and said she didn't like the way Paki was acting. I was too upset over Nandi to notice."

"She's brilliant," Rachel Wentz said. "She's on her way to medical school one day. What a story she is! She's the loveliest, sweetest woman. She's half out of her mind, she's so worried."

"We tried to send her home," Sofia said. "She wants to stay until Nandi comes back."

Zukisa probably wasn't a suspect, and she still might have her job—if Nandi survived.

I remembered how I'd been sent to the kitchen to babysit the cooks from South African Sun on Melrose in the moments before Nandi was snatched. Had they been Paki's friends brushing me out of their way while Paki cheerfully sipped wine with Sofia?

If Paki's involved, maybe Nandi's less likely to get hurt, I thought.

Paki might have made his plan to cash in on his golden child, never expecting Nandi to get hurt. But once the drop went bad, was he worried about the temperament of the gang he was working with? Was that why he'd told Sofia he was sorry?

It was still just a maybe, but *maybe* was enough to make anger coil in my chest.

"I'll take care of it," I said.

I told Marsha the story after Rachel Wentz dropped me off in front of the bookstore again. I'd decided against telling Maitlin that I had a tail. Marsha climbed out of the driver's seat to let me drive. Her eyes were glued to her cell phone's text field.

"Let me guess . . . ," Marsha said. "Women's intuition?"

"Cut her some slack," I said. "It's a hunch. I got vibes from him, too."

"I'll ask around," Marsha said as she texted someone, fingers flying. "Let's see if we can find something better than vibes on this guy."

"Who are you asking?"

"Yo' grandma. Mind your business."

I chuckled. A few hours ago, even a small chuckle would have been inconceivable.

"Let's head for San Diego," I said. "Even if Paki's tied up with the FBI, we might be able to sniff around his workplace and find something to tie him to Kingdom of Heaven."

Marsha looked at her watch. It was 3:45.

"Ten, I'll give Maitlin and her hunches the benefit of the doubt . . . ," Marsha began. "But we need to get back and stay on Simon. He's a direct route to Spider, and that's our best shot. I may be able to get our ears on Simon's home phone, if that helps. Maybe his cell, too, but that'll be trickier without custody of the phone. Paki's up to his eyeballs in feds right now."

We were having our first real argument. There was a long silence.

"Piece of advice, Ten?" Marsha said gently. "Don't get attached to Maitlin. It'll only make it harder on you if this goes to hell."

Probably Marsha's life philosophy, I thought. Once, it had been mine, too.

"Thanks, but I can take care of myself," I said.

"Just checking," she said. "Sometimes emotions sway our judgment. I know this."

The car was idling, and we had to make a choice. I wanted to jump on Paki, but I respected Marsha's opinion. Too many of my choices had been wrong so far, and Maitlin's instincts had led her all the way to Hell.

"We'll do Simon," I said. "We'll hit Paki later tonight, or first thing in the morning."

Instead of starting surveillance on Nandi's birth father, we raced back toward Baldwin Hills. There, we finally caught a break. The mechanic's truck was just driving away. Simon's engine was idling, and Simon was chatting on his cell phone in the shade of an awning, smoking a cigarette. Simon didn't look nearly as pissed as I would have been.

"Damn," I said. "He could be talking to Spider right now, and we wouldn't know."

"Patience, padowan," Marsha said, a *Star Wars* reference that surprised me. "Young the day is." She said it like Yoda. She really *was* a geek!

We stayed out of sight at the other end of the parking lot and waited for him to leave.

After five minutes, he drove off. We had almost missed him.

I remember my father complaining about long hours of surveillance when I was a kid. Often, he had to work late, and sometimes I had to sleep at a neighbor's house because he never came home. I got a taste of his old life as Marsha and I drove through Los Angeles tailing Simon O. The hours passed like years.

After he left the restaurant, he headed straight to a park in Glendale, where an equally lanky thirteen-year-old boy wearing a bright blue soccer uniform met his car. Few other kids were in sight. Thanks to us, dad was more than a little bit late after soccer practice. I was glad the kid wasn't any younger. That was at five thirty.

Great, I thought. *Paki's off on his own, and we're following the soccer dad.*

Almost as if he had a psychic burst, the kid gazed in our direction while we idled down the street, waiting. We were about thirty yards away, but he stared before he climbed into his car. Probably just admiring the 'Vette, but I was careful about my following distance. I got caught at a red light, but by then we knew it didn't matter. Simon O. was headed home.

"Maybe we'll get lucky, and Spider's at Simon's house," I said. "A rehearsal."

"And maybe Nandi will be there, too, dressed in her Sunday best," Marsha muttered, flipping through the car's radio stations, as she did every time she heard a commercial. Then she smiled sheepishly at me. "Sorry. Jokes are my way."

"Whatever works," I said. But Marsha had stolen my next thought: Nandi might be at Simon's house. *Doing what? Playing in the backyard with Simon's wife and kid?*

Simon pulled into the driveway of a quaint Craftsman almost the same shade of blue as Junior's soccer uniform, except with white trim. No other cars were parked at the house, which sat at the end of a shaded upper-middle-class street. The houses were well kept, easily worth $700,00 or more. And I didn't see any For Sale signs, which was rare during a recession.

"Nice neighborhood," I said.

"I'm not surprised," Marsha said. "Africans are this country's most highly educated group of immigrants. As a group, they do very well. Simon's brother has an accounting office about five miles from here. His wife is Kenyan, too. She's a dentist. They earn six figures, and she pulls in most of it. They're not hurting."

"Grandma told you all this?" I said.

"Pretty sharp for an old lady."

We waited for Simon to get out of his car, but he didn't. He and the kid seemed to be arguing. When the kid jumped out of the passenger seat to walk to the porch steps, Simon screeched out of the driveway. If he had turned left instead of right, he might have made us.

Next time, I definitely wouldn't try tailing anyone in a Corvette. Careful to keep out of his mirrors, I began following Simon again. Even his speed was predictable—never above the speed limit. Simon felt more and more like a dead end.

"What's Grandma saying about Nandi's birth father?" I prodded Marsha.

"Not much," Marsha said. "No arrest record in South Africa. Works as a mechanic in San Diego. If there's anything worth finding, the FBI has him in a nice, cozy interrogation room, and he's not going anywhere. Let me know if you want me to drive."

Marsha had been itching to take over the wheel, second-guessing my tactics all afternoon. I flashed my sweetest *Papa's-got-it-handled* smile in her direction.

"I got this, precious," I said. "Don't worry your pretty little head."

Marsha smiled, too, giving me the finger. I remembered where that finger had been.

If Marsha was CIA or NSA, or something else, no matter what, she could probably make people disappear if they got on her bad side. But Marsha's wild-card factor turned me on. Her body emitted a signal that made me constantly check the car's AC.

"Déjà vu, Ten," Marsha said. "For a second, you sounded exactly like my father."

"How's that rebellion going?" I said.

"It's a work of art, thanks. Too bad he never lived to see it." Her voice was quiet.

I almost mentioned how my mother had died when I was a baby; it was rolling around in my mouth, but I stopped myself. *Don't start swapping sob stories. Like Marsha said, don't make it personal.* Marsha was my partner, and an exquisite adventure in bed, but Nandi was my priority. If I faced a choice between grabbing Nandi or helping Marsha, I had to choose Nandi—and Marsha probably would, too. Or, she might just save herself. I might find out later.

I would be a fool to count on it.

Simon exited Highway 134 to drive into Pasadena, where traffic was still in rush-hour mode. After inching along, he stopped at Guitar Center, where the parking lot was jammed with the usual crowd of musicians, parents indulging their kids, and middle-aged yuppies with expendable income after their kids had moved out. A music habit is expensive to feed.

We decided to go in and blend. Even if he spotted us, we had a reason to be there.

Inside, we were met by the cacophony of shoppers testing the guitars, drums, and keyboards. I saw Simon's back as he walked into the keyboards section, not stopping to notice the guitars displayed at the front of the store. A half dozen Hendrix wannabes were strumming guitars they couldn't afford.

So far that day, everything about Simon had been consistent and bland. My heart perked up when Simon left the keyboard section and headed for the percussion alcove. It was a long shot, but he might meet Spider there before the show. My imagination was desperate.

I almost charged after him, but Marsha held my hand to slow me down. We strolled. I hoped to see a black guy about five-seven, possibly with a shaved head.

In percussion, drummers of every age sat on the drum thrones of drum sets both synthesized and real, the heavy bass beats bouncing against the walls. Shoppers in the room blended rock, hip-hop, and Latin styles, all of the rhythms crashing into one another.

Simon was standing in front of the Latin section, admiring the sets of *djembes,* congas, and timbales. My junior high school music teacher's voice came back to me as she tried to entice me to practice: *The piano is a PERCUSSION instrument, remember.* Simon picked up two shiny cowbells, one in each hand, and seemed to weigh them. After a time, he put one away and kept the other one to buy.

As he walked to the cash register, I looked at my watch: 6:35. The day was gone. Nandi still wasn't at home. I was in a Guitar Center watching a man buy a fucking cowbell.

We should have gone to San Diego, I thought.

Marsha shrugged, as if she'd heard my mind's complaint.

"Sometimes you just need more cowbell," she said.

Great. A comedian.

Showtime for Clarence Love couldn't come soon enough.

TWENTY

7:45 P.M.

At least six men in the growing line at Club Skylight could have been Spider, every bald head catching my eye. I doubted that a band member would stand in line, but I studied them all while Marsha and I were parked at a dead meter down the street. Her mini binoculars gave me a close view that was nearly useless, since I'd never seen the man's face.

Spider was a phantom. During our day working our phones while we tailed Simon, I'd talked to a friend at the Musicians' Guild who knew of two musicians with the nickname, but one was an eighty-year-old jazz player with a bad hip and the other was a female harpist with the Los Angeles Philharmonic. So it all came down to Club Skylight.

The club looked like a warehouse, sandwiched between a thrift shop and a boating supply store on a drab, nondescript street in Culver City, near the NPR station. Although most of the neighboring businesses were closed, the street-side parking was full. According to Google the club had been open for only six months, but I counted three dozen clubbers already lined up at the closed door. Most looked African, but college-age patrons of every ethnicity were waiting.

Tuesdays were billed as Afrika Night, and it was a large draw in Los Angeles's pan-African community. On my iPhone, Google found me a write-up in a *Los Angeles Times* article from March. MUSIC IS THE

COMMON LANGUAGE, read the headline in an article touting how African immigrants citywide loved the eclectic but familiar musical mix, with an emphasis on music from South Africa, Senegal, and Nigeria.

In the first photo of the band identified as Diaspora Beat, the shot had been taken in such an artsy way that the lights washed out the drummer's face; two blurry hands on the drums, his face still a mystery. The internet story included several photos of patrons dancing, and there were two clear shots of Simon, but none of the drummer. In one photo, the man I thought was Spider had his face turned away from the camera.

I just BET he doesn't like having his photo taken, I thought.

When the door opened to allow a well-dressed couple to walk inside, I saw the bouncer wave his magic wand. *Shit.*

"Metal detectors," I said, yanking my Beretta out of my pants. I slipped it into the glove compartment. "So much for the guns."

"That's damn inconvenient." Marsha occupied herself in the mirror, letting her hair down and taking off her jacket to show off her low-cut blouse. Marsha fussed endlessly with her earrings as she watched the crowd through the windshield. Did she think we were on a date?

I closed the glove compartment. "Let's scope the place, take a look in the . . ."

". . . back," she finished my sentence. "Then we knock on the door . . ."

". . . say we've got an appointment with Simon," I said. "Good. I hate lines."

Marsha laughed suddenly, still playing with her earring. "Remember how you wouldn't eat in the high school cafeteria? You said, 'Lines are for suckers.'"

I stared at Marsha, jolted. She had uncovered a memory I'd forgotten. Except for my father, no one in my circle had known me as long as she had. But it was a hell of a time for a high school reunion.

"Same plan," I said, trying to keep her focused. "We don't let Spider out of our sight. We'll follow him after the show."

"We also need his name so we can send Grandma up his ass, find out where he lives, who his friends are," she said, and smiled. "This should be fun."

Fun wasn't the word I was looking for.

"Watch out for this guy, Marsha," I said. "He'll cut you open a dozen ways."

"Brains trump blades. Let's see where he goes."

We pretended to head for the back of the line, but Marsha whipped out a pack of cigarettes, and we drifted toward the alley and six-foot fence along the side of the building. We lit up and chatted loudly about nothing, taking in the club's perimeter. In the rear, I heard the bright peal of a trumpet inside, and my heart raced. The band was warming up.

A young white woman dressed in a bartender's white shirt was smoking on the steps of the club's exit at the far rear, alongside a row of six parked cars. Marsha collected the tag numbers while we pretended to smoke. We leaned against an Expedition to hug and gaze deeply at each other for the bartender's entertainment. It was the first time I'd felt Marsha's body against mine without a hint of arousal.

"You seen Spider?" I called out casually to the smoking woman.

"Who?" she said, her face blank in the solar lamplight.

"Drummer with the band? Skinny guy, about five-seven?"

She shrugged and shook her head. No Spider, so we headed back to the front of the club.

Curious glances and a few glares followed us as we walked up to the front of the line to the closed door beside the empty ticket window. The entrance was locked, and there was no answer to our first knock. Marsha rapped on the window with a wooden bracelet I hadn't seen her put on. The bracelet did the job.

A huge, flat-faced young man in his midtwenties appeared at the window, probably a bouncer. He might be a great visual deterrent, but in a long fight, his mass would feel like wearing a raincoat made out of wet sandbags.

"Just the bar's open!" the man bellowed to be heard through the slot. "Invitation only."

I flashed my driver's license like it was a police badge. "I'm wit' da band!" I said, laying on my accent a bit thicker. "Simon said to meet him for mic check!"

Luckily, the bouncer barely glanced at my license. He nodded at the mention of Simon's name. "Okay, yeah, okay . . . ," he said. He lumbered away from the window, and the door opened with a blast of too-cool air and the smell of stale beer.

"She's with me, mon—my wife," I said, wrapping my arm around Marsha's waist.

The bouncer wasn't interested in introductions. He waved his wand lazily up and down while I raised my car keys high. He let us pass when we didn't beep.

That was the last time I was glad I didn't have my gun.

The bar was confined to a small alcove in front, with a bar counter and several tables draped in blood-colored tablecloths, lighted by fake flickering candles. A handful of couples dressed in West African patterns and L.A. chic chatted quietly, enjoying glasses of wine and beer. The room was dark enough to make me tense up as we walked slowly past the tables.

One man was too broad, another too tall, another too short. No Spider.

We floated past the archway to the main dance floor.

The inner sanctum of Club Skylight was midsize, only one level, with a vast, empty floor and tables lining the walls. Once it was full, it might comfortably have room for four hundred people. The lighting inside was an odd blue that made my skin look purple. A large projection screen on one wall showed soundless film clips that looked like Nigerian Nollywood or Ghanaian productions in everyday African urban settings.

The musicians were on the stage in the back, but not even a bartender was in sight.

I counted seven musicians under the stage's lights: Simon on keyboards, two trumpets, two trombones, an electric bass, and an electric guitar. The large percussion set had both a standard drum kit and hand drums, but no drummer yet. The wooden *djembe* drums stood like giant goblets. The brass section was playing alone, rehearsing an intricate salsa riff that sounded like a wall of sound, sharp as a knife.

The band *was* good. And I was supposed to pass myself off as a singer?

"Just remember what Mrs. Davis told us—project from the diaphragm," Marsha said. Any other time, the reference to our high school drama teacher would have made me smile.

The music stopped abruptly as Simon signaled. "*Yes!* We do it like that!"

I clapped my hands loudly as we approached the stage. "Hey, mon, that's sweet!"

Simon shaded his eyes from a footlight so he could see me. "Clarence Love!" he said. "This is the *real* band, not the one you saw at lunch."

"Yeah, I see that."

The brass players were middle aged with various stages of paunch. The guitarist and bassist were younger—the guitarist was the same man I'd seen earlier that day—but it was impossible to tell if any of them had been on the football field.

Simon motioned for me to come to the stage. "He didn't like Ray's singing," Simon said, and the band members chuckled. "He wants to audition for the lunch gig, so let's run through . . . what?" He looked at me for guidance.

"You said Marley, yeah?" I said. "Let's do 'One Love.'" It was the simplest Marley song I could think of, and I still wasn't sure I knew the lyrics.

The band groaned. To them, it was like playing "Chopsticks."

"No, no, it's fine . . . ," Simon said. "Clarence Love—'One Love.' Singer's choice."

Marsha beamed at me like a wife in front of the stage. *You can do it,* she mouthed.

I went to the mic stand. "Where's my drummer?" I tried to sound like it was a joke.

"You see him, you tell us," a trombone player said good-naturedly.

"Don't worry about Spider," Simon said. "He always shows—unless he doesn't."

They laughed. They seemed like a friendly, jovial group, like many bands I've met.

Most musicians don't play gigs for the money, that's for sure. But were any of them kidnappers?

Nervous perspiration beaded on my forehead. Marsha was already moving toward the backstage area, toward the restrooms, looking nonchalant as she peeked around. Simon counted down, and the keyboard and guitar led me into the song so quickly that I almost missed my cue.

I pulled my mic out of the stand. "'*One love . . . ,*'" I began in my best Marley impression. I won't be modest: With Simon and the guitarist singing backup, I sounded damn good.

I was just hitting my groove, walking the stage to engage with an imaginary audience, when Marsha appeared in front of the stage. One look at her face explained the sudden hot tingle that skittered across the back of my neck two seconds after I saw her eyes.

Behind me, unseen palms slapped across the waiting *djembe* drums, hard. Rapid fire.

I smelled a too-heavy dousing of CK One cologne and fresh cigarette smoke. Pall Malls.

That smell was an adrenaline bath, bringing back Nandi's face and Roman's screams.

Until then, I hadn't remembered that the knife man on the football stands smelled like cigarettes. I'd smelled him when the kidnappers closed in on me to steal Nandi away. My pores felt electrified as my heart jumped into high gear. My hand on the microphone went cold, my stage smile frozen on dry lips. I sang by rote while I met Marsha's steady eyes.

He's behind you, she said telepathically. I gave her a subtle nod: *I know.*

When the drumming got louder, I pivoted to glance over my shoulder. Spider's head was down, swaying gently from side to side, as his palms slapped the *djembes*. His head was shaved bald, gleaming from blue lights. Even without his face in view, I knew him on sight.

Spider played his own music, ignoring the rest of us. His drumming was faster than the Marley, a frenzied conversation between high and low tones. As an old jazz musician once said of Thelonious Monk, Spider found the notes between the notes. As Spider played with more intensity, the rest of the music faded into lone, stray notes.

Spider's arrival signaled the end of my audition.

"Yeah, yeah, not bad," Simon said, patting my back.

"Better'n Ray!" the bassist said.

"Too bad for you, that's not saying much," the guitarist murmured.

The band laughed, but more uneasily—except Spider, immersed in his rhythms. I glanced back at him again, and I noticed the tic Xolo Nyathi had described. His right hand was busy between beats, almost spastic. Flicking out in private amusement, practicing deadly skills within plain sight of an oblivious audience.

I felt an irrational certainty that Spider knew exactly who I was, that his knife was about to fly into the base of my skull. I climbed down from the stage, pretending to be uncertain as I turned to Simon. "I'll give you my number, yeah?"

"You've got my card," Simon said. "Call me next week, and we'll—"

"Who's this?" A husky, almost disembodied, voice. More breath than words.

I glanced back again. Spider had spoken, but he hadn't looked up from his drums.

"Clarence Love," I said when no one else spoke. "Tryin' to sing with the band."

Spider's eyes shot up to me, his head still bent over his drums. His face broke in half, part grin, part empty stare. "*Trrrying*, yes." His South African accent was pronounced. Spider was small boned, with a youthful face, in his twenties. His teeth seemed too large for his face.

The band wasn't laughing anymore. Simon shooed me from the stage as if he was embarrassed. He clapped to call the band's attention to the set list. All of the musicians paid rapt attention, except Spider.

One of Nandi's kidnappers might have been less than twenty yards from me, and I had to watch his damn show. There were no tables near the front of the stage, but Marsha and I claimed a spot at the nearest bar counter, where Spider would always be in sight. We ordered a round of drinks for show, but what observers probably assumed was a rum and Coke was missing its rum. It had never been so hard to stand still.

The band rehearsed for thirty solid minutes. I was glad when they took a break, but Spider never left the drums or stopped his brilliant performance. Recorded music filled the dance hall as patrons began filing in. King Sunny Adé. Miriam Makeba. Baaba Maal.

The guitarist walked to the bartender near us to order a beer. He had a boyish face, his hair styled in short braids. I drifted toward him, and Marsha followed two paces behind.

"How'd I sound?" I asked the guitarist.

The guitarist shrugged. "Not much range in that song."

"Yeah, mon, I know . . . hey, your drummer, he's amazing. What's his name?"

"Spider's all I know. Eight hands."

"You guys been playin' long?"

Before he could answer, Simon joined us at the bar, and the bartender slid him a bottle of Guinness before he said a word. Simon offered to refill Marsha's glass, and she agreed with a flirtatious smile. The SOB was hitting on my "wife" right in front of me, but I ignored it.

"How long's Spider played with us?" the guitarist asked Simon for me. "Three months?"

"Almost four," Simon said. "Showed up here in . . . February, right?"

"What's his name?" the guitarist said. "He ever tell you?"

Simon frowned. "Mhambi, I heard someone call him."

Marsha was listening without appearing to, swaying to the music's beat.

"Hey—Mhambi!" the guitarist called out playfully to the stage.

Spider ignored him, playing on. He never broke his rhythm.

The guitarist laughed, but Simon gave him a warning head shake: *Leave him alone.*

"Spider only likes to talk with his hands," Simon told me.

"Shit—me, too, if I could play like dat," I said. "Big up to de band! Do all your friends come to hear?" Conversation about Spider seemed to make Simon jumpy. Maybe Simon suspected that Spider was more than a musician. Maybe he *knew*.

Simon looked at me quizzically, taking a healthy swig. "Where are you from in Jamaica?" Simon said, and I felt a jolt of nerves. Was my accent off?

"Kingston," I said. "By way of Canada. Haven't lived there since I was ten."

"We met in Vancouver," Marsha said, clasping my hand.

Simon nodded, his face impossible to read. *Time to shut up*, I decided.

It was nine o'clock. Showtime.

The line outside must have been around the corner because the room filled fast, with loud conversation above the recorded music. My ears never lost track of Spider's pattering hands. While we watched the musicians file back to the stage, Marsha wrapped her arms around my neck as if we were newlyweds.

"Knows more than he's saying," Marsha said.

"Mos' def," said Clarence Love.

The crowd swelled, so packed that there was barely room for dancing, only standing. To me, it was like a time-lapse scene in a movie where one object stays the same while the scenery constantly changes around it. To my eyes, Spider was the only person in the room. The longer I watched him, the more pissed off and wired I felt. While Spider chased his musical bliss, Nandi and her parents were in misery, and Roman's children were fatherless. My lips were smiling, but it was hard to keep the death ray out of my gaze.

Call the FBI, the voice in my head insisted. But what was I supposed to tell them—that Spider was a suspect because of the way he played his drums?

"You okay here for a minute?" Marsha said to my ear at about ten thirty, when the band was in the midst of rousing classic Nigerian juju music. "Nature calls."

The song was heavy on percussion, so Spider wouldn't be going anywhere soon.

I nodded. "Yeah. Hurry back, baby."

I followed Marsha with my eyes only out of habit. She might be able to protect herself just fine, but she was still the woman I was sleeping with. If she had gone where she'd said she was going, I would have left it with a glance.

But she didn't.

At first, she waded toward the sign for the ladies' room, which was well lighted in the far rear of the club, beyond the stage. Then she zigzagged back toward the bar, blending in so well with the crowd that I lost sight of her. But I picked her up again—and she was nowhere near the bathroom. Instead, she was closer to the front exit, as if she might be on her way out.

"What the . . . ," I said aloud, watching her.

Spider was practically playing a drum solo, so I left my post and followed Marsha. I gave myself thirty seconds to try to see what she was up to, and then I would be back on Spider.

Marsha danced in place for a time, and then snaked her way in yet another direction.

I got the feeling that she was following someone. But who?

Suddenly, I knew. A tallish Asian man in a gray business suit and tie made a sudden movement, and she quickly pulled herself out of his sight in the crowd. Once his back was turned, her eyes went back to him. She reached into her purse and pulled out what looked like a BlackBerry and put it to her ear, as if she'd gotten a call. But our time tracking Simon had taught me that Marsha's "phone" was also a good camera. *Bullshit. She's taking his picture.* It was too dark for a regular camera phone, but nothing about Marsha was regular.

No one else near Marsha would have suspected, but I knew.

The drum solo ended, so I wove closer to the stage.

Spider waved to the crowd, acknowledging the applause while the rest of the band took the reins of the song. Spider was sweating. I glanced behind me toward the Asian man, and saw him grin and raise his hands above his head to clap with the appreciative crowd.

Marsha was nowhere in sight.

Someone nudged me on my left side, and I almost jumped.

"Hey," Marsha said.

"That was fast," I said.

"Line was too long," she said. "I'll hold it."

She just lied to you. The idea rolled in my head, uglier with each repetition. It wasn't the time or place to call her on it, but I didn't like it.

The band played on. I checked Marsha's face from the corner of my eye, and just when I was about to convince myself that I was only being paranoid—that maybe I'd mistaken her for another woman in a room full of Africans—I saw her glance back toward the Asian man while she pretended to watch the film clip on the large projection screen.

Gotcha. My jaw clenched. But I didn't have time to mull it over.

Suddenly, the music ended in one last, precise blast of sound.

"Thank you!" Simon said on the stage. "Next set in thirty minutes!"

The crowd roared disappointment and adoration. Spider was met by cheers when he rose to his feet. The rest of the band jumped down into the crowd, where patrons congratulated them with spirited handshakes and slaps on the back. Not Spider. He turned his back to the audience, climbing down unseen steps the other way. Toward the rear of the nightclub.

The hall behind the stage led to office and closet areas in two directions—and there were at least two exits that would take him outside. *Spider might not come back for the second set!*

"On the move," I said to Marsha, in case she was preoccupied with Mr. Asia.

"You flank right, I'm left," Marsha said. "Leave me if you have to."

And she was gone again.

At first, so was Spider. The crowd was a faceless, squirming mass.

My heart clogged my throat until I caught sight of Spider's wet, shiny scalp bobbing between patrons toward the far rear of the club. He was moving fast. I pushed myself through the tight crowd more roughly, following the drums in my chest.

DON'T LOSE HIM, OR IT'S ALL OVER.

"*Hey*—," said a man I bumped near the men's room, but I didn't linger for him to vent.

For a terrible instant, I didn't see Spider in the empty, dimly lighted hall beyond a DO NOT ENTER sign on the wall. Crates and tarps lined the passageway, but nothing else. No sign of Marsha either.

Click. A feeble sound, almost beneath my hearing. A door had fallen shut! I neared the only set of double doors it could have been, marked AUTHORIZED PERSONNEL ONLY, and reached toward the back of my pants for the gun.

But I didn't have my gun. The Beretta was back in the car, useless.

A mop in a bucket, a custodian's wide broom, and a stack of chairs sat outside the door. I grabbed the broom for its thick wooden handle, as if I had sweeping to do.

Was he in there sneaking a smoke? Visiting a bathroom? It was risky to follow, but riskier not to. I tried the first of the double doors, my thumb pressing the metal release above the handle. A small tug told me it was unlocked. I opened it half an inch, without a sound, and peeked inside. Fluorescent light peeked back out. It was a large dressing room with a bank of barred windows on the rear wall. I glanced behind me for Marsha, but she hadn't turned up yet.

Just as well, I thought. Worrying about Marsha would have split my attention. Spider was enough to occupy me.

I was so juiced on adrenaline, I barely felt my legs move as I walked inside the dressing room, which doubled as a storeroom. To my right, a small area was partitioned off as a green room with a leather sofa and a coffee table hosting a ravaged sandwich plate. Empty beer bottles stood in a circle. Three potted ficus trees were a scraggly forest dying for light. A row of four filing cabinets in the middle of the floor were a wall of privacy.

On the other side of the room, six chairs sat in front of the dressing table built into the wall, posed before a six-foot rectangular mirror framed by darkened lightbulbs. Only the overhead lights were on.

Near the dressing table, a closed door had a unisex bathroom sign.

I craned my ears, but I didn't hear a sound from the bathroom. Unless the bathroom had an exit to a room on the other side, I couldn't see a way out. If Spider was the one who'd come in, he might not be able to get out without passing by me.

But if it wasn't Spider, I was wasting precious seconds.

No time to wait for the sound of a flushing toilet. I rapped on the bathroom door.

"Anyone in here, mon?" Clarence Love called.

I tried to turn the knob. The bathroom door was locked.

"Oh hey, sorry," Clarence Love said. I slurred my words, as if I were tipsy. "Tryin' to get away from dat line. I thought only the ladies had to wait!" I faked a self-amused laugh.

No answer. My heart pounded in my fingertips on the cold metal knob.

"I gotta take a piss, mon," Clarence Love said.

Tingling hairs on my forearm made me look behind me. A shadow moved in a corner of the large dressing-room mirror, a brown arm so fast it was a blur.

A *click*, then blackness. The room was as dark as a tomb. Even the streetlights outside couldn't penetrate the tinted windows.

Clothing rustled toward me, and I dove to the floor. My broom handle *clanked* loudly against the side of a filing cabinet, like a flare to pinpoint my location.

Spider had chosen darkness. That implied comfort. Familiarity. In the dark, I was dead.

My mind snapped me a photograph of the room from my first glance, and I remembered a small panel on the wall near the door. I thrust my broom's business end at the wall, guessing where it should land. I pushed upward, trying to find the light switch.

Precious light, on my left. The ring of lights around the mirror weren't as bright as the overheads, but they came on in time for me to see Spider's knife. Spider was only the shadow behind a slender eight-inch blade.

"*Shit*—" I twisted, swinging the broom toward Spider. It hit his left side, and he gave a grunt of surprise. He backed up, and I had enough time to scramble to my feet.

At my angle, I didn't have time to get to the door.

"Fuck! What's goin' on, mon?" Clarence Love said, pretending ignorance.

That was the end of our conversation. A terrible scream slowed my blood, and I hoped it wasn't mine. But it was Spider's declaration of war. He lunged, and only my broom handle kept my arm from getting slashed to the bone.

Spider was *fast*, maybe 20 percent faster than the kid in South Africa. The fastest man I'd seen in a very long time. He parried and evaded, always spiraling in, trying to get close enough to stab. I had no clean shot, and caught only glimpses of him in the darkness, enough to get the hell out of the way, but not to counter effectively.

Don't be hypnotized, Cliff had warned me.

I scrambled away from the door, my only escape.

"*Who sent you?*" Spider rasped. "*What do you want? Who are you?*"

My disguise had held up! Spider didn't know who I was.

My luck ran out as soon as it had arrived. He shifted right, and as I followed he managed to grab hold of the handle for a moment. His left leg flashed up and fell on the handle, breaking it in half. I held on to the short end and ran, hoping to lose him at the filing cabinets. Hot pain raked across my lower back, and I yelled. Spider had drawn blood—it felt like a shallow slash, not a puncture. Hot wetness dampened the back of my shirt. *Shit shit shit shit.*

I couldn't leave my back open to him, and there was nowhere to run.

Cornered, I faced him again, armed with fourteen inches of broken broom. I fought to calm my breathing. All right. I'm not dead yet. He's faster, and has the better weapon. I'd studied Escrima, Filipino stick fighting, but I'd never faced anyone like Spider.

I was an actor to the end. "Why you killing me, mon?" Clarence Love said, dazed, while Tennyson Hardwick's mind raced for a move.

Spider sprang at me like a cat, and I struck out with my stick, knowing he would parry and riposte, or even attack the wrist. Or feint high and kick low: I'd seen his kicks, and they were almost as fast as his hands. If I didn't find a defense, I was going to experience a few moments of intense, significant pain. And then, nothing at all, ever again.

A loud *POP* behind us sounded like a fantasy of my cooling brain. But I didn't imagine the drywall that chipped away from the wall behind us, and a fresh hole. A gunshot!

In a blink, Spider pivoted out of sight behind the filing cabinets. I expected the next gunshot to put a hole in my chest.

"Where is he?" Marsha called.

Oh thank God.

"Filing cabinets!" I warned her. Maybe it was Clarence's voice, maybe it was me.

Marsha appeared in front of me, her active eyes searching for movement. She had a tiny gun I'd never seen in her steady, two-handed isosceles stance.

A clattering near the waiting area turned Marsha's head. Too late, we both realized that Spider had thrown the sandwich platter against the mirror, hard enough to shatter the glass. Sandwich wedges rained down while beer bottles crashed to the floor. While we tracked the platter, Spider reached the door with a speed that looked supernatural.

"*Door!*" we said in unison. He opened the door in a deft motion, and his body seemed to squeeze through six inches of space. We could only watch the weighted door close behind him.

I got within three steps of him, in time to hear a scraping sound from the other side. I tugged down on the latch and tried to push the door open, but it gave only half an inch before it held tight. Spider had barred the door, probably with the mop.

"He's locked us in!" I said.

"I'm fine, but we're locked in!" Marsha said. "We've lost our visual!"

But Marsha wasn't looking at me, or talking to me. Palm cupped her right ear. A microphone in her ear canal. Probably invisibly flesh colored. Grandma was in the room with us, another one of Marsha's secrets.

Marsha and I combined our weight to fling it against the doors, trying to break out. Once. Twice. Three times. I was sure I was about to dislocate my shoulder when the door gave way, and I heard the mop fall to the floor. Spider hadn't had time to slide it far enough into place to secure it.

We raced around the corner, nearly barreling into two men and a woman laughing, in a huddle. They gawked at us, their laughter stopped cold.

"You're bleeding . . . ," the woman began, concerned.

Marsha leveled her gun at the group. "Spider—which way did he go?" Her voice was in a bad mood, ready to pull the trigger.

"Who?"

"The drummer."

Three blank, terrified faces stared at us, and the woman clung to the nearest man.

"The . . . d-drummer?" one of the men said. My gut told me that somehow they hadn't seen him.

I ran for the red EXIT sign fifteen yards from us. "Take the front!" I told Marsha.

A sign on the door warned that opening it would set off the fire alarm, but no alarm sounded when I ran outside. Cool night air bathed my sweating face.

By then, more than a dozen cars were parked outside the rear door. No one was in sight, not even a stray smoker. No screeching tires betrayed an escape.

Without realizing it at first, I was whispering to myself. "No, no, no, no, no . . ."

I fell to the ground to stare at the gravel beneath the cars. It was too dark to see, so I carefully scurried from one to the next. Next, I peeked through the windows of the parked cars, looking for movement, my ears open for a surprise attack.

None came. There was nothing and no one.

"No . . . no . . . *NO!*" I wasn't whispering anymore.

Spider had melted into the night.

TWENTY-ONE

The club shut down Afrika Night early, by one thirty, and Marsha and I watched the last of the patrons reluctantly leave—none of them Spider.

The police had been called, thanks to Marsha's gun incident, but she remade herself with a change of clothes and a horrible Jheri curl wig so she could float in and out of the club. Even with a light jacket to cover my injury, I stayed outside in the shadows to avoid LAPD uniforms. I couldn't get detained again. My back throbbed from the memory of Spider's knife.

The band had played a partial second set without Spider, but the police presence thinned the crowds even before the owners announced the club was closing. I questioned patrons and employees as they left, and no one had seen Spider since the break at eleven.

Two people out of the dozens I talked to could confirm that Spider's first name was Mhambi, although no one could tell me his surname, or where he lived. When I wasn't with Marsha, I asked the bouncer and regulars about the Asian man I'd seen. The bouncer said *Yeah, we get some Chinese and Koreans in here,* but he didn't tell me anything that could help me understand what Marsha had been up to when we were supposed to be watching Spider.

I avoided thinking about Marsha while I searched for Spider. No point. But as the street emptied and the crowds disappeared, it was hard to think about anything else. Our mission had failed, and she was holding out on me. I didn't know if one fact had anything to do with the other. I didn't know a damn thing about her, except how well she lied.

By the time Marsha walked up to me after her last tour of the club, I was shaking in frustration and rage. Blame it on sleep deprivation. Marsha's mouth was moving, but I couldn't hear anything except my heartbeat thundering between my ears.

"Who is he?" I said quietly.

"Who?"

"That Asian guy you were pretending not to notice."

Her face narrowed with confusion. "Wait—what? You've lost me."

"Before the break, he was listening to the band. You took a picture. Who was he?"

Marsha's face was all confusion, like the people she'd scared shitless with her gun.

I went on, my voice chilled. "Tell me to my face you weren't tracking an Asian man. You remember: When you lied and said you were going to the bathroom?"

Marsha hooked her arm inside mine as she settled beside me against the car. Her soft eyes met mine, not blinking. "The only person I was tracking in there was Spider, just like you," she said evenly. "Ten . . . where's this coming from? I'm worried about you—"

"You lying BITCH!" I pounded my fist against the convertible top of my Corvette, two inches from Marsha's head. I've never come closer to hitting a woman. That was one of the rare times I'd uttered the epithet that rarely crossed my lips or my thoughts.

My shout turned heads. A couple of well-built brothers in mud-cloth prints walked in our direction, ready to intervene on Marsha's behalf. I took a step back from Marsha, holding my hands up as if she'd pulled her gun on me. Maybe I was lucky she hadn't.

"It's okay!" Marsha called to her rescuers. "He's my husband. He's a little drunk!"

Marsha tugged on my arm playfully, walking me toward the passenger seat. "No driving for *you* tonight!" she said cheerfully.

The men were still watching us, not quite buying Marsha's act, so I climbed into the car. Marsha followed, and we sat without moving until the men walked back to their Mustang and drove off. Nobody in their right mind wants to leap into a domestic problem.

Inside the car, Marsha's smell sickened me. I remembered my borrowed Beretta in the glove compartment and wondered what she would say if I pressed it against her temple. If she didn't shoot me first.

"I'm pissed off, too," Marsha said gently. "He got away. You learn to roll with it, Ten."

Rage boiled in me again. My hands clawed at my kneecaps. "I . . . *saw* . . . you," I said. "Get it? I'm not a fool."

"Nobody's saying you're a fool! How long has it been since you slept, Ten? Don't go batshit on me. The op went south. It happens. We have a first name for Spider now. It's a common name in South Africa, but it's better than nothing. I'll start—"

"Get out of my car."

Marsha looked at me, newly stunned. "Excuse me?"

"You heard me."

"You are *not* going to leave me here with my dick in the wind . . . in Culver City!"

"Lady, if you had a dick, I'd rip it out by the root. *Get out.*" I leaned toward her earpiece. "Hear that, asshole? She needs a ride!"

Marsha pressed her hand to her ear with an angry stare before she opened her car door. "Grow the hell up, Ten. And *you're welcome* for saving your life," she said, climbing out. "Do everyone a favor—go get some sleep."

She slammed the door.

I closed my eyes. I was too weary to curse, or even to feel.

I had nowhere else to go, except home.

3 A.M.

Dad had waited for me in his living-room recliner, but he'd fallen asleep. His gentle snores followed me as I crept into the kitchen. After the din at Club Skylight, the silence in my house was surreal and deafening. I glanced toward the stairs, but they looked like Mount Kilimanjaro, so I changed course.

I tried to be quiet as I turned on the kitchen faucet at a low stream and washed my lower-back injury with a clean cloth from the drawer. Marsha had examined me soon after Spider vanished, deciding that the bleeding had stopped, but it was an ugly gash—six inches long and an eighth of an inch deep, from my kidney to beyond my spine. If Spider had struck deeper, I would have spent a quiet evening at the coroner's office.

Dad had gotten so good without his cane that I didn't hear him until he was in the kitchen doorway. He was wearing the faded LAPD sweatpants he liked to sleep in.

"Damn," Dad said, flicking on the kitchen light to see the blood. "You found him?"

I nodded. "At a nightclub in Culver City." I paused, my tongue almost too heavy for the task. "He got away. All we got is a first name. In other words, nothing."

"He make you?"

My face was still disguised. The glue on my skin itched like hell.

"Maybe. Probably. Or maybe he just doesn't like being followed."

Both of us mulled that over while the refrigerator broke into its tuneless hum. If Spider had guessed that I was the man he'd met on the football field, I had jeopardized the drop-off again. The whole way home, I'd braced for a frantic call from Sofia.

I dabbed alcohol on my back, and it felt like liquid fire. I gritted my teeth, but part of me reveled in the pain. Pain was a relief from everything else I was feeling.

"Gonna need stitches, son."

"Not now, Dad. What's the FBI saying about Paki?" The birth father was my last lead.

"Nothing since ten. Still in interview. Maybe they held him overnight. I prolly won't hear back till morning."

"I can't just sit on my hands."

"Think that's best now," Dad said. "Don't you?"

He didn't say *I told you so*, but he didn't have to. Dad left the kitchen doorway, and I thought he might be finished with talking to me for the night. But he came back with a large first aid kit. "Marcela keeps this for me," he said. "Come on to the living room, Tennyson."

I sat shirtless on the sofa while my father tended my injury with unsteady hands. I was way beyond Band-Aids, but Dad's kit had gauze and medical tape. I helped him wrap the tape tightly from my back around my abdomen, holding the gauze in place. Not long before, I was the one who'd been trying to mend *him*. Like Octavia Butler wrote, *The only lasting truth is Change.*

My neck was exhausted, so I kept my head and eyes low.

Marcela shuffled out of Dad's bedroom in my father's rumpled terry cloth robe, sleepy. She didn't always sleep over, but now she did more and more.

"*Dios*—what happened?" she said, alarmed.

"Cut his back," Dad said. "He's all right."

Marcela was a trained nurse, but she hung back to let Dad finish his work. Some jobs are for parents alone. "Ten, I could heat up some food . . . ," she said.

I shook my head. I hadn't eaten since lunch, but food was a foreign concept as a harrowing truth settled across my spirit: Of *course* Spider had recognized me! He wouldn't have tried to kill a random intruder. Marsha had said Kingdom of Heaven liked to make an example of families who didn't play by their rules.

I might have sealed Nandi's death.

"Doesn't need food," I heard my father say, like a dream. "He needs rest."

I didn't make the decision to lie down on the sofa, but my body improvised without me. My eyes had battled with me while I drove home, and I finally gave them their way. I could have wrapped myself in that darkness for years.

Finally, I grasped the notion of wanting to stay in bed and never get up. My agent, Len, had tried to explain depression to me after his divorce, when he popped prescription pills like candy to get through his day. I wanted to call Len up and apologize to him for every bullshit pep talk I'd ever given him. I wanted to apologize to Chela for trying to convince her that control and comfort were anything except illusions. Delusions.

The world was a house of horrors. End of story. The rest was bullshit.

To me, only seconds had passed when I opened my eyes and saw Chela sitting in my father's lounger, watching me sleep. Dad and Marcela were nowhere in sight.

My back was still on fire; maybe the pain had awakened me. When I shifted position on the sofa, my spine's dull shout became a scream. Knives hurt in a much more personal way than clubs or even fists. Knives are a violation.

The living room was dark. Except for the pain, I might have been dreaming.

"What are you doing up?" I said.

"Waiting for you. Nobody told me you were down here."

"You're supposed to be asleep. It's late."

"You mean early," Chela said.

I might have dozed again. When I opened my eyes, Chela hadn't moved from her post, guarding me. She was rocking slowly back and forth in the chair, with a squeaking that sounded like a ticking clock.

"Tomorrow morning," I said, bleary, as if she'd asked me a question.

"What's tomorrow?"

"I'll start calling, like I said . . . try to find your mother."

"I don't have a mother," Chela said.

You and me both. The grief I'd always felt for the woman I'd never known shook me again. "You know what I mean," I said. "I'll work on . . . getting her consent."

"What about Nandi?" Chela said.

A fist stuffed my throat, blocking my breath. I had to confess the worst to Chela.

"I can't do anything for Nandi," I said. "I'm in the way. I probably got her killed."

"Oh, so you're just gonna buy that bullshit from the FBI?"

Only the chair's persistent squeaking kept me awake, Chela swinging slowly back and forth. The moonlight from a window caught her hair, like a halo. Was she a dream after all?

"I'm not what you think I am, Chela."

"You're not the guy who figured out who killed Afrodite when the cops were too busy to look for the real suspect? Made them look like assholes when T. D. Jackson died?"

"That guy got lucky." If *luck* was the right word for what I'd been through.

"*Bullshit,*" Chela said. "You're still that guy, Ten."

I hadn't realized my eyes were closed until I opened them again. This time, I saw a shimmer on Chela's cheeks; she was crying. Chela's tears made me sit up. My back screamed at me again, and the haze of unreality lifted. Suddenly, I was wide awake.

Chela's face was bright red. She looked as if she was holding her breath.

"Chela . . . ?" I said.

"I keep thinking about her," Chela said, her whisper weighted with tears. "Scared. All alone with these assholes. Missing her mother." She couldn't clamp back her sob.

"Hon, these are bad guys, but they made a deal with Maitlin. Besides, the FBI has a real suspect. By ten o'clock tonight, this will all be over. Nandi will come home."

I didn't believe it, but I wanted to. *Maybe if I convince Chela, I'll convince myself.*

But Chela shook her head. She leaned forward, suddenly older than her years. "Things don't just work out, Ten," she said. "That's a load of crap. The only time anything works out is when you *make* it work out. Like when I decided to stay with you instead of going back to Mother's." For the first time, Chela had said she was glad she'd never gone back to her madam.

I couldn't face the expectations in her eyes. "Chela . . ."

"I was a little kid, and I was *alone*. I was stuck in the house with my dead grandmother, hoping she wouldn't start to stink, or come back to life in the middle of the night like a zombie, thinking, 'Oh, it'll all work out somehow.' Well, guess what—it *didn't*. Not until I met you."

Chela was shaking, her sobs filling the room. The eleven-year-old inside her had never died. Our eleven-year-olds never do.

"*Shhhh* . . . sweetheart, come here . . . ," I said, reaching for her.

Chela rushed to me, folding inside my arms. We rocked on the sofa, both of us flooding in her tears. I'd always avoided holding her before, an invisible boundary. But we had crossed a threshold together, and it was finally all right.

Chela sniffed, wiping her nose on the sleeve of her T-shirt. "I know you can do it. You can find her, Ten—but not if you quit now. You're the one who's *supposed* to bring her home."

I would have chuckled if I could have. Chela had spent too much time with Dad.

"Like fate?" I said. "Since when do you believe in that?"

"Since you."

Dad cracked his door open when he heard our voices. He peered out at us, looking worried, so I raised my hand to gesture: *We're all right.* Dad silently closed his door again.

I must have been half delirious when I first woke, seeing Chela, because it was close to dawn and I hadn't realized it. The rising sun, not the moon, had shown me Chela's face.

I hugged my daughter, wondering how I'd missed the room's light.

7:30 A.M.

"I don't understand," I said to the speakerphone that was now the center-piece of my dining-room table. "How the fuck did that happen?"

Maybe there's a limit to the bad news we can absorb. I felt nothing except confusion. A heavy sigh flooded the speaker. My father leaned over the table, bracing himself with locked arms, his snowy eyebrows furrowed with outrage.

"No idea," Lieutenant Nelson answered on the phone. "My guy's just saying they lost him. He was released at about five thirty, and now he's in the wind."

He could have been speaking Mandarin. My mind didn't register the words.

"Nobody was following him?" I said.

"Tried to," Nelson said. "He evaded. Had help waiting, my guess. Ditched his cell phone so the FBI couldn't keep him on GPS. He fooled 'em into complacency. The tail was just a precaution—nobody thought he was their guy. His polygraph didn't look right, but his record in South Africa was clean."

My rage erupted, sudden and deep. *"MotherFUCKERS!"*

I picked up the first thing I saw—an empty coffee mug from the Monterey Jazz Festival I'd attended with Alice years before—and threw it against the nearest wall. The mug disintegrated, but I'd hoped for an explosion that would shake the house.

Dad put a firm hand on my shoulder to hold me still.

"His apartment?" Dad said, raising his voice for the phone.

"That's the last place he'd go, but they're keeping an eye on it. Sorry, Preach." A pause. "Sorry, Ten. That's all I've got, and don't expect any more bulletins. The feds just went into strict cover-your-ass mode."

I walked away from the phone. The storm inside me needed somewhere to go, so I paced the living room. Chela and Marcela watched from the outer ring, somber.

The FBI had lost Paki. Nandi's last chance—gone. The best-case scenario was that her father was taking her back to South Africa. Worst-case scenario, Paki's crew had panicked and killed Nandi after the FBI brought him in for questioning. Or after my encounter with Spider. Hell, they might have killed Paki, too. He might have escaped right into a landfill.

Either way, Sofia Maitlin would never see Nandi again.

"What about Spider?" I called to the phone.

"Nothing stateside yet, and I'm hearing there's a shitload of Mhambis in the system in South Africa," Nelson said. "I'll try to narrow it down, but we need a surname."

Maybe Marsha has something by now, I thought without wanting to. I didn't know if I was desperate enough to try to call her, but how much more desperate could I be?

"Least they can't pin this on LAPD," Nelson said, a company man to the core.

The room was silent until the phone spat out a grating busy signal. Dad was closest, so he rested the receiver on the cradle to bring back the quiet.

"Well, *that* bites," Chela said.

My cell phone's battery was nearly dead, so I found the charger and plugged it in before I dialed Rachel Wentz's number. Someone had to tell Maitlin that the FBI had lost their suspect.

The call went directly to voice mail. Before I left a message, I thought better of my plan and hung up. No need to drag Rachel Wentz into a legal nightmare over FBI leaks. They would find out sooner or later.

"*Vamos*, Captain," Marcela said. "Let's you and me cook up some breakfast."

Dad followed her into the kitchen, squeezing my shoulder as he passed me. I tensed, involuntarily shrugging away his touch.

My fingers played with my phone's keypad, ready to dial the number I didn't want to.

My anger was still on the surface, potent as ever. I couldn't make myself call Marsha.

I didn't have to.

The doorbell had rung by the time I got out of the shower.

TWENTY-TWO

8:05 A.M.

Marsha was a spectacle when she showed up on my doorstep with a dozen huge long-stemmed sunflowers, in a strapless summer dress that matched the petals. She looked freshly bathed, without makeup. Her raw beauty was almost enough to make me glad to see her.

"That's funny . . . ," I heard Chela mutter behind me, ". . . she doesn't *look* like a vampire."

Looks can be deceiving, I thought. I finally noticed that Chela had neglected to make it to school by her 7:20 starting time again, but a bigger problem was on my doorstep.

Marsha held the flowers out toward me, but I let her keep them.

"Can we talk like adults?" she said.

I decided not to invite Marsha inside. "Come on in, since you're here," I said instead.

Until the doorbell rang, the family had been waiting for me at the table, my father ready to say grace. A large bowl of scrambled eggs, a plate of turkey bacon, and a pancake stack waited, cooling. I halfheartedly introduced Marsha as an old friend from high school, and she glowed as if we'd thrown a party in her honor. The smile Marcela usually wore for company was absent.

"Sorry to drop in so early," Marsha said. "I see you're having breakfast."

"That'll happen at breakfast time," Marcela said dryly. She was a stickler for propriety—and maybe females can smell trouble from matching chromosomes.

Dad turned on a grin at full wattage, pulling out an empty chair at the head of the table. His eyes lapped up Marsha as if she were a bottle of Ensure. "Join us, miss. Pancakes?"

I'd never seen my father in Mack Daddy mode, but Marcela must have seen Billy Dee in him since he'd been paralyzed in his nursing-home bed. She'd paid him extra attention, so he'd charmed himself out of dying. I wanted to slap Dad for the open yearning in his eyes.

"Oh, I couldn't," Marsha said in a schoolgirl's voice. "I'm just checking on Ten."

"I'm fine," I said.

Her eyes gave me a private glint. "Are you? You seemed a little out of your mind."

My teeth tightened. "Maybe it was an allergic reaction to getting stabbed in the back."

"We're taking good care of Ten," Marcela said. "I just patched him up."

After my shower, Marcela had disinfected and wrapped my injury again, declaring that I'd avoided infection even without stitches or antibiotics—so far. My migraine medicine dulled my back's stinging. Marcela had offered me a painkiller with codeine, but I didn't want to get knocked out. A few hours' sleep had only made me feel like rolling into a grave.

I made no move to relieve Marsha of her flowers, so Dad took them instead. He handed them over to Marcela, who took them to the kitchen after giving him a chilly look.

"Come on, sit," Dad said to Marsha. "A friend of Ten's is like family."

"Well, if you're sure there's enough food . . . ," Marsha said, taking her seat.

Chela glanced back and forth between me and Marsha, deeply amused.

"Let's all bow our heads," Dad said, and inclined his head for grace.

All heads went down except for Marsha's—and mine. She mouthed *We need to talk.*

"Dear Lord . . . ," Dad began. "Our hearts are heavy as we share your bounty this morning. A child is away from home and needs your guiding hand . . ."

Let me explain, Marsha mouthed at me. I raised a silent finger to my lips: *Shhhhh.*

Marcela's evil eye shamed Marsha into finally lowering her head. Chela had to curl her lips tightly to keep from laughing.

". . . Please watch over little Nandi, and guide Tennyson, Lord," Dad went on. "We don't always understand your plan, but we know you have one for us all . . ."

Marcela broke in: "Yes, *Dios,* and please protect us from the forces of Satan, in whatever form they may take." I remembered my Sunday school lessons about how much God hates lies.

I surprised myself by joining the prayer. "And help us learn the whole truth," I said. "Help us see past falsehoods."

Dad glanced up at me, surprised and moved. "Well, amen!"

The food blessed, we ate.

8:31 A.M.

"You have a beautiful family, Ten. Chela's a triumph. I mean that. Congratulations."

Marsha walked to my corner desk after touring my screening room—or, I should say, Alice's screening room. Now it was my office, with a screen more than a hundred inches tall and nearly two hundred across when I needed entertaining. Alice used to host elaborate Oscar parties, as commemorated by rows of signed head shots decorating the walls. The only people I shared the big screen with were Dad, Chela, and Marcela. And April. I wondered if I'd gone home with the wrong woman on Monday.

"Is that really Sidney Poitier's autograph?" Marsha said, pointing to the photo above me.

I ignored Marsha's small talk. "How'd you get the gun into the club?"

"Pieces," Marsha said. Although there were two rows of movie-style seating to choose from, Marsha sat cross-legged on the carpeted floor, bunching her dress between her legs to be demure. "It's ceramic, not metal. And ceramic rounds can make decent earrings."

No wonder her earrings had been so hideous. Function, not fashion.

"And you didn't see a need to tell your partner," I said.

"I said I wouldn't tell you everything."

That was true, at least.

Marsha reached into her cheerful straw handbag and pulled out a wad of paper she unfolded twice. She laid about four creased pages on my desk beside my hands. The bad photocopies were typewritten, splotched with black marks.

"What's this?" I said.

"An apology." Then it was Marsha's turn to raise her finger to her lips: *Shhhhh.*

"What's wrong? You don't want Grandma to hear?"

Marsha showed me her right ear, then her left. No earpiece. "I'm not worried about Grandma." She indicated the pages. "Just accept my apology, please."

I started reading past the bars of solid black ink obscuring the text. Nearly half of the text was marked out, including the title at the top of the first page, so I could make out only snippets. *". . . alternately called Kingdom of Heaven, according to [DELETED], who was introduced to members of the criminal organization by [DELETED]. [DELETED] . . . has confirmed that [DELETED] met with Pakistani operatives with ties to Al Qaeda to discuss the formation of a terror cell within the United States . . ."*

I sat up straight in my office chair. "You were already investigating—"

Marsha shook her head, firmly. Her shake said *Not here.*

"I did a bad thing yesterday," Marsha said, although there were no apologies in her eyes; she was role-playing, but not for me. Had someone bugged my house? Marsha cooed, "I can't stand it when we fight, Ten. Let's take a drive together. Let's talk."

"Only if you have something to say."

"Plenty, sweetness," Marsha said.

❖   ❖   ❖

8:45 A.M.

I took Dad's laptop and my bag of supplies, including my phone charger, although I was in too much of a hurry to pull together a disguise beyond a baseball cap and sunglasses. The paparazzi had moved on to fresher blood, so no one waited in my yard.

Mrs. Katz was weeding her roses in her robe, but she came to attention when she saw me.

"Hello, Mrs. Katz," I said, waving to let her know I'd caught her staring.

Instead of answering, she pulled a disposable camera out of her robe pocket and snapped my picture. And returned to her gardening.

"Happy birthday!" I called to her. "Try the *Enquirer* first!" Only then did I notice that Marsha had turned her face slightly away the instant the camera emerged. Mrs. Katz could have caught nothing but a blur. Nice reflexes.

I headed for my Corvette, but Marsha grabbed my hand to stop me. "My car," she said, gently tugging me toward her sun-faded rose Toyota Camry. The car was practically invisible.

In fewer than twenty-four hours, in the chill of a federal holding cell, I would be asked to explain why I climbed into Marsha's car. The better question was *Why not?*

I was about to learn if Nandi's kidnappers had made further contact, or if we'd been played. The abductors might have split town with or without Nandi, using the delayed drop-off as a ruse to try to get a head start before the FBI started looking hard. After the incidents with Spider and Paki, it might be too late to bring Nandi home, but at least I might learn what had happened. Maybe I could give Sofia Maitlin that much, anyway.

And it might not be too late for Nandi. That's why I got into Marsha's car.

That's why the day took me where it did.

"They're supposed to be terrorists . . . ?" I said. After years of Christmas-light terror alerts, I was skeptical.

"This conversation is extremely illegal, Ten," Marsha said.

"And?"

Yeah, that's exactly what I said. That's where my head was that day.

"Fair warning, that's all," Marsha sighed. "Kingdom of Heaven's only ideology is the worship of green, but they cast a wide net. They're creative when it comes to making new friends. They've set up international shell companies like mushroom sprouts."

"So they're not just gangbangers from South Africa?"

"No, they're not. All immigrant groups bring crime with them. The Italians, Koreans, Chinese, Japanese, Mexicans . . . ask the Native Americans and they'll probably talk about the Pilgrim Mafia. At first, it's all just criminals organizing to stay out of each other's way, but they eventually evolve to share political coverage and information resources. The Kingdom followed this model: It's like a small multinational now. Actually, probably not so small. Some of the leadership is still in SA, but Umbuso Izulu is only the brand name."

I flipped through the pages she had given me.

". . . *[DELETED] has long purported that Kingdom of Heaven's smuggling operation, based at the [DELETED], has successfully smuggled tens of millions of dollars' worth of weapons and drugs over U.S. borders . . . [DELETED] first proposed a partnership between the Kingdom of Heaven and Al Qaeda to bring biological weapons through Los Angeles . . .*"

"How firm is the Al Qaeda tie?" I said. "Or is it speculation?"

"They're smugglers, and they're damn good at it, so that's enough to get our attention. We've had a lot of chatter in the past week. Maybe it was just about the kidnapping, but we're not sure. We don't like not being sure."

Marsha was suddenly using the word *we*, like Maitlin had when she invited me back into the investigation. Marsha's *we* didn't include me, but maybe she was opening a window.

I tested the fresh air. "What were we really doing yesterday?" I said.

"Looking for a trail to the Kingdom of Heaven. We have mutual interests, Ten."

"And the Girl Scout who wanted to do a good deed? Isn't that what you said when you bared your soul to me yesterday? That was a good moment for you, by the way."

"Who says it's not both?" she said. "Nandi's a two-year-old girl. I used to be one, too."

"How did you end up . . . ?" I didn't finish. The woman in my car had banished the shy, sweet-faced girl I'd known in high school. "You were all set to be an actress."

"I *am* an actress, as you might have noticed. Are you ready to focus?"

"Promise me you didn't know," I said.

"Know what?" Marsha sounded flustered.

"You didn't know Nandi was about to get grabbed."

"Of course I didn't know! You honestly think I would sit back and let that happen?"

You might, if you thought it would get you closer to your targets. I thought. All I knew for certain was that I couldn't believe her. But I thought there was a chance I could, just once.

"Do you know where Nandi is?" I said.

"If I knew where she was, we'd be there now."

The might of Marsha's bosses hadn't done any better than we had, and neither had the FBI. The growing futility of our mission deadened my blood.

"I heard about Paki," Marsha said, reading my face. "Nelson's a fool for calling you on your landline. But I guess he's a big boy."

Marsha was still monitoring my phones, but it seemed pointless to nag.

"Who else has me wired?" I said.

"Maybe that group we affectionately refer to as the Cowboys In Action. And I'd bet you're still on the FBI's radar," Marsha said. "Nelson's a pawn. His FBI source isn't telling him everything. They're giving you the rope to hang yourself."

"I don't get it," I said. "With Paki taking off, how can they think I'm a suspect?"

Marsha chuckled, shaking her head. "You're screwing with their case. That's enough. Do I know for sure they've got your house wired? Maybe not. But why take the chance?"

I hoped she was wrong. I could imagine breaking Nelson's nose someday, but I'd hate to see him blow his career because Dad had asked him for a favor.

"So, Mr. Sensitive . . . ," Marsha teased me. "Do you see now why I couldn't tell you everything? And why I sure as hell can't tell you more?"

"Maybe," I said. "Where was fucking me in your plan? What did that get you?"

"Orgasms," she said. "What did it get you?"

"This is about trust, Marsha."

"In my line of work, there's no such thing. Take it or leave it."

"Who was the Asian man?" I said softly, her last chance.

"Listen to you! Are we back in high school?"

"I saw you following him, Marsha. You took his picture."

"He's a figment of a sleep-deprived imagination," she said. "I didn't notice any Asian guy, Ten, or *any* other guy except Spider. I saw a long line for the bathroom, *darling*. I remembered there was another bathroom up front, but once I got closer I could tell it was more packed out there. I gave up. I had to go so badly, I nearly pissed on myself when some fool stranded me on an empty street without a car. End of story."

I didn't quite believe her, but most of me wanted to. I felt my face coloring, warm.

"Which reminds me . . . ," Marsha said, her dark eyes steady. Her voice was as calm as her eyes. "If you leave me stranded again, I might shoot you. Pulling that trigger would be a waste beyond words, and I'd probably feel really bad about it later, but I'm just warning you, Ten: I *might*. That was a bullshit move. And unprofessional as hell. You could have gotten me killed."

She was right. Dad had told me stories about soldiers getting fragged for less.

"I thought you said this was an apology," I said, touching her cheek.

Marsha didn't move away. "I suck at apologies."

"Me, too," I said. "Sorry I left you. It won't happen again."

"And . . . ?" Marsha prompted.

"Thank you for last night." I lifted her right hand from the steering wheel, and brushed my lips against her knuckles. "I owe you my life."

She smiled. "That's what friends are for."

She stopped at the red light. I leaned over to kiss her lips, my fingers playing like moths' wings against the length of her neck. Her tongue was fresh maple syrup. Her heart pulsed as her neck fell back against the headrest. Marsha's taste was genuine. Her breath couldn't lie. Her skin was all I really knew.

"Let's find our little girl," I said, cupping her chin in my palm.

"Tennyson Hardwick, you stole the words out of my mouth."

The light turned green. Marsha drove.

The FBI was probably staking out Paki's apartment, and I had no doubt I would go to jail if I got caught there. So naturally, Marsha and I zipped straight down Interstate 5 for San Diego.

I wasn't filled with hope, but desperation moves were better than no moves at all.

Spider wasn't going to stick his head up again. If I could have cloned myself, I would have checked out South African Sun on Melrose, the limo company with the mysteriously missing driver, and a dozen other leads, including Simon—but going after Paki felt like the best move. The FBI had lost Paki, so he was fair game. If I got into Paki's apartment, I might find something the FBI didn't know it was looking for.

Paki was the key, but not just because of whatever connection he had to the abductors, or Kingdom of Heaven—Paki was a piece to an even bigger puzzle that bothered me more and more in new daylight. Was he involved? Planned all of this from the beginning? Made it seem he only wanted passage to America, using Maitlin's lawyers to get him a visa, just to hook up with his home boys and snatch his own child? Christ, he would have had every opportunity to scope out her mansion, detect her weaknesses, even help plan the party. This was a nightmare.

But something was still missing.

Maybe Maitlin and her husband, Alec, had a secret relationship with Kingdom of Heaven. Could Alec's shipping connections be of use to the international smuggling operation Marsha had spoken of? Maybe the abduction was like the nightclub killing my father had described—an internal squabble that veered out of control. What wasn't I seeing?

Whatever the whole truth was, I hoped it wouldn't get me killed.

"You say Kingdom of Heaven has international ties . . . ," I said. "They approached someone from Pakistan. You mentioned Zimbabwe. Which other countries are they tied to?"

"You already know more than you're supposed to," she said. "Don't push it."

"I'm trying to crack this thing, Marsha."

"I'm helping you crack it—but it's *need* to know. This isn't Spies 'R' Us."

"What about Greece?"

"Oh, I get it—you name every country, and I eliminate them one at a time?"

"I'm not playing games, Marsha. Sofia's husband is Greek. He's in shipping. Maybe something ties him to the smuggling. What if there's a connection?"

Marsha hid a bemused smile by turning away from me, suddenly fascinated by the freeway as we drove. "I love the way you think, Tennyson Hardwick," she said. "But you're getting colder, not warmer. Nothing in Greece."

"If I can believe you."

"Throwing darts at the map won't help us find Nandi. You're wondering about Alec Dimitrakos? I wondered, too. Nothing points to him having ties to the Kingdom."

Maybe, I thought. Maybe.

"My guess is . . . ," Marsha went on after a pause. "The abduction wasn't a part of the larger scheme of things. Limited international involvement. Paki just has friends in low places."

"They sure took their time to look his way," I said.

"So I noticed. But as a wise man once told me, I'll cut Maitlin some slack. This is an emotional time. You think she's in on it somehow?"

It wasn't that. Not exactly. But I couldn't find words for it.

"I hope they don't have a guy inside Paki's place," I said, imagining John Travolta sitting on the toilet in *Pulp Fiction* while Bruce Willis snuck back into his apartment.

"That would *definitely* be inconvenient," Marsha said. "I'm just hoping their guys are easy to make. I'm pretty good at sniffing out feds."

"You and that dress might make a good decoy."

Marsha's skin was bare above her breastbone except for a string tied around her neck, so she wasn't wearing a bra. She looked like dark chocolate in a golden wrapper. No wonder my father had gawked.

"Thanks for the compliment, baby, but the bureau's not that easy," Marsha said.

TWENTY-THREE

We caught some traffic during our one-hundred-plus–mile drive down Interstate 5, but it gave us time to research.

While Marsha drove, Google Earth on my iPhone showed us that Paki's "apartment" was a small guest cottage on the property behind a two-story historical Mediterranean in North Park. The view on my screen was crisp enough to show me a potted plant on the house's windowsill.

"Shit," I said, and held my screen up for Marsha to see.

"Big fun now," Marsha said. The last time she'd mentioned *fun,* I'd nearly died.

I'd hoped Paki lived in a larger apartment building, which would have made it easier to blend in as a resident. I liked the shaded yard's cover of the guesthouse, keeping it barely in view from the photo, but we had to expect surveillance from the front and the rear, so it would be harder to get close without being noticed.

"A couple of calls from a throwaway phone . . . a few anonymous Paki sightings might keep the boys busy for a while," Marsha said. "They might pull out, if they're at the house."

I glanced at her, hoping that was a joke. "We're on the same team, Marsha. We're all trying to find Nandi. We can't muddy the FBI's investigation—I just want a peek around."

Not to mention that it sounds like a sure ticket to a perp walk.

Marsha shrugged. "Sorry. Habit."

"Who belongs on a quiet residential street on a weekday morning? Repairmen . . ."

"You need a marked truck or a van to sell that," she said. "And a uniform. No time."

We passed a large nursery on the side of the freeway, and the answer came to me in a mental lightning bolt. "Gardeners!"

Marsha gave me a look of delight, like a teacher watching her favorite student graduate.

"Genius," she said.

In a tough economy, day laborers are easy to find. All we'd have to do was swing by Home Depot and recruit a work crew. We would descend on Paki's house as a team of gardeners, in the FBI's plain view. If someone was at home in the main house to challenge us, we could put our gardening team to work at a neighbor's house. At least it gave us a reason to be nearby. Close enough to peel off to the guesthouse.

Easy money for a gardening crew. Free landscaping for a homeowner. Everybody wins.

While I drove, Marsha climbed into the backseat to change into a T-shirt and jeans from her mobile closet, a garment bag she apparently took everywhere, beside the black backpack she'd called her "burglary kit."

Her lovely sundress had been for my eyes only. I glimpsed skin as she put on her bra. If the drivers near us were paying attention, they got a peep show. Their loss if they missed it.

We tried a Home Depot about ten minutes from Paki's address, and hit the Lotto. At least two dozen workers waited in the slim shade of an awning, most of them Latino, likely Mexican, a couple of them black. A half dozen of the men wore the orange shirts of professional gardeners, and others were in street clothes.

Best of all, one of the men was in the driver's seat of a large white pickup truck. Tejano music played softly from the truck's open windows.

About time I caught a fucking break, I thought.

My Spanish would have been good enough to get by, but Marsha took the lead with rapid Spanish spoken with an accent that sounded

Mexican when she hopped out of her car to talk to the driver. He was about sixty and had a salt-and-pepper mustache and two days' worth of gray stubble. He told her his name was Demetrio.

"We've got a job we want done in a hurry," she told him in Spanish. "We need six or seven guys. You'll be back in a couple of hours. Ten bucks an hour. You'll get an extra hundred for driving them and for using your tools."

Demetrio nodded. "*¿Cual hombres?*" he said. Which men?

I sighed, scanning the group of eager workers who were gathering closer. Some were as young as sixteen, and one looked as old as seventy, their faces broiled red-brown. The worse the economy got, the bigger the knots of waiting workers. I felt uncomfortable about making the men unknowing players in our private drama, but Marsha could barely keep from smiling. For her, it was just another day at the office.

"Orange shirts," I said, pointing out six men in orange shirts. "You, brother. *Tú. Tú. Tú. Tú. Y tú también.*"

Most of the men hopped grinning into the truck bed, but a white-haired man who looked like he was in his fifties corrected me as he walked past me: "*Usted,*" he said, checking for insolence in my eyes. "Not *tú.*"

"*Lo siento, señor,*" I apologized. "*Perdóname.*"

I'd been too informal with him. In his place, my father would have jumped on me, too.

The black man bumped my fist as he climbed in. "Thanks, man. Lost my damn job."

"Glad to help, bruh," I said.

We had a crew.

Damn, we're good, I thought. *Almost scary good.* I'd known how easy it was to manipulate people as an actor, a sex worker, and a private detective, but Marsha was a master. And I was learning to think just like her.

When I offered to trade Demetrio my fresh white T-shirt for his orange work shirt, he looked confused, but was happy to oblige the boss. His shirt was damp with warm perspiration, giving me the scent of his long day. Perfect protective coloration. If someone was going to stand out, I didn't want it to be me.

I took the wheel of Marsha's car, driving slowly so she wouldn't lose our truckload of gardeners while they followed us to Paki's house. I kept them in the rearview mirror.

"If the FBI's inside the guesthouse, we're screwed, of course," I told Marsha.

"But I'm thinking they're outside, or maybe inside the main house. I'd pick a second-story window. Or maybe across the street, or in a neighbor's yard. Walking or jogging up and down the sidewalk. We're looking for a man or woman, young or older. Could be anybody."

"Who are you in all this?" I said. "Sorry, but you don't look like a gardener."

"If anyone asks, I'm the supervisor," she said. "Somebody inside the house challenges us, we're at the wrong address. We find a time to break for the guesthouse."

"The rear," I said. "We'll use the shade for cover and figure out our way in."

"Tennyson Hardwick, I could get used to working with you." Her sweet smile made me want to agree with her. I'd seen that smile in bed, in the moments before she went to sleep.

"Let's just try to get this one right," I said.

The long gravel driveway at Paki's house, as I'd hoped, was empty. The peach-colored house sat on the corner as vividly as its photograph, unchanged. A driveway led to a carport on the side of the house. Beyond that, the darkened guest cottage was nestled in trees.

Since we had the truck behind us, we pulled up to the curb. No explanations necessary.

Marsha and I barked orders: Trim the swath of grass in the front yard. Clip the hedges. Weed the flower bed. The house already looked well landscaped, but a gardener's work is never done. Suddenly, the yard was a hive, orange-shirted bees buzzing everywhere.

The sidewalk was also busy with pedestrians, another break in our favor. There were so many college students, young mothers, and joggers of all ethnicities on the street, we probably didn't need the extra cast. But with so much at stake, why not?

Apparently empty house. Busy neighborhood. *We're cool again, God. Throw a big break my way with Nandi, and I'll be first in line at church on Sunday.*

"Think I've got our guy . . . ," Marsha said, lips barely moving as we surveyed the workers from where we were leaning against the bed of the truck. "One of them, anyway."

"Is it a problem?"

"Actually, we're good. Seven o'clock," she said, pretending to wipe dirt from my shoulders. "Behind us. Waxing the black Jeep Grand Cherokee across the street. Dodgers cap. Where we're parked, we've obstructed part of his view, so he might change his vantage point. Now's a good time to make our move."

I glanced into the bed of the truck and pulled out a rake, my eyes carefully low. "Got it. I'll linger near the backyard. You ease your way back. Tell the guys to stay up front."

"Good luck, Ten," Marsha said. A gentle plaintiveness in her voice made me give her a long look. *She thinks we're wasting our time,* I realized. It stung, hard. But most of the sting came from knowing she might be right.

Rake in hand, my head covered in an olive drab gardener's cap with long ear flaps, I enlisted in my orange-shirted army.

Demetrio wandered toward the carport and backyard with his weed cutter as he trimmed the grass near the flower bed against the house, but I redirected him. "In the front only. I'll take a look around back," I told him in Spanish. Or close enough. Demetrio changed direction.

I took a last glance at the visible windows to make sure no one was watching me. Then I turned slightly to nod to Marsha. *I'm going in.*

I walked down the gravel driveway at a stroll, although I wanted to run.

A Siamese kitten crouched in the carport leaped in my path, and I almost jumped. The cat bolted into hiding. My heart was racing just like it had at Club Skylight.

I *needed* to find something, and was terrified I wouldn't.

The cottage looked small, maybe six hundred square feet, with quaint detailing that matched the main house's architecture. It had its own porch and a fairly large picture window, curtains closed. I ignored the front door and slipped around a corner, toward the back.

The cottage was built so close to the neighbor's adjoining fence that the bougainvillea bushes growing through it were a thorny passage. One look at the tangle, and I almost changed my mind. But I could see a small jalousie window, already half open, that would be easy enough to remove if I got close. Up front, I was more likely to be caught.

At least the bougainvillea would make it impossible to conduct surveillance from the rear. Even the main house's second story was obscured by a tall oak near the guesthouse, so I was already invisible. I decided to stay that way.

"You have *got* to be kidding me," Marsha muttered beside me, eyeing the bougainvillea.

I wished I'd brought hedge clippers, but I used my rake to lift a heavy bougainvillea branch whose thorns were nearly the size of roofing nails. Much of the barrier went up with the branch. "Keep this out of my way, and I'm in," I said.

Marsha took over the rake, and I squeezed behind the house to the window. At the window, I reached into my back pocket and pulled out the surgical gloves Marsha had given me from her goodie bag. Gloves on, I was ready to go in.

"Don't toss those gloves here," Marsha said. "They can get fingerprints from *inside*."

Good to know.

Jalousie windows are great for letting in a breeze, but they're a burglar's wet dream. The windows were partially open, so I started working on the glass panels, fast. Some were looser than others, but one at a time the slender panes slid out.

In less than two minutes, there was nothing but a screen in my way. My knife took care of that. I looked back at Marsha, who was straining from the weight of the branch on her rake.

"I'm in," I said. "What about you?"

"Just go," she said. "I'll figure it out."

The bathroom window was narrow, but I was slender enough to fit. A small boulder behind the house gave me enough height to swing one leg into the blue-tile bathroom, and minor contortionism put my feet on the floor. Clowns on the bathroom's wallpaper. Ugh.

My heartbeat nearly drowned out the quiet.

I was caught already if there were agents inside, so I didn't want any surprises. It's not smart to sneak up on people with guns.

"Hello?" I called. No answer.

Already, signs of the FBI's search were obvious. The small bathroom's medicine cabinet was wide open, nearly emptied, and a few over-the-counter medication bottles lay in the sink. Tylenol. Claritin. A half-used, neatly rolled tube of Crest toothpaste. A half-used, neatly rolled tube of Preparation H. Good to know both ends were getting serviced. The bathtub was filled with hand towels from an emptied cabinet on the wall above the toilet.

What the hell are you going to find that they didn't? my Evil Voice taunted.

Even in my gigolo days, when I was invited into homes by my clients, I felt like an intruder because of the boyfriend, fiancé, or husband who had no idea I was his guest. I learned to study my clients from their homes to help create a better fantasy man for them.

Paki's apartment left him a mystery to me. He might be a neat freak, or a slob, but the FBI's souvenirs made it hard to tell, except that there were no dirty clothes on the floor or dirty dishes in his kitchen sink.

I guessed that the apartment must have come furnished, because the furniture was sturdy but old, like a grandparent's home. Except for the futon, the pieces matched, had been carefully selected, and had been in the house a long time. The carpet was old, slightly stained beneath the newspaper that covered the living room floor. The FBI had apparently sorted through a stack of the *L.A. Times*. Maitlin had given Paki a new start in life, but it was modest.

Is that what happened? She let you visit her house, and you started wanting more?

Nothing was framed on the walls, except a faded Norman Rockwell print of a kid in a dentist's chair that I was sure had come with the room. The cottage was a studio, not a one-bedroom, so Paki's futon was propped up against the wall as a sofa. He had a night table on one side of the futon, and a small computer desk on the other. The computer, of course, was gone. Only the monitor and printer remained.

The futon faced a twenty-seven-inch television on a TV table against the opposite wall, next to the picture window. Paki probably kept the curtains closed to see the picture better, without too much light. The curtains were heavy, only slightly frayed at the floor. I was glad the curtains were closed, so I could walk without worrying about the window.

Paki was a soccer fan. A yellow jersey from Cape Town's Santos team lay across the arm of his futon, and I noticed a soccer magazine on his dinette table. Otherwise, the table was clear except for an apple. The apartment had been cleaned out to the bone.

"Not much to it, is there?" Marsha said.

Her voice had the too-gentle quality I had noticed before. Her voice said, *Well, Ten, now it's time to face facts . . .* Marsha's hair was disheveled, and I saw three parallel scratch marks across her forehead. And a tiny bead of blood.

"The bush got you," I said. "You're bleeding."

"I am?" she said, surprised. "Where?"

With my index finger, I gently dabbed the spot. No more blood came. I laid her blood on my tongue. The sharp taste melted down my throat and was gone.

"All better," I said. It had been several days since Marsha and I had spent a night together, I realized. I couldn't remember how long, but it was too long.

"Fuck it, we leave through the front door," Marsha said. Beat. "When we're done."

The search, to her, was an afterthought. Meaning: *We can use the front door after you finally realize there was nothing you could have done for Nandi from the instant you let her go.*

The day was caving in. The growling of strangers' gardening tools sounded absurd.

But for twenty minutes, we looked wherever we could think to look. Every inch was a football field. I couldn't let my eyes miss anything. Trash cans. The closet. Drawers. Cabinets. Under the futon. The TV cabinet. DVD cases. The walls. The refrigerator.

Paki liked to cook. There were no restaurant containers in his fridge, only pots and pans from meals he had fixed for himself on the tiny kitchen's two-burner stove. Fresh milk. Fresh fruit. The rice, flour, and spices from his kitchen cabinets were laid out across the Formica counter. He liked wine—a 2006 California Viognier-Roussanne blend was chilling in the fridge, with four more identical bottles in a wire wine rack on his counter. Good wine.

No junk food. No sweets. Paki's vices weren't culinary.

The refrigerator had a magnet shaped like the South African flag, pinning coupons. A magnet shaped like a bottle of wine, labeled Happy Cellars, pinned nothing. Was it decoration, or had something fallen?

I looked down toward the floor, at the crack between the fridge and the counter. The corner of a photograph was sticking out, so I picked it up. My heart got its hopes up. *Please let this be a photo of Paki posing with Spider outside Spider's house—the address in plain view.*

But it wasn't, of course.

It was a photo of Paki posing with Maitlin, Alec Dimitrakos . . . and Nandi. They were all in swimsuits; the photo had been taken by the pool at Maitlin's house. From Nandi's face, still as pudgy as it had been at the orphanage, I guessed that the photo was taken soon after she arrived in the States. One big happy family. Even Alec was smiling.

I almost kept the photo; once it was in my hand, it took a moment to let it go. I finally slid it under the wine bottle magnet. Then I turned away from the face that haunted me—and maybe would for the rest of my life. Whether or not Paki had been involved in Nandi's abduction, the photo's haunting rightfully belonged to him.

I toured every cranny of Paki's apartment a third time, a fourth. I flipped through his yellow pages to see if he'd scribbled any numbers, or circled any names. I checked the dusty top of his refrigerator for stray scraps of enlightenment. There were no notebooks, no addresses, no telephone numbers. No information.

My father had warned me what Hell would feel like, and Hell was all I found. Denial was lifting like a giant balloon, and reality sat hard in its place. My stomach ached, searing pain. For the first time all morning, the throbbing across my back from Spider's knife was fully awake.

What the fuck are you doing? Wearing bullshit disguises and breaking laws—for what?

Behind me, Marsha sighed. She'd stopped searching ten minutes before I had, and was now merely going through the motions. Reality had hit her much sooner.

"We knew it was a long shot coming after the FBI," she said. "Thorough is their job."

Her condolences didn't unclench my stomach.

"Maybe Paki didn't run," I said. "Maybe his people killed him."

Marsha nodded. "Crossed my mind," she said. "He'd just spent all night with the FBI, and we have no idea what he said. Yeah, maybe the Kingdom got him. But the feds might be following his leads, grabbing Nandi right now. Locking up the bad guys."

"Maybe," I said. Hans Christian Andersen wouldn't have bought that fairy tale.

I hadn't heard from Rachel Wentz or Maitlin all day. Maybe they had finally been silenced, or maybe Maitlin was too distraught to call. It wasn't a good sign if the kidnappers had been out of contact since my confrontation with Spider, with no further proof of life.

My feet needed somewhere to go after pacing tracks in the living room, so I found myself back in the kitchen. Marsha followed. My eyes traveled its surfaces, looking for what I'd missed. I tried not to notice the photo, whether it was a visual hoax or a simple tragedy.

The narrow kitchen was claustrophobic. Two steps in, and there was nowhere else to go.

Beside me, Marsha opened the refrigerator. "I'm starving," she said. She pulled out the bottle of wine and studied it. "Mmmmm. And thirsty, come to think of it."

I didn't want to eat Paki's food or drink his wine, but Marsha started searching through the assortment of kitchen supplies on the counter and in the drawers. She found a corkscrew.

"Ten, listen . . . ," she began in her *woe-is-you* voice. "We can't stay here much longer. I told the gardeners to leave when they were done, but someone might come looking."

"I know," I said.

Marsha opened the cabinet, where a few cheap dishes remained. She found two wineglasses and pulled them out. I couldn't help one last peek high on my toes to see if I'd overlooked any papers. But the cabinet was nearly bare. I felt around, and nothing was hidden.

"Ten, this happened *despite* your involvement, not because of it," she said. "You're good—I mean *really* good. You're quick. Resourceful. You've given Nandi everything you have. You're as good as anyone I've worked with—people with real training. So it's getting more and more unbearable for me to watch you beat yourself up."

She handed me the chilled bottle, and the corkscrew. My fingers went to work without my mind engaging. I've opened more bottles of wine than I can count, so my *pop* was quick and efficient.

"None of it brought Nandi home," I said.

"She may still come home. I never say never. Nothing is ever exactly what it seems."

My throat and tongue were dry. Since the wineglasses were set up on the counter, I poured one glass half full and gave it to Marsha. She held her glass, waiting for me to pour mine. I wasn't in the mood for celebrating, and alcohol wouldn't knock Nandi out of my head. But I splashed wine into my glass to be sociable.

"A small toast?" Marsha said.

"To what?"

"To hope."

Who can refuse a toast to hope? I clinked my glass against hers, gently, and sipped.

My first thought was, *Good wine*. Light and crisp. Sweet tropical citrus.

Then I sipped again, and the world rocked still. I took a third sip to be sure. The soles of my feet stung, as if I'd immersed them in ice.

"Holy *shit*," I said. I picked up the wine bottle again to stare at the label.

"Yeah—it's great," Marsha said, misunderstanding my excitement. "Let's take a bottle."

The light blue label was simply designed, and was marked HAPPY CELLARS—PASO ROBLES—2006.

The bright yellow smiley face on the label looked hand sketched. The bottle confused me. I sniffed the mouth, trying to understand. What was it that had lingered after the citrus faded? A little something vintners call "minerality." Delicious. Rare.

"Wine connoisseurs turn me on," Marsha said. "What'd you find? Hidden floral notes?"

I held up my hand to stop her jokes. I needed to think.

Finally, Marsha realized my mind was somewhere else. "What's going on?"

"I know this wine," I said. "I've had it before. In South Africa."

Marsha took the bottle and read the label. "It's a California wine."

"I know. That's what I don't get. But I've had *this* wine, with Sofia. While we were in Cape Town. Sofia Maitlin gave me a sip. It was local, from Stellenbosch. I'm sure of it."

Slowly, Marsha's face changed as she lowered the bottle, all playfulness fleeing her overly bright eyes. "Why does a South African wine have a California label?" she said.

"I'm not sure," I said.

"Could this . . . Happy Cellars be rebottling it? Why?"

"I don't know."

My fingers trembling, I pulled out my iPhone to do a quick Google search on Happy Cellars, in Paso Robles. Was it even a real winery?

It was. There weren't many listings, but I got a few bloggers singing its praises. *Best wine on our trip to Paso! I wish I could find it in L.A.!* crowed a woman who called herself Biker Gal. Happy Cellars had its own cheap website, probably from a free host. No flashing images or elaborate photography, just a home page with a photo of a vineyard and the winery's address in Paso Robles. No mention of South Africa. I scrolled through the site, looking for any winery employees. None was mentioned. No faces.

"So you're saying . . . this South African wine is in a Paso Robles bottle? At a vineyard called Happy Cellars?" Marsha said. "I'm still trying to wrap my mind around this."

I shook my head, frustrated. "I don't know. Maybe it's locally grown—but if it is, they're re-creating the conditions exactly. Probably using the same winemaker."

"I'm still confused, Ten."

My heart raced as my mind put it together. "A winemaker is like a chef. You can give ten different winemakers the same raw ingredients, grapes grown and stored in identical conditions, and they'll create ten different bottles of wine. A winemaker's creation is like a signature." Alice had taught me that, once upon a time. We had spent many lazy hours in Cape Town's wine country.

"So this wine has a South African winemaker's signature," Marsha said.

"Yes."

"You're sure?"

"There's a winery in Cape Town that uses concrete aging bins. They are more temperamental than steel drums, but they *breathe*. I'd have to taste them side by side to be sure, but . . ." Revelation swamped me. "Shit! Paki and Sofia were drinking this wine at Nandi's party. The bottle was on the table. I don't know if it was her bottle or Paki's, but I remember seeing it."

Marsha went silent, thoughtful, while I went to the wine rack to grab one of the other bottles. Same wine, same vineyard, same vintage. Had Paki gone on a spending spree?

"Wine like this . . . maybe twenty dollars a bottle?" I guessed. "It's not cheap. Paki's living on a shoestring, working as a mechanic, and he's gonna drop a hundred bucks or more on wine? Plus . . . it's a boutique winery. Paso's wine country. If you live in the Bay Area, you drive up to Napa. If you live in L.A., you drive to Paso, stay in a B and B, go from vineyard to vineyard. Most people probably buy from the source."

Unless Paki has a friend who works there, I thought.

"A gift from Sofia Maitlin?" Marsha guessed.

"Maybe, but . . . if the winemaker is South African . . ."

". . . Paki might know him," Marsha finished. She sounded awed.

"Paso Robles," I said. "If Paki's not dead, maybe that's where he ran."

Paso Robles was a four-hour drive from Los Angeles, fairly secluded, with acre after acre of grapevines. Farmers with lots of large storehouses. Barns. Privacy.

Maybe that's where they're holding Nandi. To my surprise, hope was still alive. Marsha stared at me, nearly gape jawed. "You put that together from the *taste*?"

"We need to go to Paso."

Marsha backed up two steps, blocking the kitchen doorway. "Ten, wait . . ."

"I know it's a six-hour drive from here, but this one goes to my gut."

"I need you to take a deep breath and think clearly," Marsha said, like a hypnotist.

"Wait—one minute I'm as good as anyone you've worked with, and now . . . what? You think I'm way off base? Look at the pieces: Cape Town. A winemaker. Paso Robles."

Marsha reached slowly behind her back. I hoped she was about to call in the Marines.

Instead, she pulled out her Beretta. And pointed it squarely at the center of my chest.

My mind, which had been racing, came to a dead stop. I couldn't have said anything if I'd wanted to. Marsha had the gun; it was her turn to talk.

"Put down the wine bottle, Ten," Marsha said. "Kick your pistol to me."

Shitshitshitshitshitshitshit.

"Look into my eyes," she said, "and tell me if I'm bluffing."

Marsha's eyes had been replaced by the eyes of someone I had never met.

She had moved to the doorway to stay out of my reach, I realized. Only an amateur points a gun in close quarters.

If I tried throwing the bottle at her, Marsha would shoot me as I raised my arm. I set the bottle down on the counter so hard that it splashed. I might not be able to hurt her with a glare, but I did my best. My eyes were seeing blood.

"Now the Beretta," she said. "I'm sorry, Ten."

I wanted to bang my head against the wall. How could I have been so stupid?

My hands slowly brought my gun out of my pants. I squatted to lay it gently on the linoleum and stepped back. With my toe, I kicked it in her direction. The Beretta Marsha had lent me slid straight to her feet, as if it had a homing device. She picked it up without taking her eyes off me, shoving it into her jeans with her free hand.

"I'm just trying to find a little girl," said an old man's voice that was mine.

"Put your hands on the counter," Marsha said, as if I hadn't spoken. She reached into another pocket, and I heard the all-too-familiar jingling of handcuffs.

In Paki's kitchen, I assumed the position. Through the kitchen window, the bright bougainvillea blossoms lied and said everything was fine.

"*Shit*, Marsha, *come on!*" I said. "This isn't right. You know it isn't."

Marsha tossed the handcuffs toward me, but I refused to catch them. They clattered to the floor behind me.

"Pick them up," Marsha said, slowly and carefully. "Hook one wrist, put your hands behind your back, hook the other."

"I want my lawyer."

"*DO IT!*" Marsha roared. Was her gun hand shaking slightly?

I didn't want to test Marsha's nerve, so I cuffed myself. I had done that more times than I could count, too—but usually in the bedroom.

"This is entrapment," I said. "*You* texted *me* and said you could help me."

Once I was cuffed, some of the armor faded from Marsha's eyes. She let her gun hand relax, dropping slightly. "Ten . . . I told you, I'm not a cop. I'm not FBI. This sucks on your end, but it's not much better on mine. I'm sorry, but I can't let you go to Paso."

Getting arrested would have been a nightmare, but the nightmare was getting deeper. Anger made me want to try something desperate: charge at her with my shoulder; a long, sliding side kick . . . but I talked myself down. Only confusion remained.

"Why?" I said, feeling foolish for expecting anything like the truth.

Marsha pursed her lips, blinking. She was conflicted, or wanted me to think she was.

"Nandi is an abduction case, and it breaks my heart," she said. "But my investigation is national security. If I blow a lead, thousands could die."

"If you don't care about one, you can't care about 'thousands.'" I started to shift my weight to try hooking a chair with my foot and heaving it up into her face, but even the *thought* triggered her alarms, and her gun hand snapped rigid again, the muzzle staring at my heart.

"Ten," she said. "I really, *really* don't want to shoot you."

But she would. She didn't have to say it. She had killed people before.

"What the hell does it matter to you if I go look for Nandi?" I said.

"It matters," she said. "Your leap helped me bring something very important into focus, an angle that hadn't occurred to us, and we need time to process what it means. We can't send anyone rushing in—not you, not the FBI. We need to take a closer look."

"Even if a little girl dies while you're 'processing'?"

Marsha didn't answer right away. Her eyes were forlorn.

"Yes," she said. "Even if."

TWENTY-FOUR

I work in Hollywood. I've been betrayed by friends, lovers, and strangers. But with Marsha, I'd hit the trifecta.

At gunpoint, she walked me out of the kitchen to Paki's living room. She kept me in the corner of her eye while she peeked out the curtain. The gardeners' machinery had died.

"If I can't call a lawyer, fuck you," I said. "You're not taking me anywhere."

Marsha gave me a baleful look and glanced outside again. Was she waiting for the gardeners to come looking? They were the only people who could tell anyone where I'd been.

"We'll sit tight here for a while," Marsha said. "Until my friends get here. They'll want to meet you and chat about the wine, and you'll have some time to calm down so you don't get hurt." She made it sound like a social occasion.

"In the middle of an FBI stakeout?"

Marsha's eyes flashed. "You don't get it, Ten. Screw the FBI. This is my scene now. I don't want them here, I don't want them in Paso. Your world just changed."

I didn't like the sound of that.

"And then?" I said, my voice dry. "After the chatting is over?"

"That's up to you, sweetness. But I think you need a vacation for a couple of days."

Marsha was planning to debrief me, transport me somewhere, and lock me up. The juvenile part of my mind wondered, *How could she do that to ME?*

And the painful answer was, *With effortless ease.*

"Not without a fight," I said again. "Just know that."

"That could get ugly, Ten."

"That's up to you . . . *sweetness.* And, baby, don't you dare turn your back on me. I can't wait to throw you through that window."

"Thanks for the warning. I'll just have to kneecap you first."

Marsha closed the curtain, never once turning her back as she paced. I wondered how long I had until her backup came knocking on the door. Unless they were already in San Diego, it might take an hour or more. I might still have time to talk my way free.

I stripped the steel out of my voice. "She's a two-year-old girl, scared to death—and she just wants to go home, Marsha," I said.

"You and I both know that Nandi is already dead." The sugar coating was gone.

"Until there's a body, we don't know that."

"She was dead the minute the drop-off went south. And if she wasn't dead then, she was sure as hell dead after Spider made you at the night-club. Your face was on the news, Ten."

"How easy is it to kill a two-year-old kid, Marsha? Could you?"

I almost didn't want to know the answer to the question.

"It would be tough," she conceded.

"Do they plan to kill her? Yeah, maybe. I'm just saying *they might not have done it yet.* She could be in some basement in Paso Robles with Paki, and we still have time to find her!"

"If Nandi's with her birth father, she'll probably be fine."

"*Fine?* Are you crazy?"

"I'm sorry, Ten, but I can't blow a five-year investigation because you think there might be a kid over there—especially if that kid might be dead, or with her dad."

"He helped abduct her! He's not her *dad!*"

My leg mutinied, stepped toward Marsha. She snapped into a two-handed pistol stance. "Sit down," she said. "Slowly. Or you'll never dance at Chela's wedding."

I sat. "This whole time, you never gave a fuck about Nandi," I said.

"Believe me or not, that's not true," she said quietly. Her face was flat, nearly expressionless. She was masking emotions. "I'm only with you today because I wanted to help."

"But you never thought I'd get anywhere, did you? This was just a side adventure for you. Except for that Asian guy at the club, maybe, you've just been marking time. You know what, Marsha? When your friends get here, I'm gonna tell them to go *fuck* themselves. Then, the first chance I get, I'm gonna call the people I know at the *L.A. Times* and see if they want a story on covert intelligence ops being conducted on U.S. soil and involving Kingdom of Heaven."

Maybe it wasn't the right tactic, but the truth was all I had left.

Marsha's frame sagged. "Then you might not get that chance, Ten."

"Do you think anything you threaten me with could be worse than *this*?" I said, shaking the handcuffs behind my back. "Then you haven't learned a damn thing about me."

"You're wrong," Marsha said, blinking. Her eyes looked glassy. "I've learned plenty. And there is worse. You don't want to know how much worse."

"Bring it on, bitch."

This time, Marsha took two strides toward me.

"What?" I said. "You want to fuck me one more time?"

Marsha stopped in her tracks, giving me a sick, almost hopeful, smile. "Wish I could."

"Yeah, baby." My voice was suddenly super sweet, as if my words were poetry. "Just bring that fine chocolate ass over here and let me do that thing—you know, that special thing you like. Let me tie you up and rub you down. I hate it when we fight." I puckered and blew her a poisoned kiss. The scent of her made me feel sick to my stomach. Until that day, I'd never had the taste of hatred in my mouth. "Now I know what a real whore looks like."

Marsha's face flinched. Not much, just a quiver at the edge of one eye, but I saw it.

"It's not personal, Ten. It's my job."

"And you do love your work, don't you?"

"Ten, don't make this harder than it has to be."

"That's up to you. How long before your friends get here?"

Marsha shrugged. "Thirty minutes after I call. Give or take."

Her words roared in my ears. "After you call . . . ? You haven't flipped on your tricorder so your people can hear us?"

Marsha's face was empty. "No."

I took another long breath. "Why not?"

"I don't know." For the first time, Marsha lowered the muzzle, away from my heart.

She was barely five yards from me, and I was fast. In a deadly race, I could have launched at her like a missile. I didn't. The day was coming back to life. I saw a calm, snowy Japanese garden in my mind.

"Don't," I said, trying to help Marsha see my garden, too. "Don't make the call. I was where you are the day Nandi was kidnapped—the boss wanted one thing, but the other thing was right. I should have done what was *right*. Maybe someone in Paso is trying to do what's right, too—and Nandi is still alive."

Marsha didn't answer.

But that was the first moment I knew Nandi still had a chance.

The drive to Paso Robles was six hours from San Diego, back north on Interstate 5, but we decided not to try flying. Even if we arranged a last-minute flight to Paso Robles Municipal, we figured we would still have to rent a car once we got there. Marsha could have called for a helicopter, but claimed she'd "gone black." We were on our own.

My ride in the car with Marsha was tense, mostly silent at first. We were both on our way somewhere we had no business going, with someone we had no business going with. Just being near Marsha pissed me off. We both knew we were better off with backup, but neither of us could call the people we were supposed to. I didn't dare call my father, since the FBI might be bugging my line to set me up for obstruction of justice.

Not ideal circumstances for a rescue attempt.

Marsha drove this time, so I went to work on Google Earth again to try to find a photo of Happy Cellars. The closest satellite image I got, if it was the right place, was a nondescript but large wooden farmhouse on a hill, surrounded by vineyards and at least a half dozen outbuildings. By the time we got to Paso, the shadows would be long.

"How's it look?" Marsha said.

The memory of Marsha holding me at gunpoint made my tongue swell with anger. I had to concentrate to keep a civil tone. "Looks like a big farmhouse, if it's the right place," I said. "More than three thousand square feet. Probably has a big cellar, up on the hill like that. Lots of other little buildings where they could be holding her. Sheds. A barn."

"We have our work cut out for us," Marsha said. "We'll want to separate again."

"Works for me." The farther away I got from Marsha, the better. She was insane if she thought I would ever trust her again.

"I'm putting my ass on the line for you and Nandi, Ten," she said.

"Your choice," I said. "You could have stayed behind. I don't need a babysitter."

"If we find what I think we might, we'll need more than a babysitter," Marsha said.

"If you want to talk, talk. Cryptic don't mean clever."

"You're already in deep enough to go to prison for a decade."

"I'll wash your back in the showers," I said.

"Bring a loofah, and some aloe. Jail soap is shit on my skin."

The 101 is the more scenic route to Paso, hugging the Pacific, but it would have added ninety minutes to the drive. We shot north along Interstate 5, which stretched for mile after mile with no homes or businesses in sight, mostly just craggy rocks, brown grass, and the occasional fast-food watering hole.

Until the vineyards. After we turned west on Highway 46, about sixty miles from Paso, the vineyards' lush greenery filled our windows. My hardest trials have often been waiting for me in pretty places, so the sights didn't soothe me. Even landscapes can lie.

Marsha's sigh seemed to echo my thoughts.

I removed the Beretta's magazine and replaced it again, checking the action. Memorizing its rhythms. If we stumbled on a nest of armed men, I had to be prepared to fire multiple rounds. I hoped that the loud *CLICKs* from my exercise were irritating the hell out of Marsha. *If you pull a gun on me again, you better pull the trigger, too,* I thought.

Marsha knew that if she didn't shoot me next time, I would kill her. We had an understanding, Marsha and I.

"We leave the car parked somewhere with the keys ready," I said. "Whichever one of us gets Nandi first, we take off. The other one's on their own."

"That's not how I usually do business," Marsha said.

"Your world has changed," I said, repeating her words from Paki's apartment.

"This doesn't count as an apology?" Marsha said. "I changed my mind, Ten."

"And a thrilling, heartrending moment that was. Where were you planning to take me?"

For a long time, Marsha stared at the road. I assumed she was ignoring my question until she finally said, "A federal holding cell. Off the books, so it wouldn't have been on your record. We would have wanted to host you for a few days, that's all. Keep you out of the way— scare you out of talking. No rough stuff—just intimidation, a taste of your future if you got in our way. But I would have made sure they brought you In-N-Out Burgers."

I hadn't realized my anger had room to grow. "You think that's funny?"

"You asked for the truth, Ten. I never said it was pretty," Marsha said. "Do you think that course would have been easy for me? But look at what's at stake! Did you think we haven't had another nine-eleven because no one's *tried* it? Because somehow the bad guys had a change of heart and didn't want to hurt us anymore? No. It's because there are a lot of people like me, willing to work in the shadows to keep you safe."

"I believe our former vice president called it 'going to the dark side.' Congratulations, Vader. The Emperor must be pleased."

"Grow up. This is bigger than you. Or me. Or a beautiful two-year-old girl."

Part of me was amazed by her powers of rationalization; another part understood her position, whether I wanted to or not. In her place, I might have done the same thing.

"And don't turn your nose up at my burgers," Marsha said. "After a couple of days cut off from the outside world, you would have been loving some burgers."

"A comedienne *and* a humanitarian," I said. "You're the whole package, Marsha. All's forgiven now."

Marsha turned to me as if to make a snappy comeback, but she gave me only a peek of sad eyes. I can't stomach a woman's sad eyes.

"Save it," I said, and pretended to doze against my headrest.

The dusk sky lit up Paso Robles in orange and deep violet, wordless beauty.

Once we'd talked through our plan, Marsha and I didn't speak for the rest of the drive.

6:30 P.M.

Happy Cellars appeared at the intersection the navigator had promised, a building designed like a giant wine cask, well marked by a large ranch-style wooden sign at the T created by the intersection of two dusty rural roads. The bigger farmhouse stood high on the hill, an eighth of a mile away. There were four cars parked in a small parking lot set off from the street by a row of old, cracking, wooden wine barrels. A banner hanging on the building advertised WINE AND MICROBEER BAR NOW OPEN UNTIL 9 P.M.!!!

I hadn't expected Happy Cellars to be open for business on a weekday, or so late. Most wineries in Paso rely on weekend business for wine tasting, but Happy Cellars also apparently had its liquor license to sell wine by the glass. I was glad for the chance to snoop without sneaking around. Yet.

We didn't pull into the parking lot. Instead, Marsha drove straight past. Barely slowing.

Adjacent to the public building, acres of foil strips tied throughout the vineyard winked like confetti in the dying sunlight, a deterrent against birds. The west section of the vineyard was protected by eight-foot-high deer fencing, which might trap us inside better than it kept the deer out. I also spotted nets strategically placed among vineyard rows.

Happy Cellars didn't like pests of any kind in its vineyard.

"Let's circle back around the way we came," Marsha said. "Parking lot's risky, and the car will stand out too much if we leave it by the side of the road."

"We passed an old billboard a quarter-mile back," I said. "We could pull behind it."

"*Perfecto.*"

She pulled into a makeshift turnabout that traffic had carved into the grass and turned the car around. It would be a long quarter-mile if one of us was carrying Nandi in a hurry. The distance would be greater if we were coming from the farmhouse on the hill or one of the more distant outbuildings. But there was nowhere else to hide our car in the acres of vineyards.

"Keys on the driver's-side tire," I said. "Like I said, whoever gets Nandi first leaves. Nandi is our priority. No messing around to plant bugs or whatever you want your people to do. After Nandi's clear, you can blow the place to Hell for all I care."

Marsha met my eyes. "Nandi is the priority," she said, a solemn vow.

With that promise from Marsha and ninety-nine cents, I'd almost have enough for a trip to the dollar store. But no matter what her other motives were, I had to believe that she wouldn't do anything directly to jeopardize Nandi's life. If that was true, maybe we could pull it off.

Besides, if bringing Marsha had been a mistake, it wasn't too late to undo it. *I could render her unconscious, stash her in the trunk . . .*

No. She was right: Without her to back me up, Nandi was dead. If she was there at all.

The car jounced on stones when Marsha pulled off the road to park behind the billboard, largely out of sight from either traffic direction. The billboard wasn't lighted, so the car would be completely hidden in the tall grass after dark. I just hoped that no overzealous local police or neighbors would get curious before the sun went down. There were no buildings nearby, only acres of grapevines.

There wasn't a sound around us as we climbed out of the car, except for the swishing of the tall grass as we made our way back to the road. A distant car's headlights were too far away to have spotted us. If anyone asked, we were just taking a walking tour of Paso.

My cell phone was in my jeans pocket, on Vibrate. My Beretta was hidden beneath my shirt. Marsha's was nestled in her purse. She pulled the backpack out of her trunk to make us look like hikers, so I strapped it on.

"What have you got in here?"

"A few goodies. First aid. A couple of energy bars." She looked up at me. "We have no idea what condition we'll find her in, or if they've been feeding her."

Her eyes slid away when I met them. I'll be damned. So she had a heart, after all. Maybe two-year-old girls have that effect on everyone.

"Let's make it look good, shall we?" Marsha said, slipping her hand into mine.

I almost let her hand go, but she had a point. Her palm was warm and dry against my cool, damp one. Hand in hand, we walked the steeply dipping road back toward Happy Cellars. Even after what she'd pulled on me, as far as my skin was concerned, all was forgotten.

Two crows perched above us on the deer fence made me struggle to remember the old wives' tales about crows, how many meant good luck, and how many meant bad. All I knew for certain is that a flock of crows is called a murder. The term got stuck in my head.

Nandi is here, I thought. I was so certain, nobody could have called me a liar if I'd been strapped to a polygraph machine.

"The customers are probably just customers," I told Marsha, "but anybody else at this place might know all about Nandi. They're all in on it. This might be the kidnappers' whole base of operations. They're highly armed, so we can't make mistakes."

"Damn right," Marsha said.

Our plan was simple: First, we would go inside to check the place out under the guise of being customers. Collect tag numbers. Next, we would take anything we learned to help drive our search after dark. I wasn't in a full costume, but I hoped my sunglasses, three days' worth of razor stubble, and a baseball cap would obscure my face to anyone who might recognize it.

A fifth vehicle had pulled into the parking lot while we were gone, a huge mud-caked white Ford pickup truck with an empty gun rack. I wondered who was carrying the rifle, and where they were. I listened for a child's voice or laughter, but all I heard were laughing crows.

HAPPY CELLARS—EST. 1987 read the lettering that looked like it had been branded into the wooden sign posted on the barrel beside the road.

Internet research suggested that Happy Cellars had been a local staple for years, but had passed into new ownership five years before, after the original owner died. The new owner, a man named George Wesley, had been mentioned in the minutes from a city council meeting after his application for a liquor license earlier that year. But George Wesley, whoever he was, had kept his name off the internet otherwise. I'd gotten several hits from the name, which was common, but no more for a George Wesley in Paso Robles. His local address listing matched the address for Happy Cellars, as if he didn't exist otherwise.

The building that housed the tasting room had once been a small house, with a stone path and a patio swathed by grapevines overhead. Squashed grapes and shrinking raisins dotted the patio floor. A bell tinkled when we pushed inside the heavy, aged oak door.

We were greeted by a giant yellow smiley face poster with a psychedelically colorful border, a relic from the 1970s that matched the bottles. The interior smelled like incense, but not as earthy or spicy as the incense in Little Ethiopia, more like candy. The Stones' "Sympathy for the Devil" played from a hidden speaker, just barely loud enough to register above the conversational buzz. The front half of a powder blue VW Bug was propped against the wall as if it had driven into the room, buffed and shined for ambience.

Happy Cellars had tables instead of a bar, each table decorated with a working Lava lamp. The tables were crafted from glass tops fitted over modified wine barrels. There were couples or groups at half of the tables, twelve people talking and laughing quietly. None of the patrons looked up when we walked in. Three of the tables looked like couples out on a date, and one was home to three hunters sharing a pitcher of beer. I didn't see anyone behind the counter.

"Hey, folks! Help you?" said a woman's perky voice.

The woman, holding a broom behind the door, was white, about sixty-five, slightly overweight, her silver-specked hair hanging past her shoulders hippie style. Her face was all ruddy friendliness. She looked like the cool grandmother who'll let you stay up late.

"We'd like to taste some wine . . . ?" Marsha said.

"After six, we only sell by the glass," Granny Hippie said, blue eyes flashing merrily. I heard a whisper of exoticism in her accent. German? "If you like it, I'll give you twenty percent off a bottle."

"Sounds like a deal," I said. "Let's check it out, baby."

"What's your pleasure?" the woman said.

"Got a good Viognier?" I said.

The woman's face brightened. "Soon as you walked in, I knew you were a man of good taste. And you, miss?"

"He's my wine guy," Marsha said, smiling at me adoringly. "I'll have what he's having."

Granny Hippie winked. "Between you and me, Chardonnay drinkers just don't know any better yet. Go on and seat yourselves. I'll bring out two glasses of our 2007 Viognier."

Yes, there was an accent buried underneath her carefully enunciated banter. She masked it well, but it was ground in deep. She was pretending to be someone she wasn't, too.

She knows something, I thought.

Pleeeeezed to meetcha, the speaker whispered. *Hope ya knowww mahhhh name . . .*

I wanted to press my gun to her throat and introduce myself. The Stones laid down a hypnotic beat as I followed Marsha to a seat by the window while she laughed about something imaginary I'd done in San Francisco earlier that day.

Everything dropped into slow motion, following the song's mournful beat. The table of hunters laughed endlessly over a missed shot during hunting season. Granny Hippie ambled across the room, checking table by table for anyone who wanted to spend more money. Two college-age girls showed each other photos on their cell phones, giggling. A white-haired couple sat taking it all in as they held hands across their tabletop.

Did I hear Nandi's high-pitched voice from over my shoulder, near the counter?

Wishful thinking, it turned out. The sound was only the sad psyche-delic whine from Hendrix's electric guitar in "Red House," bleeding from the speakers after the Stones. Feeling so close to Nandi—but knowing how far I still had to go—made me ache from sitting still.

The wine arrived instantly, served with a hearty smile. I smiled right back.

Through an archway leading to the rear, where one of the two saloon-style doors was frozen ajar, I spotted a black man in the kitchen. My breath turned to ice. *Spider!*

But he was taller, with wider shoulders. Not Spider—but was he South African?

I wrested my eyes away from him, finally remembering to sip my wine.

Marsha didn't need prompting to know where I'd been looking. She saw the guy in the kitchen, too. She was still wearing a phony smile, but her eyes sparked.

The man in the kitchen was talking to someone, and he sounded agitated. I couldn't see the people he was talking to, but under the music I heard traces from their conversation. There might be two or three other men back there.

"Gonna swing by the men's room," I told Marsha. The men's room was also in the rear, not far from the kitchen's swinging doors. At least I would get a better peek.

Marsha nodded. *Be careful,* her eyes said. "Hurry back, baby."

My heartbeat rocked me as I walked the room's length across those wooden planks. I kept my face slanted away from the kitchen doorway, but my eyes roamed behind my sunglasses.

A second man was still out of view from my angle as I walked by the kitchen. But I caught a glimpse of the third man, whose head was bent as he took a bite out of a sandwich.

Paki.

TWENTY-FIVE

SHIT. **I INSTINCTIVELY** hiked up my shoulder to hide my face as I ducked toward the bathroom. Paki was alive! Did that mean Nandi was alive, too?

A few words drifted my way, but I couldn't distinguish Paki's voice in their hush.

"... and when they arrive, then what?"

"... what have I been telling you ... ?"

Their words shifted into a language with clicks, losing me as I reached the bathroom.

My hands shook on the bathroom doorknob as I let myself in. I couldn't have pissed a drop even at gunpoint, so I didn't try. I waited a few years, flushed the toilet, and came back out.

To my relief, I heard the same trio of voices in the kitchen, more agitated.

"... but then it's a disaster ..." Paki's voice.

"It's a disaster already! Can't you see?" A rational whisper I didn't recognize.

I lingered as long as I could, pretending to tie my shoelace just beyond the kitchen doors. But the conversation drifted back into a language I didn't know. I never heard Nandi's name.

I wanted to burst into the kitchen instead of going back toward my seat, but I pulled myself away from the men's conversation. All I could do in the kitchen was bring out my Beretta, and it wasn't time for that yet.

Too many innocent people could get caught in the crossfire or taken hostage. I'd end up dead or in jail, and Nandi in a grave. Like Dad had told me, I had to weigh every decision like gold.

I joined Marsha at the table and scooted my chair so that my face wouldn't be visible from the kitchen. She clasped the top of my hand: *What's up?*

"Our buddy who recommended this place . . . ?" I said. "We can thank him in person."

Marsha glanced nearly imperceptibly toward the kitchen. "*Love* to," she said.

"But we'll have to wait. He's still out hanging with his friends."

"How many friends?"

"Two," I said. "Maybe more. Popular guy."

"How are you doing back here?" Granny Hippie said, hovering at our table.

That time, I heard her Afrikaner accent loud and clear. She was South African.

WHERE THE FUCK IS NANDI? my mind screamed at her.

"Doing all right," I said instead. I tried to wipe loathing from my face, fixing a neutral smile. She didn't seem satisfied; she'd noticed that I'd barely touched my wine. I raised my glass slightly. "What's that mineral taste?" I said, low enough so my voice wouldn't carry to the kitchen. I'd noted the same crisp minerality in Paki's wine bottle. And Maitlin's.

Granny Hippie grinned. "We use cement barrels for aging. That's what you're tasting."

"Wine is so confusing!" Marsha said. "Red. White. That's all I know."

Granny Hippie and I shared a superior smile over Marsha's ignorance.

"Is that common? Cement barrels?" I said to Granny Hippie, pretending I gave a shit.

"We're the only ones in Paso. Stainless steel is easier to disinfect, but we're kind of old-fashioned here." *Like in South Africa*, I thought, but I didn't have to ask. "I've got a Viognier-Roussanne blend you might like better," she offered.

"I'll give this one a chance," I said, with a smile to ease her load. "No worries."

Granny Hippie winked. "They pay me to worry."

"I like this," Marsha said. "Bring us a bottle. It'll go great with the food at our party next week."

"Pretty *and* smart," Granny Hippie said. "Be right back."

The kitchen door swung shut behind Granny Hippie when she went to the back, but no one came out. I was worried that Paki might leave, but the quiet babble of voices went on despite Granny Hippie's presence.

A gasp came from behind me. "Where do I know that face . . . ?" a woman said.

I didn't have to turn around to know that she was talking about me.

"*Shhhhh*. Don't be rude," hissed the woman's companion. From the sound of it, they might be college kids who weren't much older than Chela.

When I sipped my wine again, my hand was unsteady. Marsha's eye noticed my hand's quiver, so I exhaled slowly, looking for the calm eye in the waiting storm.

"We better take off before it gets too dark," I said. "We promised the kids."

"Mommy and Daddy to the rescue," Marsha said. Our eyes locked, bound in purpose.

"I'll stay in and pay."

"Great. I'll be right outside." I was on my feet, trying not to look like I was in a hurry.

"I *definitely* know his face . . . ," the voice said. "Damn! Now it'll drive me *crazy* . . ."

Keeping my eyes and face away from the giddy voice behind me, I leaned over to kiss Marsha's lips gently; I'm not even sure it was for show.

The older man and woman sharing a table close to the door gazed at us as if we were a time machine. Their smiles encouraged us to cherish each day like our last, each night as if we might not live to see tomorrow. On my way out, I smiled back to show them I got the joke.

You never know when it's your last chance.

✦   ✦   ✦

7:35 P.M.

I waited for Marsha around the corner from the tasting room's entrance, near a Dumpster that smelled like rotting fruit. The still parking lot and empty roads were wrapped in long gray, orange, and purple shadows. Neatly planted rows grew in every direction. Tourists might have seen beauty, but all I saw was the perfect seclusion for hiding an abducted child.

Lights burned in several windows in the house on the hill at Happy Cellars. The house was brick and had a reddish hue, I realized, just like the Hendrix song. I counted three cars parked up at a circular driveway in front of the house, but there was plenty of room for more cars out of my sight. The farmhouse looked busy.

I still had more than an hour before the sky went fully dark, but I wasn't going to let Paki out of my sight. There was nowhere for Paki to go on foot except into the grapevines, which weren't dense enough to conceal him even in dim daylight.

Paki wasn't going anywhere without me.

While I waited, the older couple left and climbed into their vintage VW bus. They drove away as Rare Earth blared through their open windows.

"Turns out she knew you from a *cell phone commercial*," Marsha said, joining me outside. "Let's walk before she tries to get an autograph."

"What about Paki?" I said, hushed.

"We'll watch him from a distance."

A distance turned out to be back at our car, but Marsha's high-powered binoculars put us right back where we'd been. I hoped we looked like bird-watchers to anyone who drove by, but we lowered the binoculars when cars approached.

We'd chosen a low-traffic road a quarter-mile from the vineyard entrance, but we were high enough on a hill that the vineyard spilled down below us, and our views of the corner tasting room and the farmhouse were unobstructed. The growing darkness made it hard to see even with binoculars, but I had a clear view of Happy Cellars's front door and the driveway. The doors opened and closed as patrons left; no more came in.

A large red Chevy Tahoe pulled into the vineyard's driveway, but it veered beyond the parking lot and drove up toward the house instead.

"They've got company," I told Marsha, and let her take a peek.

"Uh-oh," Marsha said. "This looks like bad news. And now Paki's on the move."

"Where?"

"Getting into a car with two other black males. The white Honda Accord."

My recurring nightmare was unfolding for yet another night.

Marsha handed me the binoculars. The world bobbed wildly until I found the barrels, near the parking lot. A flash of white reverse lights caught my eye. The white Honda Accord was backing out of its parking space.

"Then we follow him," I said. "He'll take us to Nandi."

"We need to stay on the house. I have to bring in my team, Ten . . ."

The Honda didn't turn toward the driveway that led to the road. Instead, it swung the other way—toward the house. The car veered along the same path the red SUV had followed.

"He's going to the house!" I said. "Screw your team."

"That red SUV says this isn't a two-person job." I'd never heard Marsha so anxious.

"Call whoever you want," I said, "but I'm going in for Nandi. You can stay here."

"Going in by yourself doesn't help Nandi. You need me."

"Maybe I do. But I can't ask you to risk your life over this."

"You didn't ask," she said. "I offered."

"Then we're already in this, Marsha. You should have made your call in San Diego."

Marsha shook her head, sighing. She glanced at the sky. "Twenty minutes, and we can go in. But that's pushing it. It's safer to wait another hour."

"We can't wait an hour."

"We probably can't wait twenty minutes."

We left it at that—a plan neither of us liked.

"What are we up against in that SUV?" I said.

"If I'm right? Three or four armed men, maybe more. Well trained.

That's in addition to however many others are already here. It might be you and me against an army, Ten. This is about recon, not engagement. Engaging is our last resort. If we engage, we get zapped. These guys aren't shy about pulling the trigger."

The odds didn't feel good for any of us suddenly. The air in the parked car was thin. We hadn't thought to turn on the air conditioner.

"Do you have a number?" I said. "Someone I call if this doesn't work out?"

"Yeah, I'll give you my boss's number. And his email address, his Social Security number, and a map to his house." Marsha gave me a sarcastic sneer. "No more wine for you."

"Your *family*, Marsha," I said. "You know how to reach mine."

Marsha's face was still in the day's last light. "No thanks." A quiet beat. "Just look up my family. You're the detective. It would almost be worth getting killed to be a fly on the wall."

"Not by a knife," I said, stretching to relieve the pressure against the wound across my lower back. "B'lieve dat, mon."

"Hell no. Definitely not a knife."

If and when I saw Spider again, there would be no question of knives: I would shoot him dead at ten paces.

Marsha and I waited for the dark.

8 P.M.

The sun finally slipped past the edge of the sky, a dim pink ghost. Marsha's dark features blurred if she walked too far from me, and her bland clothes lost their color. Holes appeared in mounds of parched soil as we walked, trying to swallow our feet.

By the time Marsha and I walked back to the Happy Cellars driveway, the hunters' pickup and a Volvo were the only vehicles left in the business parking lot. It wasn't closing time yet. There was no light except a single one on the porch that lit up the front door. In the light from the window, I saw Granny Hippie lean over to serve a table. But she didn't see us.

We walked past at a brisk, nonchalant pace. *Now you see us, now you don't.*

There was no way they would keep Nandi near the tasting room, since so many outsiders came and went. If Nandi was on the property, she was either in one of the outbuildings, or somewhere inside the main house. Our instincts led us to the place where we were most likely to find answers: the house on the hill.

The brick colonial house loomed above us, waiting. Two stories. A big house to search.

We left the gravel driveway leading up to the house. It dead-ended into fence and gate. The fence was topped with razor wire, and light from the house painted the top edge a dull yellow. We'd be bloody targets trying to climb that. The gate was chained, and the chains were joined with a nasty-looking Master Lock padlock. It looked to be high end, one of the ones they market as "unpickable." Marsha *tsk'd* and reached into the backpack.

"What do you have in there?" I said. "Some kind of pick gun?"

She gave me a smug smile. "Better. A cigarette lighter."

"Hell of a time for a smoke."

It wasn't really a cigarette lighter. The little gold cylinder was more like a mini blowtorch.

"And . . . a Brymill Cry-AC liquid nitrogen storage system," Marsha said. Next, she pulled a silver cylinder about the size of a small hairspray can from the bag, and handed it to me. It weighed about two pounds, and felt warm.

Was it a bomb? I held my breath. "What . . . ?"

She thumbed the torch, and played its blue flame over the lock. "Now watch carefully, in case you need to do this. You heat the metal up for about a minute. The torch will raise the temperature to almost three hundred degrees." I watched in fascination. After about a minute, she raised the second cylinder, and flipped up the four-inch spout with her thumb. "Watch what happens when hot metal meets minus two hundred degrees."

"What is that?"

I heard a hiss, saw whitish fluid or vapor gush out in a stream. "Liquid nitro," she said. "Warts, skin tags, skin cancer. Plastic surgeons love this stuff, and so do I."

The lock was covered with hissing frost. She smacked it with the base of the blowtorch . . . and the lock fell into pieces, like broken glass.

I seriously reconsidered the harsh words I had directed at God. Marsha might be my guardian angel after all.

She bagged her equipment, and we opened the gate and slipped into the vineyard. We left the road and waded into the sea of leaves and stakes pointing high. Without venturing too far in, we had a passage roughly parallel with the path to the house. The scent of grapes was sweet perfume all around us.

We didn't dare use flashlights, so we trusted our eyes to guide us through the maze of plants, which grew up above our waists. I'd noticed that a portion of the vineyard had nets over the grapes, which would make movement more difficult. There would be no avoiding the nets if the main driveway was closed to us while we were escaping with Nandi.

And we would get that far only if we were lucky.

Marsha hummed "One Love" softly to herself as she dodged stakes and branches. Sometimes she whispered the lyrics, her voice almost playful. Marsha seemed to have made peace with dying in the field a long time ago. She'd risked her life for a lot less than a beautiful African child. Shit, she might have thought dying this way would erase a truckload of sins. I've got my own trucks lumbering behind me.

The vineyard rows stopped within three yards of the fence around the main house. The last part of our approach would be in the open.

"Wait," Marsha said, crouching. She produced night vision binoculars, which reminded me of Roman. I hoped she would have better luck with them. I saw a prick of light ahead.

"There's a guy smoking in the red SUV parked out front," Marsha said. "Probably a lookout. The people we've been tracking are very cautious."

"Good thing we don't plan to use the front door," I said, reaching for the binoculars.

The profile in the vehicle's driver's seat was surprisingly crisp, although he sat a football field away from us. He was an overweight man nursing a cigarette, two fingers near his face, his elbow propped in the open window.

He didn't look South African. More like Asian. Chinese, maybe?

Surprise, surprise, I thought. *An Asian connection.*

I didn't call Marsha on her bullshit about the Asian man I'd seen her tracking at Club Skylight. I had heavier business on my mind right then.

Up close, the dignified estate looked more like a castle, impenetrable. We had to find a way inside or we couldn't help Nandi.

"There's probably a rear garage door," I said. "Kitchen door?"

"Or open windows," Marsha said. "Maybe they let in the cool air after dark."

I took another peek through the binoculars: The living-room windows behind the white porch swing looked like they were open—directly in view of the red SUV. Off-limits.

Still, if those windows were open, maybe some others were, too. The side of the house closest to us was windowless on the ground floor because of the garage, but there would be more windows in the rear.

"Let's go get our hands dirty," I said.

The run to the house was steep, at least fifty yards, most of it uphill. The ranch-style fence circling the house was only decorative, without any wires between the boards. We squeezed through the fence easily, barely slowing down.

We should be the FBI, I thought. *We should have let them send a team.* But it was too late for second-guessing. The feds had lost Paki, and I had found him. Marsha's people, whatever shadowy alphabits they hid behind, hadn't known about Happy Cellars.

At the rear of the house, there was a large open patio with a shaded table and six chairs under the yard's sole two trees, both large oaks. An old plastic wading pool was full of water that looked clean. The pool made my heart leap. *Please please let Nandi be here . . .* On the far side of the patio, the wall jutted outward to create space for a dining room or sunroom with banks of shuttered windows. Were people moving beyond the shutters?

Daylight suddenly sprayed across the lawn in our corner of the yard. We were within five feet of the rear wall, and we'd tripped a motion-detecting security light. It would have been smart to run back toward the vineyard, out of the light's way. Instead, we both ran toward the house—and the light. No turning back.

We hid against a crevice in the wall just beyond the light's reach, close to the patio but out of view if anyone peeked out of a shutter in the sunroom. An oak tree helped shelter us. We were both breathing hard from our uphill sprint. My heart caught as I braced for the sound of a warning siren. A bell. A barking dog.

Blessed quiet.

The light glared down from a corner of the house's rear. I hoped it was on a timer and would go off by itself. The mounted light's motion-sensing panel was pointed in our direction, but we could dodge it as long as we hugged the wall. I was sure there was a matching light on the other side of the house, near the sunroom. If *that* one came on, someone would see it.

I took advantage of the light while we hid, glancing *up*. A second-story window almost directly above us was halfway open, with room to be pushed higher. An easy fit.

Could I climb in from the tree? I took a step closer to the tree to try to map the patterns of its branches. The top branches had been sawed away from the window, but I could get close enough to put my foot on the ledge. If plan A didn't work on the ground floor, I had a plan B.

The security light suddenly switched off. Darkness again.

Beside me, Marsha exhaled with relief.

There was definitely movement behind the windows.

To avoid tripping motion sensors, we stuck to the wall and stayed low to the ground as we inched across the rear patio toward the sunroom.

A door! It was slightly recessed into the wall, so we hadn't spotted it at first glance, but it appeared like the promise of hope. I gestured for Marsha to stay back, and put my ear to the door, listening for voices or movement. Nothing. With a silent prayer, I tested the knob.

Locked. I was about to ask Marsha to repeat her freeze trick when two men came into view in the adjacent window, lighting cigarettes as they spoke in anxious Xhosa or Zulu. They were in the kitchen, I guessed, and we were at the rear kitchen door.

"So much for the easy way . . . ," Marsha whispered behind me.

We pushed on toward the sunroom, crouching to avoid being seen. The rectangular kitchen window came next, well lighted with fluorescent bulbs. The kitchen was large, with a chef's island and bar stools, the counters covered in plastic produce bags. Two men unloaded food from the refrigerator, their backs facing us.

I saw movement in the far-left corner, inside the adjoining butler's pantry. At the butler's pantry window, I finally heard a man's voice, and the loud *clink*ing sound in what might be a sink.

". . . think they came all this way for excuses and bullshit?" an angry man's voice said, laden with a South African accent. But he was not an Afrikaner. His voice was lower pitched than Paki's, but their accents were similar. "Do you know how you look to them now? You look like a fool who can't do business without tripping over your feet. A silly winemaker!"

Marsha joined me, pressing her ear close, too.

"Leave her at a gas station toilet in Santa Barbara," another man said. "What's the difference?" His voice had a similar accent, triggering strong recognition in my mind, but I couldn't place it. Not yet.

"The difference between *HAVING* a *witness* and *NOT* having a witness. You've seen how clever she is! You surprise me, really!"

"Paki says they will pay anything, as long as—"

"Paki is a fool! She is the noose they will hang us all by, boss. And now, of all times, you look like another greedy *tsotsi*. Like a small-time kaffir back in Cape Flats!"

"But . . . ," the boss said, lowering his voice tenderly, out of hearing, ". . . is almost the same age."

The other man spoke angrily in Xhosa, I guessed, and the only word I recognized was *Mhambi*. Spider. It was the only word I needed to hear. My heart raced into the house without me while I listened at the window. A trusted adviser was pushing to have their boss give Nandi's execution order. And Spider and Nandi were inside. I was sure of it.

The voices suddenly grew fainter as they walked away.

". . . can compensate Paki for his loss . . . ," the boss was saying, casting off his doubts.

And they were gone.

"Damnit . . . ," I whispered. I motioned Marsha forward, and we crawled closer to the sunroom. Traces of muffled conversation led me to the sunroom's windows.

Under the cover of darkness, beside a hibiscus hedge, we risked taking a peek.

There were eight men in the large sunroom, where a long outdoor patio table doubled as a conference table. But no one was sitting down.

Everyone ignored the fruit-and-cheese plate and wine bottles on the table. The room looked restless.

A balding Asian man paced in an Italian suit and tie, and the four other Asian men, all younger, wore casual street dress, including baseball caps. They all looked like undercover cops, but they weren't cops. They were bodyguards.

One was stationed in the doorway. Another stood beside the window, his back facing us. They had created a formation in the room, ready for trouble. If we tripped the motion sensor by the window, everyone would notice the light.

The man at the doorway across the room hiked his chin in my direction, and I quickly pulled away. "Careful," I whispered to Marsha. "Twelve o'clock."

Marsha's wide eyes didn't move or blink for ten more seconds. Finally, she pulled back.

Holy shit, Marsha mouthed to me.

You know them? I mouthed back.

Marsha nodded, looking dazed.

I was about to ask for an introduction when a booming voice floated through the window. "Ah, Mr. Yi, please accept our apologies," said the South African man I'd heard in the butler's pantry. The adviser. "We have been concluding a very delicate—"

An angry voice cut him off, so muffled that it took me too long to realize that the balding man in the suit was speaking Chinese. Marsha's head shot up to stare into the room again.

"Mr. Yi is very, very disappointed in so many delays," said a cultured English accent. One of the Chinese bodyguards sounded like he'd learned English at Oxford. He was about thirty and wore his hair long. "And this foolhardy distraction has already jeopardized so much. All the media headlines! He wanted to make this trip personally—"

"And we are so honored he did!" the Kingdom's adviser said, in diplomacy mode.

I risked another peek into the room, too. A short black man wearing slacks and a dress shirt entered, and I recognized him instantly—he was the cook I'd been sent to babysit at Nandi's birthday party. His kitchen laborer's bearing was gone, replaced by a princeliness no one in the room could ignore. Everyone straightened to their full heights when the African walked in.

As soon as he spoke, I also realized he was the boss I'd heard through the window. His voice was the same, but he now spoke with a high-bred English accent, matching the translator's like a common language.

"Mr. Yi, please accept my personal apologies," said the South African kidnapper who sounded English. He made a practiced bow. "We are resolving this awful and embarrassing situation as we speak . . ." He was also the short man from the football field, the one who had wrested Nandi from me at gunpoint.

An instinct to lunge at him through walls and windows nearly overwhelmed me.

More irate Chinese from Mr. Yi followed, but I had heard enough: Nandi was a point of contention with the Asians, and she had run out of time.

Spider wasn't in the room—where was he? Heading for Nandi's room with knife in hand?

"I'm going in now," I whispered to Marsha.

She waved me off, straining to listen to the men's conversation. She motioned: *How?*

"I'll climb the tree," I told her. "There's an open window up there."

Marsha glanced at the tree. It was a seventy-footer. If I slipped, it would be a long way down. While the rant in Chinese continued through the window, Marsha nodded.

"Do you need the backpack?"

Marsha shook her head. "Not as much as you will. I can get this door open by the time you get back—and hopefully the smokers will be nicotine flush and back in the house. If you have to shoot someone . . ." The idea stopped her in midsentence. "Let's hope one of us can run like hell while carrying a two-year-old."

I nodded. Suddenly, I didn't want to leave Marsha alone.

"Come up with me," I said.

Marsha shook her head. "Ten, I have to stay and listen. I need ten minutes." She was almost whining, crouched by the side of a house like a schoolgirl playing hide-and-seek. "If I have to, I can create a distraction. Go get Nandi." She raised her finger to her lips: *Shhhhhh.*

Inside the sunroom, the translator took his turn: "Mr. Yi says this is unacceptable behavior . . . and he is baffled as to why you would have pursued such a public and distasteful act at such a sensitive time for all of us . . ."

Marsha was lost in her surveillance, holding what looked like a phone up close to the window. A listening device? A recorder? Hell, she might have had a goddamn periscope.

I wanted to be mad at Marsha for switching priorities in the middle of our mission, but I found myself worrying about the man smoking in the red SUV. And the men at the meeting inside, who might see her through the window.

But Nandi needed me more than Marsha did.

Ten minutes, and I'll be back with the prize, I thought. *Be here.*

TWENTY-SIX

8:35 P.M.

Midway up the tree, my foot slipped against the bark. I flung my arm out to catch a branch overhead—and I triggered the same security light we'd set off before. The side of the house closest to the vineyard lit up like it was midday, providing enough light past the patio that Marsha's outline against the house came into sharper focus.

I hugged the tree like a lover, not moving as I tried to blend in. There was a rustle as Marsha ducked in the hedges near the sunroom. I counted the seconds, my arms aching from my awkward grip.

The man standing at the sunroom window pushed the blinds aside and stared outside.

I expected him to look down toward Marsha—instead, he seemed to stare straight at me, as if he knew exactly where I was perched. My torso was hidden from his angle by the branches, but my face was in plain sight, resting on a V in the tree.

We seemed to be staring eye to eye. I almost reached around for my gun.

When the light finally went off, my arteries drowned in an adrenaline surge. My limbs seemed numb, but I held on. The man in the sunroom closed the blinds again, and stayed at his post.

The rest of the climb raced by. My hands found their holds and my feet followed, just like I was playing in the old ficus tree I conquered daily in our yard when I was a kid. The branches near the window, chopped off at the ends, were strong enough to hold me, so I could look inside.

There was a nightstand light on in the room, which was smallish and sparsely furnished, like a guest room. There were shopping bags of clothes on the bed. I saw pajamas from the kids' TV show *Dora the Explorer,* still carrying the price tag. Could Nandi be in the room?

The idea almost froze me on the windowsill. My imagination fed me an image of Nandi sitting upright on the bed, smiling and happy to see me. But then I realized that the door to the room was wide open, not locked. And no one was in sight.

An empty room was the next best thing to Nandi being there.

Fresh from my practice at Paki's house, my knife sliced an X through the screen. A quick couple of taps, and I raised the open window high enough to let me inside. The next thing I knew, my feet were on a carpeted floor, soundless. I had penetrated the fortress.

But I didn't have time to celebrate. There were footsteps coming in the hallway. Fast.

I rolled across the floor, landing behind the door just as a voice boomed nearby.

It was Paki, talking to someone as they walked briskly past. ". . . but they swore it would never come to this!" He sounded distraught, breathless.

"They are not reasonable like you and me," said the black South African who had been counseling Paki in the wine-tasting room. "What is a child to them? They only know money! Don't interfere with my brother. There is already talk—"

"She is my *child!*"

"Yes, Paki, yes, but if Mhambi thinks you are a problem, I am afraid for you . . ."

The voices faded again, moving past. *She IS my child. Nandi was still alive!*

They might have been on their way to see Spider, from the sound of it. If I got to them first, I might be able to sway Paki to help with a rescue. His friend might be halfway sane, too. Either way, I didn't have time to think it through.

I only glanced around before I slipped into the hallway to follow the men, mostly to make sure there weren't security cameras mounted in the corners. Paki and his friend turned a corner to my right.

I'd entered the house in a room near the top of a winding staircase. A tile floor gleamed up at me from the lower level. I heard rapid, angry Chinese downstairs, from the sunroom—Mr. Yi's mood had not improved—but I didn't see anyone milling around in the foyer, or posted at the door.

Keeping close to the wall, I dashed after Paki.

They had reached a small side corridor, and were walking toward a closed door at the end.

Paki's friend was pleading with him in Xhosa, warning him. Genuinely worried.

Paki rapped on the door, hard. "Mhambi!" he called. "You must talk to me!"

Spider was in the room. Was Nandi there, too? I stayed hidden around the corner from Spider's room, but that left me exposed in the upstairs main hall. After a glance at the other end to make sure no one else was coming, I slipped my hand around my Beretta, ready to draw.

A click around the corner as Spider's door opened. Even in another language, I recognized the voice from Club Skylight. He sounded annoyed.

Paki's friend spoke to Spider, trying to placate him. His fear needed no translation.

"I've bought clothes!" Paki said, breaking into English. "I can take her away with me."

"You?" Spider said.

"Yes, me! I am her father!"

"And with such a father as you, it is more merciful to put her out of her misery!" Spider said. "You'll be paid for your tears, Paki, and I'll be paid for mine. They should make you go to the basement and wipe up your own shit."

I wanted to turn the corner and shoot Spider on the spot. I wished I had a silencer on my gun the way people do in movies—but in the real world, silencers are really only sound *suppressors*, and they're louder than silencers in movies. And I didn't even have that.

But I had my lead.

They argued a while longer in Xhosa, but I wasn't listening anymore. As soon as I heard the word *basement*, I bolted toward the stairs.

I raced down the spiral staircase, running far ahead of ideas or plans. My eyes swept the ceilings, still looking for surveillance cameras. None so far.

At the bottom of the stairs, I almost ran headlong into the chest of the stout Asian man I'd seen smoking outside in the red SUV. He had a newspaper curled under his arm, fresh from a bathroom break. His linen jacket was pushed aside by the barrel of the AK-47 assault rifle. A very nasty gun. The black gleam nearly made me trip on the last steps.

Done, I thought.

The actor in me saved my life. I never broke my stride. Never reached for my gun. I maintained my breezy pace, giving AK-47 a *Whassup* nod as I rounded the staircase. *Places to go, things to do, man.* He nodded back, grunting in response. To him, I was another one of the Africans. Hell, maybe we all *do* look alike.

I was dizzy from adrenaline, but I didn't have time to recover. I would be lucky if I had sixty seconds to find the basement. Where was it?

I veered away from the sunroom, to the other side of the house. If my search took me toward the sunroom, I'd have no choice—but it was no place to start if I wanted a chance.

Each door and archway might be full of promise, or death. I shunned open spaces, looking for corners, shadows, and furniture to keep me out of sight. I pursed my lips to keep from calling out Nandi's name. Would she hear me? And who else would?

The foyer and living room looked empty, so I darted to a narrow reading room with a fireplace, an antique grandfather clock, and a love seat beside a row of bookshelves. Two voices approached, speaking Xhosa or Zulu. I shrank behind the grandfather clock just in time to conceal myself as they passed. Not Spider, but I was sure they were armed.

There were at least twelve men in the house, and those were only the ones I knew about. Marsha had been right: They might as well be an army.

For a full five seconds, I ignored the inconsolable, wailing cries that pierced me. Since the sound captured the way I felt, I thought it was in my mind.

It wasn't. Somewhere near me, Nandi was crying.

The cry was muffled, but the sound seemed to surround me. I gazed down at the floor and fell to my knees to put my ear against the cold tile. The cry sharpened.

Nandi was *beneath* me! My fingertips rested against the tile, as if to memorize the place where I had found her. My heartbeat raged and thrashed in my fingers. I might have tried to dig through the floor if I'd had a shovel ready.

Even then, I didn't dare call to Nandi. The floor was thick, and my voice would carry much farther inside. I still heard the two men talking in the hall.

I looked around the reading room for a door that might lead to the basement. Nothing.

A one-eyed peek around the archway into the foyer. The two Africans were standing in what might be the kitchen doorway, twenty-five yards away.

I leapfrogged to the small corridor beside the reading room, and found an alcove with two closed doors on opposite sides. In the alcove's rear, there was an entrance to a butler's pantry, perhaps where the boss and his adviser had been standing when Marsha and I overheard them. That might mean I was within only a few yards of the back door, and my only backup. No conversation or stink of cigarette smoke: They must have gone. If Marsha had opened that door, we had egress.

But I didn't have time to check on that door, or verify that Marsha was ready for us. Nandi was in the basement, and Spider was on his way. Nandi's cries followed me into the alcove.

When I opened the door closest to me, a stench floated out. The driver with the AK-47 had nervous bowels, and a spritz of air freshener hadn't helped erase the scent. I closed the door to the guest bathroom, softly.

The second door looked only wide enough to be a broom closet, but why would a broom closet need a padlock? The blowtorch was the easy part; I've used them before. I counted slowly to sixty as the flame flared against metal. I smelled the wood around the doorknob getting singed as the heat grew. The liquid nitrogen was actually more iffy. Two hundred degrees below zero is as corrosive as flame, but less familiar. The hissing sound was deafening to me.

Frosted. Thumped. Metal cracked, and I caught the pieces in the backpack. Only a hole remained where the doorknob had been. I wouldn't have much time in the basement.

The two men near the kitchen went on with their endless conversation. They weren't leaving, and they might wander back at any time. Fighting not to rush, I reached for the door.

I pushed the door open, expecting a guard just inside. A light was on above the doorway. My only Xhosa flashed to my mind: *Molo,* I would say. A friendly hello and a smile. One word might buy me enough time to knock him down the stairs.

Molo. Molo. Molo.

No one was there to greet me at the top of the concrete basement stairs, but Nandi's cry burrowed into my ear. Holding my breath, I slid inside and pulled the door closed.

I don't remember pulling out my Beretta, but it was in my hand, ready to fire. I crept down the stairs, my eyes watching for blind angles. I expected to see a muzzle flash with every step. *Hold on, Nandi, I'm almost there.*

It was pitch dark at the bottom of the stairs. Nandi's cry was everywhere.

I touched the wall closest to me and found a dimmer switch. I turned on a chandelier, which looked misplaced, and it cast pale spikes of light across the unfinished room.

The basement was large, only partially finished, with industrial-grade carpeting. Giant rolls of brown carpet leaned against the walls, and other piles were covered by tarps. A washer and dryer sat silently behind me, beneath the stairs. The only furniture sharing the huge empty floor space was an old picnic table and benches.

Far across the room, I saw an overturned playpen.

But no Nandi. No one in sight. Now that I was here, she'd gone silent.

"Nandi?" I finally called out. "It's Mr. Ten."

An answering wail.

I ran toward the playpen and its sharp smell of urine and feces. A dirtied Barbie doll sat on top of a discarded diaper soaked brown. A child's cup had spilled to the floor after the playpen fell over. Nandi had begun her escape without me.

"Sweetheart? I'm here to take you home," I said, raising my voice as loudly as I dared.

In my imagination, Spider was already there and it was too late. I turned to aim my gun toward the stairs, sure he was standing there. He wasn't. My joints were trembling in hidden places I hadn't known about, slowing my movement.

Keep it together, Ten . . .

What looked like a trail of discarded animal cracker pieces led me to an overturned laundry basket in the corner behind the playpen. The crying was coming from the basket.

Nandi already sounded petrified, so I didn't want to startle her by wresting away her protective basket. I kneeled down to stare past the white plastic bars to the small face inside.

Two frightened, damp eyes stared back at me.

"Nandi?" I said gently. "I'm here to take you home. But you need to be very quiet. We don't want the bad people to hear us." I had been rehearsing for Nandi since the football stadium.

"I want my *BOTTLE!*" Nandi screamed, furious that I hadn't brought one.

And she was right. If I'd brought one, she wouldn't have been screaming.

"*Shhhhhh,* hon, please please don't cry," I said. "Your mommy's waiting for you, but we can only see her if you're quiet." Energy bar! What had Marsha said? I shucked the backpack, opened the zipper, and dug around, producing a foil-wrapped granola stick. Nandi's eyes went wide when I pulled it out, and peeled it. She held her chubby hands out, and I gave it to her. She jammed it into her mouth and chewed greedily.

"Now as soon as we get you home," I began, "your mommy—"

"*MOM-MEEEEEEEE!*" Nandi shrieked, trying to conjure up her mother. I was horrified by the idea of rendering a two-year-old unconscious, but I might have to. I didn't have a sedative. The only other ways might hurt her.

My Beretta and I checked the basement door. Spider's ghost was running toward us again, but he was gone when I blinked.

Desperate to distract Nandi, I tugged at the energy bar. "Gimme! I'm hungry."

"*Mine!*" Nandi objected.

I was bringing her back down from the cliff.

"Can't I have just one bite?"

"No!" Nandi insisted.

I pretended to sigh with disappointment. "Well, then go ahead and be a little piggy. Hungry as I am, I might eat *you* by accident." I don't know where I found the jollity.

Slowly, the laundry basket lifted, and Nandi's full face came into the light.

She was not the same child I had seen on the football field. Her face was so changed, I would not have recognized her. It wasn't just the dirt that shadowed her complexion, although the dirt alone broke my heart. Her nose and cheeks were caked with dried mucus. Her hair was matted with dried baby food. She was naked except for a Dodgers T-shirt that hung past her thighs, and had been white before it turned gray. The child hadn't been groomed in days.

The abductors had taken better care of Nandi when they thought they were sending her home. Once their plans changed, Nandi's treatment changed. How long had it been since she'd been fed, or had a diaper changed?

For the first time, there was utter silence in the laundry room.

"Nandi, you know how there's good guys and bad guys?" I said, risking more tears.

Nandi nodded fervently while she chewed, as if she'd been studying the subject.

"You and me, we're the good guys—but the bad guys are coming. And I want to take you away, but the bad guys will hurt us if they find us. So we have to be *very quiet*. Understand?"

I didn't dress it up like a game this time. I stared straight into Nandi's eyes and talked to the part of her that already knew.

"My bottle?" she said, still negotiating despite a mouth full of granola.

"I'll get you a bottle as soon as we get away from the bad men. I promise."

"I want it *now*."

There was no time for further negotiation. I sat Nandi across the crook of my arm. She already seemed lighter than she'd been at the football stadium. Her T-shirt was damp, probably from urine. I felt so filled with rage that I planned to come back and lay waste to the whole house after I got Nandi home.

Nandi's crying started again—much more softly, but much too loud. Still, we had to go.

I didn't see any windows or other doors, so I carried her to the stairs.

We were halfway up when the basement door cracked open.

That time, I knew it wasn't a trick of my eyes. I leaped backward, landing on the floor silently while air *whooshed* from Nandi's lungs. I darted around the corner as a lone man's footsteps descended.

"What happened to this door?" a man's voice said.

Spider.

In one version of that night, Nandi was completely silent. Spider never saw us around the corner, distracted while he investigated Nandi's overturned playpen. While his back was turned, I hit him in the base of the skull with the butt of the automatic, hard enough to send this King to the Kingdom.

That version died when Nandi wailed. My hand over her mouth only made her cry harder. "Hey!" Spider said, chiding Nandi. "How did you get—"

When Spider turned the corner from the stairs to look for Nandi, he came face-to-face with my Beretta.

"*Get back!*" I said. "Stand against the wall!"

Under different circumstances, the childlike O of surprise on Spider's face might have been comical. His hands flew above his head, and he fell back against the wall, blinking.

When the startled moment passed, Spider grinned at me as if we'd just shared an adventure. His teeth grew large. "Shit, man, you got me, eh? It's just you! The one from Skylight? I thought you were the FBI!

Oh, you scared me . . . I saw your face on television. You're the actor who works for Sofia Maitlin! I should have known you."

His easy banter was a ruse to distract me. Even knowing that, I almost forgot.

"*Shut up*, Mhambi," I said. "Step away from the stairs."

The grin was gone. "Or what, cowboy? Is that what they call you in movies? The white cowboy?"

"Live or die. Your choice."

For five excruciating seconds, Spider didn't move. He was already testing me. Spider gave a bitter laugh. "After you shoot me, then what? Who's outside that door, actor? You shoot me, they all come running. Tell me: Then what?"

"Then you'll still be dead."

"I should be dead ten times over," Spider said, shrugging. "What's death to me? What about you, actor?"

"If you die, too?" I said, also shrugging. "Why not?"

Spider *tsk*'d. "Is that what you want for Nandi? Bullets and blood?"

"Better than starvation."

"Nobody's starving this girl!" Spider said. "Eish! She's very fat, this one. Put down your gun. My conscience won't let me kill this little girl. I was coming to take her to her father—her *real* father. He's going to take her where she belongs."

He didn't try to hide the lie in his voice, but I still wanted to believe him. Nandi wailed, clinging hard to my neck. She might not have known everything, but she knew enough.

"Conscience?" I said. "Try again."

"You're a madman to come here," Spider said, his voice tinged with admiration. "I told my boss we should have killed you before. Look how far you've come, actor!"

"You think I got here by myself?" I said. "The feds are arresting everyone at your meeting right now, including Yi and your boss. It's over— *get down on the floor.*"

A glimmer of hesitation in Spider's eyes. My gun felt heavier with its growing power.

I had logic on my side, after all: What kind of fool would try a rescue without backup?

But when Spider spread his arms akimbo, my heart plummeted.

"That's what you want?" I said. "You'd rather die than let me take her?"

Instead of answering, Spider stepped toward me, his face placid. Taking his time, Spider lifted his tunic to reveal his knife sheath. With a flourish of his fingers, he reached for his knife. He slowly fanned it in the air.

My gun arm was so rigid that if I breathed too hard, I would pull the trigger.

"Don't make me!" I said. "*I will shoot you* before I let you hurt her."

I heard voices upstairs, and I realized that Spider had left the door ajar. The two men I'd heard near the kitchen were only a few yards from the basement door. Right above us.

"Where's your FBI raid?" Spider said, voice low. He was enjoying his game.

Suddenly, my Beretta felt light enough to float away, powerless. All of the moisture in my body turned to dust. No single gun would keep me alive in a basement with only one exit. The basement was my prison.

Where was Marsha? Was there a chance that, even now, she was making her way down the stairs? Could she have already called for backup? How much time did I need to buy us?

"You have a problem with your rescue, actor," Spider said. "A *big* problem."

I took a step backward, maneuvering the picnic bench between us. I'd already killed Spider in my mind, imagining how Marsha and I could prop the picnic table up to stave off the bullets from upstairs as long as we could. Bullets and blood were surely coming. My eardrums sang from Nandi's cries; I was sure they must be bleeding inside.

"You pull the trigger," Spider sneered, "we both die. My way, one of us has a chance."

"Your way?"

"No gun," he said. "No bullets. Just you and me."

"*Mhambi!*" a voice boomed from upstairs. "Still so much noise! My ears!"

I dodged back to the corner, out of sight. My gun never left Spider, and I'd pinned him. He couldn't make it past me to the stairs without getting shot. We were stuck with each other.

Spider's unblinking eyes stared through me.

"Then close the door!" he called upstairs. "Or come do it yourself!"

The men complained, but the door slammed shut.

"Put the gun down," Spider said.

"Not so fast." Warily, I made a wide circle away from Spider, toward Nandi's overturned playpen. Spider twitched like a batter ready to steal second, but my steady gun barrel and unblinking eye held him in place.

"That's the agreement—no gun," Spider said. "You will do this thing."

"Why?"

"Because I know you," Spider said. "I knew you in the dressing room. At the nightclub. You have trained for many years. But you have never had the moment I offer you."

"And what the hell is that?"

"You will not do this to save your life. Or the child's life. You will not do it for Sofia Maitlin, or the FBI. You will use all of those things as an excuse."

"Why?" I was only half listening, trying to think of a better way to save Nandi.

"Because you are tired of playacting," he said. "Of pretending to be men you are not. You want to know who you really are."

"And you know who I am?"

"No," he said, voice seductive. "I know who *I* am. All your life you have sought the answer to a question you could never speak. You have trained, and sweated. I know. I did as well. The difference between us? I did not seek this out, trying to become something I feared I was not. My father gave me this, Ummese Izulu, the Zulu knife. As his father gave it to him. What did you do? What is the American way? Did you drift from school to school, digging shallow holes while the gold you sought was just a few strokes deeper beneath your feet?"

Shit. Had he been talking to Cliff? "You're talking nonsense."

"After we dance, you and I . . . if you survive, you will understand my words."

He was wrong. He didn't know me. I knew who I was, and his head games couldn't change that. This wasn't about whatever warped significance a monster like this might find in the death games he had played from the cradle. This was about a child's life, and there, he had offered a possibility of survival.

I could do it. I could take this fool.

I ignored the stench from the playpen and righted it. Nandi could get out by herself, but maybe I could keep her clear for a while.

"Just wait," I said. *"Don't you fucking move."*

"This is how you talk in front of a little one?" Spider said, and *tsk*'d again.

Nandi struggled as I lowered her into the playpen with one arm. I had to drop her without being careful, pushing her away when she tried to hoist herself back to my arm. Nandi's cries turned to shrieks. She hated the playpen.

With one of my arms finally freed, I backed to the wall and grabbed the end of a tarp, yanking on it. Paint cans fell over loudly, one of them spilling white paint across the carpet.

"Hey!" Spider said. "Clumsy man. Don't shoot me if it's your fault that they come."

I dragged the tarp to Nandi's playpen and tossed it over her. Nandi's cries became more frantic once she was denied light, but the tarp was heavy enough to mute the sound and hold her in place longer. It gave me more than I'd expected.

I just hadn't wanted Nandi to see what was about to happen in the basement.

Spider's eyes were like a cat's as he watched my gun. "Give me your decision!" Spider said, irritated. "You prolong her suffering."

"Like you give a damn."

"Even a dog should not suffer," Spider said. "I never make innocents suffer."

"She's already suffering!" I said, scanning the shelves and the floor for something I could fight with. But I always had one eye on Spider. For all I knew, he could throw that knife as well as stab and slash. A single blink, and that deadly blade could fly.

"There!" Spider said, pointing.

I didn't look. "What?"

"A knife for you."

Instead of turning my head as Spider had probably hoped, I stepped toward the wall where he was pointing. I never lost sight of Spider's body mass in my target sight. For half a second, I peeked where he had pointed: A knife in a leather sheath hung on the wall beside a tall box of Borax. A hunting knife, by the look of it. It was about nine inches overall, with a five-inch blade and black Micarta handles and a nickel-silver finger guard.

All right. I could work with this.

Nandi was rocking and shrieking in her dark playpen, but it was harder to hear her.

Where was Marsha? *Is there another way out of this?*

My heart was making up new rhythms. If I've ever been more afraid—facing off a killer with Nandi at arm's length—I don't know when it was.

But Spider was right about one thing: I was a fighter. I was afraid, like all fighters, but fighters have more than their fear when they face an opponent. I had training and hard-won experience, and no part of my mind could accept failing Nandi. My fear was my power.

Yeah, you scare me. But I've trained too long and too hard to just get chopped up. It ain't gonna happen.

With one eye on Spider, I shook the knife free from its sheath. I had the blade in one hand, the Beretta in the other. I wanted to save Nandi so badly, I struggled to control the wall of breath that held back a nauseating ocean of adrenaline. Concentrate on exhalations only.

Don't gulp air.

"Relax," Spider said. "Put down your gun. No matter what happens between us, I will take her to her father. The girl will live."

He's gonna call for backup as soon as you put the gun down, my Evil Voice said. *You should have shot him already. No one will hear.*

But I couldn't believe my lies, or Spider's. Anyone on the ground floor would hear a gunshot. And just as Spider recognized me, the story from Xolo Nyathi in Little Ethiopia had shown me who Spider was. Ceremony mattered to him. Killing Nandi was just his job.

Nandi's shrieks spurred me on. Even muted, the noise would bring the others back soon, with or without Spider.

I ejected the magazine and laid it on the shelf, out of easy reach. I rested the gun beside it. Spider and I stood a dozen yards from each other, both armed with knives. Spider didn't move at first, staring at me with what might be awe, or just pity.

"A man crazy enough to come here . . . ," Spider began, ". . . is worthy of a dance. But I warn you: This will not be quick."

A shudder went through me, the memory of pain, starting at the small of my back.

Spider gave me a small bow, his eyes never leaving my face.

Our race to death began.

TWENTY-SEVEN

TIME, NOISE, AND thoughts vanished.

The basement. Nandi. Everything, forgotten.

Spider was my world, tunnel vision collapsing everything to a single bright point. He made a loud clicking sound, advancing, his arms swirling like a Bollywood dancer, two arms waving like snakes—one harmless, one deadly.

I watched the center of Spider's chest, soft focus, watching his hands with my peripheral vision. He came straight in and I flinched back, startled.

It had been a feint. Spider grinned, as if in that moment he had learned everything he needed to know. But the grin was only for an instant. His bearing had changed since his bow. He planned to kill me with meticulous elegance. And glee.

Spider stalked me, left, then right. I tried a low cross kick at his ankle, Filipino style, and grazed him. He slid away like Astaire, recovered, and drew me in with a pretense of imbalance. I slashed at his left wrist, aiming at the radial nerve and brachial artery. But it was another feint, and his hand wasn't there anymore. I never saw how he did that, but suddenly there was pain in my left forearm.

I retreated in a flurry of low kicks, anything to keep him from coming straight in as I wrapped my mind around the pain. How had he stabbed me? He had known where a visual blind spot would be when he pulled my attention right.

Fuck! This wasn't a self-defense art. This was a killing technique, for hunters of men. *Wake up fast, or you are dead.*

Spider twisted behind me, and I felt another jab as he stabbed me in the ass—only two inches of fierce pain, but a world of humiliation. He could have killed or crippled, but had instead chosen to shame me. The hunting knife flew out of my hand, skittering six inches away.

Spider sighed, as if my dropped knife annoyed him. The world stood still. I swear he allowed me the two seconds I needed to grab the knife as he closed in.

He grinned at me. "You are not as entertaining as I had hoped," he said.

My foot struck the backpack, and I kicked it up into his face. He had moved sideways left, but for a moment his lethal right wrist slowed, and I grabbed it with my left. I should have twisted then, but the damaged forearm failed me, and he twisted free—but not before I shot the fastest kick to the groin I could manage. He twisted his thigh into it, blocking, and almost stabbed the calf before I could retract it.

Damn, he's fast!

I had to kill him. I'd always known it, but now it sank in: I *had* to kill him, and soon. He could have killed me twice already. The next time he brushed against me, I would die.

My left arm and stabbed gluteus throbbed, but I forgot my injuries when Spider's snake dance advanced again. Spider was angry now, and that knife came so fast that my counters to his ankles barely disrupted his rhythm enough for me to stay away.

Spider stabbed at me six times from six directions in less than two seconds. I needed every bit of evasive footwork I had ever practiced to stay at a distance. I knew where his kill zone was: I just couldn't get close enough for mine.

When Spider's blade sank into the meat of my right calf, I thought my leg had been cut off. Only fear of alerting Spider's friends stanched the scream in my throat. A red cloud of dizziness tried to cover my eyes, but I blinked it away. I stumbled over my backpack, and went down. The knife spilled from my hand. Again.

Spider's eyes glittered. He was having the time of his life. He stared down at me, savoring the moment.

I was about to die.

Nandi's crying had stopped, as if she knew.

A tiny voice from beneath the tarp: "Mis-ter Ten?"

My world turned to water from fear, shame, and pain. *This is it.*

"She will not suffer as you will," Spider said, weaving around me, choosing his killing position. "*You* made this happen. You fools shot the boss's nephew. *Eish!* Why didn't you keep the agreement? You have *forced* me to do this terrible thing! We have children, too. You have felt nothing yet. For forcing me to kill a child, I have more pain for you. I will give you a thousand cuts, and *piss* in every one of them. When you are an eyeless, lipless thing, I will make you crawl across the floor and kiss my ass to end your agony. Or . . . you could beg me now. Up, onto your knees and beg me to make it quick. Go on, *actor.* Play the coward. The role of hero doesn't really fit, does it?"

He was monologuing, ready to lay me and his sins to rest. I groaned as I rose to my feet, right leg buckling a bit. I bent down one vertebra at a time to reach—

But I didn't go for the blade. Instead, I collapsed back down to the floor with all the untelegraphed speed gravity could offer, rolled, and lashed out with both feet into Spider's crotch. Or would have, if Spider hadn't stumbled back, flowing with me like my own shadow. I thumped his right thigh, and his blade nearly cut my ear off, slashing my right cheek instead.

Shit!

My calf was on fire. I shut down the pain and closed in for a head butt so hard that it echoed. I was in so much pain already, I barely felt it. I somehow wrapped firm fingers around Spider's knife hand, avoiding the blade.

Finally—my kind of fight.

We went to the ground, a ball of knees and elbows. We rolled three times. I elbowed him in the nose once, trying to drive it through the back of his head. His eyes crossed. *Damage. Good.* I slammed my back into one of the metal shelves, pulling Spider with me. We were twisted up, my right arm behind the leg of the shelf, and he didn't give me room to pull it around. I was trapped on the floor between Spider and the shelf.

Spider was no longer stunned. He began stabbing at my left wrist, scraping and cutting. I yelled out when he hit bone, but he missed the arteries. In a moment he would orient, and work himself free. Then I'd be dead.

The back of my head thumped against my backpack. My right arm cast around, looking for the items that had spilled out. A cylinder? The torch? I needed to grab *something*.

My fingers found the cold metal canister, nearly as big as a can of hair spray.

Liquid nitrogen.

I flipped up the nozzle on the can, snaking the arm that held it around the leg of the shelf.

Almost blindly, I pointed and pressed.

Spider saw the can coming a half second before the blast hit him from ten inches away. His eyes opened wide, and he tried to turn his head. But even Spider wasn't that fast.

The liquid nitrogen hit the left side of his face in a blast, freezing his skin faster than it could send pain signals. His left eye sealed shut. For a precious second he was shocked, body rigid. Then he convulsed, as if he'd been struck by lightning, throwing me off.

But he still held his knife.

I unhooked my arm from the shelf and rolled clear. I seemed to be floating above the room, watching both of us. Outside myself. Time was frozen.

I had never met the man facing off with Spider, his bloodied face as impassive as a block of ice. That man frightened me, but I was glad he was on my side.

Spider's right eye blinked hard, shedding tears from stray flecks of frozen hell. His left eye wasn't working, and I saw something other than pain on Spider's face: fear. No other opponent Spider faced might have lived long enough to see that expression.

But fear wasn't enough. Spider had to die.

Time unfroze. I took a long, sliding step to close the distance between us, turning my hip, and jabbing a left heel kick into his ribs that dropped him where he stood. The kick might have hurt me as much as it hurt Spider.

But finally, blessedly, Spider's knife flew out of his hand as he collapsed to the ground. He groaned, a primal, guttural sound, staggering back to his feet.

Without his knife to fear, I went straight at him. I hit him so fast in the throat that I didn't see my own hand move. He stumbled back against the wall, clutching at the damage. He didn't even have time to gurgle before I elbowed his head and spun him with an Indonesian *puter kepala* head throw. Dropped him to the ground and followed him down, wrapped my legs around his waist from behind, snaked one arm around his neck, and wrapped the other arm around his head to try to get the leverage to choke him, a modification of judo's *hadaka shime san*, "naked strangle."

Spider was a thoroughbred, but I was an alley cat, had roamed from school to school in search of . . . I'm not certain what. I may not have gone deep, but I'd gone wide, and in that basement, in that terribly bright moment in time, all those parallel lines of training had joined in infinity.

Parallax.

Spider thrashed, still incredibly strong, his convulsion powerful enough to lift us both from the ground before we crashed back down. I couldn't get the leverage I wanted, so I reached up and sank my teeth into his ear. As his blood filled my mouth with the taste of molten copper, he tensed involuntarily. I twisted his flesh in my teeth, bearing down harder in my death grip. My arm must have felt like a metal pipe across his throat.

Spider clutched at me, bucking like a bronco frantic to throw its rider. When my head hit the ground, hard, I barely noticed the shower of sparks. I bore down.

I held on for my life, and for Nandi's. I shifted my grip, and bore down against unresisting flesh. I couldn't afford to take a chance, not against someone as dangerous as this. I held on until Spider's twitching stopped.

Strange. The sound, when it came, was more crunch than snap.

For precious seconds, I heard only my rasping breaths. My whole body shook as I considered a marvelous thing: *No snapping sound. Who would have thought?*

I pushed his limp body away. He looked very like a sleeping child. So small, now.

All of me hurt. Everything bled. I didn't think I could stand up, but I knew I couldn't stay on my knees.

Nandi was crying. There was still an army upstairs. This wasn't over, not by a long shot.

I forced myself up to my feet. My right leg was jelly, preoccupied with its pain. When calf muscles flexed, I felt Spider's knife afresh. With each limping step, he stabbed me again. But while I felt the pain, it was in my body, not in *me*.

I know that sounds strange, but it's the only way I can describe what I was experiencing.

Nandi was crying, but first I needed my Beretta. I hop-jumped to the shelf as fast I could between pulses of pain, grabbing the magazine and loading the gun with fingers that were steadier than I had any right to expect. I trained the gun toward the stairs. I thought I heard six or seven sets of footsteps, but no one came. I thought I heard heavy breathing, but it was mine.

Nandi was crying.

I must have been a horror, covered in blood. I ran to the laundry room's sink, between the washer and dryer. The faucet was tight from lack of use, but I turned on a thin stream of water, glad when the pipes didn't moan. I grabbed an undershirt from a heap of dirty clothes on the dryer and wiped my face and hair. I cupped water in my hands and let it wash over me. I watched the sink fill with pink water. My blood.

Nandi was crying.

"Coming, honey!" I said.

I tore off my ripped and bloodied T-shirt. I grabbed at the first dark item I saw from the pile of clothes; it looked like a teenager's hooded black cotton jacket. The right leg of my jeans was soaked with blood, but the jacket covered the rest.

I probably needed a tourniquet, but Nandi was crying.

I ran to the tarp and pulled it off the playpen. I dragged the tarp to Spider and laid it over him. I didn't look at his face to see if his eyes were open or closed.

Nandi was sitting in filth in a corner of the playpen, her face bright red with terror as she stared up at me. But she stopped crying.

My smile was a damn good one. My smile was the only thing that might save our lives.

"It's Mr. Ten, Nandi," I said cheerfully. "We're going now. You need to be very quiet."

Nandi nodded, watching my smile.

She didn't cry. She wobbled to her feet on fat legs.

Her face aglow with trust, Nandi reached up to be lifted into my arms.

Nandi, it turned out, was small enough to hide in a laundry basket piled with clothes.

She wriggled restlessly, but her face and limbs didn't show. And the crying had stopped.

She weighed only about twenty-five pounds, but my slashed arms made carrying her a torture separate from walking. And walking was its own fierce challenge. Climbing steps was three times as hard as walking.

I listened at the door. The voices were gone.

"Remember—if we make noise, we lose," I said.

Nandi didn't make a sound to answer. The basket trembled against my bleeding arm, but I tightened my grip around it. My Beretta was in my right hand, wrapped inside a T-shirt. Nandi was bundled in clothes, so I could afford to drop her in a hurry and squeeze off quick rounds, if it came to that. Then I would have to improvise.

My foot was bracing the door slightly ajar, and I pushed it open, emerging into the brightly lighted hall with the black hood pulled up over my head, shoulders hunched. Just a guy bringing up the laundry.

Should I go upstairs, or toward the back door?

The open window upstairs might have been easiest, but I didn't trust myself to carry Nandi safely down the tree. My body wanted to rest on the floor; that's the natural thing a body does when it's bleeding so much. The skin on my face was cold, and I felt dizzy when I breathed fast. If I was going into shock, losing too much blood, I couldn't count on climbing down the tree.

It had to be downstairs.

I staggered in place, staring toward the front doors. They were a straight walk twenty feet across the living-room tile, and mine for the taking. AK-47 would be curious, but his car was parked only a few painful steps from the front door. If necessary, I could shoot him.

The locks didn't need keys from the inside. The door might be unlocked from AK-47's toilet break. He might not pay any attention to me and my basket of laundry.

I tried to see it unfold in a way I could believe.

"Hey!" a voice chided me. He was one of the men I'd heard before, approaching me from the reading room. I lowered my head, relying on my hood to shield me. I turned away, walking slowly toward the butler's pantry behind me, away from the front door.

"*Molo*," I said pleasantly in Xhosa, as I would speak to a friend. It only meant *hello*, and it sounded like I would need something stronger.

"'*Molo*'?" he mimicked me, and berated me in Xhosa or Zulu. Shit—wrong word. I kept up my steady pace, walking away. He followed me, his voice rising. He'd mistaken me for someone else, which had bought me a few seconds, but I would have to shoot him before long. I walked slowly to put it off as long as possible. Gunfire would only make everything harder.

In my mind, I was standing at the top of Table Mountain. That's how calm I got. Another phrase came back to me from a long-ago visit to Cape Town. A useful phrase.

I stopped walking, waiting for him to reach me. My back was still turned to him.

"*Ndicela uxolo*," I said. *Sorry.* It was the only clicking word I knew, with clicks on the *c* and *x*, which I'd practiced to impress Alice. I shifted my head toward him as if to make eye contact, stopping just shy of showing him my profile. I engaged him with sincerity, adding a dash of deference. "*Ndicela uxolo*, boss."

He started to say something else, but I took another step forward and punted his balls up into his throat. He made a sucking-lemons face and dropped to his knees, clutching himself, a thin, strangled scream escaping his lips for the second before the ball of my foot struck his temple squarely. He hit the ground like a bag of bones.

I set the basket down, dragged his body to the cellar door, and threw him down the stairs.

A dark spot on the floor caught my eye.

I had left a smudged trail of blood from my bleeding calf. Trying to clean it up might only make it worse. The next person in that hallway would see the blood.

Moving as quickly as I could, I left the cellar door and headed back to the alcove, which led to the butler's pantry. I had reached the rear of the house.

A window inside the butler's pantry stared out at the backyard's night. I'd been beneath that window not long ago, where I'd overheard the boss and his adviser deciding to kill Nandi. The window was high and would have been an awkward climb, but I tried to unlock it. It might have been bolted, or maybe I was losing my strength. I wasn't sure. I was light-headed.

The sound of the breaking window would attract attention, too.

I walked through the length of the butler's pantry, which was large and well stocked, and emerged in the rear of the bright kitchen. The other end of the kitchen led to the sunroom. The summit between the men was still under way. I saw at least four, only twenty feet from the kitchen door. One of the Asian men paced in the doorway, and I barely ducked back into shadow in time for him to miss me.

The door I'd seen outside was the kitchen's back door, midway between the butler's pantry and the sunroom. Marsha had promised to unlock the door for me, and she would be waiting.

Thank God. Marsha is here.

She might be Nandi's last chance.

I would hand off the basket to Marsha, stay behind to cover them. Marsha could make it to the car with Nandi. The keys were with the car. The plan ended with Nandi getting home and me getting shot dead, but despite its flaws, the plan wasn't bad.

As long as Marsha was there.

Nandi was wriggling, so I bounced the basket to soothe her. "*Shhhhh . . . ,*" I said.

"I'm hungry," she said, whining but not crying.

"*Shhhhhh.*"

Once Nandi had quieted, I moved to the kitchen. I tried to hide my limp, walking with an urgent pace, as if I had important tasks. It took two tries to get the knob to turn.

"Who's that?" someone said from the sunroom.

I was way beyond *Hello* and *Sorry.* Keeping my head down, my finger ready on my trigger, I pulled the back door open. It opened inside the house, so I could shield myself longer. I couldn't see anything except gray in the darkness.

"I'm here!" I called out.

"Hey!" a voice challenged from twenty paces behind me, and closing. It might have been the same man who'd followed me earlier.

"I've got her!" I said, taking a step outside. I felt the air on my face.

I made out the pale flowers on the hibiscus bushes near the sunroom. I glanced up at the tree, silhouetted against a bright, swollen moon.

A man, unconscious or dead, lay on the ground outside the door.

But Marsha was gone.

TWENTY-EIGHT

OKAY, I THOUGHT, staring out at the dark, still yard. Impossibly calm.

All thoughts and plans halted while I watched myself move.

I tossed the laundry basket to the side of the house, where it rolled gently to the wall. Nandi cried out in protest, but she was clear. I whirled back toward the kitchen doorway and fired twice at the thin Asian man who was ten feet behind me. He dodged back into the kitchen, yelling as my second shot snapped his shoulder around. The T-shirt wrapped around my gun glowed hot. Fabric burned.

The security light came on like a noonday sun. Nandi crawled out of the laundry basket, crying in plain view. I pulled Nandi toward me by the back of her collar. I scooped her into my arms and ran for the darkness, and the fence.

POP POP.

Glass shattered as a gun was fired from the sunroom. Soil jumped beside my foot.

"He has the girl!" the boss man said.

The gravel driveway back to the road was too far in the wrong direction, so the driveway wouldn't have worked, regardless of the headlights sweeping toward me on the road.

I ran in the grass. Downhill. So fast that my feet tripped as often as they didn't, like falling while upright. I caught my balance at the fence, and the basket fit through the rails with ease.

My body howled with pain, but the howl was far away, like a distant hurricane. I ran with Nandi into the vineyard.

When I collapsed, stumbling, to my knees, I was sure I'd been shot. The world rocked into focus. Grape leaves scratched my face and eyes. Nandi's grip on my neck nearly choked me, but the sudden drop to the ground stopped her crying cold.

"*Shhhhh,*" I said, resurrecting my smile. "It's okay. It's okay."

That was the best I could do. Those few words drained my breath.

I waited for my heart to seize up, or for everything to melt away. The men shooting at me might kill me, but I was dying already. I'd killed Spider quick, but he'd killed me slow.

"Get lights out here!" the boss's English accent said.

They weren't firing anymore, but they were looking. Even in hunting country, gunfire will attract the neighbors' attention.

I checked the distant glow of Paso Robles's night lights to orient myself. They were east, and our car was parked northwest of the farmhouse. The keys were with the car.

"*There!*" someone said.

I cradled Nandi over my shoulder, my hand resting across the tiny bones in her back.

When I crawled our first step since my knees had buckled, my leg cramped, and I nearly yelled out. The earth near my face smelled sweet when I stumbled down. Nandi wriggled against me, whimpering, but never fell or made a sound.

The voices were getting closer, a *swishing* of men walking briskly through the vineyard, closing in with regimented precision, just like at the football field.

"*Shhhhh,* it's okay," I lied. "It's okay, Nandi. It's okay."

I rubbed her back, and Nandi's whimpering stopped. Her weight rested against me. Nandi was tired, too.

A crackle in my ear, a foot away. I made out a man standing over me, breathing hard. I raised my gun, but I knew I was too late. He had seen me first. I was already in his sights.

"*Don't move!*" the voice said, a harsh whisper. "Mr. Hardwick. It is Paki."

My gun's muzzle leveled on his chest, and my finger caressed the trigger. The man I had become in the basement wanted to shoot Paki most of all.

But Paki hadn't called for his boss. For an instant of silence, hope danced.

"What do you want?" I said.

"*Quiet*," Paki said. "Is she safe? Let me see her."

Paki stepped closer, out of the shadows, kneeling beside me.

We weren't dead yet. But someone had a powerful flashlight. The beam swept down the rows to our left.

"Give her to me!" Paki whispered, reaching for Nandi.

"No way," I said, angling her away from him. My Beretta was in his face.

Leaves thrashed and soil danced behind us. Six gunshots, popping firecrackers.

Paki pulled me out of the way of a bullet that singed my ear as it passed. When I stumbled, Paki kept me on my feet. When I didn't know which way to run, he steered me. I just held on to Nandi and kept quiet during the pain; and that took every drop of strength that remained to me.

Paki is the last person I want to credit for saving my life, or Nandi's. But he did.

The shooting stopped, replaced by cursing and fevered consultations. The voices fell farther and farther behind us. Paki kept me on my feet.

Still not dead.

I pulled my arm away from Paki and staggered a step on my own. Pain hammered me, but I stayed on my feet. "Northwest," I whispered. "I parked a car. Through the fence."

"Too far. There is a car in the barn," Paki said. "A service road behind the vineyard."

The barn seemed an impossible distance away, at least forty yards up the hill. Barely visible in the dark.

Headlights approached from our left, bigger and brighter with every heartbeat.

A voice behind us barked orders in angry Chinese. We were fucked in every language.

We crouched low. I took a painful step, avoiding the headlights. Stakes and plants churned beneath the truck's undercarriage as it bounced toward us. The headlights followed us.

A large flashlight switched on from the barn, as bright and final as gunfire at close range.

We were cut off. Life narrowed down to single breaths. The truck's roar was loud now.

I covered Nandi's eyes so she wouldn't see the monster truck, and she didn't fight me. She seemed to be falling asleep on my shoulder, lulled by the jouncing.

Excited calls approached behind us. The truck was close enough to show its white paint.

"We will die here!" Paki said.

I tried to stand, but stillness had stolen what remained of my strength. Nandi pressed herself against me. There was a strange peace to seeing what the end looked like, knowing I had done more than I had known was possible. Nothing left undone.

Fate trumps everything. Everything that begins must end. Even Nandi understood that. I wondered what all the struggle, all the fear and striving, had been about.

Flashlight beams bobbled through the vineyard, blinding me.

"'Row, row, row your boat, gently down the stream . . . ,'" I sang for Nandi.

"I didn't know!" Paki whispered, talking to God. "She wasn't supposed to be harmed!"

Nandi's breathing slowed. She was near sleep. I wasn't far behind. We would sleep together. Both of us had earned our rest.

"'Merrily, merrily, merrily, merrily . . .'"

The truck's engine was a lion's roar.

"'Life is but a dream . . .'"

Nandi lay on my shoulder, warm and quiet despite the noise. The grape leaves rustled around me, and it seemed I could see every vein, every imperfection, every budding grape. Each breath was a sip of wine. The moon and stars were glowing embers in a cloudless sky.

Beautiful. Perfect.

The winds came with a mighty beating fury, as if to carry us all into the sky. Light poured down, brilliant beyond daylight.

Until I saw the helicopters, I thought I had died.

TWENTY-NINE

THE VINEYARD SWARMED with activity as the night got darker.

I recognized some of the alphabet soup on the windbreakers—FBI and ATF—but most of the men who had rescued me were in street clothes, without letters to announce them. I hadn't seen Nandi since a gleaming gold badge pulled her from my arms.

Nandi cried for too long after that, but she had been quiet for an hour. I hoped the helicopter had hurried her back home. I would have called Maitlin to tell her that Nandi was safe, but my cell phone was long gone. I'd watched a perp walk of fifteen people parade past, but it was hard to feel satisfied when the wheels of justice were rolling over me.

"I work for Sofia Maitlin!" I said, hoarse from trying to explain myself. The knife wounds were an agony, but pain was better than prison.

I was handcuffed to a gurney, so I didn't have a choice about being loaded into the ambulance. Maybe I was being arrested, but I wasn't sure. I didn't know who was taking me into custody, or where I was going. I thought I'd recognized a sunburned face—he'd been wearing a Hawaiian shirt the first time I saw him—but I was too disoriented to place him.

These are Marsha's people, I thought. If so, the cavalry came with a price—but maybe that meant Marsha wasn't hurt. If I knew that, the rest might be easier to take.

I tried to make eye contact with the shaven-headed brother loading me into the ambulance, human to human. He looked more like a soldier than a paramedic. "This was a rescue, man," I explained calmly. "I tailed Paki here with a sister named Marsha Willis. I haven't seen her since I left her standing outside the kitchen door. I just want to know if she's all right."

Marsha might have vanished after calling in the troops, or been injured before they arrived. She might be dying in the vineyard somewhere. I couldn't stand not knowing.

The medic shrugged with a curt shake of his head. *Tell it to somebody else, man.*

And slammed the ambulance door.

All I know is that it wasn't Cedars-Sinai.

Tight-lipped doctors and nurses examined me—including X-rays—decided I didn't need surgery, gave me a blood transfusion, and patched me up. No one offered me painkillers, but I would have refused anyway. I wasn't sure my mind was sharp enough to keep me out of prison.

I didn't know how much time had passed, or if it was night or day. The vineyard seemed like a dream with a happy ending for Nandi, but a different one for me.

While the medical staff swabbed and stitched me like a NASCAR pit crew, I sat under the harsh fluorescent lights and remembered Marsha telling me that the deal I made to free Nandi might be prison. She'd told me in plain English.

So that's the next thing, I thought, with no particular feeling. All I wanted was sleep.

If someone had offered me a bed, I might have signed my name to anything.

But I was far from sleepy. The pain, and the wondering, kept me wide awake.

After the doctors finished their work, I was brought to a conference room furnished with a small square table and a single iron chair. My hands were cuffed in front of me, which was hell on my bandaged wrist. I had been handcuffed for hours.

And sitting, period, wasn't fun. Considering.

The room was too cold, with no clock and a reflective picture window that was obviously a two-way mirror. There was nowhere to lie down, so I tried to rest my head on the table. I learned pretty quickly that it was better to sit upright. I didn't try to pose for anyone. Despite my discomfort, I was glad for the quiet.

Maybe I slept. I'm not sure. I was alone in the room for at least two hours. Longer.

Three agents—two men and a woman—finally opened the door and came inside. I didn't expect good news, but I was glad to see them. If I was going to prison, I wanted to know.

They stood over me, one on either side, the third straight in front.

The man facing me had wild eyes and a beard that needed trimming. He definitely wasn't FBI. The second man looked Latino, gray-flecked hair cut stylishly, wearing a plain navy blue sweat suit. The woman, big boned and in her thirties, looked more officious in a schoolmarm's skirt without a wrinkle.

All of them were dressed to disappear in a crowd, unremarkable.

"You can call me R.J.," the bearded man said. "We're gonna hang out for a while."

"My name is Tennyson Hardwick," I said, my mantra. "I work for Sofia Maitlin."

R.J. held up his hand, but politely: *no need.* He slipped his hand into his pocket and pulled out handcuff keys. A practiced turn and my wrists were free. I hadn't realized how uncomfortable they were until they were gone.

R.J. went on: "This is Reiter, and this is Ramirez. The three R's."

He smile was tame, but his eyes stayed wild.

I was tired, so my eyes might have been a little wild, too. I'd needed to take a piss for hours, but I didn't give them the satisfaction of asking. I didn't trust R.J. removing my handcuffs.

"I need to make a call," I said.

R.J.'s smile widened, suddenly looking sincere. But he shook his head. "Don't think so."

"You're saying I can't call my lawyer?" I said.

Still smiling, R.J. nodded slowly, as he would to a child. "Get that out of your system?"

"I don't talk without my lawyer."

"Good thing that chair's comfortable," R.J. said.

After two hours, the chair was far from comfortable, handcuffs or not. I needed to be in a bed, probably a hospital. I hurt. *Sonofabitch*. It was going to be a long night. Or day.

R.J. lit a cigarillo that smelled foul, far too close to my nose. "There's a dead man back there, Hardwick. And your fingerprints are all over that cellar."

Too many fingerprints for denial. I gambled on the truth.

"A kidnapper," I corrected him. "On his way to murder Nandi. He attacked me with a knife, so it was self-defense. I'd do it again." The memory of Spider in the basement was hazy, as if I had watched it on a movie screen. In memory, I watched another man, a lethal man without hesitation or doubt. I'd waited my whole life to meet him.

"Whoa, whoa." R.J. laughed, and the others chuckled. "He's still dead. Chill out. Chill out—get it? The ME said that the tissue damage to his face and eye looked like extreme cold. There was a liquid nitrogen container on the floor. Wonder if that had anything to do with it."

"You're kidding," Reiter said. She sounded impressed.

"Liquid nitro?" Ramirez said, peering down at me. "Classic."

At any moment, they might all start slapping my back and inviting me out for whiskey shots. I wondered what was waiting at the end of the bullshit.

The room was gray with smoke. My throat wanted to cough, but I refused.

"We like you, Tennyson," R.J. said. "We like you a *lot*."

The others agreed. Reiter patted my back firmly, an old buddy. The impact sent a bolt of pain through my right leg, already stretched in a painful position. My teeth gritted. I made no sound.

"There's just a couple of problems with your story," R.J. went on, his voice sober. "Actually, they're pretty damn big problems. So we're gonna take some time and clarify."

"Shouldn't take more than a few hours," Ramirez said.

"A few days at most," finished Reiter.

They said it like they were joking.

"The Marsha thing, for starters," R.J. said. He consulted a file folder. "Marsha . . . ?"

"Marsha Willis."

"Yeah, Marsha Yvonne Willis, Hollywood High School?" R.J. said.

"Yeah," I said.

"She lives in Canyon Country. We just talked to her on the phone. Nice lady." I didn't like where the tone of his voice was going. "The Marsha thing is bullshit, Tennyson. Marsha Willis didn't go with you to Paso on a covert op. She wasn't helping you rescue an abducted child. Tonight's soccer night."

He gave me the folder.

A sharp color printout of a driver's license photo of a woman named Marsha Willis Henderson stared up at me. The years had filled out her cheeks, but her nose was exactly as I'd remembered from *A Raisin in the Sun*. I didn't have to look at the rest in the file, although I saw a headline in a story where she was named her school's teacher of the year.

The woman I had known as Marsha shared her complexion and height, enough to be her sister, but it wasn't her. I knew right away. *Shit.* I hadn't checked her out because I'd thought I knew who she was. Since *I'd* proposed the name to *her,* I'd never been suspicious.

I could have been pissed off, or sad, but I still had a little of that odd sensation of floating outside myself. I tried, but I couldn't feel anything.

"She played me," I said. "She lied."

"Someone's lying," Ramirez said. His eyes were sober, too.

"This is our entire conundrum," R.J. said. "We talk to Marsha, who turns out to be a junior high school drama teacher of the year—and then we've got you. You, by the way, have broken a pretty alarming number of federal laws. I don't know how well you've been briefed, but you are in a shitload of trouble."

"I haven't been briefed, actually," I said.

"The FBI is writing a book on you as we speak," R.J. said. "Usually that's the bad news. But in your case, that's the good news."

I couldn't resist. "Then what's the bad news?"

"You seen that TV show . . . ? What's the name?" R.J. asked Ramirez and Reiter.

"What show?" Reiter said.

At first, I thought he was talking about my old series, *Homeland*. I'd played an FBI agent working with the Department of Homeland Security.

R.J. snapped his fingers. *"Without a Trace,"* he said. "It's about people who've disappeared, right? One day they're here, then *bam*, they're gone. That's a fascinating show."

He was looking at me again, the wildness back in his eyes.

"You ever heard of the Patriot Act?" R.J. asked me.

"For fighting terrorists," I said.

"For example," R.J. said.

I suddenly realized how hungry I was. I wondered again if it was day or night.

"That's got nothing to do with me," I said. I wanted to force him to say what he was hinting at. "I'm not a terrorist."

"But you're an *interesting* guy," R.J. said.

"Fascinating guy," Ramirez agreed in a singsong voice.

R.J. went on. "And if we decide we want to talk to you for a while, get to know you better, we can keep you around as long as we need to. But nobody wants that," R.J. said.

"Pain in the ass," Ramirez said.

Cold-steel reality unfolded in my head: I was in an interrogation room in an unknown location. My body felt butchered. I had been promised a long stretch in prison. I had just lost my oldest friend. I had barely survived the night, and a man had died at my hands.

No. I had *killed* a man. For the first time in my life I'd stilled a beating heart. Wasn't I supposed to feel something about that? Anything at all?

He was dead, I was alive.

I wondered how many people R.J., Ramirez, and Reiter had killed among them, or what measures they were willing to take when they wanted information. I didn't get along with most cops already—but they weren't cops, or anything like it.

I wished they were. I understood the rules with cops. There were no rules in this room. There were ends, and means, and God help anyone caught between them.

R.J. folded his arms, sighing for me. We both understood my predicament.

"As for the dead guy, it's your word against a witness," R.J. said. "Our witness, it turns out, has a lot of surprising things to say."

"What witness are you talking to? Paki?" I said. No one answered, but Paki was probably on a crusade to keep himself out of prison. "He sold his daughter out for ransom. He'll say anything to stay out of jail."

"But what will *you* say to stay out of jail?" R.J. said.

I finally got it.

"This is all about my statement," I said. "My official story to the FBI." Stone silence from the three R's.

"Let me guess . . . ," I went on. "You don't want me to mention a certain female operative."

R.J. smiled, approving. "That's a good start. But you're missing the big picture."

"Bigger than lying to the FBI?" I said.

R.J. leaned closer to me, those wild eyes at the bridge of my nose. "You're not thinking too clearly, are you?" R.J. said.

I didn't blink. "I'm thinking very clearly," I said.

"I hope so," R.J. said. "People who don't think weary me."

I thought about my bed at home. Wondered what Dad and Chela were going through, worried about me. Those were the thoughts R.J., or whatever his name was, wanted me to have.

"The way I see it," R.J. said, "you have two choices: Sit here and piss on yourself for the next few days, or you can play it smart."

My heavy bladder pulsed, taut. "I'm listening."

"Here's what happened," R.J. said. "You got drunk. You mouthed off at two guys in a bar. Or four. Whatever your ego can handle. They jumped you. You passed out. You lost track of time."

No one who knew me would believe that story.

"You never met anybody in covert ops," R.J. went on. "You've never heard of Kingdom of Heaven."

"You were never in San Diego," Ramirez said. "Or Paso. Or Happy Cellars."

Reiter finished: "You haven't seen Nandi since the failed drop."

They had my story all worked out.

"The FBI found Nandi," I said, trying the lie out on my tongue.

R.J. smiled. "Damn right."

"Best agents in the world," Ramirez said.

"God bless America," finished Reiter.

We worked out the story a bit longer, and I thought they might be willing to let me go home soon. When I asked to use the bathroom, they cheerfully agreed.

R.J., Ramirez, and Reiter were gone when I was brought back to the interrogation room, but lunch was waiting for me on the tiny table—a bag from In-N-Out Burger that smelled like Heaven in a wrapper. Inside, the double cheeseburger and fries were still warm.

It was the best damn burger I ever tasted, just like Marsha promised.

Wherever she was. Whoever she was.

We were both invisible that day.

The man who had killed Spider and rescued Nandi was somewhere in the room, somewhere in my body. But he wasn't me.

If he wasn't me, then . . .

A voice from the dead whispered in my ear: *"After we dance, you and I . . . if you survive, you will understand my words."*

Spider's words. He claimed to have found the answer to my life's question.

And now, so had I. I thought he'd seen the fighter in me, because that was what I'd always thought I was seeking. Instead, what I'd found was a killer. He had known it from the beginning.

Cliff had told me I'd make a breakthrough in six months. I had gone to a place beyond my dreams, and it had taken only six minutes.

Of all the teachers I had ever known, how very strange that, in the end, a little South African named Spider had been the best.

THIRTY

I LOST ABOUT thirty-six hours after the shoot-out in the vineyard. By the
time an unsociable FBI team dropped me off at my front door, it was
seven o'clock in the morning the day *after* Nandi got home. I didn't know
what day of the week it was. My street fascinated me, as if I'd never seen
it before, shiny cars and colorful gardens. The gardens reminded me of
Paki's house.

There were no paparazzi waiting. I wasn't a part of their story anymore, and that was fine with me. Anonymity has its advantages.

I hopped up my walkway with my crutches. My right leg was wrapped
and braced.

"Holy *crap!*" Chela said when she opened the door. Her face twisted,
as if the sight of me hurt her feelings. I hadn't expected the tears in her
eyes. "Ten, are you okay? What the—"

"Better than the other guy," I said, a rote joke that made my stomach
drop. "I'm fine."

"What the hell, Ten?" Chela said. "Nobody knew anything. Your
agent called and said Sofia Maitlin was trying to find you. Nandi's back
home, but you're gone? No calls, no cell phone? We went to the freaking
morgue last night!"

"*Shhhhh.* It's okay," I said, and hugged her. I could have been talking
to Nandi.

Dad stood in the doorway with a new wooden cane, eyeing me to see if he believed me. He watched the unmarked FBI sedan drive off until it turned the corner, out of sight.

"What happened?" Dad said when I didn't offer a story.

"Nothing," I said. "Bad night. Too much to drink. Couple of guys jumped me."

The cover story was the plainest way to tell Dad I couldn't talk about it. He'd never known me to be drunk in my life. I trusted Dad with my secrets—but like Marsha said, I didn't know who was listening.

"Next time, pick up a damn phone," Dad said, and I wondered if he'd believed me until I saw the comprehension in his eyes. We would talk later. Privately.

"Were those cops?" Chela said, and gently led me into the foyer.

"They let me off with a warning," I said.

Someone stirred on the living-room sofa, and it wasn't Marcela. At first, I didn't recognize the tall young man sitting there, his wiry hair mussed from sleep. He was olive skinned, with a thin, dark mustache. Had an agent been sent to my house?

"Hey, Mr. Hardwick," said a voice that was deeper than I remembered. "Sorry I crashed out. Chela was going crazy."

His name came to me. *Bernard Faison.* Chela's boyfriend.

"I said it was all right, Ten," Dad said. "He slept on the couch."

As far as you know, I thought. When I was in high school, I asked Dad if I could spent the night on a girlfriend's sofa—and he looked at me like I was crazy. Chela grabbed my arm, as if to restrain me. I hid my flinch so she wouldn't know she'd hurt me.

"He was helping us check hospitals!" Chela said. "He drove me all over after school yesterday, then he got us Taco Bell. I don't know what we would have done without B., Ten."

Bernard unfolded, standing at his full height, and he was taller than I remembered, too.

"No big deal, Mr. Hardwick," Bernard said modestly. "Glad you made it home. Go easy with the . . . you know . . . *drinking.*" He stage-whispered the word with a disapproving look.

Chela held his hand, and for a moment I was forgotten. Bernard filled her eyes.

"Thanks, man," I told Bernard, "but I wasn't expecting company." I

didn't want Bernard up in Chela's room with her, and I didn't want anyone except family in my living room.

Bernard's face went flat. "Oh. Right. You're probably . . . tired."

Chela looked mortified, but my bandages kept her civil. "He needs to
sleep it off, baby," Chela told Bernard as she led him to the door, casting
me a look over her shoulder.

Was Chela in love with him? If I didn't hurry and adopt her, she
would be grown.

The stairs would be hell on my leg, so I stopped at the sofa for a while,
pushing Bernard's blanket aside. Chela stayed outside with Bernard for a
long time, an emotional good-bye after their first trial together. Bernard's
stature had risen while I was gone. *Glad to help, B.*

The news on TV didn't bother me anymore, since the story wasn't
about me.

BIRTH FATHER ARRESTED, the caption on CNN's screen read. Footage taped the previous day showed a proud police procession following
Maitlin and her husband as they brought Nandi home. Nandi was all
cleaned up, with bows in her combed hair. I hoped Maitlin would never
know exactly how her child had looked and smelled in the basement in
Paso Robles.

Watching Sophia and Nandi waving and grinning for the cameras
in front of Maitlin's house, it looked like mommy-and-daughter day at
the park. Their joyous smiles were identical. *Ebony and Ivory,* I thought.
Living in perfect harmony on my HD flat screen.

Next came footage of Happy Cellars, where police vehicles still
crowded the farmhouse.

". . . a harrowing scene in tranquil Paso Robles last night, halfway
between Los Angeles and San Francisco, when helicopters descended
on the vineyard where Nandi Maitlin was being held . . . one kidnapper
is dead, and the FBI made at least a dozen other arrests, including Paki
Zangwa, the South African national who is Nandi's birth father . . ."

Paki's mug shot. He took a good photo even when all hell was breaking loose.

For irony's sake, the network showed footage of Maitlin's *The Vintner.* Maitlin, in Victorian dress, was running between rows of ripe grapes
toward an impossibly beautiful sunrise.

When Marcela arrived with a small bag of groceries, I had to submit to prodding and wrapping all over again. She grudgingly admitted that the doctors had done a good job with my injuries, but she clucked because I hadn't been admitted to a proper hospital.

"A knife again?" she said, without being told. She could tell by the marks.

"Clumsy me," I said.

Marcela held both of my hands, trying to get past the crazy. "That knife came only inches from an artery in your leg. *Cinco minutos,* and good-bye. And your face!" She looked mournful, gazing at my slashed cheek, like a ruined Picasso.

"I'll never drink again," I said. Except maybe the occasional glass of wine. Maybe.

I noticed intricate African designs on Dad's cane. It was the one April had bought in Little Ethiopia, I realized. "April came by?" I said.

"Checked in on you yesterday," Dad said. "Worried, like the rest of us."

Like everyone else I knew, I owed April a call. I had given up on getting my phone back. Once I could stand up again, I would need a new cell phone—but I no longer felt incomplete when I was out of touch with April. The people I needed to talk to were already here.

"Where's the vampire lady?" Chela said, returning from her long good-bye. "Was she with you when you got jumped?"

"Nah," I said. "She's moved on. Rolling stone kinda thing."

"Good," Marcela said fiercely. "I didn't like her."

"Seemed all right to me," Dad said, and Marcela breezed away with her medical kit.

"Why aren't you getting ready for school?" I asked Chela. "Go on. I'll still be here when you get back."

Chela sighed, ready to protest. Instead, she wrapped an arm around my neck, careful to steer away from my bandages. "You better be, Dad," she said.

Dad.

My heart, which had felt dead for days, sparked back to life.

After Chela went upstairs, Dad sat beside me on the sofa, without help except from his cane. His sigh wasn't from exertion; it was a leftover worry set free.

"Sorry, Dad," I told him. "It was out of my control. I couldn't call."

Dad patted my knee. "Grateful you're in one piece, more or less. Thank you, Jesus."

On TV, the newscaster said the FBI would be giving a press conference the next day.

"Feds pulled it off after all . . . ," Dad said, almost a question.

"Looks that way."

"Caught a lucky break?"

"Real lucky," I said.

We left it at that, for the time being. Dad was so proud of me, he couldn't help smiling. He patted my knee again.

The last faces I saw before I dozed off to sleep were Maitlin's. And Nandi's.

Smiling.

I had made it up to my bed by two o'clock, when Len Shemin called. By then, I had slept and not much else all day. Any interruptions felt like dreams; only sleeping felt real. I was sleeping so hard, I didn't have rooms for real dreams.

"Is this your number now?" Len said. "The home number? All this time, I never had it."

"For a while," I said.

"Before I forget, Spike wants to know when you can be on the set," Len said. "They called this morning—so you're still in. Let's both give thanks to the movie gods."

I tested my body, trying to sit upright. All of me roiled with pain, even in places the knife hadn't touched. I vowed to start painkillers by bedtime.

"I can't do it before next week," I said. *Or a hell of a lot longer.*

I hadn't taken a good look at the scar Spider had left on my cheek, but I might need more than makeup to go back in front of a camera. I didn't have the heart to tell Len yet. Until right then, I hadn't thought about it.

"Next week? Really?" Len said, deflated. Delaying the scene wouldn't sit well with the producers. "Okay. Let's say Monday."

"Monday's not gonna happen, Len," I said. "I need a week. At least."

"Is there something you need to tell me, Tennyson?"

"Nothing I need to, and nothing I can. Sorry, man."

The line was silent while Len pouted. Len knew I didn't divulge most of my secrets, but he hated to be left out of the Sofia Maitlin saga. "Well, I heard back from Rachel Wentz," Len said finally. "She says it's fine. Just show up at the gate."

"When?"

"She said anytime. They're in all day. Thank God the little girl is safe. I hardly slept a wink this whole time. Tennyson, just tell me this . . ." He struggled to find diplomatic language.

"No, I'm not fucking Sofia Maitlin," I said. "Now, before, or ever."

"Thank you," Len said, relieved. "I hate to ask, but it's for your own good. Let this whole stink die, and we'll get you back to work. Six months from now, it's all behind you."

It would never be behind me, but Len didn't need to know that either. "I'll update you on the shoot," I said, as if I juggled movie shoots every day.

None of that mattered. All I could think about that day was Sofia Maitlin's smile.

If Len had known what I wanted to ask her, he wouldn't have helped broker our meeting.

He would have begged me not to go.

The paparazzi encampment down the street from Maitlin's house had thinned, but a dozen cameramen and three news vans sat hoping for footage of Maitlin taking her rescued daughter out for an ice cream. Or to the nearest airport. Where do you run?

No one took notice of the cab that pulled up at Maitlin's gate. The bandage across my cheek looked almost as bad as the bloody scar. Since ugly is a sin in Hollywood, nobody glanced at me twice.

I didn't remember the name of the man at the security gate. He was on Maitlin's staff, the one who'd reminded me of a college football player. Like me, he had aged.

He didn't greet me, since I was a reminder of our shared disasters, and lost friend. I didn't ask when Roman's funeral was scheduled, and he didn't say so. Maybe I had missed it. He gave me a weak, pained nod and opened the gate.

Carter. That was his name. The guilt in his eyes pissed me off. I had slept off my guilt as I lay in my bed thinking of Maitlin's smile.

"You, me, Roman . . . we did good work, Carter," I called as the cab drove me by. He glared like he thought I was being sarcastic. "It wasn't our fault."

"Whatever gets you through the day," he said.

Soon, Sofia Maitlin might need a new security team to protect her from her old security team. She really might.

"Wait for you here?" my cabbie said, taking a break from his Bluetooth. My cabbie was African, maybe Ethiopian. His name on the visor was Dawit.

"Yeah, hang out awhile," I said. "This won't take long."

Walking to Maitlin's door was a return to the scene of a nightmare. The shiny pebbles in the driveway only reminded me of our frenzied search for Nandi, doomed before it started.

Pretty isn't the same as happy; it only looks that way.

The housekeeper who'd stood with me beside Nandi's kidnapper in the kitchen opened the door. The memory passed between us, too, unspoken. She pursed her lips.

"Please follow me," she said.

Somewhere, Nandi was laughing. With the ceilings up to the sky and a foyer as large as a courtyard, Nandi was suddenly all around me. I'll never be able to describe that sound, but it made me promise myself a date with Dad to church. It almost put me in a better mood.

Riding on Nandi's laughter, I didn't mind so much that the housekeeper was leading me across the length of the house, toward the back. I hadn't planned to see the backyard again.

I saw Maitlin through the sliding glass door before we reached the patio—she and Rachel Wentz were sitting at a shaded table near the pool, the same table where they'd been on the day of the party. The day Paki was sitting with them.

"Mr. Hardwick!" a familiar voice exclaimed behind me. Zukisa, the nanny, was overjoyed to see me. Her dark, lovely face glowed. She rushed as if to embrace me, but stayed clear of my crutches, bouncing on her toes. "We have her back with us!"

"I heard," I said. "How's she doing?"

Zukisa's smile faded fast. "It is still difficult," she said. "She doesn't sleep well. Cries and cries. Won't stand the dark." Her South African accent made each word a poem.

"Don't try to put her in a playpen," I said before I could stop myself.

Zukisa's eyes widened: *How did you know?* She nodded. "Yes . . . it will take time."

"She's got that," I said.

I wanted to return Zukisa's smile, but I couldn't. I wasn't sure what I thought of her. I didn't know where she fit yet. She hadn't worked at Children First, but what if she was connected to Paki somehow, too?

"Are you going to be all right, Mr. Hardwick?" Zukisa called after me as I followed the housekeeper through the door.

"I will be," I said. *One day.*

Rachel Wentz and Maitlin both stood up when they saw me coming on my crutches, but they didn't move otherwise. Their conversation stopped dead.

Rachel Wentz was dressed for a day at the office, and Maitlin was in shorts and a T-shirt. I noticed her light dusting of makeup only because of the bright sun. Two brown ducks squabbled over bread in the water in the nearby duck pond.

Rachel Wentz glanced at Maitlin with a face for a funeral. Then she picked up her BlackBerry and stepped toward me, resting her hand on my shoulder. I wasn't sure what I thought about Rachel Wentz either.

"My mind can't fathom it," Wentz said. "Thank you so much for everything you did to help Nandi. We'll never forget it. *Anything* I can do for you, don't hesitate. Call us about your compensation. I'm going to start dropping your name. You're a genuine hero, and that's a rare thing in this town."

The old Tennyson Hardwick's fortune might have been made.

The new Tennyson Hardwick stood, and watched, and kept his thoughts to himself.

"Anyway . . . ," Wentz said, looking pained. She turned to give Maitlin a long hug. "It's in God's hands . . . ," I heard her whisper.

Then she gave me another pinched smile, and left me alone with Maitlin.

Neither of us said anything until I heard the glass patio door slide open and close again. Only the ducks were close enough to hear us.

"I'm sorry I can't bring Nandi out," Maitlin said. "I just don't want to remind her . . ."

"She's seen enough blood," I said.

Maitlin's cheeks went pale. She sat again, as if her legs had given out beneath her.

"Seat?" she said weakly.

"No thanks. It hurts when I sit down."

Maitlin glanced at me, appraising my injuries. Then she looked away, toward the still water of the swimming pool. "I thought she'd drowned, at first," Maitlin said. "When Zukisa and Roman came to the table and said Nandi was missing, I was afraid to look in the pool. Just last night, I dreamed she was at the bottom of the pool. This damn pool has always scared me. I wanted Nandi to have somewhere familiar to come home to, but . . ." She shook her head. "I can't stay in this house. It's torture to sit out here."

The green lawn was empty, but I could see the phantom pirate ships, one red, one blue. A part of me would always be fused to this spot, searching.

"Nandi told us," Maitlin said after a pause, still not looking at me. "Last night, she said, 'Is Mr. Ten here?' She said Mr. Ten took her away from the bad men. She said you got cut with a knife. I didn't know what to make of her story, but now I see for myself. I don't know how you did it, but . . . thank you."

"The FBI found Nandi," I said, because I had to.

The mention of the FBI made Maitlin wipe away tears with a waiting tissue box. "Paki . . . ," she sighed. "He's not a bad man. I think he met some bad people."

"We all meet a few of those." Maitlin had mentioned him first. "Was it in Cape Town? At the winery?" I said. "Was that where you first met Paki?"

Maitlin glanced up at me, a silent plea. But my eyes didn't give her anywhere to hide.

"Yes," she said finally. "He was the on-site mechanic there. Handy-man, plumber . . . he did everything. We were shooting *Vintner*. Almost three years ago."

"And?"

She stared at the tabletop. "And . . . I was foolish."

Until she said the words, I might have been talked out of believing it. "You slept with him?"

"It was more than that," Maitlin snapped, as if she were offended. "For six weeks . . . we were lovers. The whole world knew my husband was cheating on me, and in walked beautiful Paki. I cared about him—encouraged him to go to school. He was bright. He speaks four languages! He came to my room at night. No one on the set knew."

"But you were engaged to a billionaire," I said.

"Yes." Instinct made her look around to make sure we weren't being watched.

"And you got pregnant?"

Instead of answering, Maitlin nodded, her head tilting slightly forward. "I was almost suicidal. I couldn't tell Alec. We were just getting past all the scandals, working toward a marriage contract. He felt guilty for what he'd put me through, so he was feeling . . . generous."

Seventy-five million dollars. And that was if the marriage only lasted less than ten years. If they made it a decade? Maitlin would be able to buy her own studio.

Maitlin went on: "I felt trapped. I couldn't tell Alec, and I couldn't bring myself to get rid of the baby. I hid my pregnancy almost the entire first trimester, even from Alec."

"Did you tell Paki?"

"No," Maitlin said. "We thought . . ." She stopped herself. She hadn't meant to say *we*. Since she hadn't been working in league with her husband, that left Rachel Wentz.

"Don't blame her," Maitlin said, reading my mind. "The first thing she told me was, 'You have to tell your fiancé.' But she didn't know Alec like I do. He never could have married me. He's much too proud. It would have shamed his family in Greece."

It's not like they could have pretended the baby was his, I thought. Alec's family would still have its date with shame, no doubt.

"And there was all of Alec's money," I said.

Maitlin's ears turned red. "It had been less than a year since my parents were killed, and Alec's scandals on top of that. I was a wreck, Mr. Hardwick. I lay awake nights for months out of sheer terror that someone would find out I was having a baby. And I couldn't take sleeping pills, antidepressants, tranquilizers—nothing. That was my diet, and I stopped when I got pregnant. I changed the way I lived."

"How did you sell a six-month spiritual retreat to Alec?"

"Alec always knew I had a spiritual life—I spent a month in Tibet right after we met. I told him we were both about to start a new life, and I wanted to cleanse myself before I went to the altar. He would do anything to make me happy. Besides, Alec has his own life. A villa in Florence, his family castle in Greece, and compounds in Mexico and Buenos Aires. He wrote me a few sad letters, but I think my absence only made him more desperate to have me."

"He never knew you were pregnant?"

"No one in America did," Maitlin said. "Except Rachel."

Of course. I reminded myself never to turn my back on *that* shark.

"Nandi was such an easy baby." Her voice grew soft, as if she were talking to her daughter.

My throat was burning. I poured from the crystal water pitcher on the table, with thinly sliced oranges perfectly arranged across the ice cubes. I needed a drink to hear the rest, and water would have to do.

Maitlin went on: "I'd met Bessie in Cape Town, at a publicity event while we were shooting *Vintner*. She had a lovely orphanage—I couldn't forget it. All it needed was some sprucing up. More money for staff. And I thought . . ."

"Why not adopt your own baby?" I finished, when she didn't.

"It sounds . . . ," Maitlin began, but stopped again. Maybe she'd never heard the words aloud. "An actress named Loretta Young did it in the 1930s. She was pregnant with Clark Gable's illegitimate child, and her contract with her studio had a morals clause. She fled to Europe with her mother, and later ended up adopting her own child. Rachel told me that story once. So many of my friends were adopting . . . and I saw an answer. Even Alec liked the idea of adopting a child—we talked about it. I could be Nandi's mother, but without the shame of an affair. Why should she begin her life under such a cloud? I pledged my heart to Nandi under the moon and left her in the care of people I trusted. People I *researched*."

Mama Bessie's days in the orphanage business were about to end, I guessed. I wondered where her children would land after all of the dust settled. Children like Oliver.

"What about Zukisa?" I said.

"No!" Maitlin said, raising a trembling finger. "She has no ties to Children First. We met her independently, during a nationwide search for a nanny. She still doesn't know. I'm sure of it."

If that was true, Zukisa might be the closest thing Nandi would ever have to a mother.

"Why South Africa?" I said.

"I didn't know where else to go. I trusted only Bessie—that woman was making miracles happen on a daily basis, and she needed resources. I gave her a large contribution, and *every penny* went to the children and that facility. And she took care of Nandi. You saw Children First—it's impeccably run. I knew my baby would be safe there. Bessie worked with Rachel to fast-track my application. I visited Cape Town whenever I could, and they smuggled her out to the hotel for visits. It was months, but it felt like a lifetime. I lost twenty pounds from the stress. That day you came was my first visit to the orphanage since Nandi was there. We thought it was time to go public."

"How did Paki find out?"

"I don't know," Maitlin said. "From the photos? She looks so much like him. Or, maybe someone from Children First overheard something and told him. Bessie's had leaks before—that's why the crowd was waiting for us. He never told me how he found out."

"Did he try to blackmail you?"

"It wasn't like that . . . at first," Maitlin said. "When he contacted me, he was hurt. Angry. He had feelings for me. That was one of the reasons I stopped seeing him, at the end. He had a fantasy of us together, and he got nasty when I told him I was marrying Alec. He said I should bring him to America to help raise his daughter. I didn't want him within a thousand miles, but he insisted. It came through my lawyers, so I was terrified Alec would find out the truth. But Paki never put it in writing, never said we had a secret. I didn't want to fight with Paki, but I couldn't give up on Nandi. Fame and money have certain privileges. My lawyers had connections in the State Department who fast-tracked a work visa. Alec never knew the rest. Everyone was happy. I thought it was over."

Maitlin looked exhausted. She drained her glass and stared at the pool again. Her hand was shaking. She didn't try to hide it.

"Did you know that Paki was involved with Kingdom of Heaven?" I said.

I couldn't help trying to make my voice gentler.

Maitlin shook her head, resolute. "Absolutely not. I'd never heard of them. I still can't believe it. Maybe he knew someone at the winery in South Africa, if they're connected. A friend? Maybe he told the wrong person, and got swept up into something. He would never hurt Nandi. I'm sure of that."

I could have told Maitlin that Paki saved Nandi's life in the vineyard—and mine—but neither of them deserved the grace.

"You didn't know about the plan to kidnap Nandi?" I said.

"Of course not!" Maitlin said, losing her battle against her sobs.

"But you had suspicions about Paki," I said. "And you didn't want to call the FBI."

"*They said they would kill her,*" Maitlin said, spraying a whisper through gritted teeth.

"Yes. And once the FBI started sniffing around Paki, your secret would come out."

That was the plain truth of it. That was why Roman was dead. Why Nandi and I had almost died together in the vineyard. Maitlin had been afraid Paki would say too much. Paki bore responsibility for the kidnapping, but Maitlin's lie had opened the door.

From the agony on her face, Maitlin had never heard the sound of the truth spoken aloud. She looked breathless, gazing at me with something like wonder. Slowly, she shook her head. "I just didn't think he could . . ."

". . . lie as well as you?" I finished for her.

"I love Nandi!" Maitlin's eyes spilled tears. "You don't know how much."

I was tired of standing on my crutches in the sun, and tired of talking to Maitlin. My slashed arms ached from holding myself upright.

"Who told you about me and Paki?" Maitlin said. "The FBI?"

"You just did," I said. "I had a suspicion. Like everyone says, she has your smile."

"What now?" she said, suddenly shrunken.

"It'll leak. Paki's probably already talking. Billionaires have a lot of friends, and people who want to be friends. He'll hear the truth. I thought you might want a last opportunity to tell him yourself. You owe him that dignity, at least. But you better hurry."

I watched her eyes glass over. Somewhere deep in there, she was trying to find a way to spin this, to make it work for her. Then her face went blank, porcelain. The momentary glimpse into the real woman was gone.

Maitlin smoothed hair away from her forehead, the only strands out of place.

"Well, Mr. Hardwick, I'm sure my lawyers will settle any outstanding matters with you. I'm very tired," she said, standing. "And I hope you'll understand if I need to be with my family."

"Indeed you do," I said. "I just wish I'd had a better home to bring Nandi to."

Sofia Maitlin smiled, her eyes dancing with madness. It was quite a performance. I wondered if even she knew when she was acting anymore.

I wondered what child protective services would make of a mother like Maitlin when the social workers came to take a much closer look at Nandi's life. But Maitlin had money, and money could make problems go away. As they say, we can't choose the people we're born to.

"Maitlin," I said. "We've been through enough for me to tell you the truth."

"Yes, please."

"I hope they take her from you," I said. "I hope they give Nandi to Zukisa."

Her eyes watered, but the rest of her face never changed.

I turned around to limp back toward the house and the waiting cab.

Nandi was still shrieking and laughing somewhere inside the palatial house when I returned, and Zukisa was laughing with her. Nandi's voice was so tiny, she sounded like she could fit in the palm of my hand.

What would Zukisa do after she heard the news about Maitlin? Would she quit, or weather the storm for Nandi's sake?

At least Nandi will be rich enough to afford therapy, I thought.

At the front door, I paused to savor the echoes of joy one last time. Nandi's laughter healed my face enough to smile.

THIRTY-ONE

THREE MONTHS LATER

The Good Earth in Studio City throws down a great Oriental chicken salad, so I ate there whenever I worked my new gig at CBS. Work was only two or three days a week, but my face was popping up on *The Young and the Restless*. It was good to be back on TV.

I remember when a soap actor could be set for life. Now the soaps were struggling—even *The Guiding Light* got canceled. But I would have steady work for at least two months. Len had advised me against taking the job, but I felt lucky to get it.

Lenox Avenue had finally wrapped—Spike said he liked me better with the scar—but the release date was half a year away. At least. I wasn't a movie star yet.

Hollywood is all about waiting. If you don't stay busy, you lose your mind. For a change, my mind wasn't on work. I was consumed with my home.

I'd found Nandi, but I couldn't find Chela's birth mother.

I'd made hundreds of telephone calls and two weekend trips to Minnesota in a month, and I'd mostly gone in a circle between rehab centers, hospitals, jails, and drug dens that always took me back to *I don't know*. Chela had given me permission to let it go, but I couldn't live with failing her. Maybe we store up feelings in one place, and that's where mine were.

I'd become obsessed with finding Patrice Sheryl McLawhorn, and I was running out of time.

That day, I was supposed to be memorizing lines, but I had my search notes spread across the table, trying to decide where to look next. The trail was paper thin, but it seemed to be leading to Canada. I was ready to go wherever I had to.

Someone sat down across from me in my booth.

I didn't have to look up. Her coconut oil scent said it all.

"I'm sorry, but I don't know you," I said to the woman across from me.

"Are you sure?" said the woman I'd called Marsha.

Her hair was cut in a page boy, dyed red-brown instead of black, the color of dried rust. Her haircut changed everything about her face, making it sterner at some angles and softer at others, but her body was the same. White jeans could hardly contain her.

I'd been trying to decide how I felt about Marsha, too. I still wasn't sure.

"You went to my high school. I'm sure about that part," I said. She'd known about Mrs. Davis and the jokes I made in the cafeteria.

She nodded. "We walked past each other in the hall every day my junior year."

"I went through yearbooks going back ten years," I said. "Which one are you?"

"Marsha," she said. "Let me be Marsha. Any other name I give you would be a lie, too."

Her voice was soft, tentative. "I was the kid nobody noticed, Ten. You were a god, and you smiled at me for no reason one day. Maybe you just felt sorry for me, but I've had a crush on you ever since. So there—now you know my secret. It just wouldn't be a good idea for you to know my name."

My memory flashed me a glimpse of gold-rimmed eyeglasses. Nothing else.

Landing in bed with a woman I'd believed was an old high school friend had taken me back to the beginning of myself, for a while. I'd enjoyed the feeling. If I believed her, I could capture some of the feeling, at least. But believing was hard for me.

The nearest diners were far away, across a large room, so Marsha and I could talk.

"We almost died when you left," I said, my voice low and even. "I could barely walk."

"I was under orders," she said. "After I called in, it was up to the FBI. The choppers were waiting in Atascadero, five minutes away."

"If Paki could keep us alive that long."

"Poetic justice, isn't it?" she said.

In other words, Nandi and I had survived by chance. Like Marsha had told me once, she wasn't good at apologizing. And I was crazy if I thought she'd come to offer me an explanation.

Marsha wanted something. And since she was already oiled up, I figured it was something big.

I ate when my salad arrived, refusing to let my reminiscences with Marsha kill my appetite. I asked the waitress to bring Marsha an iced tea, too.

Under the table, Marsha's foot climbed my calf, toward my left thigh. Such an obvious tactic disappointed me, until I felt myself getting hard. I hadn't had sex since the last time with Marsha, and my body recognized her touch. Every toe that ran across the bulge in my lap had its own caress. She nudged with her big toe, and ten of mine curled in response.

"You are a freak, I'll say that," I said. "And from me, that's saying something."

"I'm parked outside," Marsha said. "I have a big backseat."

"My father told me never to get in cars with strangers."

Marsha smiled, as if my willpower made her proud. "You did good work out there, Ten. You impressed me. You impressed my . . . friends. You're a natural."

"Is this where you offer me a part in a movie?"

"Sure," she said. "It's only acting."

The growing earnestness on her face made me laugh.

"I have a gig for you," she said. "You're the perfect person to save my ass."

I stopped laughing. "You've got nerve asking me for anything, lady."

Marsha looked at me with amnesia. "What do you mean?"

"You piggybacked on my investigation to get closer to Kingdom of Heaven," I said, just loudly enough for her to hear. "You compromised me and nearly got me killed. I was deprived of civil rights during an unlawful interrogation and imprisonment—and the burgers were good, thanks, but not good enough. What the hell makes you think I would work with you?"

"Nandi's home, isn't she?" Marsha said quietly.

We sounded like lovers having a spat. In a way, I guess we were.

"The end justifies the means?" I said. "I've heard that song before. The very worst offenses in the history of the world were justified like that."

"That was one of the *good* days," Marsha said. "There are stars on the wall at Langley—one for everybody who didn't make it—and they're a reminder that some days go bad. There are a lot of stars, Ten. I don't take the good days for granted."

If Marsha considered our day at the vineyard a good day, we had different definitions.

"I've got lines to memorize," I said.

"I'll tell you more," Marsha said.

Curiosity killed the cat, I reminded myself. But I was already listening.

Marsha scooted beside me in the booth, pretending to sample my scallions. When she leaned against me, her skin draped me in body heat. "You're not the only one who got in trouble. You rescued Nandi, so you made out better than I did at the vineyard. The meeting was interrupted before I could get what I needed. That vineyard in Paso was one end of a ball of yarn we've been unraveling for five years. Remember where we met? In Malibu?"

My mind flashed an image of her nakedness against the Pacific.

"Hard to forget that," I said.

"I was surveilling a beach house. We've been there a year. The house belongs to a man named Fong, an arms dealer high in the Chinese organization. If I could have gotten the information there, my employers wouldn't be on my ass.

"He has a young, beautiful wife. Raised in Hong Kong. Speaks perfect English. She's a movie and television fan. I think you'd like each other. And while you were liking each other, you might be able to . . . plant a little listening device in the house."

"You don't have people who do things like that?"

"There are limits to resources, and license. For diplomatic and other reasons, we can't do anything that might embarrass the State Department."

"So it could only be done by someone you could leave high and dry."

"Someone who would, of course, be very well paid for that risk."

I had heard enough. "No thanks," I said. "Been there, done that."

Marsha whispered in my ear. "The husband might be working with terrorist cells to develop a smuggling network. An ear in the right place could save thousands of lives . . ."

Marsha's voice trailed off as the waitress returned with her iced tea. I hadn't realized that Marsha's hand had wandered to my lap, barely concealed by the table. From the startled look on the waitress's face, she'd seen more than she expected. She hurried away.

"*Well* paid." Marsha squeezed my crotch. "Among other perks."

"Not my line of work," I said, gently moving her hand. I scooted a safe distance away, to the edge of the booth. "I'm not getting my balls shot off seducing some Chinese mastermind's wife. Or locked up for breaking and entering, or worse, when you decide you don't know me anymore." I leaned forward. "I do not trust you. There is nothing in this world you could say to get me back into this madness."

"Well, if that's how you feel," Marsha said. Then she pulled a manila folder out of her white leather bag. She rested it on the table, although she never let it go. The folder was marked with a single name typed on a label: PATRICE S. McLAWHORN.

Chela's birth mother.

Marsha pulled out a full-color eight-by-ten photo. It was a surveillance photo from a grocery store parking lot, as clear as a studio's. It was the same white woman I'd seen in Chela's photo, with thirty more pounds and fifteen more years, her hair dyed red. She didn't look like a junkie, dressed in a skirt and jacket she wore to an office. I couldn't see Chela anywhere in her.

"This is it," Marsha said, watching my eyes devour the photograph. "Everything you need. Home address and number. Work address and number. Her biography. Once she signs her consent, your adoption application will race like lightning. You'll be Chela's legal father before her eighteenth birthday. This woman has gone to great lengths to forget who she used to be."

"Quid pro quo?" I was seething that she was trying to trap me. For an ugly flash, I remembered the man in the basement. I pushed the folder back to her half of the table. "Don't dangle people I care about over my head," I said. "Help with strings is just a threat in lipstick. Not a path you want to walk with me."

"Not at all, Ten," she said, and pushed it back. "This is yours. A gift for an old friend. But I would like you to listen to me for a minute."

"One minute."

She smiled. "Most people are bored to death all of their lives, Ten," Marsha said. "They're hamsters on a wheel. That's not you. Most people let the shitstorm they call their past cripple them with guilt. You look for people to save. You thought you were an actor who solves problems. No, Tennyson. You're a problem solver who acts. And playtime is over. What happened out in the vineyard, Tennyson? Who were you in the basement?"

I stared at her, swearing she didn't deserve the truth, knowing that Marsha, like Spider, already knew it.

Marsha pressed on: "You had some rough moments while we were looking for Nandi—but you were *alive*. I can't be Marsha the soccer mom; I need this rush, and so do you. This is who you really are. I've seen it up close."

I remembered Cape Town, and how April had tried to bring me into the light. Marsha was pulling me in an entirely different direction.

Just like Spider.

I stared at the woman in the photo, Chela's mother, close enough to touch.

"My soap has a crazy shooting schedule," I said.

"I suspect this is a night job, baby."

Marsha smiled. She had me, and she knew it.

When it comes to our children, sometimes there's nothing we won't do.

Of course, sometimes our children are just our excuse.

EPILOGUE

THE CHINESE BUSINESSMAN'S wife was beautiful: tall, regal, and oval faced. Shiny jet hair grew down to her waist. Her milk-colored silk blouse fell across her modest chest like a royal cloak. Her dossier said she was thirty, but her petite body lagged by a decade. I would have noticed her even if I hadn't been looking.

She was having a drink, as she did every Thursday after her spa visit. I strolled in her direction across the crowded hotel bar.

Ignoring a beautiful woman is the only way to get her to notice you, so I walked past her and slipped onto a bar stool about six feet farther on. Two stools sat between us, empty.

"Hey!" the bartender greeted me. I'd seen him the night I rescued Nandi. I hadn't been able to place him, but I did now. He was about fifty, balding, and paunchy—and wearing the same Hawaiian shirt he'd worn renting Hummers in Malibu for Marsha. Still sunburned.

"What can I get you, Ten?" he asked.

"Chocolate martini."

A girl who looked too young to drink grabbed my arm. "*Omigod!* Can I get your autograph? I hate your character on *The Young and the Restless*! You're such a great asshole!" I thanked her for the compliment.

The bartender handed me my martini and snapped on the bar's mounted TV, where the DVD was already cued. "I was just watching you," he told me, winking. "Mr. Big Shot."

The DVD was dailies from *Lenox Avenue.* In them I stood nose to nose with Denzel in a replicated speakeasy, both of us in 1920s double-breasted suits. I barely recognized a close-up of my face—and the scar I was still spending a fortune to fix, but that wasn't quite gone yet.

"Or you'll do WHAT, man?" my voice said from the screen, ready to kill or die.

The footage seemed alien to me. I couldn't judge it. It must have been good, because Denzel had said he'd never want to meet me in a dark alley . . . but wanted to work with me again. Spike said I'd really captured the aura of a crazed killer.

Spider and I would have had a good laugh about that.

She slid onto the bar stool beside mine.

"That's you in that movie?" She had an English accent, by way of Hong Kong.

"It hasn't come out yet," I said. "That's just footage from the shoot, eight hours on the set with Denzel. Someone's gonna kick your butt for having this, Mario. Those studios don't play with their money." His name wasn't really Mario, just like Marsha's wasn't Marsha. But Mario would do.

While I joked with the bartender, my mark's eyes drank me in like a chocolate martini.

"It must be very exciting to be in movies," she said. I'd never met a model who didn't want to act.

I gave her my full attention over my shoulder, and turned on The Grin. If the light caught my face right, she would squirm in her seat.

"Movies are one way I get excited," I said.

She squirmed. In her gaze, we were already befouling her husband's bed.

"My friends call me Ming Ming," she said, slipping her delicate hand into mine. Her birdlike thumb brushed the pulse point on my wrist. "Your name is . . . ?"

"Hardwick," I told her. "Tennyson Hardwick."

ACKNOWLEDGMENTS

TANANARIVE DUE

What an incredible journey Tennyson Hardwick has been! Thank you to Blair Underwood for dreaming Tennyson to life, and to Steven Barnes for walking with me in the dream every day as my coauthor and life partner. Thanks to my longtime editor, Atria Books Vice President and Senior Editor Malaika Adero, and to publisher Judith Curr at Simon & Schuster for understanding exactly what we wanted to accomplish with this series. And thanks to Todd Hunter at Atria for always making sure we're on track.

Special thanks to the NAACP for awarding us a 2009 NAACP Image Award for *In the Night of the Heat*—as a child of civil rights activists, that resonates very deeply. The memory will endure as one of the most magical moments of my life. And thanks to Go on Girl! Book Club for the honor of naming us 2008's Authors of the Year for *Casanegra*.

We are humbled and grateful.

Thanks to my literary agent, John Hawkins, of John Hawkins & Associates; and to my film and TV manager, Michael Prevett, at The Gotham Group.

Many thanks to the people in my circle who helped us research this novel—with a special shout-out to my Facebook "family," which really came through in delightful ways.

Any mistakes herein should be blamed on me, not on my sources.

First, thanks to the Old Soldier.

Thank you to photojournalist and producer Miki Turner, for her impressions of Cape Town. (I was visiting vicariously through you!)

Thanks to social worker Stacie Ottley and family attorneys Elizabeth Schwartz and Deborah Wald, for advising Tennyson during his plans to adopt Chela.

Thanks to Lisa Getter Peterson—you know why.

Thanks to retired Col. Frank Underwood, Blair's father, for his grace and service.

Most important, thanks to my family: My parents, John Due and Patricia Stephens Due; my sister Lydia Due Greisz; and my sister Johnita Due, for blessings to last a lifetime. Thanks to my husband, Steve; my son, Jason; and my stepdaughter, Nicki; for my new home.

Adoption is a subject very close to my heart. It would pain me to believe that the events in this fictitious story would make anyone hesitate to adopt a child, either domestically or abroad (although it is usually much cheaper to begin the search at home).

The children need us. It's not as hard as you might think.

Your child may be only a few keystrokes, or a phone call, away.

STEVEN BARNES

As always, no book is written in a vacuum—many hands and minds collaborate to shape human lives, and it's those humans who create things like detective novels. Tennyson's world is always a great place to play. *From Cape Town* has special significance, because I have loved the espionage genre so much, for so long, and this has been the first time I've even wet a toe in that pond.

With that in mind, first thanks must go to the Old Soldier, who pointed me in the direction of fascinating truths concerning the American intelligence community and warned me when the fiction got too close to literal truth. His contributions can be found in every chapter, and it is one of the unfortunate realities that those who are most helpful in such matters sometimes cannot be thanked by name.

The owners and operators of Chronic Cellars in Paso Robles, California, who educated us about wines and the differences between concrete and wooden tanks over glasses of absolutely smashing Merlot. I heartily recommend them.

The Kingdom of Heaven is fictional. But all immigrant populations contain predators as well as good, honest people searching for a new life. We hope no one will mistake our fantasy for any sort of reportage. The "Knife of Heaven" technique is also fictional, but like the South African martial art of Piper (which it strongly resembles), created by Nigel February, is based on Zulu spear and knife techniques. Piper is absolutely lethal stuff, and I simply couldn't resist borrowing its approach.

Thanks to Guru Cliff Stewart, who manifests here as "Cliff Sanders," a melding of his name and that of Sijo Steve "Sanders" Muhammad, two of the creators of the Black Karate Federation and simply insanely accomplished martial artists, as well as being true gentlemen and scholars. I am honored to count you as friends and teachers. God is good.

To my family, the greatest treasure of my life. My soulmate, Tananarive. I just adore you. My son, Jason, who lives absolutely at the center of my heart. My wonderful sister, Joyce, and her children, Steve and Sharlene, who brightened difficult holidays. And last but certainly not least, to my darling daughter, Nicki, taking her first real steps into her dream.

Go get it, kid.

BLAIR UNDERWOOD

> "Gratitude is the Heart's Memory."
>
> —FRENCH PROVERB

As *From Cape Town with Love,* our third Tennyson Hardwick novel, is released, my heart abounds and I am exceedingly grateful for this opportunity to acknowledge and remember so many who have supported this endeavor from its inception.

So let us begin with *conception*. First and foremost, I salute and honor my parents Col. (Ret.) Frank and Marilyn Underwood, who instilled in me the passion for the imagination, a work ethic to see a dream to fruition, and faith to progress to the next condition. Contextually, this story speaks to family ties, specifically parent/child relations. Tananarive Due, Steven Barnes, and I unanimously agreed that it would be most appropriate to dedicate this novel to the ones who gave us life, our parents. So Mom and Dad, this one is for you!

Well, Tananarive and Steven, the saga continues. I am most appreciative to have been given the privilege of collaborating with you these past few years. Though I am enormously gratified with *Casanegra* and *In the Night of the Heat*, what is most enjoyable about this journey is that each subsequent novel gives birth to a brand new set of challenges and unique adventures for "Ten." As both he and our series evolve, I find myself desperately wanting to delve even deeper and continue to walk in his shoes for decades to come.

Désirée, my bride, you make me feel as though, with God and you by my side, I can move mountains. I pray that you will forever feel my gust of wind under your wings as I feel your perpetual wind beneath mine.

To my seeds, Paris, Brielle, and Blake, your inquisitive nature and wonder of the world before you utterly inspires me. As you grow up, never lose your childlike spirit. The seeds of all possibilities lie within it. Protect that spirit.

To my family, Frank Jr., Marlo, Mellisa, Jackson, Owen, Carter, Austin, Kelly, Khloe, Kamden, friends and relatives far too many to name, the words "thank you" are woefully inadequate. Suffice it to say, I acknowledge and honor you for allowing me to share your walk through this life. Each one of you has been instrumental in shaping and affecting my life in wonderfully profound ways.

To Lynne Andrews, my cousin, they say that the squeaky wheel gets the oil. Largely due to your presence in our household, there are no loud squeaks, squawks, or otherwise. Thank you for your spirit of light and helping to keep everything running smoothly.

Ron West, my manager and friend, "one more again." Thank you for believing in my crazy journey through the minefields of this thing called

Show Business. You continue to work tenaciously on my behalf and for that, I thank you.

Lee Wallman, we've traveled to countries around the globe and it is always great fun. As often as we greet each other with an elongated "helloooo," know that I am honored to have you as my publicist and hope to never say good-bye.

Deborah Ainsworth, Tommy Morgan, Gary Reeves, and Maria Savoy, you encourage, insulate, and motivate me more than you will ever know. Thank you for always having my back.

To Diane DaCosta, because of your example of leadership in this literary arena, I felt emboldened enough to try my hand as well. You are truly courageous and I am honored to call you friend and family.

To the readers and enthusiasts of our series, because of your continued patronage we are humbled by yet another opportunity to present the next chapter in the life of these characters that we have all come to know and love.

Ralph Waldo Emerson once said, "Ideas must work through the brains and the arms of good and brave men, or they are no better than dreams."

Because of the bold and innovative brains and arms of our publisher, Judith Curr, and her exceptional colleagues at Atria Books, including Christine Saunders and Todd Hunter, this series has transcended dreamstate and has become reality. Judith, for your quiet strength of leadership, undying support, and discerning grace, I am eternally grateful.

Malaika Adero, this is now our fourth book together, and you continue to be an exemplary editor, as well as one who possesses an extraordinary spirit of warmth and kindness, not to mention great hair. I thank you.

Lydia Wills, you remain an inspiration and the keeper of "coolness."

To all the cohorts at the Paradigm Talent Agency, as well as Patti Felker, Eric Suddleson, and Bruce Gellman at Felker, Toczek, Gellman and Suddleson, many thanks for your constant guidance, motivation, and support.

If "tomorrow belongs to the people who prepare for it today" and "the past ain't nothin' but 'prologue,'" then because of all of you, the future of Tennyson is so bright, you might wanna whip out those sunglasses!